MONTANA!

The tenth triumphant novel
in the WAGONS WEST series—
stories of courage and excitement about the
pioneering men and women who wrest the riches of
mountains and plains from gunslingers and savages
for a growing country's glory.

WAGONS WEST

MONTANA!

AMERICA'S PROUDEST TRAILBLAZING MEN AND WOMEN CARRY FREEDOM'S SPIRIT ACROSS THE GREAT DIVIDE TO A WILD AND DANGEROUS TERRITORY.

TOBY HOLT—

Heroic son of wagonmaster Whip Holt, he maps a new direction for his destiny that leads to a woman's love . . . and an imposter's deadly plot.

CLARISSA SINCLAIR—

A passionate young bride who fights to keep a husband's love and trust—even if it means finding the courage to kill.

BETH MARTIN—

The beautiful, spoiled daughter of Major General Lee Blake, her growing jealousy threatens to destroy a marriage; her impetuousness to endanger a life.

HANK PURCELL—

A young gunslinger who swears vengeance in
his hunt to track down his father's killer.

THUNDER CLOUD—

Courageous Chief of Chiefs of the mighty Sioux nation,
a man educated in the white man's language and ways,
determined to drive them from his people's land.

SADIE "MA" HASTINGS—

Leader of a ruthless outlaw band, her guns blazed
with a special hatred aimed at ending
Toby Holt's chances of happiness.

EULALIA HOLT—

Handsome widow of the legendary wagonmaster,
she tests a son's loyalty with her
desire for a new love.

SUSANNA BRENTWOOD—

Wife of a brave military commander,
she captures the spirit of Montana in print,
until she herself becomes its hostage.

YALE MYERS—

Grizzled, burly, and dangerous, neither blizzards
nor armed men can stop him from claiming
a secret cache of gold.

Bantam Books by Dana Fuller Ross
Ask your bookseller for the books you have missed

WAGONS WEST ★ TENTH IN A SERIES

MONTANA!

DANA FULLER ROSS

 Created by the producers of
White Indian, Children of the Lion,
Saga of the Southwest, and
The Kent Family Chronicles Series.

Executive Producer: Lyle Kenyon Engel

BANTAM BOOKS
TORONTO • NEW YORK • LONDON • SYDNEY • AUCKLAND

MONTANA!

*A Bantam Book / published by arrangement with
Book Creations, Inc.*

*Bantam edition / April 1983
2nd printing . . . September 1984*

*Produced by Book Creations, Inc.
Chairman of the Board: Lyle Kenyon Engel*

ISBN 0-553-22925-7

Published simultaneously in the United States and Canada

PRINTED IN THE UNITED STATES OF AMERICA

H   11 10 9 8 7 6 5 4 3

Plan of Fort Shaw

ICE HOUSE · BAKERY

CORRAL

BLACKSMITH · ORDNANCE

B · B

QUARTERMASTER

B · B

HEADQUARTERS

GUARD HOUSE

QUARTERMASTER

B - BARRACKS
O - OFFICERS QUARTERS

MAGAZINE

FORT SHAW
—Montana—

RON TOELKE ·82

MONTANA!

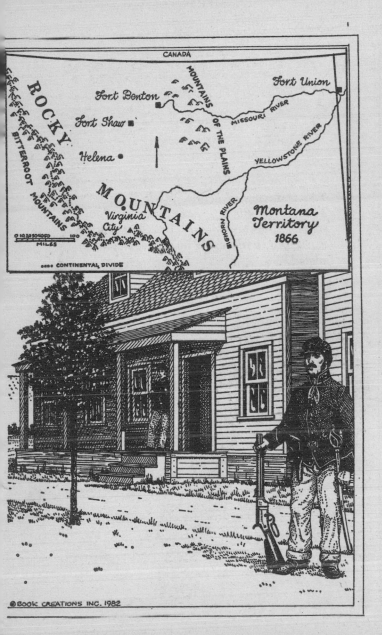

I

At first glance Toby Holt bore a startling resemblance to his late father, Whip Holt, the legendary mountain man, trapper, and hunter, who was responsible for so much of the development of the American West. Toby had the same lanky, lean build, moving with the grace of the natural athlete; his hair was the same untamed dirty blond; and his pale blue-gray eyes had a penetrating quality that made them seem to bore into and through the object or person at which they were looking.

There were differences between father and son, of course. Toby had fought valiantly as an officer during the long years of the Civil War. In addition, he had spent virtually the entire year since the war ended laying out a route for the new transcontinental railroad to the Pacific Northwest. Perhaps the greatest difference between Toby and his father was too subtle for almost anyone to notice: The son had enjoyed the benefits of a higher education, not to mention the excellent training of his mother, Eulalia. As a result, Toby's speech was more literate, his manners more polished.

Toby Holt looked up from the document he had been reading and glanced out toward the distant snow-capped mountains that lay to the east of his family's ranch house in Oregon. Then he grinned at his good friend and partner, Rob Martin, the surveyor who was working with him on the all-important railroad route.

"We can still back out of this if you want to," Toby said. "It's not too late."

Rob, who was Toby's height and had red hair, chuckled as he reached for the paper. He could not imagine Toby backing out of anything that he had made up his mind to do. They had been close all their lives; Rob's parents, Dr. Robert Martin and the former Tonie Mell, had crossed the continent to Oregon with Whip and Eulalia Holt in the first wagon train to the Pacific Northwest. Most recently, the two young men had formed a partnership with their good friend from Oregon, Frank Woods, who was currently working the lumber camp in the Washington Territory, sending Toby and Rob their share of the profits.

Rob scanned the paper briefly and saw that it was dated six weeks earlier in late February, 1866. It bore the signature of Andrew Johnson, President of the United States, and was written on White House stationery.

The document itself was very simple, directing Toby Holt and Robert Martin to continue with their survey for a railroad line and specifically instructing them to proceed without delay to the Montana Territory for the purpose of determining where the railroad line would be laid there.

"Why in thunderation would we want to back out?"

Rob demanded. "We've known for weeks that this presidential order was coming, and we've just been waiting for the weather to improve so we can carry it out."

Toby chuckled dryly. "If you think the Washington Territory was uncivilized and barbaric," he said, "wait until you see Montana. It's primitive! The better part of it looks precisely as it did when Lewis and Clark first traveled through it sixty years ago. As a matter of fact, it hasn't changed much since the thirties and forties when mountain men like Kit Carson and my father were leaders in the fur trade."

"All I know about Montana, really," Rob said, "is that the western half of the territory is very mountainous and the Continental Divide is located there. The eastern half is a lush prairie land and has a number of cattle ranches being established there, so it can't be all that uncivilized. What's more, a great many people raced into the territory in the gold rushes of the past fifteen years. From the stories I have heard, it was as hectic there as it was in California and in Colorado."

"The tidal wave of gold seekers passed through Montana, and practically none of them settled there," Toby replied. "As I say, the better part of the territory is still in its natural state."

"All that is going to change in a great hurry," Rob said humorously. "Beth has been insisting that she is going to move to Montana when we get to work out there, and that she's going to set up a base that we can call home. I've tried to talk her out of it, but you know my wife. Once her mind is made up, nothing will stop her from trying to get her way."

Toby's smile faded, and his heart sank at Rob's mention of his wife. The problem was ever present, and just the thought of it paralyzed Toby Holt.

The difficulty was that he had grown up with Beth Blake, the daughter of Cathy and General Lee Blake, his parents' closest friends. Their mothers had confidently expected them to develop a romantic interest in each other, and, consequently, they had done just the opposite: They had drifted away from each other. Not until he had returned to the ranch after nearly being killed fighting in the Civil War had the sobered Toby realized that he actually cared for Beth, and by that time, it had been too late. Toby was already married, and Beth became betrothed to Rob, soon thereafter marrying him. Thus even after the death of his wife, from whom he had been estranged, Toby was not free to pursue Beth.

"This is none of my business," Rob said with a touch of embarrassment, "but I've been wondering lately if you and Clarissa are going to marry."

"I honestly don't know what I'm going to do," Toby confessed. Certainly his partner knew that he'd been having an affair for some months with Clarissa Sinclair, a widow from Philadelphia, who lived in the Washington Territory. The truth of the matter was that he couldn't decide whether he cared enough for Clarissa to marry her. Images of Beth still intruded, and he felt in all fairness to himself, as well as to Clarissa, that he should get Beth out of his system once and for all before he even contemplated marriage to someone else.

Rob tactfully dropped the subject. He knew more than he was revealing; he had heard, for example, that Eulalia Holt was urging her son to marry Clarissa and that young Cindy Holt, Toby's teenage sister, had become another of Clarissa's champions. Certainly he had no desire to add to Toby's pressures. Besides, right now he and his wife were going to go up to Washington to spend some time together, alone, in the lodge Rob and

Toby had built. Rob Martin would have enough pressures of his own coping with his beautiful, impetuous wife.

The mountains of Montana, wild and remote, with many peaks soaring thousands of feet above sea level, brooded in white-capped, silent majesty and set the tone for the territory of which they were an integral part. To their east lay the lush prairie grasslands and meadows, a continuation of the lands to be found in the Dakotas. Buffalo attracted by the vegetation roamed in large numbers, and it was the fertility of the land that had lured settlers here. Rugged and hardy ranch owners, who found the climate and soil perfect for the raising of cattle, were beginning to move into the territory and were establishing homesteads, most of them separated from their neighbors by vast distances.

The isolation, the difficulties of travel, were responsible for most of Montana's problems. The territorial legislature met rarely. The first governor of the territory had resigned in disgust, and the second was dead, widely believed to have been murdered. The administration in Washington as yet had been unable to find a willing replacement for him, just as it was unable to find individuals willing to work as marshals or sheriffs.

Bands of outlaws roamed through the populated sections of the territory, robbing the inhabitants and then disappearing into mountain refuges. The settlers were also harassed by sporadic Indian raids. Of late, large numbers of Indian warriors were arriving in the eastern part of the territory, all of them mounted on their small, swift horses, and all of them wearing war paint.

Had the Montana settlers been in a position to

check more closely, they would have realized that the Indians were traveling to a conclave in the hill country that led to the mountains. They came from every direction except the west, and some traveled singly, others came in groups. Some were old friends and had fought numerous battles against the wagon trains of the settlers all the way from Iowa to the Continental Divide. Others had never seen a white man but had heard blood-curdling tales, in song and in story, of the greed and rapacity of the whites.

"Why have we been called here?" they asked each other as they set up their tents of animal skins.

The reply was always the same. "Only Thunder Cloud knows."

Thunder Cloud was the Sioux chief of chiefs, the undisputed leader of the nation's seven separate, distinct subtribes. He had been elected to his high post a decade and a half earlier, and he had lived up to the highest expectations of his colleagues and supporters.

Thunder Cloud was no ordinary warrior. Educated by early missionaries in what became the state of Iowa, he not only spoke and understood English, but could read and write the language, as well. He kept abreast of the activities of the white men, whom he despised, by reading their newspapers; and by avidly following the battles during the Civil War, he had become an expert on military strategy and tactics.

Tall and rugged, with an aquiline nose, deeply bronzed skin, and penetrating eyes, Thunder Cloud resembled the American Indians who were popularized in the illustrations for the stories by James Fenimore Cooper. Habitually closemouthed, he confided in no one and was regarded as something of an enigma even by the few colleagues who were relatively close to him.

More than one hundred war chiefs of the Sioux had gathered in a hidden valley in the Mountains of the Plains, located in the heart of the Montana Territory. Until Thunder Cloud arrived, they whiled away their time by hunting. In addition to the vast herds of buffalo attracted by the splendid grass of the plains, the area abounded in deer and moose, elk and antelope. Flocks of ducks, geese, and quail flew northward overhead toward their summer resting places in Canada, and the lakes and rivers were full of trout, salmon, and other prized fish.

Thunder Cloud had an instinctive flair for the dramatic, and he arrived in the valley at a moment when his subordinates were beginning to become restless and bored. He rode into the encampment with an escort of twenty-five young warriors, each of them carrying a distinctive Sioux lance, a long, perfectly balanced polelike weapon that braves were taught from earliest boyhood to hurl while mounted on their galloping horses. For his noon meal, Thunder Cloud selected portions of the hearts and livers of a moose and an elk, a deer and an antelope. This was not accidental, and as word of his selection spread through the camp, the wiser and more experienced of the warriors realized that he had deliberately chosen a symbolic meal.

At last he was ready to speak, and he summoned the war chiefs and warriors to his campfire. They surrounded it, sitting cross-legged in a circle on the ground, their arms folded in front of them. For this special occasion Thunder Cloud had worn a headdress of feathers that encircled his head and trailed down his back. He had also revived an old custom of the Iroquois of upper New York state: Over his shoulders he wore a robe of buffalo skin decorated with dyed porcupine quills that formed various geometric patterns.

Not the least of Thunder Cloud's attributes was his talent as a speaker, and he did not disappoint his listeners. He addressed them in a deep, mellifluous voice that was capable of expressing a full range of human emotions, and as he talked, his listeners felt first sadness, then anger, and ultimately even outrage.

"My brothers," he said, "how good it is to share fresh, roasted meat with my blood brethren of the Sioux! How I have longed for this day!" He slowly scanned his audience, and whenever he saw a familiar face in the throng, he nodded, his dark eyes brightening.

Most of his audience was composed of mature men, Thunder Cloud's contemporaries who remembered their own youth in far-off Iowa, which lay to the east. There was no need for the chief of chiefs to remind them they had been slowly pushed westward by the pressure of the colonists who had come from the east and set up their homes and established their farms on the lands that had belonged to the Indians.

Thunder Cloud appeared to be a mind reader. "How far back we go together!" he exclaimed. "How many winters we have been friends. How many summers we have ridden together on the hunt for buffalo."

He had struck precisely the right note, and his listeners stirred. They and he were attached by strong bonds of shared memories, and in their nostalgia, they were ripe for whatever he chose to propose to them.

"Long ago in the time of our fathers," Thunder Cloud said, "all the lands that lie west of the broad Mississippi River belonged only to the Sioux and to our friends from other nations. Then the white men came. Their appetites were huge. Little by little they took our lands from us to build their towns, to create their farms, and to excavate their mines. Little by little we were pushed farther and farther to the west. Until now, for we can go no farther." He gestured in the direction of the distant snow-capped peaks of the Continental Divide.

His listeners nodded, and a grizzled subchief of the Sioux shouted, "The mountains are a final barrier. We can retreat no farther."

"We can retreat no farther." Thunder Cloud repeated the words with seeming relish. "In the eastern part of this land called Montana, and on the plains of Dakota, there is game without number. There graze vast herds of buffalo. There, as my brothers know, are elk and moose, deer and antelope for all. In this paradise, this great hunting ground, which we shared with the Blackfoot, who make their home in the northern Plains, and with the Cheyenne, who live in the Wyoming country to our south, we have found contentment. But even here the white man has no intention of allowing us to live in peace!"

"Thunder Cloud speaks words of truth!" a young warrior shouted.

The chief of chiefs appeared to ignore the interruption. "Far to the east," Thunder Cloud said, "on the far bank of the Mississippi River, I have seen a terrible invention of the white men. It is an iron horse, an instrument made of metal that belches great clouds of smoke and that travels at high speeds on beds of shining rails. The iron horse carries fifty men at a time, perhaps a hundred, perhaps even two hundred. It carries all of their belongings as well, and it could be used to transport a whole herd of buffalo in safety."

There were some in his audience who had never

seen railroad trains, and they were fascinated by his description. Those who knew railroads realized he was not exaggerating and nodded somberly.

"The first settlers who have come into the region," he said, "have traveled by wagon train. How well we know these horse-drawn wagons of the white men! But those who will follow these first settlers expect to travel by iron horse!" His voice rose in wrathful excitement. "No longer will they come in tens or in ten times ten. Now they will travel by the hundreds, and they will spread out through our hunting grounds like a plague of locusts or grasshoppers!"

His auditors were becoming aroused, and they began to move restlessly.

"When an Indian steals," Thunder Cloud declared scornfully, "he is clever. He moves silently in the night, and he makes no sound as he takes that which is not his. But the white man is arrogant—as he always is. Believe me, my brothers, it is good that I know the tongue of these pale-skinned serpents. They actually dare to boast that they are going to build the shiny rails that will carry the iron horses to our hunting grounds. They are so certain they will succeed that they boast in advance of the benefits they will enjoy."

He shook his fist above his head, and his listeners echoed him by doing the same.

"What say you, my brothers?" Thunder Cloud demanded fiercely. "Are we going to sit back and do nothing? Are we going to be like helpless women when the white men come in their iron horses to steal our hunting grounds from us?"

His words had the desired effect. More than one hundred warriors were on their feet now, brandishing tomahawks above their heads and shouting, "No! No!"

The chief of chiefs quieted his audience with a series of sharp, abrupt gestures, and they sat down again.

"We are of one mind, my brothers," he said grimly. "We will drive away the white men who have settled in our hunting grounds and have cut down our forests to build homes and barns and fences. We will take their cattle and their horses, and we will burn their homes to the ground, causing the settlers to flee for their lives. The white man must be driven from this favored land!"

An elderly warrior, his hair flecked with gray, was so carried away that he unleashed a bloodcurdling war cry. Instantly the air was filled with identical cries from his comrades.

Thunder Cloud was not yet finished speaking, however, and he quieted the crowd with great difficulty. "Wait, my brothers, and hear the last words that I will speak to you this day," he said. "We will drive the white settlers from our land, we will take their livestock and destroy their homes, but when possible, we must avoid killing them."

A strange hush fell on the assemblage, and the warriors looked at each other in puzzlement, wondering if the chief of chiefs had lost his wits.

"My reasons are simple and plain," Thunder Cloud declared. "White builders have erected a number of forts in Montana. Soldiers occupy those forts, and they are arriving in ever-increasing numbers. They are splendid fighting men, and they have a great talent when they aim their firesticks. Thus, we must avoid at all costs starting a full-scale war with these soldiers. Though our numbers are greater than their numbers, our weapons are not the equal of their weapons.

"There will not be war, however, if we allow the

settlers to live. I will be satisfied, well and truly satisfied, if we drive the settlers out of our land. This we will do. When their horses and cattle vanish and their homes are smoldering ruins, they will become discouraged, and they will leave."

The leaders of the Sioux looked at one another and nodded in surprised approval. Only someone as infinitely clever as Thunder Cloud could have devised a scheme that would rid Montana of the hated white settlers but would avoid a full-scale war with the troops, whose expertise with modern rifles the Sioux had learned to respect greatly.

One major question was still unsettled, however, and an elderly subchief climbed slowly to his feet. "What of the men who will come to Montana to determine the path that the shiny iron horse rails will take?" he wanted to know. "Will we also drive them out of Montana?"

Thunder Cloud's dark eyes glittered. He said, "Once we have completed our task of driving out the settlers who are desecrating our hunting grounds, we will turn our attention to the men who chart the path for the iron horse. At that time we will teach them and their masters a lesson that will be long remembered. We will kill them with our bows and arrows and our tomahawks, and we will take their scalps as symbols of the victory that will be ours when the last white man leaves the Montana hunting grounds!"

After spending almost a full year in the nation's highest office, President Andrew Johnson, who had been so unexpectedly thrust into his role by the assassination of Abraham Lincoln, had grown accustomed to his surroundings and his work. Painfully honest and blunt, the

former senator from Tennessee had as many enemies as
he had partisans, and although he enjoyed the presidency
and hoped for another term, his foes were determined to
block his ambition.

The undeclared candidate, who was winning their
support, was the Chief of Staff of the U. S. Army, General
eral Ulysses S. Grant, who was popularly regarded as
the commander who had won the Civil War. Amiable almost
most to a fault, Grant saw to it that he made few enemies,
mies, and he was beginning to develop ambitions of his
own for the presidency.

The newspapers of the major cities of the Eastern
Seaboard were filled with speculation about the next occupant
cupant of the White House, and the talk inevitably affected
fected the relations of Johnson and Grant. They met
frequently in the line of duty, and the tension that both
felt began to show plainly. Both were polite, trying hard
to behave like gentlemen, but the strain showed, even
though their mutual ambition was one subject that neither
ther ever mentioned.

"I asked you here, General," President Johnson said,
"to discuss the new railroad in the West."

General Grant opened the top brass button on the
tunic of his uniform in order to obtain greater comfort.
"Ah, yes," he said, "the central route from Wyoming to
California."

"No," the President replied pleasantly, in spite of
the effort it caused him. "I'm referring to the northern
route that will go through Montana to the state of Oregon
gon and the Washington Territory."

Grant reacted as though he had been rebuked. His
smile vanished, he sat erect, and replied in a low voice,
"Yes, sir."

"In the very near future," the President said, "as

soon as the snows in the high Rockies melt, the team that performed for us so successfully in the Washington Territory is going to do the same for us in Montana."

"Pardon my ignorance, Mr. President," the general said, "but just who comprise this team?"

Andrew Johnson was surprised. "Why, Toby Holt and Rob Martin, of course."

General Grant's politeness was studied. "You say they're competent, sir?"

"Very," the President replied crisply. "Toby Holt is the son of Whip Holt, and that ought to be enough credentials for anybody. But the fact remains that he did a splendid job in the Washington Territory, and so did Martin, his surveyor partner."

"With the Congress clamoring for action in the building of the railroad, Mr. President, can these two gentlemen operate quickly enough to satisfy the politicians?"

"It's a question of whether they can respond fast enough to meet the demands of industry. There are dozens of factory owners who are eager to open major trade with Oregon and Washington. With Puget Sound as the railroad's terminus, the trade with the Orient will also be highly lucrative. So it's businessmen, not politicians, who are the ones who need to be satisfied." The President didn't appear to realize he was administering a rebuke.

General Grant didn't want Andrew Johnson to think he was currying favor, and he hesitated before replying. "Perhaps the army can help speed the task, Mr. President, and complete the route for the new railroad in less time than it would otherwise take."

The President looked interested.

"Major Isham Jentry is an extremely capable officer

with considerable experience in surveying, and he also knows a great deal about railroads. I recommend that we assign him to work with Holt and his partner."

"It can do no harm, certainly, to send him out," Johnson said at last. "I urge you to write a letter to young Holt and tell him that competent help is on the way."

"I'll do that," Grant said, and reaching for a piece of paper and a lead pencil, he scribbled a note to himself.

"That still leaves the basic problem in Montana unsolved," Johnson said, frowning.

Grant knew about the state of affairs in Montana, but he waited for the President to elaborate.

Johnson turned to a table behind him, which was piled high with papers and documents, and after searching for some moments, he reached for a packet of letters tied together with a cord. "If you'll read these," he said, throwing the bundle to Grant, "you'll see just how bad the problem is. These are all letters from settlers in the Montana Territory, complaining about conditions there and asking for help from the federal government. All of them sing the same tune. They've suffered raids by bands of Sioux Indians, they've lost cattle and farm implements, and even their homes and barns have been burned down. The Indians seem to take sheer delight in malice for its own sake. As if that were not enough, gangs of desperadoes are also operating in the territory. People like the notorious crew headed by a woman." He searched his mind for her name. "Ma Hastings, I think she's called."

None of what General Grant heard was news to him, and he listened patiently. "I think you'll find that by summer, Mr. President, the army will have the situation under control. The Indian raids will stop abruptly, and so will the activities of the robber gangs."

Johnson was a man who dealt in specifics and wanted more than vague reassurance. "How so?" he demanded.

"The overall commander," Grant replied with a touch of asperity, "is Major General Leland Blake, who is the officer in charge of the Army of the West. There's no one more competent in uniform today!"

"I know Lee Blake, and I am familiar with his record," the President replied a trifle abruptly. "I quite agree with you. He's exceptionally capable. But that doesn't answer my question. What's he doing specifically to end the reign of lawlessness in Montana?"

"He's dispatching a full regiment to Fort Shaw in Montana," General Grant replied. "The troops are all experienced fighting men, all war veterans. And they are being commanded by Colonel Andrew Brentwood, a highly decorated hero of the war, in whom Lee Blake has great confidence. I can't say that I blame him. He's the nephew of the late Mrs. Blake."

"I'm not disputing Colonel Brentwood's credentials," the President said, unconsciously raising his voice. "But where is he? Why aren't he and his regiment already in Montana, restoring order and establishing a rule of law? The territory is part of these United States, you know, and I can find no excuse for reigns of chaos and terror there!"

Grant took the criticism personally, and he, too, became strident. "The passes through the Rockies that lead from the Pacific, where the regiment is currently stationed, are six to twelve feet deep in snow. The troops can't be moved until the season is farther advanced and the snow melts!"

Andrew Johnson was not satisfied with his explanation. "I find it odd—incomprehensible, in fact—that the situation was allowed to deteriorate so badly. How does it happen that the regiment is only now being sent into the territory? Why wasn't it stationed there last year in time to prevent these outrages that are making life so miserable for our settlers?"

General Grant had a difficult time keeping a lid on his temper. "Ever since Colonel Brentwood's unit was formed a year ago," he said, "he and his men have had their hands full! They've been busy fighting the Nez Percé in Washington. You may recall, Mr. President, that the Indians there revolted, and the army had its hands full."

"Montana," the President said, "must be made safe once and for all for American citizens. It must no longer be a land where outlaws find sanctuary and where Indians terrorize the settlers."

When a President of the United States spoke in that tone, only one reply was possible. "Yes, sir," Ulysses S. Grant said.

Andrew Johnson had worked himself to a fever pitch. "We're a supposedly civilized nation," he said, "and we're living in the second half of the nineteenth century, a supposedly civilized age. So I find such activities intolerable in any territory where the flag of the United States of America flies."

Grant again said, "Yes, sir."

President Johnson spoke crisply, with finality. "Send a telegram without delay to Lee Blake," he said. "Tell him you're acting on the instructions of the Commander in Chief. Instruct him to send Colonel Brentwood's regiment to Montana with the greatest dispatch as soon as weather conditions are reasonably safe." As far as he was concerned, that settled the problem.

General Grant fumed as he rode back to his own War Department headquarters in his carriage. He regarded Lee Blake as exceptionally competent, and he hated to interfere in any way with the operations of a subordinate's command. But in this instance he had no choice. The Commander in Chief had given him a direct order, and he was required to obey it. As soon as he reached his desk, he immediately started to work, drafting a long telegram to Major General Leland Blake at Fort Vancouver in the Washington Territory, across the Columbia River from Portland, Oregon.

The open-air cooking fire could be seen for miles on the vast prairie of eastern Montana, but the members of the band, eating their supper around it, were indifferent to the reflection it cast. Hard men with wooden faces and expressionless eyes, they either squatted or sat on the ground and ate stolidly in silence, tearing the buffalo meat apart with their fingers and wolfing down the baked beans that were a staple of their diet. If they seemed arrogant, they had good cause: They comprised the Hastings gang, the most feared band of cutthroats, gunslingers, and robbers in the entire West, and they were conscious of their standing.

Sitting alone, conversing with no one, was a woman with closely cropped gray hair. Sadie "Ma" Hastings, the widow of the founder of the band and currently its head, often was mistaken for a man. She wore a man's broad-brimmed hat, open-throated shirt, breeches, and boots; a pair of six-shooters dangled from the ammunition belt around her middle; and she displayed no delicacy, no hint of femininity as she gnawed the meat from a bone.

To her left was her elder son, Clifford, who was thirty-one years of age and very good-looking. He was stocky, solidly built, and bore a strong resemblance to his mother. It was said that if Ma Hastings cared about anyone on the face of the earth, it was Clifford.

There was an aura of mystery that surrounded him, largely because he rarely participated in the raids that the band conducted. He was generally recognized, however, as half of the brains behind the gang's activities. It was Clifford Hastings along with his mother who planned every robbery and issued precise instructions to the men on how the action was to be carried out.

Newer members of the gang, like the laconic, ugly Slim Davis, were inclined to believe that Clifford was endowed with a yellow streak that made him afraid to participate in actual combat. But the older members of the band knew better. He was a deadly shot, as cool in an emergency as his late father. The old-timers insisted that he was merciless, utterly lacking in fear, and they warned the newer members to stay on the right side of him. His only known weakness was his penchant for visiting brothels whenever he had money in the worn leather purse he carried in a shirt pocket.

Seated near Clifford, gorging himself on food, was his younger brother, Ralph. Ma Hastings ignored him, as did most of the others, and only Clifford glanced in his direction from time to time to make sure that he was all right. Ralph Hastings was, to put it mildly, a problem. Short, fat, and in his mid-twenties, Ralph had two obsessions. One was food, and the other was the raw gin that was available from the peddlers who crossed the territory on foot.

"Ralph ain't too bright," was Ma's judgment of her younger son, and the members of the band agreed. Only Clifford knew better. Ralph was sensitive, and his older brother suspected that he drank to excess because he was secretly ashamed of the way that his mother and his brother earned their living. It was an unwritten but inviolable law of the band that Ralph was to be left behind and not participate in any of the group's activities.

As Ma put it, "My Ralph, he means good, but he's an awful slow draw, and his aim ain't worth spittin' at. So we don't lose nothin' by leavin' him with the packhorses."

Both Clifford and his mother well knew that Ralph's trouble was not due to his poor aim or his inability to draw a weapon rapidly. Usually he had consumed so much gin by the time a raid took place that he was useless. But this was a subject Clifford and his mother did not discuss. The less said the better.

Ma threw into the fire the bone on which she was chewing and wiped her hands on the sides of her breeches. Rolling a cigarette with one hand, she picked up a twig in the other. Reaching toward the fire she lighted the twig and used it to light the cigarette. It dangled from one corner of her mouth as she surveyed her subordinates, taking her time as she looked first at one, then at another. "Everybody here?" she demanded. "Nobody's missin'?"

Clifford made a rapid count. "We're all here, Ma," he replied.

"You boys was grumblin' to each other the last couple o' days," Ma said, "because you thought I was ridin' ya too hard, traipsin' from one end o' Montana to the other. Well, it ain't accidental that we pitched our camp right here where we're sittin' now."

Something in her tone, rather than her actual words, caught their attention, and all eight members of the band, along with Clifford, watched her closely. Only Ralph seemed lost in thought as he continued to gaze vacantly into the fire.

"Any o' you boys ever heard tell of a feller called Pete Purcell?"

There was a silence, which was finally broken by Slim Davis, whose voice sounded as though he had a mouth filled with pebbles. "If we're talkin' about the same gent," he said, "there was a Pete Purcell down Wyoming way who was supposed to be the best gunslinger in the whole West. I heard tell that one time he even stood up to Whip Holt and got away with it."

Ma Hastings snorted impatiently. "There ain't a man alive," she said, "that ever stood up to Whip Holt and lived to talk about it. Don't believe every tall tale ya hear, Slim. I'll say this much, though. From what I hear, Pete was a gunslinger and a first-rate one at that. He also happens to be one o' the best judges o' horseflesh anywheres."

The men knew that Ma was not talking for her own entertainment.

"What happened to him?" Slim asked.

"Well, I was told Pete got married to a little gal he met down in Wyoming," Ma said, "and a year later, when she died havin' her baby, he grieved somethin' awful. That's when Pete reformed. He ain't sighted down his barrel or pulled a trigger in sixteen years!"

Slim was fascinated. "How come?"

"He had this kid, ya see," Ma replied. "A boy name o' Hank. Pete had to be a ma as well as pa to the kid, so he swore he was goin' to change his ways, and damned if he ain't kept his word.

"That ain't sayin' he's lost the knack o' handlin' firearms," Ma went on. "He's still as dangerous as any man you'll find anywheres. So we're goin' to need to be real careful and cautious."

Clifford, who already knew what his mother had in mind, calmly plucked a weed and chewed on the white root at its end.

"It just happens," Ma said, "that Pete Purcell raises the finest horses you're gonna find for miles and miles around. He's been sellin' one or two a year, and his customers are so blamed anxious to get them that they pay his price, no matter how much he asks. Well, I got to thinkin', and the way I see it, we need some new mounts. I don't see no reason why Pete should be greedy and take all the profits. He should be willin' to share with those who're in need, like me. So we've come here, and right this minute we're sittin' no more'n a couple o' miles from his ranch. Now that we got full bellies, I think we're gonna ride over there and relieve Pete o' some o' his horses."

Members of the gang chuckled softly as they exchanged glances. Ma, as always, was thinking of their welfare, and that's why they swore loyalty to her.

Clifford took charge, and there was a ring of authority in his voice. "There's no moon tonight," he said, "which is why we planned our raid accordin'ly. Everythin' depends on our timin', which has to be just right. I'm gonna draw you a sketch o' the Purcell ranch, and I want you to come around me now and pay attention." He picked up a stick and began to draw squares and circles in the dirt near the fire. "Here's Purcell's house," he said. "A hundred yards or so from it is his corral. They're the only two places you got to worry about." He pointed the stick as he spoke. "Bob, you'll open the corral gate. That is your only job. You six will ride inside, lasso a couple o' horses each, and lead them out. Your job is the ticklish one, and you can't hesitate. You got to drop your ropes just right over the heads o' the horses, and don't scare them. Because once that gate is open, they'll streak for daylight if they get half a chance."

"Be they wild?" a member of the gang wanted to know.

Clifford shook his head. "High spirited, not wild. Purcell not only breeds fine horses, but he trains them real good, too." He looked at each man in turn. "Any questions so far?"

"What about me?" Slim Davis demanded. "What do I do?"

"I was just comin' to you," Clifford said. "You and me have a special job. Seein' as how we're the best marksmen in the crowd, we're goin' to keep watch on Purcell's ranch house, and if Pete comes chargin' out and starts to raise his rifle to his shoulder, we do away with him, and we do it neat and clean, as well as fast."

"You're comin' with me, Cliff?" Slim could not hide his surprise.

Clifford spat into the dirt. "You already heard that Pete Purcell was a gunslinger second to none. I been doin' a lot of figurin', and it's like I told Ma, we can't afford to take no chances. So you and me will ride herd on old Pete. And the minute we see him startin' to use one o' the boys as a target, we'll put our own lead into him. Everybody got it straight?"

One by one the men nodded. Each of them knew his assignment, and there were no questions.

"I guess we'll be on our way then," Ma said, and without further ado, started across the prairie toward the place where her horse was grazing.

The others followed her example, and bolts clicked as they checked their rifles for the task that lay ahead.

Only Ralph remained sitting at the fire. When he was alone, but not until then, he reached into a hip pocket, drew out a pint bottle of gin, and raising it to his lips, downed half the contents. He coughed, gasped, and then a complacent, satisfied smile spread across his moon face. The gang could risk their lives for all he cared; he was happy to stay right where he was for the rest of the evening.

The kitchen of the small, unpretentious ranch house was bare, devoid of all ornamentation. A pair of old curtains covered the window; they had been washed so frequently over the years that they were threadbare and scarcely served the purpose for which they were intended. The kitchen table was of unpainted pine, as were the chairs, and on the small, utilitarian wood-burning stove two battered pans still simmered.

Seated at the table was tall, rangy Pete Purcell, his heavy tan emphasized by the freckles that dusted his nose and by his sun-streaked hair. Opposite him, concentrating on a mammoth steak, was his sixteen-year-old son, Hank, who bore a startling resemblance to his father and gave promise of being even taller and huskier when he stopped growing.

Pete ate methodically, shoveling his own steak and fried potatoes into his mouth, chewing them thoughtfully, and getting the next bite ready even before he swallowed. Suddenly he pointed his knife. "Hank," he directed, "eat your salad greens!"

The boy made a face. "Aw, Pa! Do I have to?"

"It strikes me you're gettin' kind of big for a visit out back o' the woodshed," Pete told him, "but I am still bigger'n ya, and I can still whale ya. I'm bringin' ya up the way your ma would've if she were still livin', and ya know blame well she would've insisted that ya eat your salad greens. She was always harpin' on me to eat greens, and that's why ya have to do it."

"How come I gotta eat greens, when you never touch 'em, Pa?" he demanded.

Pete chewed thoughtfully as he pondered the question. "The way I see it," he said, grinning, "ya got me ridin' on your back, boy, but I ain't got anybody pesterin' me, and that's the difference between us. If your ma was still here, you bet I'd eat vegetables and salad greens twice a day. But I can't hardly stomach 'em, so I don't touch 'em. But your situation ain't the same as mine." He chuckled sympathetically.

Hank couldn't help laughing, too. Then he picked up his fork manfully, speared a large quantity of lettuce in his salad bowl, and cramming it into his mouth, chewed and swallowed rapidly. There was no appeal from his father's ruling, as he well knew. They had been inseparable ever since Hank's mother had died in childbirth, and his father meant everything to him. But he knew that his late mother's slightest wishes were still law. His father had confessed to him freely, for instance, that he had been a gunslinger in Wyoming and Utah but that he'd reformed after he had become a father. He had walked a straight, narrow path for sixteen years.

Pete watched his son wolfing down lettuce and nodded in approval. "That's more like it," he said.

"I always do what ya tell me, Pa," Hank replied seriously.

Pete raised an eyebrow. "Ya finished your book learnin' for the week?"

Hank returned to his steak, and with his mouth full, he merely nodded.

"Did ya put shoes on the colt yet, like I told ya to?"

Again the boy nodded.

"Let me see now." Pete frowned in concentration, trying to catch his son out. "Here's one for ya. What did I tell ya is the first rule of firearms?"

Hank swallowed a mouthful of food and grinned. "That's easy," he said. "Ya taught me never to draw a gun unless I mean to shoot, and never to shoot unless I mean to kill."

Pete was highly pleased. He had taught his son all there was to know about guns, and Hank had proved to be an excellent pupil. He was now nearly as good a shot as his father, though the boy had made a solemn vow to Pete never to use a gun unless he needed to protect himself or his loved ones. Leaning across the table, Pete grasped his son affectionately by the shoulder. "You're smart, boy," he said. "Smart as they come."

Pete relaxed, and they ate together in a companionable silence. Hank stood and refilled their plates with fried potatoes and then took several slices of steak from the other pan. "Might as well finish up this here beef," he said. "It'll be too tough by mornin' to eat."

"Might as well," Pete answered, and helped himself.

The silence was broken by a loud, squeaking noise, the sound of the corral gate being opened.

Pete tensed immediately, his meal forgotten. He leaped to his feet and, glancing out the window, saw six men on horseback in the corral, rounding up the mounts that were his pride.

"There's robbers out yonder," he said hoarsely, and immediately took his rifle from the wall pegs on which it rested.

Hank needed no urging and ran for his own rifle, which was propped against a far wall.

"I'll handle this, boy," his father told him. "Don't you start mixin' in unless I call for ya."

Hank wanted to protest, but his father's word was still law, and he didn't say a word.

Pete quietly opened the door and stepped outside.

The thieves were professionals, he could see that much very clearly. A lasso had been thrown over the head of each horse in the corral, and the animals were quickly being led out into the open. The whole procedure was smooth, rapid, and amazingly efficient.

Pete started to raise his rifle to his shoulder, but he had no opportunity to aim, much less to fire. Before the rifle butt even reached his shoulder, a single shot sounded sharply, and Pete Purcell crumpled to the ground, a bullet placed neatly between his eyes.

"Ya got him, Slim!" Clifford Hastings called. "Nice shootin'."

"Ain't no one can shoot like Slim Davis!" Slim laughed.

"Now let's get out o' here," Clifford called.

A helpless rage, combined with an all-consuming sorrow, shook young Hank Purcell. Tears stung his eyes, and he shook his head to clear his vision. Flattening himself against the open door so the raiders would not notice him, he stared hard at the man called Slim. Concentrating his whole being on the man, Hank committed every detail of that face to memory. Never would he forget the man called Slim, never would he erase the picture of his father's killer from his mind.

Recognizing the futility of striking single-handed against so large a number, he closed his eyes and stood rigidly until the hoofbeats of the raiders died away.

Then he saw that he was alone and the corral was empty. His lifeless father lay sprawled in the dirt at his feet.

The night that followed remained forever unclear in Hank's mind. The sun sank behind the snow-capped peaks to the west, and he dragged himself to the yard at the rear of the house. There, next to the pine that marked his mother's final resting place, he dug a grave for his father. He never was able to recall actually burying Pete; apparently he blocked the horrors of that experience from his mind.

But when dawn broke over the Dakota prairies to the east, the fog that enveloped Hank Purcell lifted, and he remembered everything from that moment with the utmost clarity.

Picking up his rifle, he dropped to one knee at the graveside. He was dry eyed, and his voice was slightly hoarse when he spoke. "Pa," he said aloud, "I aim to remember every last thing ya ever taught me. I know ya told me never to shoot 'cept in self-defense, but I'll never rest until I do to your killer what he done to ya. I pledge ya my sacred word that I won't rest until the no-good bastard called Slim is six feet underground!" Rising stiffly, he walked to the barn, where his two-year-old gelding was housed. He was fortunate, he supposed, that his horse hadn't been in the corral with the others, or he would be without a mount now. He saddled the animal, then carefully locked the barn, and returning to the house for his bedroll, he locked the doors behind him. There was little, if anything, of value that he was leaving behind, other than his memories.

He mounted his horse and paused for a moment to look back at the pine tree. On one side of it stood his mother's grave, on the other side was the freshly turned earth of his father's. His jaw tightening, his green eyes blazing, he turned his mount and headed for the north, in the direction he had seen the bandits ride off.

II

Fort Vancouver, overlooking the Columbia River on its north bank opposite the town of Portland, Oregon, was a busy place, as befitted the headquarters of the Western command of the United States Army. Commissioned and noncommissioned officers on night duty in the headquarters building worked late, as usual, and oil lamps burned in many offices. In the barracks there were lectures and demonstrations in progress, and everywhere a sense of bustle and purpose prevailed.

Only in the private house of the commander in chief of the Army of the West, did absolute peace prevail. Major General Lee Blake, tall, gray haired, and distinguished, a hero of both the Mexican War and the Civil War, sat at the head of his dining room table and watched the handsome lady seated opposite him pouring coffee.

Eulalia Holt, looking radiant, with her thick, dark hair hanging loosely down her bare shoulders and cascading over the top of her off-the-shoulder gown, cer-

tainly didn't look like the mother of Toby and Cindy
Holt. She had recovered from the devastating blow she
had suffered when Whip Holt, her husband, had been
killed in a mountain slide with Lee's wife, Cathy, the
previous year, and there were no dark shadows beneath
her eyes now.

There was no denying that she was a middle-aged
matron, but Lee reflected that she bore a surprising resemblance to the lovely, high-spirited girl she had been
when they had crossed the continent together in the first
wagon train to Oregon.

That was when he had won Cathy van Ayl as his
bride, and Whip and Eulalia had been married, also.
The two couples had been close for more than a quarter
of a century since that time, and Lee felt, now that he
and Eulalia were the only survivors, that they were
drawn together by special bonds.

"Aren't you having any more coffee?" he asked.

She smiled and shook her head. "At my age," she
said gently, "I find that more than one cup at night
keeps me awake."

"In that case," Lee said, chuckling, "I'm forced to
make the same confession to you. Shall we go up to the
point and see the view instead?"

"I'd love to!" Eulalia said eagerly, and they rose
simultaneously to their feet.

A few minutes later they were strolling arm in arm
up to the pinnacle behind the buildings of the fort to the
artillery lookout that afforded a splendid view of the
river and of Oregon beyond it. Eulalia was wearing a
cape of beaver to ward off the chill, and Lee had
donned his greatcoat and his gold braided senior officer's
hat.

They were silent as they walked, both of them content, both of them very much at ease with each other. They had been frequent companions since the grim tragedy that had robbed them of their respective mates, and they found great solace in their close friendship.

At last they reached the summit, and Eulalia leaned on the rail and looked at the lights in Oregon on the far side of the river.

Lee Blake concentrated on her, rather than on the view. "I—I've been wanting—very much—to have a talk with you," he said.

She turned to him and was surprised to note that he was somewhat flustered and was encountering difficulty in speaking clearly. Guessing the nature of his problem, she smiled at him in encouragement.

"We've known each other for a great many years," he began tentatively.

"More years than either of us cares to recall, I'm sure," Eulalia said lightly.

"Of course," Lee went on, "you had your life with Whip and your children, and I had mine with Cathy and Beth, so it was only natural that we never developed a close relationship. Then when tragedy struck us simultaneously almost a year ago, it pulled us together."

"Yes, that it did," she replied. "You'll never know how much you helped me to overcome a terrible time."

"You did the same for me," he said. "In fact, you saved my sanity. And that's no exaggeration."

Eulalia reached out and put a hand on his arm. "Lee, my dear," she said, "I remember all too clearly that you proposed marriage to me several months ago, and I told you at that time that it was premature, that we were still too close to our losses to be able to think clearly."

"I well remember the occasion," he said, "and I have waited until now. Do you still think it's too soon?"

Not trusting her voice, she made no reply in words and shook her head.

Lee's face reddened. "I've had very little practice at this sort of thing," he said, "so you will have to forgive my blundering approach. But I've been wondering—that is to say, I've been hoping—I mean—"

"Yes, my dear," she said, smiling as she interrupted him, "I'll be very pleased and proud to become your wife."

His relief was so great that he exhaled very slowly. Then he recovered and, taking her in his arms, kissed her gently.

Eulalia had been kissed by no man other than Whip in more years than she could remember. But Lee's kiss felt good, and she was warm, secure, and safe in the knowledge that she was cherished and that she wanted this man as much as he wanted her. Her arms tightened around his neck.

After a time they moved apart. "We'll be very wise if we go back to the house before we indulge in more of that kind of thing," he said in a strained voice. "It wouldn't do at all to have some junior officer and his fiancée come up here and stumble onto us."

Eulalia couldn't quite control the giggle that welled up in her. "I suppose I'll become accustomed to thinking of preserving a dignified front for junior officers and the young women they're going to marry," she said. "I'll do my best to remember it."

"You'll do whatever you please," he told her. "I think it's miraculous that we're getting together."

She looked up at him, her blue eyes luminous. "It is rather astonishing, you know. I was worried, for a time, about certain things, as I saw us growing closer and closer to each other."

"What kind of things?" he demanded, challenging her.

Eulalia took his arm, and they started down the path that would take them back to his house. "I had two worries," she said. "One of them was that memories of Whip and of Cathy might come between us and spoil whatever happiness we could attain together. I've thought about that problem long and hard."

"So have I," Lee told her soberly, "and it was not until I was quite sure, in my own mind, of where both of us stood that I was presumptuous enough to propose to you a second time."

"Michael Holt was a very special man," Eulalia said softly. "I have many wonderful memories of him, and I shall carry those memories with me until the day I die. By that same token, I know that Cathy was a very special person, too. A rather wonderful person. I knew her as well as one woman can ever know another, and there is no doubt in my mind that she will occupy a special niche in your heart as long as you live. Neither of us would be the kind of people we are unless we felt that way. But I don't think the ghosts of Whip and of Cathy are going to interfere with our relationship."

"I'm quite sure of it, too," Lee said. "Wherever they are now in the afterworld, I'm quite sure they're rejoicing that you and I have found each other and are going to be getting together. This may sound foolish of me, but I have the feeling it's what they would have wanted for both of us."

She considered his statement, weighing it, and ultimately she nodded.

They walked the rest of the way to the house in companionable silence.

When they moved indoors, Lee removed his hat and coat, then helped Eulalia with her cloak, and again taking her into his arms, kissed her soundly and at length. She stepped back from him and was slightly breathless. "We're not finished talking yet," she said. "It's not fair to distract me that way. You're destroying my ability to think clearly."

He grinned at her. "I refuse to apologize."

"Very well, sir," she replied with spirit, "please don't. But I want you to listen to me. I said that as I saw our situation, we have two problems. We've discussed one of them."

They walked side by side into the living room, and Lee went to a table where he kept several cut-glass decanters and looked at her questioningly.

She shook her head. The general poured himself a small brandy but did not give her a drink. "I'm bracing myself," he told her.

"We're not alone in the world, either of us," Eulalia said a trifle grimly. "We have children to consider, and their feelings about us are bound to have an effect. We already know the resentment your daughter feels about our seeing each other. Thus, you can imagine what Beth will say when she and Rob return from the lodge in Washington and she hears we're going to be married."

Lee grimaced and then sipped his brandy. "If I know Beth," he said, "she'll try to raise the roof with me. She's found it very difficult to accept the loss of her mother. She views the rock slide as an unnatural event, and she feels that Cathy was taken from us prematurely."

"So she was," Eulalia said, "but the important thing

to keep in mind is that we did lose her and that now life must go on."

Lee nodded, and his voice was like steel as he said, "Whatever my daughter's problem may be, I refuse to let our lives be affected by it. Beth has a very clear choice. Either she accepts our marriage, in which case we'll welcome her with open arms, or she won't, in which case we'll have virtually nothing to do with her."

"There's no need to take that strong a stand," Eulalia murmured.

Lee shook his head. "I'm sorry, but that's my decision. I'm going to let nothing come between us or influence us, and that's final!"

She realized this was not a time to discuss the matter in depth with him, so she changed the subject slightly. "I don't foresee my daughter creating any problem whatever for us," she said. "I know Cindy will be genuinely pleased. She likes and admires you enormously, and I think she will very happily accept our marriage."

He smiled and nodded. "That's a relief," he said, "because of all our children, she's the only one we'll have at home, and it would be unfortunate if she were at odds with her stepfather."

"I can't imagine that happening," she replied.

He took another sip of his brandy and looked at her quizzically. "What about Toby?"

"I honestly don't know how Toby will react to the news," Eulalia said. "Certainly he must realize that you and I have dinner here several evenings a week, and when we aren't here, we're eating at my house. It must have occurred to him that we have something other than an ordinary friendship, but he's very much like Whip in many ways. He becomes almost Indian-like in personal

matters and is so inscrutable that it's impossible for anyone, including me, to tell what he thinks."

Lee's voice became strident without his realizing it.
"I believe," he said, "that Toby will have enough on his
mind that he won't be able to concern himself too much
about our marriage."

Surprised by both his tone and his words, Eulalia
looked at him inquiringly.

"This is privileged information," he said, "so it isn't
to be repeated."

It occurred to her that she would be privy to a
great many government secrets from this time forward.

"I had a confidential telegram just today from General Grant," he said, "and conditions in the Montana
Territory are chaotic. There's a major Indian uprising
brewing there, and the Sioux are going to raise holy hell
anytime now. In addition to that, bands of thieves are
pillaging settlers' homes and murdering innocent people
all over the territory."

"Oh, dear," she murmured.

"Those factors, combined with a very difficult terrain, are going to create conditions that will keep Toby
and my son-in-law, Rob Martin, fully occupied," he said.
"I'm sending Andy Brentwood's regiment to Montana as
soon as the weather permits—on the direct orders of
President Johnson—but as competent an officer as Andy
is, I don't expect him to perform miracles. As I say,
Toby is going to have no opportunity to worry about his
mother's remarriage."

Eulalia meant what she said when she told Lee
Blake that she had no idea how her son would react to
the news of his mother's forthcoming remarriage. But
she was determined to find out, and the best of all pos-

sible ways, she thought, was to hold a confidential talk with Clarissa Sinclair, Toby's houseguest who was staying at the ranch. Clarissa had recently sold the boardinghouse she owned in Washington and was spending more and more time with Toby in Oregon. Certainly it seemed just a matter of time until the young couple got married.

From what Eulalia saw of Toby and Clarissa when they were together, she strongly suspected that they were having an affair, though since they were sensible, grown-up people, this was not her concern. Eulalia was determined to find out from Clarissa what Toby felt about his mother's remarriage, reasoning that the younger woman well might know things that Eulalia herself knew nothing about.

Fortune smiled on her that same night when Lee took her home. She found that Toby had already retired, and Clarissa, clad in a dressing gown, was in the kitchen, boiling a pot of water.

Eulalia halted and quietly studied her. She herself was far from short, but Clarissa, who was five feet ten inches tall, towered above her. The younger woman had red hair and green eyes, and she was big boned yet well proportioned, with broad shoulders, a high, firm bust, and an incredibly tiny waist. Her hips were svelte, and her legs were exceptionally long. She moved with surprising grace for a woman her size, and Eulalia could see why Toby found Clarissa so attractive.

Eulalia gently cleared her throat to notify the guest of her presence.

Clarissa looked up slowly, in no way surprised, and smiled. "Good evening, Mrs. Holt," she said pleasantly. "I hope you don't mind my taking over in your kitchen this way, but I suddenly felt that I wanted a cup of tea before I went to bed."

"By all means. Have some tea if you wish," Eulalia told her, "but wouldn't you prefer some hot chocolate?"

The young woman laughed. "There goes my diet," she said. "You've found one of my secret weaknesses."

Eulalia moved to the stove and took charge. "I shouldn't have hot chocolate, either, but I think I will. So we'll both be very wicked." She laughed.

Clarissa's giggle was conspiratorial, too. Then she looked at the older woman and said, "I'm glad we are doing this, Mrs. Holt. I've been wanting to have a private chat with you for some time."

"No more than I've wanted one with you," Eulalia replied. "Why don't you start?"

"There's something that has been bothering me," Clarissa said. "I'm sure you're aware of the fact that Toby and I have been sleeping together, and I don't want you to get the idea that I'm that kind of a person."

Eulalia patted her on the shoulder. "I'm not sure that I know what kind of a person you have in mind, but I can assure you I have only good thoughts about you."

"I—I'm glad," Clarissa said, and continued to speak bluntly, as she always did. "I was married once. Unhappily married, and my husband, who drank to excess, was killed in the war. For the first time in my life I fell in love after I met Toby, and that is why I have given myself to him."

Eulalia measured out the chocolate and stirred the milk, which she had started to heat on the stove. "I've had no doubt in my mind that you love Toby," she said. "If I didn't know it, I'd realize it from the instant that I saw you looking at him."

Color rose to Clarissa's face, and she looked even more attractive. "I didn't realize I was that transparent."

"You aren't to anyone except me, perhaps," Eulalia assured her.

Clarissa was relieved, and even pleased, that Eulalia had taken such an interest in her.

"The big question, it strikes me, is whether or not Toby loves you. Does he?"

Clarissa took a deep breath and replied slowly. "I'm certain he does, Mrs. Holt. If I weren't convinced of it, I wouldn't still be sleeping with him. I believe with all my heart that Toby does love me. Unfortunately, he doesn't yet realize it. He's still a little in love with someone else."

"What do you mean?"

"As I understand it, for many years you and the late Mrs. Blake campaigned quietly, but diligently, to promote a romance between Toby and Beth Blake."

"I'm afraid I must plead guilty to that," Eulalia said.

"They wanted nothing to do with each other, which was only natural, but after a time, Toby began to appreciate Beth's good qualities. Only then it was too late, for Beth got married to Rob Martin. Still, I know he remains rather enamored of her."

"What a pity!" his mother said.

"Isn't it?" Clarissa was as calm as she was realistic. "Toby is endowed with great good sense," she said. "It's one of his more attractive traits. So I have been waiting quietly for him to settle down to earth again and to realize that Beth means nothing to him. You see, I'm convinced that sooner or later—and I hope it's going to be very soon—he'll wake up to the realization that I'm the woman he's wanted all along. When that happens, he'll marry me—I hope." She forced a smile, but it was obvious that she was making a great effort.

"I admire your perseverance, as well as your honesty," Eulalia told her as she added the chocolate to the hot milk and stirred it. "You're in a thoroughly unpleasant situation, and you need to show a great deal of character and a lot of patience."

"I don't have too much choice, do I?" Clarissa said, and smiled without bitterness. "I'm neither a saint nor a martyr. It just so happens that I know my man. At least I'm convinced I know him, and I'll be very much surprised if my estimate of him is wrong and he turns away from me. It isn't easy to wait for him to see the light and come to his senses, but I console myself with the thought that ultimately I can't lose."

Eulalia studied her and nodded, admiration in her expression and in her voice. "You won't lose," she said. "I'm sure of it, too."

Clarissa thanked her.

Eulalia filled their cups with the hot chocolate, and the other woman carried them to the kitchen table.

A generation separated them, yet Eulalia felt completely at ease with this young woman. "As long as we're talking in confidence," she said, "perhaps you can be of help to me."

Clarissa's eyes widened. "I can't imagine how," she said, "but I'll certainly be glad to try."

Eulalia took a deep breath. "You're the first to know this," she said, "and I'll be grateful if you'll keep the information completely to yourself for the present. I'm going to marry General Blake."

Clarissa remained calm and smiled quietly. "I must admit I'm not surprised," she said. "Ever since I've known you, I've kept thinking how right you seem for each other."

"Thank you. I take that as a compliment."

"That's the way it was intended," Clarissa said. "You both have qualities that I greatly admire, and surely those same fine qualities are what drew you to each other in the first place."

"We do have much in common," Eulalia said. "But it is nice, all the same, to hear that someone else thinks so, too." She hesitated for a moment. "How do you think our children are going to react to the news?"

Clarissa paused before speaking. "You probably already know this," she said at last, "but Beth Martin will be very antagonistic."

The older woman nodded. "I do know, and so does General Blake. I just wish we could do something to alter her attitude."

Clarissa pondered the statement briefly. "I don't know if you can. I'm afraid Beth's an unpredictable, unstable person just now. She misses her mother desperately, and even Rob, who should be first in her life, is unable to help her. It seems she just can't understand the tragedy, can't understand why her father isn't reacting exactly as she is. She doesn't see that for the very reason General and Mrs. Blake were so happily married, he'd want to be married and find happiness again. I think it's as simple as that."

"You may be right," Eulalia said. "But for all of our sakes, I hope she starts to see reason."

"I hope so, too," Clarissa said.

"I'm not in the least worried about Cindy," Eulalia said.

"Your confidence in her is justified, I'm quite sure," Clarissa told her. "She's always been very close to you, I gather, and in her opinion, you can do no wrong. If you've elected to marry General Blake, she'll accept that without questioning it in any way."

Eulalia nodded, and in spite of her attempt to remain tranquil, she grew tense. "What about Toby?" she wanted to know. "I'm asking you because I believe you're better acquainted with him these days than I am."

Clarissa sipped her hot chocolate and stared at the nearest kitchen window, in which she saw the reflection of the logs burning in the hearth. "Toby," she said, "adores you, and he also worships the memory of his father. I also know he respects General Blake a great deal. But I'm afraid I can't, for the life of me, predict how he'll feel about your news."

"I was afraid of that," Eulalia murmured.

"If he's troubled," Clarissa said, "I think it's likely that he'll come to me and talk about the problem. If he does, I'll do my best to set him straight and to convince him that your decision is by far the best and most sensible for both you and for General Blake."

The older woman moistened her dry lips. "Thank you. I just hope that Toby comes to his senses soon and realizes what he's missing by not being married to you. You have no idea how much I look forward to having you in the family as a daughter."

Major Isham Jentry was tired after his long journey across the continent from the District of Columbia, and he was relieved that he had at last arrived in eastern Oregon. In another day or two, he would reach the Holt ranch, outside Portland, and his long journey would come to an end.

He had traveled by train from Washington City to

Independence, Missouri, and then had gone on horseback from that takeoff point for the rest of his journey, following the by-now highly traveled Oregon Trail. Accustomed to traveling on his own for long distances, Major Jentry was nevertheless surprised to discover that, in his mid-thirties, he had somewhat less stamina than he used to have. Consequently, he hoped that Toby Holt and Rob Martin, to whom he had been assigned by General Grant on the personal directive of President Johnson, would consent to grant him a respite of a day or two before they took off with him for the mountains of Montana.

He was looking forward to the survey for the railroad line. After devoting many years to a study of potential railroad routes, he was facing the greatest challenge of his life. It would be nice, all the same, to do nothing for forty-eight hours before setting out for the rugged wilderness of the territory where the railroad line would be laid.

Isham Jentry didn't know the name of the small Oregon community where he was spending the night, but that scarcely mattered. He had found a small, exceptionally comfortable inn, and the proprietor and his wife, Jim and Nolane Brennan, had not only put him up in a very comfortable room but had also given him the best meal he had eaten in weeks. Now, feeling sated and at peace, he decided to take a brief stroll in order to stretch his legs after spending day after day in the saddle.

There was a genuine feeling of spring in the air, and Brennan and his wife were sitting on the porch of the inn, drinking tea, when the major emerged into the open.

"Going to see the sights of the town, mister?" the innkeeper asked, chuckling.

"Something of the sort," Jentry replied, as always slightly surprised when people thought him a civilian. But he knew there was nothing else they could think since he was on furlough and was not in uniform. He would be outfitted when he arrived at Fort Vancouver and his surveying assignment began.

"You can see just about all there is to see from here," Mrs. Brennan told him. "There's the post office, and next to it is the general store, and beyond that is the sheriff's office. Oh, yes, and the bank is just across the street on our side, with our dentist renting space on the second floor. And that's about it."

The major chuckled and explained that he was just intending to get a breath of air before he turned in.

"If you like flowers," the innkeeper's wife told him, "be sure you stop at the garden down at the end of the block. After the warm weather we've had for the past week, some of the crocuses are in bloom."

Jentry thanked her and started off on his stroll. The night was clear, the sky was star-filled, and the moon was so bright that he could see the few buildings of the little town in full detail. Reaching the corner, he paused dutifully to bend down and look at the little flowers that bloomed at the base of a thick evergreen hedge.

Major Jentry never knew what hit him. The burly, barrel-chested man loomed up behind him, a knife gleaming in one hand, and he plunged the blade into the victim's back. The blow was expertly directed, and Isham Jentry was dead before he crumpled to the ground.

The killer removed the blade, wiping it on his victim's clothing, then flipped Major Jentry onto his back and expertly, swiftly, rifled his pockets.

Taking no time to read the papers, the thief was delighted to see that the documents included identification, an important-looking letter from the War Department, and best of all, a considerable wad of paper money.

Jamming the booty into his own pocket, the man hurried off down the street, and moving with a speed that was not in keeping with his bulk, he soon disappeared from sight, to where his waiting horse was tied.

Jim Brennan and his wife, who had witnessed the entire incident, were almost paralyzed by the tragedy, which seemed to happen in an instant. They continued to gape as if in a trance, and finally the innkeeper grasped his wife's arm. "Come on," he said. "We'd better report all this to the sheriff's office in a hurry!"

Reluctant to go to the scene of the crime themselves in the event the killer was lurking nearby, the couple headed directly down the street. Moments later they were seated in the office of the deputy sheriff, who heard their story, managed to calm them, and immediately sent two assistants in search of the killer.

"Now then," he said, "you say you saw the man who put a knife into the guest at your inn?"

"Yes, sir," Brennan said. "The moonlight was nice and bright. Too bright, as a matter of fact. The dirty swine pushed a knife into our guest as calm as you please."

The deputy sheriff picked up a quill pen and dipped it in a jar of ink. "Describe the man to me, if you please."

Mrs. Brennan started to reply.

The official shook his head. "Your turn will come,"

he said. "One at a time. I want to hear what your husband has to say first."

Brennan described the murderer to the best of his ability. Then his wife did the same, and the deputy sheriff jotted down descriptions on which they concurred.

"That should give us enough to get a start on," he said. "I'll send someone to the nearest telegraph office to wire every post office in Oregon, California, and the Washington Territory right off. You've been very helpful, both of you, and I thank you for the information."

Before the couple could leave, an assistant came to the door. "We found the body, sheriff," he said, "just where Mr. and Mrs. Brennan said it was, but we couldn't find any trace of the killer. We know it was a professional who did the job because of the way he knifed his victim and turned his pockets inside out."

The deputy sheriff shook his head and frowned. "You say you have no idea of the victim's identity?"

Jim Brennan shook his head. "No, sir," he said. "We only rent a few rooms at the inn, as you know, and we never require identification from our guests. The gentleman paid for his night's lodging and for his supper—and for his breakfast tomorrow morning, too, come to think of it. After I showed him to his room, I was talking with him when he unpacked his saddlebags, and there was nothing in them that could identify him, either. What do we do now with his horse?"

"I'd advise you to keep the animal for the present," the deputy told him. "Very often when a person is missing for any length of time, his family makes inquiries, and we're able to trace him in that way. If you don't mind keeping the animal and feeding it, that is—"

"Of course, we will," Mrs. Brennan said, interrupting. "That's the least we could do for the poor fellow."

"I'll keep you informed of any leads we get," the deputy sheriff told the couple. "Between now and then, if you should happen to think that you've seen the murderer previously and can identify him positively, that would be very helpful."

"I'm afraid, sheriff, we've already told you all we know," Jim Brennan replied. "I don't know if the motive was robbery or what it was."

"Console yourselves with the thought that the whole situation will be clarified sooner or later," the deputy sheriff replied. "The days when people were killed indiscriminately in this part of the world are ended. Oregon is a full-fledged state now, and we catch killers, and then we string them up."

"If it's all the same to you," the innkeeper said, "I think I'll load my pistol and keep it on my bedside table at night."

"That's a very wise precaution," the deputy told him. "I'd do that if I were you."

Sixteen-year-old Cindy Holt, her hair in pigtails, stood before the wood-burning stove and turned the strips of bacon sizzling in an oversized frying pan.

Clarissa Sinclair, standing beside her, was even busier. She was toasting bread on the flat of the stove, keeping one eye on the pot in which the coffee bubbled, and deftly frying eggs, flipping them over gently at precisely the right moment.

Toby Holt came into the kitchen, followed by his ever-present companion, his shepherd dog Mr. Blake. Seeing Clarissa and Cindy, Toby paused and grinned. "Well," he said, "you make quite a team."

Clarissa replied without looking up. "Your mother is always cooking for us, and we figured the very least we could do is to prepare a meal for her for a change. Will you go to her bedroom and call her, Toby? We're ready for her now."

"You bet," he replied, and hurried off down the corridor, Mr. Blake choosing to wait in the kitchen for a possible handout from Clarissa or Cindy.

A few moments later, the family was seated around the breakfast table. "This is a lovely surprise," Eulalia said. "I can't thank you enough for being so thoughtful." She smiled at Clarissa, then at her daughter.

"It's about time you slept a little bit later in the morning, Mama," Cindy said.

Eulalia shook her head. "Oh, I've been awake for a very long time. I've been trying to figure out how to broach something to you and Toby, and I finally decided to come straight out with it."

Clarissa encouraged her with a sympathetic smile.

"Toby, Cindy," Eulalia said, "there's little need for me to tell you what I thought—and still think—of your father. He was the most extraordinary man I have ever been privileged to know, and I had twenty-six wonderful years of marriage to him. We had a few difficulties, it's true, but we ironed them out before Toby was born, and I don't think we ever had a serious disagreement from that period until his untimely death."

Cindy nodded gravely, but Toby looked perplexed, wondering why his mother was eulogizing his father.

"We met," Eulalia continued, "when we crossed America together in the first wagon train that came to Oregon. Let me remind you that our closest friends on that long and perilous journey were Cathy van Ayl and Lee Blake."

"We know all that, Mama," Cindy said, a trace of

impatience in her voice. "You've told us all about the wagon train lots of times."

Eulalia ignored the interruption. "As you've seen for yourselves," she went on doggedly, "Lee Blake and I turned to each other for consolation when your father and Lee's wife were taken from us in that terrible rock slide last year."

Cindy listened intently, her face solemn. Toby, however, felt his nerves growing taut, even though he didn't understand why he was reacting as he was.

Clarissa nodded rather emphatically to Eulalia. Bracing herself, her tone unconsciously defiant, Eulalia went on. "Gradually, without our realizing it, the essence of our relationship changed. Last night Lee Blake did me the honor of asking me to become his wife, and I accepted him."

There was a moment of electric silence at the table. Then Cindy jumped to her feet, her bacon, eggs, and toast forgotten. Racing around the table to her mother, she threw her arms around her and hugged her fiercely. "I'm so glad for you, Mama!" she cried. "Gee! This is wonderful!"

Toby realized he had to say something. He forced a smile, even though his face felt stiff and unyielding, and he said lamely, "My felicitations to you and to General Blake, Mama."

If Eulalia was aware of the fact that her son was less than enthusiastic, she did not show it. "We've had time only to make a few very basic decisions," she said. "Cindy, you're still in school, of course, so you'll live with us."

"I'm glad, Mama," the adolescent girl replied sincerely.

"General Blake's duty," Eulalia went on, "requires

him to live at Fort Vancouver for the present, and as he has a large house there, ample for all of our needs, that's where we'll make our home. I hope you'll come there often, Toby, and as for you, Clarissa, you'll always be welcome, too."

Though Toby remained silent, Clarissa said warmly, "Thank you, Mrs. Holt. I appreciate this more than I can tell you."

"I have no intention of selling this ranch, however," Eulalia said emphatically. "This was your father's heritage to his children, and someday it will go to both of you. The horse-raising business is still very profitable, and we'll continue it."

"Good!" Toby said heartily. "That makes a great deal of sense." He knew that Stalking Horse, the Cherokee who was his father's dear friend and who had been the foreman of the ranch ever since the Holts moved there, would continue to run the ranch as he had done in the past. The hired hands all looked up to him, and the ranch had prospered under his and Whip Holt's supervision.

"Ordinarily," his mother said, "you'd be expected to take the reins here. But you have your own career to pursue, and you're going to be off in Montana with Rob for many months. So it isn't fair to ask you to give up your own life and tie yourself to the ranch. But you and Cindy will inherit it jointly one day, and when that time comes, you will be free to dispose of it as you please."

"I'll want to keep it always," Cindy said fervently.

Her brother smiled at her. "I anticipate no serious problems," he said. "I'm reasonably certain you will get your wish."

Eulalia glanced at the grandfather clock that stood in one corner of the kitchen and rose hastily to her feet.

"You'll have to forgive me," she said, "but I have so many things to do today. The general's gig is coming across the river for me in forty-five minutes, so I've really got to hurry." She fled in the direction of her bedroom.

"Cindy," Toby said, "you might want to take Mama her coffee. Even though she's in a rush, she'll still want to drink it."

"Sure," his sister said cheerfully, and balancing her mother's cup and saucer carefully, she went off toward the bedchamber.

Toby returned to his bacon and eggs and ate stolidly, his face revealing nothing. Clarissa studied him in silence for a time. "Well?" she asked at last.

He forced a grin. "I'm as happy for my mother as Cindy is," he said.

Clarissa continued to regard him unblinkingly. "I doubt that very much," she replied. "You don't sound it, and you don't look it."

"All right, then," he replied at last, giving up the pretense of being interested in his breakfast and pushing his unfinished plate away from him. "I am jarred by the news, and I don't mind admitting it to you. Yes, I suppose I saw this coming, and I guess it was inevitable, but the fact remains that I am going to have to get used to the idea of my mother's remarriage."

Clarissa thought she could help him by speaking forthrightly on the subject. "Here's how I view the situation," she said. "Your mother is still young and enjoys the best of health. Furthermore, she is still an exceptionally attractive woman."

"That she is," Toby was forced to agree.

"In my opinion, it would be wrong of her to bury herself here at the ranch with memories of her late husband. If she were to do that, she might as well be dead herself. She has many years of useful living ahead of her, and I think it's wonderful that she is planning to re-marry. It certainly is what I would do if I were in her place and found a man as thoughtful and considerate and good as General Blake."

Toby drank some coffee to hide his confusion and to give himself time to compose himself. He realized that he had to agree with Clarissa, even though he was highly uncomfortable with the idea of his mother's re-marriage. It all seemed to be happening so fast! But if he opposed his mother, he knew he would be placed in the position of standing in the way of her happiness, and that was the last thing on earth he wanted to do.

Suddenly a feeling of panic assailed him, and un-able to think clearly, feeling uncontrollably restless, he jumped to his feet and ran outside toward the stables.

Clarissa was astonished. She followed him to the door and called after him, "Toby, what's the matter? Where are you going?"

He made no reply for the simple reason that he literally didn't know where he was going. All he knew was that he had to get away from the ranch and have some breathing space.

Clarissa remained standing in the frame of the kitchen door, her expression pained, her body trembling. She knew Toby was upset, but the way he had run from her, without so much as a kind word or gesture, suggest-ed that perhaps he didn't love her after all.

Saddling his horse quickly, Toby checked to make sure that his pistols were in their holsters and then rode off at a gallop into town. It seemed that all the events of the past year—his father's death, his mother's intended remarriage, the marriage of Beth Blake to Rob Martin—

had suddenly come to a head. He was badly disturbed, and he had to get away to sort out his thoughts.

Scarcely aware of where he was going, he rode through the rutted streets of Portland, which was now a bustling, sprawling city. He took no note of the passersby, many of whom knew him and called out in greeting, and he didn't dismount until he arrived at Jack's Saloon, a place that he often frequented when he went into town for meals. Jack had been a cook in the army and prepared first-rate meals, though the place was deserted when Toby walked in, the breakfast crowd having already come and gone. Jack was behind the bar as usual, and his nephew, an eleven-year-old boy named Buddy, was clearing the last of the tables, taking the dirty dishes into the kitchen.

Toby and Jack greeted each other in monosyllables. Toby asked for a mug of black coffee, then took a table in the back of the dining area.

The proprietor realized that Toby Holt had come to work out a problem and had no desire to engage in conversation. So Jack got a mug of hot, black coffee from the stove in the kitchen, took it to Toby's table, and placed it in front of him, then left him alone.

Toby was so deep in thought that he failed to note the arrival of two cowhands with stubbles of beard on their faces. These men were strangers to town, having recently found jobs at a ranch in the area, and though it was still morning, they had already consumed enough liquor to be in a troublemaking mood. They sat at the bar, ordered whiskey, and looked around for a victim at whom they could poke fun. They began to speak of Toby disparagingly, but Jack gave them a warning. "I wouldn't get him riled up, gentlemen," he said. "That there is Toby Holt, the son of Whip Holt, who's as good a shot as his old man ever was. You don't want to tangle with him."

One of the cowhands laughed rudely, obviously not familiar with the Holt name. He spewed a stream of saliva at a spittoon on the floor, indifferent to the fact that he missed it. Whether a crisis would have developed was difficult to say, because at that moment Buddy returned to the main barroom from the kitchen, where he had just deposited some glasses. Now he assiduously began to sweep the floor.

One of the cowhands nudged the other. "Hey, look at that; he's wearing an apron! Do you suppose it's a fellow or a girl?"

"Can't rightly tell from the looks of things. The only way we can make sure is by seeing him or her dance. Hey, you," he called. "Start dancing for us."

Buddy paid no attention. Drunks at the bar were no novelty to him.

But the pair were not to be denied their fun. They pulled out their six-shooters and pointed them at the boy's feet. "Dance, damn you!" one of them called angrily. "Or else we'll make you dance!"

The sound of the shouts roused Toby Holt instantly from his reverie. His own six-shooters were in his hands as he took in the situation at a glance. A hard, grim line formed around his mouth, and he called out to the cowhands, "Put your guns on the bar."

When the men hesitated, Toby called out again, "Now!" To emphasize his point, he fired his gun at a spot only inches in front of one of the cowhand's feet. "Either you put your guns on the bar or I'll make *you* dance!"

The men slowly obeyed, their eyes never leaving

Toby's as they placed their weapons on the bar behind them.

Toby looked at them hard eyed. "Now slide those guns down to the end of the bar. Go on!" he shouted, and the two nervous cowhands did as they were told "You just made a contribution to Buddy," Toby said, "as a way of paying him for the torment you subjected him to. He'll get a pretty penny for selling them."

One of the men started to protest, but the expression in Toby's eyes stopped him.

"If I were you," Toby said, "I'd clear out of this bar and leave town. I'd leave it awful fast because I'm not feeling any too generous these days, and if I see either of you again, I might just take in mind to put a bullet between your mean eyes."

The two men had heard enough, and slapping some coins on the bar for their drinks, they quickly took their departure, not concerned with their dignity as they stumbled and fled.

"I warned you," Jack called after them, "not to monkey around with Toby Holt!"

Buddy, still stunned by the rapid developments, bent to the floor to pick up something that had dropped from his pocket.

Toby made an effort to be kind to the lad. "What's that you have there, Buddy?" he said, and took a grease-stained, much-handled photograph from the boy It was a picture of a girl. "Hey," Toby said, "she's right nice looking. Who is it?"

The boy swallowed hard. "That's my sister," he said. "She went off to live with a feller, and they went down to San Francisco way. The last I knowed, they busted up, and we lost track of her. We don't know what's become of her, but we keep hopin' that she's all right and she'll show up here one of these days."

"Sure she will. You just have faith," Toby said, hoping that he sounded sufficiently encouraging. Returning the photograph to the boy and paying Jack for his coffee, he took his leave, and as he mounted his horse to start back to the Holt ranch, his own situation was suddenly clarified.

Yes, his mother's coming wedding was a source of distress, since it would be difficult to see her married to a man other than Whip. But what was really upsetting to Toby was the realization that the solidity he had felt in life was gone and that he had to depend entirely on himself now. It was up to him to arrange his life; it was up to him to create the relationship that he obviously wanted with Clarissa. He had been living with her, of course, and was responsible for her. If they quarreled and parted at this point, he had no idea of what would become of her, and he knew he could blame only himself. That was wrong, and he'd never forgive himself if anything bad happened to her.

He knew now what had to be done and spurred his horse to a much faster gait.

When he arrived at the ranch, he was vastly relieved to see that Clarissa was standing outside, leaning on a fence post. Her face was averted, and fortunately for his peace of mind, he didn't see the tears in her eyes or on her cheeks, her reaction to his abrupt leave-taking earlier in the morning.

Dismounting rapidly, Toby tied his horse to a rail and announced, "You're just the person I want to see."

"I'm here," she replied quietly.

"I want to talk to you," he said, sounding more belligerent than he intended.

Clarissa was a woman of spirit and was not daunted by his tone of voice. "What do you want to talk about?" she demanded.

"Marriage!" he heard himself say to her. "It's high time that you and I got married, don't you think? We've been sleeping together for long enough, and as I don't believe in affairs any more than you do, I think it's time we ended the whispering campaign that's bound to be going on around us."

Clarissa was shocked. She had sworn to herself, and had told him, too, that she would marry him only if he was very sure that was what he wanted, but the suddenness of his proposal suggested that he was motivated by reasons other than his love for her. Yet now that she actually faced the decision, her resolution weakened. She loved Toby, and the events of the morning had made her believe she might be losing him. Now that she had an opportunity to keep him, her thinking was colored, and she was helpless to reject his proposal.

Not trusting her voice, she nodded. Toby instantly took her firmly in his arms and kissed her passionately. Carried away in spite of herself, Clarissa returned his embrace and kissed him fervently.

At last he released her, conscious that they were outside the ranch house and could be seen by the hired hands. He allowed some space between them.

"This was—rather sudden, wasn't it?" Clarissa asked breathlessly.

Toby shook his head. "We don't have much time to hem and haw," he said. "Rob and I are going to Montana as soon as the weather permits, and I had to get my personal life straightened out first."

What he told her was the partial truth, but there was something else about his sudden decision he was unwilling to admit: He was unsure if he had proposed to Clarissa out of his love for her or out of a sense of duty, a feeling of being obligated to her. Whatever the case, his decision was made, and the die was cast.

Toby's unexpected proposal to Clarissa, and her abrupt acceptance, took his mother completely by surprise. She was delighted, however. That evening after supper with the young people, when she and Lee Blake were alone in the parlor of the ranch house, she was able to express her thoughts freely.

"I couldn't be happier for Toby than I am," she said. "Clarissa is a marvelous young woman, and she's going to make him a wonderful wife. But I dislike—intensely—their idea of being married by a justice of the peace and then sneaking off to Toby's lodge in Washington for a quick honeymoon. In years to come, they'll regret what will look to so many people like a surreptitious wedding."

Lee nodded. "You favor a real wedding, then, I take it."

"Indeed I do! The problem is that Clarissa does not have a relative in the world. She's completely alone, and she doesn't know many people here in the Pacific region. The only way she can have a real wedding is if we give it for her."

"I don't see that as a problem," Lee replied, smiling. "In fact, it will be good practice for our own wedding. If Clarissa wishes, I'll be pleased to give the bride away."

"I'm sure she'd love it, Lee!" Eulalia said enthusiastically. "She already thinks the world of you, and what I think of you—well, I'm not going to tell you because I don't want to give you a swelled head. You're really so sweet and considerate to think of doing all of this."

"It's what you want, isn't it?" he asked simply.

Eulalia knew she was the most fortunate of women. She was going to have a second husband as kind and thoughtful as her first.

She threw herself with zeal into preparations for the wedding of Clarissa and her son, engaging the minister, inviting friends, and arranging for a buffet meal to be served at the ranch house following the church ceremony.

In the days immediately prior to the wedding, Toby saw very little of his bride, who was frantically busy with the wedding dress and trousseau that her future mother-in-law was giving her as a wedding gift. He had to curb his annoyance, but his spirits improved when he received a letter from Tumwater, Washington. His partner, Rob Martin, was writing to inform him that he and Beth would be returning from their stay at the lodge in Washington a scant twenty-four hours before Toby's wedding.

"I reckon I'm in luck," Toby said to General Blake. "Rob is going to be showing up here just in time to solve the problem of who will be my best man. I assume he'll agree."

"I don't think there's much doubt of that," Lee told him.

"This is good news," Toby said, "but I have no idea when I'll be able to pass it along to Clarissa. It seems like she and my mother are spending all their days at the dressmaker's."

Lee Blake chuckled. "Let me give you some paternal advice," he said. "Weddings are strictly women's business. We're almost excess baggage, and we're wise if we keep our mouths shut, do strictly what we're told, and stay out of the way. It's much easier on us, and the wear and tear is vastly reduced."

Toby laughed dutifully at the general's sense of humor, simultaneously realizing that Lee Blake was behaving magnificently, which was more than he could say for himself. He had yet to comment on the general's coming marriage to his mother, and he realized that the longer he delayed in bringing up the subject, the more difficult it would become for him to broach it. There was no time like the present, so he squared his shoulders, cleared his throat, and thrust out his hand.

"I haven't said anything about you and my mother, sir, because I haven't quite known what to say. I'm very attached to my mother, as I suspect you know, and my father's memory will always be very important to me. But my mother believes she's going to be happy with you, and that's all that I want for her. So I wish you what I wish her— the very best of everything good."

After a lifetime of associating with young officers, Lee well knew the effort that Toby had made and, for that reason, appreciated his words all the more. He gripped the younger man's hand hard. "Long before you were born, Toby," he said, "I knew that your mother was a very special person. I've never lost sight of that fact all through the years, and I'm sure not forgetting it now. You can relax in the knowledge that I'll be as gentle and as kind and as generous as I'm capable of being. I don't pretend that I'm going to be able to fill your father's boots. Whip Holt was a good friend and was one hell of a fine fellow in every sense of the word. I have no intention of competing with him, either, for your mother's affection, or for yours and your sister's. You can rely on me, and so can your sister."

When Toby replied, his voice was surprisingly

husky. "You know, General," he said, "next to my father,
I respect and admire you more than any other man I
know." Ashamed of his show of sentiment, he turned
away abruptly.

Lee Blake quietly rejoiced. Toby hadn't completely
accepted his mother's forthcoming marriage, but at least
he was opening his mind to her situation, and that was
all to the good. Now if his own daughter reacted in the
same way, he and Eulalia would have clear sailing.

The vacationing Rob and Beth Martin returned to
Fort Vancouver at noon on the day prior to the
scheduled wedding of Clarissa and Toby. The Martins'
trip to the lodge in Washington had been intended to
ease Beth's distress over her father's courtship of Eulalia,
and also to give the young couple a chance to spend
some time together alone. In the beginning, as they rode
high into the Washington mountains and made camp for
the night before arriving at the lodge, it appeared their
trip was going to achieve all that they had intended.
Beth seemed to thrive in the fresh air and in the mountain heights, and she was as happy and vivacious as she
had been when Rob had first fallen in love with her.
Beth became totally enamored of Rob once again as he
expertly led them through mountain passes, shot down
game for the evening meal, and prepared for them a
snug, comfortable little shelter out of tree limbs and
pine boughs. That night they made love gently, ten-
derly, and they were relaxed, totally at peace with one
another.

But when they arrived at the mountaintop lodge
that Toby and Rob had built, their newly discovered
happiness was shattered. Beth completely lost control
when she saw the site where her mother and Whip Holt

had been buried in an avalanche, and running to the spot—near which Toby had erected a special monument—Beth fell to her knees and began to sob.

Perhaps Rob should have anticipated just such an outburst, for Beth had taken her mother's death very hard. She found it impossible to accept that her lovely, warmhearted mother had met an early death in a freak accident, and she was also unable to accept her father's apparent acquiescence to his wife's death, which was how Beth viewed the fact of his seeing another woman less than a year after the tragedy.

All Rob felt was frustration, for he didn't know how to talk to his wife anymore or how to make sense to her. He stood beside her as she wept, his hand on her shoulder, hoping Beth's inner turbulence would eventually subside so they could have a normal married life, uncomplicated by outside matters.

Beth did indeed seem to calm down, and they stayed at the lodge for two weeks, but whatever rapport they had achieved on the ride up into the mountains had been lost. Beth became sullen and uncommunicative, and though she didn't engage in any new emotional outbursts, she nevertheless treated Rob like a stranger. That was what he was to her now, though she prayed that in some way her husband would reach out, even if it meant simply holding her in his arms as if he really cared. But he never did this, seemingly afraid that any such intimacy with his wife might make her become emotional all over again.

When they arrived back at the fort, they found no one at home at the Blake house, and they went to the nearby home of Beth's cousin, Colonel Andrew Brentwood, and his wife, Susanna. The sprightly, warmhearted Susanna promptly invited them to stay for dinner.

Andy Brentwood inspected his blond, blue-eyed cousin, Beth, and had to admit that she was exceptionally pretty, the spitting image of her late mother. He was also forced to agree with his wife's wise estimate that she had become highly unpredictable after her mother's death.

They went to the dining room table, and Susanna, who was in the latter stages of her pregnancy, busied herself ladling asparagus soup from a tureen into individual bowls. "You've missed a lot of excitement around here," she said, smiling broadly. "All sorts of things have been happening."

"Like what?" Beth demanded imperiously.

"Let me guess," Rob said, and was silent for a moment. "Judging from your expression, Sue, and from that silly grin on Andy's face, I immediately conclude that your news is romantic. So I'll take a wild leap into the dark and say that Toby Holt is finally going to marry Clarissa Sinclair."

Susanna clapped her hands together. "No wonder Beth married you, Rob," she cried. "You're too clever for words. Indeed they are marrying—tomorrow—and you're scheduled to be best man."

Rob was pleased and smiled broadly, but Beth smirked. "I never thought that Toby would marry the Sinclair woman," she said. "Men so seldom bother to go through a ceremony after they've been living with a woman."

No one replied to her snide remark, and Beth knew she had been unnecessarily cruel, but she found the news that Toby was going to be married unsettling. It had pleased and somehow comforted her to think of him

as a bachelor who was quietly and privately pining
away for her. Toby's marriage to the very attractive,
red-haired Clarissa spoiled the image of him that she
was cherishing.

Andy Brentwood privately hoped that his wife
would mention that Eulalia Holt and General Blake
were intending to be married, too. But Susanna was
leaving that chore to her husband. She knew, as he did,
that Beth would disapprove, and she reasoned that it
was his duty as her blood relative to break the news to
her.

Andy procrastinated, waiting until they had finished
their soup and he had carved and served the meat before he broached the matter. The tall, thin young officer
had faced enemy fire consistently and unflinchingly for
four long years of the Civil War, and he did not intend
to shirk his duty now. "Toby and Clarissa aren't the only
romantic couple in the area," he said. "Your father and
Eulalia Holt are going to be married, too, Beth."

Beth paused with her fork lifted partway to her
mouth. Her jaw dropped, and she stared at her cousin in
total disbelief. The color drained from her face, and
Andy wouldn't have been surprised had she fainted.

The silence that followed was so tense that Susanna
found herself talking rapidly and a trifle too loudly in
order to fill the sudden void. "As we understand it," she
said, "they are planning a very quiet wedding because
they feel that, in view of last year's tragedy, any other
kind would be inappropriate."

Beth still did not speak, and Rob felt he had to say
something. "When are they planning to marry?"

Susanna shrugged. "They haven't set a date yet,"
she said. "We had dinner with them the other evening,
and they wanted to wait until you two came home so

they could discuss the matter with Beth. They're anxious to defer to your wishes, Beth, just as they're taking the wishes of Toby and Cindy Holt into consideration, too."

"That's very kind of them, I'm sure," Beth said in a voice that was like acid.

Andy saw no reason to evade central issues. "I've been sorry for General Blake for the past year," he said, "He's been wandering around like a lost soul, and so has Mrs. Holt. I don't know what they've suffered, and I can only imagine the hell they've been through. But I know this much after spending several evenings with them: They're happy and relaxed together, and they deserve all the joy they can get in this life."

"Amen to that," Susanna said, taking a firm stand beside her husband.

Beth opened her mouth to say something, changed her mind, and, instead, devoted herself to her meal. She ate with single-minded concentration, and when she spoke, it was to relate amusing incidents that had taken place while she and Rob had been staying at the remote mountain lodge. She did not refer again to the subject of her father's marriage to Eulalia, and when she and her husband took their leave after dinner, intending to return to her father's home, she was unnaturally bright. But it was plain that her gaiety was forced.

When they entered the house, however, the sight of the furnishings, all of them selected by her late mother, robbed Beth of her self-control. She wheeled on Rob, her fists clenched, and cried in a choked voice, "How dare he do a thing like this!"

Her husband had been expecting a reaction of some sort, but her vehemence was so great that he was startled by it, and he didn't know what to reply.

"How dare he insult my mother's memory by marrying that woman!" She was weeping now and shouting loudly through her tears.

Rob tried hard to answer her logically. "Mrs. Holt," he said, "was your mother's closest friend. As for her being 'that woman,' as you called her, I don't think the attack is quite justified. She's been universally recognized as one of the first ladies of Oregon for many years."

Beth was beyond reason. "She's a temptress!" she screamed. "She took advantage of my father's natural grief and snared him for herself."

Rob knew she wasn't being logical. "You seem to forget that Mrs. Holt was suffering from a great shock herself," he said. "She lost her husband. That couldn't have been very easy for her."

Beth faced him, her feet apart, her fists clenched, and her eyes blazing. "She was suffering so much," she said, sneering, "that she couldn't wait to set her cap for my father. She recognized a good catch when she saw one, and she couldn't wait until she could claim him for herself."

Rob realized Beth was making no sense, that she was driving herself into a state of unthinking hysteria. The problem was only aggravated by the fact that Beth had been unable to find sexual release in her marriage, that Rob loved and respected her so much that he instinctively and habitually treated her in bed like a lady. What Beth unconsciously craved was to be treated as a woman, far more passionately than Rob had treated her thus far.

"Please calm down," Rob told her. "Your father may walk in at any moment, and you don't want him to see you in this state."

Her face was so contorted with rage that she lost all

vestiges of her natural beauty. "Let him walk in!" she screamed. "I'd love to confront him this very second. I want to tell him how contemptible and low he is to have forgotten my mother so soon after her tragic accident. He's been lusting after that woman so hard that he's lost his balance."

Rob felt sure she would be thoroughly ashamed of her outburst when she regained her emotional stability. He knew he had to silence her and somehow force her to become calmer, but he had no idea how to accomplish that end. "Please, honey," he said. "You don't know what you're saying, and you can't possibly face your father in this condition. You don't want to hurt him, and you'd be inflicting a grievous injury on him if you spoke to him this way."

"I hope I do hurt him!" She waved her arms frenziedly. "I hope I hurt him so badly that he'll bear the scars for the rest of his days!"

Rob had tolerated enough, and unthinkingly, not bothering to weigh the consequences, he took a single step forward, raised a hand, and slapped Beth smartly across one cheek. The blow was not hard enough to do her any damage, but the impact stunned her.

They stared at each other in shocked silence. Rob was abashed, but he did not apologize for his sudden outburst of violence. He was afraid that if he did beg Beth's pardon, she would indulge in another emotional rampage. Thus, he said nothing.

Beth stared at him in wonder, and in some way that was mysterious to her, her anger drained out of her. She still felt contempt for her father and for Eulalia Holt, but certainly her rage had subsided, at least temporarily. She looked at Rob as though she were seeing him for the first time, and in a sense, that was true. In the back of her mind, she wondered if perhaps after all, there was a passionate, forceful side to Rob. She certainly hoped there was.

III

Yale Myers congratulated himself smugly and reflected that his good luck was continuing. He was wanted on charges of murder and of robbery in more states than he cared to remember, but he was safe from the authorities now, and it appeared that he would be untouchable for the foreseeable future.

His system, he decided, worked perfectly. He made it a practice, after he killed a man, to assume the identity of his victim, and he had found that a careful study of the documents, letters, and other papers that he stole from the bodies of those he murdered stood him in remarkably good stead. Once away from the scene of the crime, he was accepted without question, and he continued to play the role until he became bored or his wanderlust got the better of him. Then he repeated the whole process.

Myers had learned all he needed to know about the identity he was now assuming, that of the man he had killed in the eastern Oregon town. He was now Major

Isham Jentry, an expert on the building of railroads, and it mattered not to him that he knew nothing whatsoever about the subject. The letter he carried inside his coat pocket told him what he should do next. He was to report to Major General Lee Blake at Fort Vancouver in the Washington Territory and was to join Toby Holt and Robert Martin in determining a route for the new railroad line that would be built across the Montana Territory. Realizing that Montana was still a largely uninhabited wilderness, he knew he would be safe there for many months to come, and he was pleased, too, because he had heard that precious minerals, such as gold and silver, were abundant in the high mountains of the western part of the territory. If his good fortune continued, he might find a vein of gold or silver and never have to worry again about the source of his next meal.

Myers had no idea whether the late Major Jentry had left a wife and children somewhere in the East. For his own practical purposes, it was easier to assume the identity of a bachelor, beholden to no one. That gave him a freedom of movement that he would otherwise be denied.

Crossing the turbulent Columbia River by commercial ferry, he made his way toward Fort Vancouver. The sight of an armed sentry at the gate of the palisades gave Myers momentary cause for pause. Uncertain how to act in his role of the major, he was relieved that he was wearing civilian clothes, since he had never in his life saluted. He approached the sentry and, not deigning to dismount, took Major Jentry's identification from his inner pocket.

The sentry unfolded it, read it, and immediately stood at rigid attention as he saluted.

Myers was pleased by the man's reaction and raised

his own hand vaguely to the broad brim of his hat in response. Then he carefully took the identification document back from the sentry.

"May I ask where you're going now, sir?" the soldier asked respectfully.

"I'm here to see a general, name of Blake."

The sentry took pains to remain formal. "The office of the commanding general of the Army of the West is located in the headquarters building, sir," he said. "You see the fork in the road up ahead yonder? Take the left-hand route and follow it till you come to a two-story building painted white, with a flagpole in the yard in front of it. That's the headquarters where you'll find General Blake."

Myers thanked the man and was surprised when the sentry again saluted as he started off down the road. Apparently, he thought, Major Jentry had been someone of importance. His mood improved still more, and he was in high spirits by the time he reached General Blake's headquarters building.

A short time later, Myers made himself at home in the general's office, slouching in an easy chair.

Lee Blake was somewhat surprised and dismayed as he studied Major Jentry. The man's white shirt was soiled and much in need of laundering. There was black dirt beneath his fingernails, and his dark hair needed to be cut. Furthermore, he had shaved carelessly that morning, and stubble showed here and there on his swarthy face. To say the least, he did not look like an officer who would enjoy the confidence of the army's high command in Washington. "So you're the expert in railroading whose arrival we've been so anxiously awaiting, Major," Lee said.

"Well, I don't like to blow my own horn, General,"

Myers answered jovially—far too informally for an officer of middle rank addressing a major general, "but that's what they seem to think in Washington."

His breeziness was so marked that Lee could not fail to note it and was not impressed by the man or his manner. "I'll introduce you to one of your new partners, who happens to be in the office this morning," Lee said, "and then I'll arrange to have you assigned to the B.O.Q. I'm sure you'll want to get cleaned up after your long journey."

Myers had no idea what B.O.Q meant, but a warning bell nevertheless rang shrilly in his mind. Ordinarily he paid scant attention to his appearance, but the general was exceptionally neat and so were all the other officers he had seen on his way into this private office. As a major, he assumed that he, too, held a rank of some significance, so it would be wise to make himself presentable at the first opportunity.

The general sent an aide for Rob Martin, who was spending the morning at headquarters studying maps and charts of the Montana mountains. His son-in-law soon appeared, and Lee introduced him to Major Jentry. "I'm sure you two will have no lack of subjects to discuss," Lee said, "but don't pounce on him too quickly, Rob. Give him a chance to settle into the bachelor officers' quarters first."

So that's what B.O.Q. meant! Myers was relieved.

An aide conducted them to a nearby building, and Rob said he would return in an hour. Myers's instinct for self-preservation promptly asserted itself, and he took a bath, went to the post barber in the same building, and turned his dirty laundry over to an orderly. He was infinitely more presentable when Rob returned. His good fortune was even better than he had realized. For however long he would remain at Fort Vancouver, he would be given three meals a day in the mess hall on the ground floor, he had a comfortable private room, and the orderly service provided him with free servants. His spirits buoyant, Myers wanted to celebrate.

"I don't suppose you got a bottle of whiskey handy," he said.

The surprised Rob shook his head.

"You happen to know where I can get hold of some?" the man persisted. "I feel like having a nip or two to celebrate."

"You'll find no hard liquor at Fort Vancouver," Rob told him. "As I'm sure you realize, its use is forbidden here, except in the private homes of senior officers."

Myers hastily covered his tracks. "Oh, sure, sure," he said. "I know all that, of course. I was just looking forward to relaxing a mite after coming here all the way across the country. It's one hell of a long trip."

"So I've been told," Rob replied politely, hoping that his reaction to the man was mistaken. Major Jentry appeared to be something of a boor. "The chief of operations at headquarters," Rob said, tactfully changing the subject, "has some really first-rate maps and charts of Montana. In fact, I was studying them when you arrived here this morning. I'd think it would be very much worth your while to look over them."

"You bet," the man replied vaguely, without enthusiasm, telling himself that he could examine maps until he was blue in the face but would glean nothing from them.

His lack of enthusiasm struck Rob as odd. "Of course," Rob said politely, "you probably know all there is to know about Montana."

The last thing that Myers wanted was to be regarded as an expert; there was no telling when he might be required to show off his alleged knowledge. "I'm sure I still have plenty to learn about Montana," he said vaguely. "It's like any place. You never really know it until you've been there."

"Oh?" Rob hid his surprise and replied politely. "I had the notion that you were already familiar with the territory."

Myers chuckled. "I can't imagine where you got that idea," he said. "I've never set foot in Montana in my life. Never had any reason to go there, come to think of it. Until now." There. He'd said more than enough and called a halt before he went too far. One of the problems with impersonating a stranger was the danger that he would talk too much and give himself away.

Rob could scarcely wait to start talking business. "Do you have any special notions or ideas regarding the building or location of the rail line through Montana?" he asked.

Long practice in impersonation enabled Yale Myers to reply glibly and easily. "I never believe in counting chickens until the eggs are hatched," he said. "I think we'd be smart to wait until we get there and see the land for ourselves. Then you and I and the third member of the team can analyze what we're inspecting, and it will be much easier and more realistic to make any decisions at that time."

Rob felt rebuked and knew that Major Jentry was right, but at the same time, he felt deeply disappointed. He and Toby had been expecting to be joined by an army officer who knew the territory well and was thoroughly conversant with the problems of constructing a railroad line there. Unfortunately, this was far from the case.

Not that it mattered. What really bothered him was the personality of the man with whom he and Toby would be so closely associated in the months that lay ahead. He had been looking forward to a speeding up of the entire process, but now it seemed likely that they would be taking their time, plodding, putting one foot in front of the other.

Regardless of what Rob thought, he knew all too well that he and Toby held their commissions from President Johnson, acting on the authority of Congress. Apparently Major Jentry was operating under the same authority. For better or worse, they would be required to work together. Therefore, he would have to make the best of the situation.

Toby and Clarissa had agreed to Eulalia's wishes to have a formal wedding, but they still wanted to keep it small, with only family and close friends in attendance. Privacy, however, proved to be impossible; the Holt family was too well known. The church was crowded with well-wishers, and every pew was taken. Many of the guests, knowing that the bride had no relatives in the Pacific Northwest, deliberately elected to sit on Clarissa's side of the church. Also in attendance was Clarissa's close friend, the former Bettina Snow, who with her little daughter, Lucy, had crossed the continent with Clarissa when they had first come out to the Northwest. Bettina had married Frank Woods, and the three members of the Woods family had come down from Washington for the wedding.

Toby, standing near the altar with Rob Martin beside him as his best man, surveyed the throng as he waited for his bride to come down the center aisle. Never had he seen so many familiar faces, and he estimated that just about everyone he had known in the years of his childhood and adolescence was present. It wouldn't have surprised him had he been told that virtually the entire company of those who had crossed the United States in the first wagon train to Oregon had turned out to honor him and his mother.

Of all those present, he was more conscious of Beth Martin than of anyone else. She was demurely attired in a tailored jacket and skirt, but they were a brilliant scarlet in color and caused her to be particularly noticeable. He was right when he guessed that she was wearing more makeup than usual, but he had no idea that this was deliberate on her part to conceal the ravages to her face of the crying spell she had suffered the previous night when she had thought again of her father's coming marriage to Eulalia.

Beth caught Toby's eye and smiled at him. He grinned at her in return and suppressed the sudden longing he felt for her. This was no moment to think of any woman except Clarissa!

Beth continued to smile steadily. Toby became flustered. It didn't occur to him that she was flirting with him deliberately; he knew only that he had never seen her looking warmer or more desirable.

Then Clarissa appeared at the back of the church clad in a gown of ivory lace and satin, and he put everything else out of his mind. Clarissa was radiant, her eyes luminous as she moved slowly down the aisle on the arm of Lee Blake, who was wearing his full-dress uniform of a major general. When Beth saw her father, she stiffened, her mouth setting in a thin, hard line.

When Lee drew near to the front pew, his eyes met Eulalia's, and he smiled. Her own smile told him how pleased and proud she was that he had made this effort for her son and new daughter-in-law. He told her silently in return that the gesture was the least he could do for her happiness.

As the clergyman led the young couple through the marriage rites, Eulalia raised a tiny lace handkerchief to her face and dabbed at her eyes from time to time. Lee, who had joined her after leaving Clarissa at the altar, moved closer to her, as if to give her added strength with his presence.

"I now pronounce you man and wife," the clergyman intoned at the ceremony's end.

Toby enthusiastically kissed his bride, and the grinning couple moved happily up the aisle, both of them appearing to be in something of a trance.

The entire party rode out to the Holt ranch, where a simple buffet meal of cold turkey, cold sliced beef, and cold salmon was served. Everyone drank to the health of the bride and groom with a punch that Ted and Olga Woods—Frank's parents—had mixed for the occasion.

Lee and Eulalia stood beside the bridal couple in the receiving line, and to an extent, this was their wedding reception, too. They were well acquainted with everyone present, from the older people who had made the monumental transcontinental journey with them, to the children who had been born after the company had arrived in Oregon.

Eulalia and Lee were too proud of each other and of their relationship to dissemble, and when they admitted to the more discerning among the guests that they, too, were going to be married, word spread rapidly through the gathering.

Beth Martin created something of a stir when she approached the newlyweds to offer her felicitations. She shook hands with Clarissa, wishing her the best of ev-

erything, then paused in front of Toby, deliberately
reached up her hands to his face, and kissed him soundly.

As the startled bridegroom was the first to discover,
it was no token kiss but was impassioned and lingering.
He became tense until Beth finally released him, and
without moving on in the receiving line to his mother
and her own father, she turned away abruptly, joined
her husband, and demanded a glass of punch.

Clarissa, who had witnessed the unexpected incident, did not indicate by a word or a change in expression that she was aware that anything amiss had
taken place.

Then the musicians who were hired for the occasion
began to play a waltz, a dance whose popularity was
spreading from Europe to the New World, and Toby
promptly led his bride onto the floor of the parlor, from
which the rugs had been removed. Soon the room was
filled with dancing couples.

Eulalia stood with Lee, her hand on his arm, as
they watched the couples whirling around the room. "I
told Toby that he and Clarissa have set us such a good
example that we're going to do the same thing in ten
days," she murmured. "I certainly didn't expect them to
cut their honeymoon short, but he insisted that they're
going to be here. He said that he'll soon be on his way
to Montana in any event."

Lee was quietly pleased that Toby and his bride
would attend his and Eulalia's wedding. Apparently his
future stepson had meant every word he said when he
wished the general well on his forthcoming marriage to
Eulalia.

Eulalia's grip inadvertently tightened on his arm.
"Did you speak to Beth?"

"I did," he said grimly, his face growing taut.

"Well, how did she react?" Eulalia prodded.

"She didn't." He failed to realize he sounded cryptic.

She controlled her temper. "What did she say?"

"Nothing."

"She doesn't learn every day of the week that her father has set his wedding date," she said with a touch of asperity. "Surely the girl made some sort of reply!"

"She didn't say a word," Lee replied, "not one blessed word."

Eulalia was silent for some moments. Then her jaw jutted forward, and a stubborn, determined look came into her eyes. "You and I," she said in a quiet, even tone, "are being married in precisely ten days. Our children have been invited to attend as our only witnesses."

"Exactly," Lee said, "and if Beth elects to absent herself from our wedding, that's her privilege, and we'll say no more about it!"

The wedding festivities became even livelier, and when they were at their height, Toby and Clarissa sneaked away. He said good-bye to his dog, Mr. Blake, whom Cindy would be looking after while Toby and Clarissa were on their honeymoon, and then the young couple changed into traveling attire and went to the rear of the barns behind the house. There Stalking Horse had awaiting them two saddled geldings and a pair of packhorses with supplies and the clothing they were taking with them. Demonstrating his usual skill. Toby avoided detection as he guided his bride down the path that led from the Holt property to the river.

They crossed the Columbia by ferry and then set out for a small country inn where Toby had written for a reservation.

They arrived at the establishment shortly before

sundown, and after eating supper there, they went upstairs to their room, which was comfortably furnished and had a delightful view of the Washington countryside. There they shed their clothes unselfconsciously and were soon in each other's arms, kissing each other hungrily. Then they went to the large, four-poster bed to continue their lovemaking.

It was the first time they had slept together since they had become husband and wife, and as Toby said afterward, "I don't know why this should be, but I felt different."

"Of course," Clarissa replied. "So did I. I was far more secure and solid. I was no longer worried about what people might think of our sleeping together, and we were both able to relax totally, just concentrating on being ourselves."

The next day, they rode from early morning until dusk, and when they finally arrived at the lodge that Toby had built high in the mountains, they prepared supper, using supplies they had brought with them. Toby promised to catch some trout for their breakfast the following morning.

The next day, they went to the high mound of boulders and rocks that marked the final resting place of Whip Holt and Cathy Blake. Here, near the inscribed stone monument Toby had erected to the couple who had lost their lives so tragically, they stood in silence, each of them lost in thought.

"I'm fortunate," Clarissa said at last, "to have known your father before he was taken from us. I hope he approved of me."

"I know he did," Toby replied. "He told me as much."

She was silent for a moment. "I never really knew Mrs. Blake. Is Beth very much like her mother?"

Toby shook his head. "Not in the least," he said. "Cathy Blake was a courageous, straightforward woman. Not that Beth isn't courageous," he added hastily. "That isn't what I meant." He groped in vain for words. "I'm not sure just what I do mean."

Clarissa was sorry she had raised the subject.

Toby persisted. "Cathy Blake was calm and sweet and kind of shy, all things that Beth isn't. I remember my father saying that he'd seen Cathy lose her temper only when she felt someone was the victim of injustice." He shook his head, ran a hand through his hair, and said apologetically, "I'm making Beth sound like a spoiled brat or a monster of some kind, but she isn't either of those things. Actually, she is very generous. She gave me Mr. Blake, my shepherd dog—he was just a puppy at the time—when I was recuperating from the wounds that I had suffered in the war. She didn't have to give me the dog, goodness knows, but it was one of those impulsive gestures. She just wanted me to have him, and Mr. Blake and I have been the best of friends ever since."

Despite Toby's assurance, Clarissa still vividly recalled how Beth had turned away from Eulalia and her father without even speaking to them in the receiving line at Clarissa and Toby's wedding. "Will Beth be at your mother's wedding, do you think?"

Toby shrugged. "I've known Beth Blake—Beth Martin, I mean—since we were both very small children, and a great many years ago I gave up predicting what she would or wouldn't do next. I doubt if she herself knows what she's going to do or how she's going to act, and I'll admit to you, just between us, that I feel a mite sorry for

Rob. He's living on the edge of a volcano that may erupt at any time."

His analogy was good, and Clarissa agreed totally. "While we're on the subject of Beth," she said slowly, "there's one thing I can't understand about her. Maybe you can explain it to me."

"I'm not very good at understanding her myself, but I'll try."

"I must be honest with you," Clarissa said. "I freely confess that I was badly disturbed by the way she kissed you at our wedding. That was no token kiss, no kiss of friendship. It was the way a woman kisses her lover. I've been married twice now, and the only men I've ever dreamed of kissing that way are my two husbands. Why did she do it the way she did—especially at our wedding reception?"

Toby reddened and instantly decided to be as forthright as he could in his response. "I wish I could answer your question, Clarissa, but I can't," he said. "She took me completely by surprise, and I must admit to you that I wondered about her later. She's only been married a short time herself, and—well, it was my wedding, after all, and I didn't feel that her gesture was very appropriate. I'm afraid I'm completely in the dark."

Clarissa knew he was being sincere, and she slipped her hand into his as they started back toward the porch of the house. "I'm not all that well acquainted with Beth Martin," she said, "so I could be mistaken about her, and if I am, I humbly beg her pardon. But it seemed to me that she kissed you as she did in a deliberate gesture. She was serving a warning notice."

"On whom?" Toby asked in bewilderment.

"On her husband, for one, and on me for another. She was saying, in effect, that just because she has a husband and you had now acquired a wife was no reason to believe she couldn't have you for her own if she wanted to."

Toby unexpectedly found himself plunged deep into a whirlpool of strange, conflicting emotions.

Clarissa had naturally anticipated that her husband would be quick to deny the possibility that he might develop any special relationship with Beth and would say that he was a happily married man. To her astonishment, however, he remained silent and appeared lost in thought all the way back to the house.

Clarissa had loved Toby for a very long time, and now, at last, a miracle had occurred, and she had become his wife. She did not intend to allow anyone to come between them, to permit anything to spoil their marital happiness. If Beth Martin tried to interfere, the risk was hers alone because Clarissa would do anything to ensure that her husband devoted his attention exclusively to her.

"You're going to your father's wedding," Rob Martin said grimly, "if I've got to hog-tie you, throw you across my saddle, and carry you into the Holt ranch house over my shoulder. You can hate it, you can have hysterics after we leave the place, and you can rant and scream at me until you're hoarse. But you're going to be there and watch your father marry Mrs. Holt!"

Beth did not dare to argue with her husband. His display of strong feelings secretly aroused her, and she couldn't help wishing he would act this way more often, especially when it came to their lovemaking. But in that area he was unassertive and almost indifferent, and all she could do was sulkily agree to attend the wedding.

When the day actually arrived, she astonished Rob

by dressing in one of her more attractive gowns, putting on makeup, and going off with him in an extremely cheerful mood, as though she had been looking forward to the event for a long time.

He had no idea how much the effort cost her, but she appeared to be expending no effort whatever. On the contrary, she seemed to be behaving naturally, kissing Eulalia when she and Rob arrived at the ranch house, extending an exceptionally cheerful greeting to Toby and Clarissa, who had just returned from the lodge, and gossiping with Cindy as she frolicked with Mr. Blake.

The only other guests in attendance were Eulalia's brother and his wife, Claiborne and Cindy Woodling, whose property adjoined the Holt ranch. Beth was charming to them as well, and they could not help responding in kind to her.

The wedding went off without any problems. Toby stood with a fixed smile on his face throughout the ceremony, looking straight ahead, and only Clarissa guessed that he was feeling turbulent emotions, which he was going to great pains to conceal.

Beth averted her face from the ceremony and closed her eyes when her father kissed Eulalia at the conclusion of the service. She clenched her fists so tightly that her knuckles turned white, but a moment later she was smiling, completely in control of herself. She was the first to bestow hugs and kisses on the bride and groom.

Beth's unexpected pleasantness gave the wedding party a new dimension, and everyone who came to the ranch house after the ceremony enjoyed the celebratory dinner.

In Toby's mind's eye, he could see his father sitting at the head of the oak table where Lee Blake now sat, but he tried hard to dispel the image. It refused to disappear, however, so he was relatively quiet, but the others were enjoying such hilarity that only Clarissa noticed that he was somewhat withdrawn.

The impending departure of Colonel Andrew Brentwood's regiment for the Montana Territory made it impossible for General Blake to get away on a honeymoon. Therefore, in order to give him and Eulalia at least a few days of privacy, Cindy was staying at the ranch house with Toby and Clarissa, while Beth and Rob had arranged to move to the Portland house of his parents, Dr. and Mrs. Martin.

Eventually a Holt carriage took the bridal couple to the waterfront, where the general's gig waited to carry them across the Columbia River to the north bank. No sooner did they depart than Beth and Rob left, on horseback, for Portland.

The moment they left the Holt ranch, Beth's manner changed dramatically. Her cheerful effervescence seemed to drain out of her, and she appeared sullen and withdrawn. "Under no circumstances," she said, "am I going to stay anywhere in the vicinity of Fort Vancouver while you go off to Montana. Seeing my father and that woman acting like lovebirds would make me positively ill."

Rob was weary of her scenes and said nothing, hoping her sour mood would soon pass. She persisted, however. "I've decided I'm going to Montana with you."

He had expected this and looked at her sharply. "Beth, I've given this matter a lot of thought, and I've decided that it's impossible for you to go."

"Why is it so impossible?" she countered. "Susanna Brentwood is going to Montana, and she'll even have her baby there!"

"Her husband," Rob said slowly, "happens to be the colonel commanding the regiment that's going to be stationed at Fort Shaw in Montana. Surely you know enough about the army to understand how that system works."

"Indeed I do," she replied. "The wives of other senior officers will be going to Montana, too. You can bet your last dollar on it. And the work that you and Toby are doing is every bit as important as the responsibilities that are carried by a battalion commander or a regimental staff officer. So if their wives can go, I can, too!"

Rob was afraid she failed to understand the situation. As the daughter of a major general, she had always been able to bend the rules and regulations in her favor, and she blithely assumed she could continue in that vein. He was convinced, however, that she was doomed to be disappointed. He and Toby were civilians, not commissioned officers, and they had no claim on quarters at Fort Shaw or the protection that the regiment afforded the wives of the families of its ranking officers. Rather than say anything to discourage his wife, however, he fell silent, preferring to avoid another scene if it was at all possible to do so.

Had he been able to see Beth's face, which she had averted, he might have been less sure of himself. Her chin jutted forward, and an obstinate gleam had appeared in her eyes. In one way or another, she was determined not to be left behind.

The following morning Rob went off to Fort Vancouver to meet Major Jentry, whom he was going to escort to a meeting with Toby Holt at the ranch house.

Beth insisted on accompanying her husband, saying that she had business to attend to at the army post. She seemed reluctant to go into detail, but once she had assured him she had no intention of seeing her father and Eulalia, he asked no questions.

They parted at the headquarters, and Beth went straight to the house of her cousin, Andy Brentwood. There, Susanna greeted her and, pleased to see her, insisted that she come into the kitchen for a cup of coffee. They sat down together, and Beth smiled and nodded. "I've been meaning to tell you how well you look, Sue," she said. "I think I envy you."

"The doctor assures me that I'm healthy," Susanna replied, "and he sees no reason why the baby should be anything but healthy, too, though he's fairly certain I'll deliver a few weeks late. Andy and I are looking forward to his arrival. Or her arrival."

"Do you want a boy or a girl?"

Susanna shrugged. "Both of us had definite feelings on the subject at first, but we've changed recently, and we'll be satisfied with a baby of either sex."

"That's very wise." Beth began to lead up to the subject that had brought her here. "I cannot help wondering whether you're going to be frightened or at least ill at ease having your child in Montana, so far from civilization."

Susanna shook her head. "Not at all," she said. "The commandant's house at Fort Shaw is very comfortable, from all that we gather, and the regimental surgeon will be at the fort. He'll have a fully equipped dispensary, so I'll be as well off there as I'd be if I stayed right here. The important thing is that Andy and the baby and I will be together."

"I envy you," Beth said tremulously, then sighed.

She rarely displayed any sign of weakness, and her cousin's wife looked at her curiously over the rim of her coffee cup.

"Rob and I," Beth explained, "are going to be separated for months and months. Depending on the progress that he and Toby make in laying out the railway line, we could be forced to be apart for as long as a year."

"I sympathize with you," Susanna said warmly.

"The worst of it, in a way," Beth continued, "is that I'll be forced to stay with Rob's parents in Portland or with my father and my new stepmother here at Fort Vancouver. I must be honest with you, Sue, and tell you that I can't even contemplate living under the same roof with the newlyweds. It would be too much of a strain on all of us."

Susanna nodded as she sipped at her coffee.

"As for Dr. and Mrs. Martin, they're lovely, charming people, but I don't really know them all that well. Besides, they're busy with their own lives, and in spite of their assurances, I know I would be in the way if I stayed there."

"I know just how you feel," Susanna said.

Still looking sorrowful, Beth waited until Susanna refilled her cup before she spoke again. "I can't help wondering," she said, "whether there might be a house at Fort Shaw that is going to be vacant. A house that I could use."

Susanna immediately brightened. "How very clever of you," she said cheerfully. "Andy has told me that the fort was built to house a very large regiment, larger than the one that's going to be stationed there, so there must be at least one officer's home that will be vacant. I can't imagine any reason why it couldn't be made available to you."

Beth had known about the arrangements at Fort

Shaw but simulated surprise. "This is wonderful news," she breathed. "Just wonderful."

"I don't know whether Rob will be spending the better part of his time in the mountains in the western part of the territory or in the plains that lie to the east," Susanna said. "But wherever he may be, the fort is centrally located, and I don't care how busy he is, I'm sure he'd find the time to visit you—at least for a day or two occasionally."

"And that," Beth said emphatically, "is better than a separation that goes on and on."

"Of course it is!"

"There's just one hitch to all of this," Beth said slowly. "I'll grant you that Andy is my first cousin and that I've been close to him all my life. But I'm still the daughter of a general who happens to be his superior officer. If I go to him and request that he make a house available to me, I'm putting him in a terrible spot. If, for any reason, he's reluctant to give me the quarters, he may nevertheless still feel he has to give in to my wishes, regardless of what he feels is best for the army and for his regiment."

"How very kind and thoughtful of you to think of Andy in all of this!" Susanna exclaimed, and fell silent as she pondered. "I have it!" she said at last. "There's no need for you to speak to Andy at all. No need for you to say a single word to him. I will go to him on your behalf, and I'll present your idea to him as though it were my own. In that way, by leaving you completely out of the picture, he won't feel under any sense of pressure to give in to your wishes."

"This is so generous of you that I don't know what to say," Beth replied.

"Nonsense!" Susanna said forcibly. "My husband

and I are able to discuss every subject under the sun—freely and without restraint. It will be a simple matter for me to talk to him about finding you suitable housing at Fort Shaw!"

Beth was elated. Susanna had taken the bait that she had offered and had swallowed it whole. Andy would surely be enthusiastic about the suggestion that his cousin accompany Susanna to Fort Shaw. Not only would she be company at a difficult time in Sue's life, but as the idea would appear to have originated with his wife, rather than with Beth, he was certain to agree to it. Therefore, Beth reflected, she would truly be free of her father and that woman at last.

So far, Rob Martin thought as he and Major Jentry disembarked from the ferry and began to ride the short distance to the Holt ranch, he was far from impressed by the major's knowledge of the problems that awaited them in Montana. Whenever Rob had tried to talk about the difficulties that they would encounter in finding a suitable route across the high mountains of the Continental Divide, Jentry had merely smiled and nodded, but had contributed virtually nothing to the conversation.

On the other hand, the major had been appointed to his position by General Grant personally, so it was unfair to judge Jentry prematurely. Perhaps he was one of those engineers who was relatively inarticulate in the give and take of conversation but who shone in the field when confronted by actual problems. There were many such engineers and surveyors, Rob knew, and he warned himself not to allow his thinking to be colored by his personal dislike of the man.

"This here is some spread," Yale Myers said appreciatively as he gazed out across the broad, rolling acres of the Holt ranch. There were any number of outbuildings, in addition to the impressive clapboard and brick main residence, and Myers could count quickly at least one hundred prime horses grazing in the fields.

Rob agreed politely that it was indeed a choice property, and Myers laughed coarsely. "Believe you me," he said, "if it was mine, you wouldn't catch me riding up into the high mountains to earn a living. I'd stay put right here and live off the fat of the land!"

Rob had to admit that he was candid, to say the least.

Myers slowed his horse to a walk as he took in every detail of the ranch house and its auxiliary buildings. "Man alive," he muttered, moistening his lips, "there's money here, real money."

The remark was crude, totally inappropriate coming from a supposed officer and gentleman. But Rob had to assume that Major Jentry was of a different breed. The officer corps of the army had been vastly expanded during the Civil War, and any number of men who didn't fit the customary mold had been admitted to the service. The major must be one of them.

As they drew nearer to the ranch house, Toby's shepherd dog appeared from behind the building and streaked toward them, running at full tilt. Suddenly the animal halted, and, ears pointed and erect, tail extended stiffly behind him, he sniffed at Major Jentry. Then Mr. Blake gave a low, menacing growl and bared his teeth. The dog looked as though he would lunge at the man at any moment.

Yale Myers instinctively reached for the pistol he carried in his belt.

"Down, Mr. Blake!" Rob shouted. "Down, boy!"

Toby heard the commotion, opened the door, and taking in the situation at a glance, he hurried into the open, caught hold of the animal's collar, and managed to quiet him. "You can put your gun away now," he said pointedly.

The man reluctantly slid his pistol back into its holster.

"I don't know what's come over Mr. Blake," Toby said apologetically. "He's ordinarily an extremely friendly animal who gets along just fine with everybody." Still holding the dog's collar with his left hand, he extended his right. "In any event, welcome to the ranch, Major."

"Thanks very much." Myers made a mental note to dispose of the dog at his first opportunity. He disliked and mistrusted animals in any event, and this shepherd apparently had penetrated his disguise, which was more than any humans had been able to do. The dog had to go.

Mr. Blake refused to be mollified, alternating between menacing growls and a high yipping sound that sounded like a baby's cry. Toby, embarrassed by the animal's inexplicable behavior, left Mr. Blake outside as he went into the house with Major Jentry and Rob. He remained conscious of the fact, however, that the dog had sprawled on the ground just outside the front door and remained alert, watching and waiting for his new enemy to reappear.

Myers did not respond to small talk, a fact Rob had previously discovered, and which Toby now attributed to the unsettling effect of the scene made by Mr. Blake. Trying to put the guest at ease, he broached the topic of their coming journey to Montana and of some of the dif-

ficulties that he expected they would encounter in the
mountains.

Major Jentry replied in monosyllables.

Then Clarissa came into the parlor, carrying a tray
laden with a coffee pot, sugar and cream, and several
cups and saucers. The effect she had on the stranger was
immediate and startling. Myers stared hard at the handsome young woman, his surroundings completely forgotten.

Clarissa's flesh crawled. She had the sensation that
this stranger was mentally undressing her, slowly and
with relish, and she could not rid herself of the notion.

Toby presented the guest to his wife, and Major
Jentry extended his hand, which made it necessary for
Clarissa to respond in kind. He grasped her fingers
firmly and held them far longer than was polite.

The man's touch made her squirm inwardly, and
she wanted to scream. Never before had she reacted this
negatively to a total stranger, and her revulsion was so
great that she was incapable of thinking clearly. All she
knew was that she had to escape as quickly as she could.

Yale Myers's mind raced. The tall, big-boned
woman was the most desirable woman he had ever encountered, and he knew that he wanted her, that he had
to have her. What was more, her husband, who would
be going off on the railroad expedition to which the late
Major Jentry had been assigned, was certainly very
well-to-do if he could afford to live in this large and
grand a house.

Therefore, Myers concluded, he would solve his
multiple problems simply and efficiently. He would wait
until he and his two companions arrived in the vast wilderness of the Montana mountains. Then during an absence of Rob Martin's, which he would contrive if he

found it necessary, he'd kill Toby Holt. Obviously Holt's widow would inherit his estate. So he would get both the woman and her inherited money by marrying her. Then his troubles would be over. He continued to stare at her, naked lust in his eyes.

Unable to tolerate the man's lewd, penetrating gaze any longer, Clarissa made an excuse and left the room. She made up her mind, however, that she would not mention her feelings to Toby. He, after all, would be required to work closely with the major, to live and travel with him for months at a time. She had no desire to be the cause of bad blood between them. . . . She was determined to keep her peculiar reactions to herself.

Twenty-four hours after their unsatisfactory introduction to Major Jentry, Toby and Clarissa were sitting in the kitchen of the ranch finishing a dinner of beefsteak and bread when they heard hoofbeats outside and were pleased to see that Rob Martin was calling on them.

But it was soon apparent that Rob was in a furious mood, and he wasted no time explaining what was wrong. "My wife has really gone and done it!" he said. "She won't tell me how, but she's arranged to go to Montana, too."

Toby blinked in surprise, and Clarissa's heart sank, although her face remained expressionless.

"Andy Brentwood is going to give her the loan of an empty house at Fort Shaw," Rob went on. "She's going with the cavalry escort that's taking the wives and children of the regiment's senior officers to Montana."

"Well, leave it to Beth to get her way," Toby said, trying to lighten the mood, though Rob still fumed and Clarissa looked pensive.

Suddenly Clarissa spoke up. "I want to go to Montana, too," she said quietly.

Toby shook his head. "I'm afraid that's out of the question, honey," he replied, a note of obvious regret in his voice.

Under no circumstances did Clarissa intend to give Beth Martin access to Toby while she herself remained separated from him by hundreds of miles. "If Colonel Brentwood was able to make the arrangements for Beth, he can also make them for me," she said. "After all, you and Rob are engaging in the same mission."

Toby exchanged a quick look with his partner, who was patently embarrassed.

"You and Beth," Toby said gently, "aren't in the same situation. For one thing, she's Colonel Brentwood's cousin, you're not. For another, she's still the daughter of the commanding general of the Army of the West, and I daresay that made it a great deal easier to assign a house at Fort Shaw to her."

Clarissa refused to give up. "In case you've forgotten, Toby," she said, "General Blake is now married to your mother, which makes you his stepson. I should think that ought to count for something. In addition to which, I hardly need remind you that Colonel Brentwood was your commanding officer during the better part of the late war, and from all I've gathered, you were quite close to him."

Toby realized it was futile to argue with her, but nevertheless he tried to set the record straight. "General Blake and my mother," he said, "have been married for only a few days. I don't think it would be right for me to take advantage of my new relationship with him this soon after his wedding. As for Andy Brentwood, he had a great many officers under his command, and I don't think he's in a position to do personal favors for all of them."

It was typical of Toby, just as it had been of his late father, to refuse favors from anyone. As Whip had always said, "I'll pay for the pleasures I can afford. As for others, I'll do without."

Clarissa nodded, apparently accepting his dictum as the final word on the subject. However, she did not intend to allow the matter to rest.

Toby and Rob soon departed for Portland to buy some additional surveying equipment they needed for their mission. Clarissa waited until they were gone, then changed into her black velvet dress with ruffled neckline and her plumed hat, complete with an ostrich feather, which Toby swore was the most attractive headgear he had ever seen. In the meantime, she had asked one of the hired hands to saddle a horse for her, and as soon as she was dressed, she mounted the mare and set out for the ferry, which took her and her horse across the Columbia River to Fort Vancouver.

Two companies of recent recruits were distracted from their drill by her proximity as she rode past the parade ground where they were at work. Clarissa rode straight to the building that the officers of the first Montana regiment were still using as their headquarters, and within a few minutes she was admitted to Colonel Andrew Brentwood's office.

"I'm honored by this visit," Andy said, smiling and rising as Clarissa entered his office. "I suppose you've come to the fort to see your mother-in-law."

Clarissa shook her head and replied with typical bluntness. "I have come to Fort Vancouver only to see you."

Andy was taken aback by her candor and rubbed

his lean jaw. "What can I do for you, Clarissa?" he asked, responding in kind to her statement.

"Is it true that you're providing a house for Beth Martin at Fort Shaw and giving her safe conduct there with the cavalry escort?" she asked.

Andy nodded.

"My husband," Clarissa said, her tone so gentle it could have been conversational, "shares Rob Martin's assignment from President Johnson to lay out a route for a new railroad that is going to span North America from the East Coast to the West. He and Rob will go as equals, and neither will have authority over the other. This is precisely the way they worked in Washington."

Andy, failing to understand the point she was making, looked at her quizzically.

"I request that the same privileges be offered to me that were granted to Beth Martin," Clarissa said, and favored him with a warm smile. "I've heard countless stories from Toby about how fair and honorable you were as his commanding officer. So I'm sure I don't need to tell you that I'm prepared, if need be, to take this issue all the way to the top. I'll write to General Grant if I must, and if I get no satisfaction from him, I'll go all the way to President Johnson."

Andy roared with laughter. "I haven't the slightest doubt on earth," he said, "that you would indeed go to both General Grant and President Johnson if I refused your request. My wife told me that Toby had married a woman with extraordinary spirit, and Sue was right, as usual."

Clarissa continued to smile sweetly, but her eyes were guarded, watchful, as she awaited his decision.

"In the first place," he said, still chuckling, "your request is eminently fair and reasonable. Please understand that Beth is receiving no favors because she's my relative or because she's General Blake's daughter. I agreed that Beth could come for the simple reason that I don't believe in separating a man and wife for an extended period of time, if it isn't necessary. The house Beth will occupy at Fort Shaw would sit empty without her, and it will cost the government nothing to have her use it. As for her escort, one of my troops is taking a number of army wives and children from here to Fort Shaw, regardless of whether Beth travels with them. Now, in direct response to you, Clarissa, I'll be very happy to extend to you exactly what I've offered Beth. The regiment leaves tomorrow, so you'll have to be ready to go then. The house you'll be occupying is furnished, but you will require linen, towels, and bedding, as well as silverware and dishes and some pots and pans. You will have to find room for anything you take with you in one-half of a covered wagon that will be supplied for your use."

She tried to thank him, but Andy was not yet done speaking and held up a hand to silence her. "You might check with Beth," he said, "and find out what she's taking, because neither of you will want to duplicate the other's list."

Clarissa looked at him blankly.

"You and Beth will be sharing the house at Fort Shaw. I am sure you would both prefer houses of your own, particularly when your husbands are free to visit you, but I'm afraid this is the best I'm able to do for you."

Clarissa felt as though she had been kicked in the stomach by a mule. She was overjoyed by the realization that her separation from Toby would be temporary and that they would, in one way or another, see each other from time to time throughout his assignment to Montana. But her pleasure was tempered by the knowledge that she would be forced to endure the company of Beth Martin day and night for the foreseeable future. She could only hope that Beth would concentrate on her own husband and would forget whatever interest she might have in Toby Holt.

IV

The settlers in eastern Montana were alert to the dangers of raids by the Sioux, who were making life miserable for them and their neighbors. It was late one night in the spring, and at the McGraw house, the rancher and his son were sleeping with their rifles within easy reach. Even the rancher's wife kept a loaded pistol beneath her pillow. All four of the hired hands in the bunkhouse also kept their weapons close at hand at night, as they did during the day, ready to take action the moment they knew an attack was in progress.

But the Sioux, using tactics devised by the wily and brilliant Thunder Cloud, had anticipated the reaction of the settlers and took evasive action accordingly. On this particular night, a band of braves, forty strong, divided into small groups as they approached the McGraw property, each unit having a specific goal. One unit was assigned to kill the horses in the corral. This was a primary function, as it made pursuit by the settlers impossible. Another group went to the barns and outbuildings behind the ranch house with the mission to slaughter every chicken and pig they encountered. A third unit roamed through the fields and disposed of all the cattle. A fourth and final group had the most difficult task of all. They were ordered to wait until the others had wreaked their havoc, and then they were instructed to shoot flaming arrows into the main dwelling and the bunkhouse, causing the occupants to flee for their lives.

After performing these deeds, the warriors were strictly enjoined to leave and to return to the main body of Sioux as rapidly as their horses would carry them. If their victims fired at them, they were to return the fire only to the extent needed for self-defense. It was important that neither the rancher, his family, nor the hired hands were killed.

It was sufficient, Thunder Cloud had emphasized, that they were destroying property and, even more important, doing away with the rancher's means of earning a living. With his livestock dead, his horses killed, and his cattle slaughtered, he would look at what was left of his house, and knowing he could no longer pay his hired hands their wages, he was certain to give in to the tearful pleas of his wife and to leave Montana for another area, where the natives would be more hospitable and he could earn his living in peace and in safety.

The raiders carried out their assigned tasks with a smooth perfection that had been polished by frequent practice. Everything went precisely as Thunder Cloud had planned it. The chickens and hogs were killed with tomahawks and knives, and the remains were left where they fell. The Sioux resisted their desire to take the animals with them for food. The horses in the corral were killed, which was unfortunate, as the Indians always favored good horseflesh. More than one hundred and thirty head of cattle were slaughtered and left to rot in the pastures. Then the rancher's home and the bunkhouse were set on fire, and the Indians crept away, satisfied that their night of terror had been effective.

On the same night, at almost the same hour, a far different scene was enacted at a ranch only a few miles away. There, Ma Hastings and her gang conducted a raid of their own.

Clifford Hastings entered the engagement himself, and he and Slim Davis killed without mercy, disposing of the rancher, his wife, and their three children, as well as murdering the two hired hands asleep in the bunkhouse.

As was their custom, they ransacked the place before setting fire to it. They took several horses and drove the better cattle before them as they departed. Meanwhile, other members of the band went through the clothes closets and the wardrobe trunks of the rancher and his family and took items of personal property that they thought might have some value in a resale market.

Now only one step remained before the place was put to the torch, and Ma Hastings gave the order herself.

"Before we set fire to the place and hightail it out of here, boys, I want you to scalp every last body you find." She gestured toward the limp corpses of the rancher, his wife, and their three small children. "Remember," she said, "we want to make it look like this place was attacked by the Sioux."

Slim Davis and another member of the band hastened to obey. Drawing sharp knives from their belts, they calmly and quickly scalped each of the dead. They had no qualms about performing these deeds, nor did they feel any remorse. It was important that the Sioux be blamed for the theft and murders, and that Ma and her gang not be suspected.

One by one the band mounted their horses and, laden with booty, started off toward their rendezvous.

Slim was the last of the gang to depart. He went into the kitchen of the looted house, intending to light a firebrand from the flame that still flickered in the wood stove. To his surprise, he saw a chicken cooking on a spit and hastily removed it before expertly setting fire to the dwelling. Then, mounting his gelding, he tore the chicken apart with his bare hands and crammed the still-warm meat into his mouth as he rode to safety, leaving death and destruction behind.

The Eleventh United States Cavalry began to move onto the Fort Vancouver parade ground, their ranks ruler-straight, their mounts moving in perfect unison as they passed the reviewing officers, Major General Leland Blake and their own commanding officer, Colonel Andrew Brentwood. Their sabers flashed in the sunlight as they saluted. The troopers of the Eleventh knew they had no peers in the army, and their pride was reflected in their bearing as they followed their regimental flag. They were unique; they comprised a hard-riding, equally hard-striking force, and they were proud of the mission on which they were being sent. Every member felt certain that by the time the unit was finished with its job, Montana would be pacified.

In the grandstand behind the reviewing officers sat the wives and children of the officers and senior noncommissioned officers, who would be traveling to Montana themselves, leaving later that day with an army escort. This was a special occasion for them, too, and they applauded as troop after troop marched with precision down the length of the parade ground.

In the place of honor, holding a seat in the first row of the grandstand, was the commanding general's new wife, Eulalia Blake, who was experiencing her first troop review since her marriage. Conscious of her need to demonstrate impartiality, she applauded each troop with equal enthusiasm.

Eulalia was flanked on her left by her daughter, Cindy, and on her right by her daughter-in-law, Clarissa. They, too, were enjoying themselves thoroughly.

Notably absent was General Blake's daughter, Beth Martin, and it was assumed that she was not attending the review because she was so busy with last-minute preparations for the wagon train journey that would take the dependents to Montana. After all, military reviews were nothing out of the ordinary for General Blake's only daughter.

Off to one side of the reviewing stand, watching the parade, were three men inconspicuously attired in civilian clothing. The members of the presidential railroad surveying team also were leaving on their mission later in the day.

Toby Holt and Rob Martin, alumni of the Eleventh Cavalry, with which they had served with distinction in the Civil War, were absorbed in the mechanics of the review and watched the parade with the experienced eyes of retired officers. Toby's dog, Mr. Blake, sat beside him and was definitely on his good behavior, neither barking nor making any attempt to accompany the horsemen as they swept in rank after rank down the field.

Also present was Yale Myers, still masquerading as Major Isham Tentry. He knew nothing about military reviews and cared even less. The gyrations of the units on the parade ground meant nothing to him. He found it far preferable to pretend to be watching the review, while in actuality he was surreptitiously watching Clarissa Holt. He occasionally moistened his lips, as his resolve strengthened. He would go with Holt and Martin to Montana, where he would somehow go through the motions of making a survey for the railroad line. Actually he would be looking out for himself, as always. If possible, he would love to get his hands on enough gold or silver to enable him to retire from his disreputable profession. In any event, he would find an opportunity to dispose of young Holt and then would claim the widow as his prize. The mere thought of bedding Clarissa aroused him, and his eyes gleamed as he clenched and opened his fists repeatedly. He had been in great luck the evening he had killed Major Jentry, and he felt that his good fortune would attend him from this time forward.

The regimental band, which had played a medley of lively march tunes, finished its last piece as the rear guard passed in review. Only then did Beth Martin appear, entering by way of the rear of the grandstand and quietly taking an aisle seat.

Susanna Brentwood was conscious of her belated appearance and was disturbed by it. Susanna knew about Beth's hostility to her new stepmother, and the knowledge made her uneasy. Perhaps she should not have interfered and suggested to her husband that quarters be found for Beth at Fort Shaw in Montana. It would appear that an explosive situation would be building within Beth; and Clarissa Holt, sharing a dwelling there, far removed from civilization, would receive the brunt of it.

Well, Susanna reflected, the arrangements were

made and were final. She could only hope that all would
be well when they settled in the Montana wilderness.
Beth was mercurial and spoiled, and Susanna could only
hope that Clarissa's sound common sense would prevent
an unseemly incident.

When the parade came to an end, the reviewing officers, participants, and civilians joined their wives and
families, and all of them adjourned to an area commonly
called "the pit," where large barbecuing facilities were
available. Here sides of buffalo and venison were roasting, and dozens of chickens were cooking on spits over
smaller fires. Men of the garrison were in attendance,
long barbecue tables had been erected, and General and
Mrs. Blake, as the host and hostess, moved slowly through
the throngs, greeting the soldiers and wishing them and
their families Godspeed on their separate journeys to
Montana.

Rob Martin was acutely aware that his wife had
made a belated appearance at the parade, but he decided this was not the occasion to chide her for her
tardiness. They would be separating immediately after
the meal, and he had no idea when his duties would
permit him to pay her a visit at Fort Shaw. So he didn't
want to mar their last moments together by upbraiding
her and creating an argument.

Toby Holt took great pride in introducing Clarissa
to various former comrades-in-arms, and his pride in her
was so obvious that his bride was secretly delighted. It
was true that Toby seemed to be aware of Beth's location in the throng, Clarissa reflected, but perhaps she
was reading more into his attitude than was actually
there. In any event, during the long separation that
loomed ahead, she vowed to remind herself of the

pleasure Toby had taken in presenting her to his former colleagues as his wife.

Clarissa had to contend with an unexpected problem: No matter where she and her husband wandered prior to the serving of the meal, Major Jentry seemed to be following her. Clarissa found his bold, covetous stare disconcerting. Certainly he was making no secret of his desire for her; she could not recall ever having seen such licentiousness stamped on a man's face.

Clarissa was strongly tempted to call Toby's attention to the fact that Major Jentry appeared to have nothing better to do than to keep her under surveillance. But she refrained, not wanting to cause any unnecessary problems. She would be leaving for Montana herself in a very short time, and it was possible, even probable, that she would not encounter the man again. Of much greater concern was that she not do anything to place her husband's mission in jeopardy. The establishment of a transcontinental railroad was a matter of utmost importance, and she wanted to make certain that she said and did nothing that would hinder the swift development of that end.

When the food was finally served, Toby and Clarissa, along with young Cindy, joined Eulalia and her new husband at one of the picnic tables, and Andy and Susanna Brentwood soon brought their plates to the same table. It could not have been accidental that Beth and Rob Martin did not appear, however, and elected to eat elsewhere.

Susanna quietly kept watch and noted that Beth had carried her plate to a table far removed from that which her father and his bride were occupying. Rob seemed disconcerted when his wife went in the opposite direction, but he shrugged, then dutifully followed her.

Susanna made a mental note to repeat her observations to her husband before their separation. She knew that it was imperative that Andy be informed of any undercurrents that might ruffle the tranquillity of Fort Shaw.

As the last of the meal was served and consumed, Colonel Brentwood nodded to the sergeant who served as the regimental bugler. Within moments the crisp notes of a bugle call floated across the picnic area, and the members of the Eleventh Cavalry were recalled to duty.

Husbands kissed their wives and children and hurriedly mounted their horses and joined their units. Andy Brentwood spoke in private with his wife for some moments, then turned and bade farewell to Eulalia and Lee Blake. He had already held an official business meeting earlier that day with the general, and they had nothing left to say to each other now except for a final farewell.

The railroad surveyors were scheduled to accompany the regiment for the first forty-eight hours of their march. It was time for them to take their departure, too.

Clarissa clung to Toby's arm as he hastily bade farewell to his sister, his mother, and her new husband.

"I hope you love your new home and new school in Fort Vancouver," he said to Cindy. "And remember, if you have any problems, you've got two wonderful parents you can go to."

Eulalia and Lee smiled at each other, pleased at Toby's remark.

Clarissa walked with her husband to the stable where his stallion was saddled and waiting, as was the packhorse that carried his bedding, his other personal belongings, and supplies for a protracted journey. His rifle, a new weapon manufactured during the latter days of the Civil War, was in its saddle sheath. Clarissa had noted earlier that one of the two pistols in Toby's belt had been his father's and that the hilt of the knife that protruded from a sheath carried the initials W. H. It was obvious to her that Toby was carrying these weapons not only for protection but also for sentiment's sake. She made no mention of them, however, not wanting their parting to be any more painful than it already was.

"I had hoped," Toby said, "that I could ride as far as the Montana border with you and the escort troop, but you're not taking the same route. Rob and I—and Major Jentry, for whatever he may be worth—have work to do in the mountains west of the border before we actually cross into Montana. So I've got to leave now with Andy's regiment."

He was repeating what he had already told her, but Clarissa knew he was unhappy over their impending separation, and she felt flattered. She reminded herself, as she had so often in recent days, and as she would do repeatedly in the months to come, that nobody had forced Toby to marry her. Though it had been sudden, he had still proposed to her of his own free will, and he had shown every sign of being in love with her. Certainly she could not doubt that he would miss her, just as she would be lonely without him.

"For someone who has always been independent-minded," he said, "I don't mind telling you that I'm going to miss you something fierce."

"Me, too," she replied, and smiled up at him. It was wonderful how reassured she felt in his presence. Only when they were separated did she feel unsure of herself, suffering doubts about their relationship, caused by her worry that he still privately imagined himself in love with Beth Martin.

"Between now and the next time we see each other," Toby told her, "be careful. On the trail to Montana, stay close to the wagon train at all times and don't ever wander out of sight of the cavalry escort. And once you get to Fort Shaw, don't go traipsing off into the wilderness. Always stay within sight of the fort."

Clarissa was touched by his concern. "I'll do exactly as you've told me," she said. "Never fear, and just remember, Toby, dear, that I've already crossed the Great Plains and the mountains by wagon train on my journey across the continent when I first came to Washington. I know how to behave, and I give you my word, I'll take no risks."

"Good," he said as he embraced her.

She slid her arms around his neck. "The same advice holds true for you," she said. "I saw the risks you took in Washington when you felt the cause of justice had to be served, and I beg you to remember that you're a married man now, so act accordingly."

"I won't forget it," he said. "But my father was a married man, too. That didn't stop him from being Whip Holt, and I can't forget, now or ever, that I'm his son."

Rob Martin soon showed up and mounted his horse. Beth materialized beside Clarissa, and the two young women stood together as their husbands rode off, with Mr. Blake trotting happily beside his master's mount. Major Jentry brought up the rear, and as the trio started off, he twisted in his saddle and looked back at Clarissa, leering at her, his lips twisting in a crooked smile.

The evil in the man was so great, so overpowering, that Clarissa was staggered. She wished that she had given in to her instinctive desire to warn Toby that his companion had shown such a strong interest in her. But it was too late now, and as she watched Toby ride

through the gate of Fort Vancouver, with the major
directly behind him, she could only hope that her husband would realize himself that his companion was un-
trustworthy.

The women and children were guided to the far
end of the field, where a large number of covered wagons, each pulled by its own team of horses, were assem-
bled. The dependents would begin their own march
within a short time, escorted by the single troop that
had been assigned by Colonel Brentwood. Most of the
clothes, household belongings, and other property that
the women were taking with them had already been
packed away in their wagons. But there were last-
minute additions. Beth Martin had forgotten two leather
clothing boxes for which she had to find room, and Clarissa Holt struggled with a box of copper pots and pans
that she and Toby had been given as a belated wedding
present. Some of the small children were insisting on
taking toys with them, and most of the women were taking the precaution of bringing extra sides of bacon,
hams, and baskets of oranges from California and apples
from Washington. The journey, although it would not be
long by wagon train standards, nevertheless promised to
be arduous, since the Continental Divide had to be
crossed.

General and Mrs. Blake arrived at the scene, accompanied by young Cindy, and ignoring the chaos, they
went from wagon to wagon to bid the occupants the
best of good fortune. When they reached the wagon occupied by Beth and Clarissa, Eulalia threw her arms
around her daughter-in-law. "I envy you, Clarissa," she
said. "I didn't realize it at the time, but some of the most
exciting days of my life were spent on the wagon train
that brought us to Oregon from the East."

"That's right," Lee added. "The experiences that we enjoyed on that train influenced and marked us for the rest of our days."

Lee approached Beth, his arms extended. The young woman stiffened, and as he embraced her, she averted her face at the last possible moment so that his kiss landed on her blond hair rather than her face.

Beth's reaction was so subtle that her father had no idea she had rebuffed him. Eulalia was aware of the slight, however, and so was Clarissa.

There was no need for words between them. They exchanged a swift glance, and Eulalia felt reassured to realize that her daughter-in-law would take no unnecessary risks and would trust Beth only when such faith proved to be unavoidable. Clarissa, for her part, was cognizant of her traveling companion's faults, and she intended to be on guard against them.

Two sergeants assigned to duty as monitors rode from wagon to wagon, warning the occupants that they were going to leave momentarily. There was a last-minute bustle as property still unpacked was hastily shoved under the canvas-covered hoops and places were taken.

Beth Martin picked up the reins and awaited the signal to set her team into motion. Clarissa Holt, seated beside her, placed both hands on the cumbersome brake, ready to release it the moment the signal was given.

Eulalia Blake felt a strange sense of shock as she looked at the two young women sitting on the board of the covered wagon. In place of Beth, she saw the young woman's mother, Cathy van Ayl, to whom Beth bore such a strong physical resemblance. In place of the red-haired Clarissa, she saw herself. A quarter of a century had passed, but she realized that time was somehow standing still.

Scarcely aware of her agitated state, Eulalia slipped a hand through her husband's arm. Lee Blake knew precisely what she was feeling and thinking, however. The clock had turned back for him, too, and in his mind's eye he also saw his first wife, Cathy, and his present bride, Eulalia.

"I wish them the many years of fulfillment and happiness that we've known," he murmured.

Finding herself surprisingly close to tears, Eulalia could only nod.

"Wagons ho!" shouted the troop commander, who was acting as wagon master.

The workhorses strained against their harnesses and began to plod forward. The creak of leather was soon drowned by the louder, squeaking noises made by the wooden wheels as the cumbersome wagons began to roll forward. The monitors moved up and down the line, instructing the occupants of each wagon when to start, and soon the whole line was in motion.

Eulalia and Lee stood motionless as they watched the wagon train leave the fort and begin its journey. Their thoughts were far away on an earlier wagon journey, and Eulalia could only echo the thoughts that her bridegroom had expressed. She hoped with all her heart that her daughter-in-law and her stepdaughter would know the great joy of living that she and Cathy van Ayl had been privileged to experience in their respective marriages to wonderful men.

The excited occupants of the various wagons had no idea that they were making history; they were too filled with the spirit of adventure to think clearly. Only the captain who was serving as the wagon master could see the situation in its true perspective. He alone knew that the arrival of this train in Montana would mark a turning point in the history of the territory. The taming of Montana by the forces of civilization was well and truly under way.

On the day after the departure of the regiment and the wagon train of dependents to Montana, Eulalia Blake found it necessary to make a journey into Portland. Cindy had an appointment to be checked by Dr. Martin, who had brought her into the world and had attended her ever since that time. The girl also needed new clothes, so a trip to the dressmaker's was essential.

It was strange, Eulalia mused: Cindy had been completely happy wearing a boy's shirt, trousers, and boots to school when she had lived at the ranch. Now, however, she had transferred to the secondary school at Fort Vancouver and suddenly decided that she needed to look like a lady. If her mother had suffered any doubts that she was maturing, she certainly knew better now.

Leaving her daughter at the dressmaker's, where fittings were expected to take a considerable period of time, Eulalia went on about her own business, attending to various errands. She bought some ribbon at a notions shop, obtained a length of cotton cloth recently arrived from New England by ship, which she intended to make into some new army dress shirts for Lee, and then went on to the Portland post office.

On a bulletin board directly opposite the main entrance, stood a large poster: *Wanted, Dead or Alive.* Beneath the heading was an artist's drawing of Yale Myers, and it was a remarkably good likeness. The text offered a reward of five hundred dollars for any information leading to the capture of the man, who had committed three separate murders in California.

No mention was made of the killing of Major Jentry, for the simple reason that his body had not been identified, and although the murder was similar to others perpetrated by Myers, the man had not yet been formally charged with it.

Eulalia had met the man she had known as Major Jentry on several occasions in recent days, and although her mind had been filled with various personal matters in these exciting times, she undoubtedly would have recognized the illustration on the poster had she paused to study it. But as she approached the bulletin board, her curiosity mildly aroused, she heard someone calling her name.

Every Oregon settler who had known and admired Whip Holt and his wife had felt deep sympathy for his widow and, in recent days, rejoiced in her remarriage to a man of great stature in the community. The people of the area had learned of the event from a front-page article in the local press, and consequently, Eulalia found herself surrounded by well-wishers.

Standing only inches from the bulletin board, Eulalia replied graciously to those who surrounded her and wished her happiness. She was always surprised to discover that she was a personality of prominence in the community. Virtually everyone in Oregon, or so it seemed, knew her and sincerely wished her happiness.

Deeply flattered, she made no attempt to cut short the conversation. She stood quietly, pleased by their concern for her, and chatted with them at some length.

A hasty glance at the clock that stood directly above the post office counter told her that she would be late unless she picked up Cindy without delay. Knowing that General Blake's personal gig would be picking her up for the ride across the Columbia River to Fort Vancouver, she had no desire to keep the sergeant in command and the members of his crew waiting for her. She mailed her letters—the task that had brought her to the post office in the first place—and then took her departure, moving quickly down the street to the dressmaker's.

Eulalia left the post office so quickly that the poster and its subject matter completely slipped her mind. The face of Yale Myers continued to glower at all passersby from the bulletin board, but his current secret was still safe, and no one knew or even suspected that he was masquerading as Major Isham Jentry.

Thanks to the meticulous, rigorous training that Hank Purcell had received from his late father, he was completely at home in the Montana wilderness. If Pete Purcell had seen his son in action, he would have known that his efforts had not been wasted. Although only sixteen years of age, the boy conducted himself with the assurance of a man at least twice his age.

Hank had made his camp directly below the crest of a wooded hill, a height that was unapproachable on two sides; the remaining two sides could be seen plainly by anyone located near the crest. That meant that the boy could not be taken by surprise. He had selected a site where the grass was lush and rich to provide his horse with fodder and where a swift-flowing mountain stream provided ample water. He had collected a large supply of firewood for his primary purpose, and he went about his duties with single-minded zeal.

He had shot a large deer with his rifle, bringing down the animal with a single bullet, and after butchering the carcass expertly, he was smoking the meat. This was a laboriously slow process, not only in the smoking but also in the cutting of the meat into strips and hanging them over the smoke. Still, Hank endured his labors with equanimity. He knew the meat would be needed for his continuing survival, and he was prepared to spend as much time as necessary smoking it over the low fire he had made.

While the meat was cooking, the boy continued to work diligently on the deerskin, curing it slowly and carefully as his father had taught him to do. Eventually, after stitching the pieces together with deer sinews, the skin would provide him with two bags to carry his smoked meat.

The fact that Hank was alone, living in the wilderness, in no way dismayed him. He had his rifle and ample supplies of ammunition, as well as a knife. In his bedroll he also had packed a frying pan, eating utensils, and salt. In addition, he had taken with him a Colt revolver that had belonged to his father. With all these things, he would have more than enough to meet his requirements for the many months ahead. No one would rob him, no one would cheat him, and anyone who crossed his path would do so at his own peril. Like Pete Purcell before him, Hank had been forced into the role of a gunslinger, and he intended to play the part to the hilt.

The boy astonished himself with his patience. He was in no rush, and every move he made was calculated and deliberate. Somewhere in Montana there lived a band of robbers, one of whose number was named Slim Davis. Ultimately Hank's path would cross that of the gang members. He might not recognize the horses they had stolen from his father's ranch, and he was reasonably sure that he would not recognize most members of the band. But he was dead certain he would know Slim Davis at a glance, for the portrait of the man's face had been burned indelibly into his brain. When they next met, no matter what the circumstances, Hank intended to put a bullet into Slim Davis's head. The killer of Pete Purcell would suffer the same fate that he had inflicted on his victim; no force on the face of the earth was strong enough to cause Hank to change his mind. The evening Hank's father had been shot, Slim Davis had signed his own death warrant.

Taking from his belt the knife that had been his father's, Hank sliced a small piece from the meat that was cooking over the smoking fire. He tasted it, chewing thoughtfully, and decided that another night and day of smoking would do it no harm. Very well, then. He would wait until this same time tomorrow before he took his departure, and in the meantime, he would continue to work on the curing of the hide.

Standing and stretching, Hank shaded his eyes as he gazed out beyond the cliff into the valley that stood below. There was no human habitation there and no sign of any other person in the area. He was alone, and he was content to have it that way.

Thanks to the careful training he had received from his father, he knew Montana well. He intended to ride from one end to the other in his search for the gang that included Slim Davis, and he would make no specific plans until he found the band. Then he intended to execute Slim swiftly and surely. His mind functioned slowly and methodically. He was drained of all emotion—or so he thought. He had no idea how deeply he had committed himself to the enterprise or how desperately he yearned to avenge the murder of Pete Purcell. Only when his father's killer lay dead at his feet would the boy be satisfied, for only then, he thought, would his father truly rest in peace.

V

It was a lovely, sunny day in Baltimore, with a salt-laden breeze from Chesapeake Bay blowing across the city. The students at the old Conservatory of Music crowded onto the stone steps of the building, enjoying the unusually mild weather between classes.

The main door opened, and a young lady emerged into the open, so deep in thought that she was oblivious to her surroundings.

Conversation died away as the students became aware of her presence, and they stared at her in admiration and respect. All of them knew her as the conservatory's most distinguished graduate student, and without exception, the other young men and women looked up to her.

No one was surprised that Millicent Randall was in such deep thought that she recognized no one as she slowly descended the stone steps, with the black leather case containing her favorite flute tucked under her arm. Virtually everyone in the school had heard her playing that afternoon the "Thirteenth Grand Solo in A Minor" by Tulous, and knew that she was still under the spell of the difficult music. There were those who would have claimed that the musical piece was far too difficult to be interpreted by an amateur flutist, but anyone who knew Millicent Randall recognized all too well that she was the first to seize such a challenge and prove the so-called experts wrong.

She bore little resemblance to the other female students, for she was somewhat older and did not bother to use cosmetics to conceal the fact that she was already in her mid-twenties. She was richly clad, too, indicating a considerable financial gap between her and the other girls at the conservatory. But her appearance was so decorous and neat that she was beyond criticism.

Of medium height, with dark brown eyes and hair of almost the same color neatly gathered into a bun at the nape of her neck, she appeared at first glance to be a rather plain-looking woman. But she also gave the impression of dainty femininity, and a stranger would have been startled to learn that the faculty of the conservatory regarded her as the most promising musician of her generation.

Knowing she had done well with the Tulous solo, in spite of the doubts expressed by her professor, she remained in a special dream world as she walked the short distance to the horse-trolley stop and waited for a streetcar, which would take her to an important engagement.

After she had waited only a short time, a trolley approached, pulled by a team of four powerful work horses. Still lost in her pleasant daze, Millicent boarded the car and paid the fare of five cents to the conductor.

Then, as she moved forward through the throng, intending to find a vacant seat, Millicent was startled when she felt a heavy, masculine hand move quickly across her breasts and then her buttocks. She emerged swiftly from her reverie.

As civilized and sophisticated a city as Baltimore was, Millicent knew all too well that there were many roughnecks in the town, and she saw that she was surrounded by four or five shabbily dressed young toughs, all of whom were grinning at her. One in particular eyed her boldly, and when he spoke, it was immediately apparent that it was he who had taken liberties with her.

"Just because you're a lady ain't no reason for ya to avoid my lovin'," he said in a harsh, grating voice. "Try me out, and then tell me ya don't like it!"

The gentle look of preoccupation on Millicent's face had vanished. Her dark eyes flashed, the lines around her mouth hardened, and her jaw became taut. Saying nothing, she slowly raised a hand to her head and removed a long steel hatpin from her hat. Then, without warning, she jabbed it with all of her strength into the hand of her tormentor.

The young man howled in pain and surprise as he stared down at the blood spurting from his hand.

Millicent Randall looked hard at him, then at each of his companions in turn. "If I were you," she said, wiping the blood from her hatpin on her victim's heavy woolen shirt, "I would leave this trolley car instantly. If you linger here, I shall be compelled to prefer charges against you and have the constabulary escort all of you without delay to the lockup. I consider your conduct a menace, as well as an insult to my sex, and nothing would give me greater pleasure than to see all of you sentenced to terms in prison!"

The young men had heard enough to realize they had chosen the wrong woman for their game. They promptly scattered and, with Millicent watching them closely, leaped to the ground before the trolley halted at its next stop.

Replacing the pin in her hat, Millicent found a vacant seat. She smoothed her skirt, folded her hands in her lap, and was a model of propriety for the rest of her trip.

When Millicent alighted from the trolley, a glance at the clock above the entrance of the Baltimore Hotel told her that she was on time for her appointment. She was pleased, for punctuality was a virtue that she cultivated. The doorman knew her and smiled, tipping his hat to her as he opened the door.

Millicent made her way quickly to the rear of the ornate, baroque lobby, where the principal conversation piece was the huge chandelier of cut glass that had been imported from the royal palace in Vienna years earlier and had been removed for safekeeping during the years of the Civil War. The leader of the string quartet playing a selection of Strauss waltzes had been a fellow student at the conservatory, and feeling as all musicians did toward her, he bowed low.

Millicent returned his salutation with a smile and a quick nod of her head, then looked around at the tables where ladies and gentlemen were drinking tea and eating rich pastries. She saw her cousin at once and started toward his table. She might have known that he, too, would be on time.

The family resemblance between Millicent and James Randall was strong. He, too, had dark brown eyes and hair, and he looked refined and neat, his suit, cravat, and highly polished boots bearing silent evidence of the fact that he was in sound financial condition. But he wore a black patch where his left eye had been, a reminder of his service as a captain in the Army Corps of Engineers during the Union's recent struggle with the Confederacy, and the hair at his temples had turned gray.

He rose to his feet when he saw Millicent approach the table and bestowed a kiss on her cheek.

"Thank you for coming, Jim," she said. "I knew I could count on you."

"I became rather worried when I received your letter saying that it was urgent that we meet as soon as possible," he replied. "It's a great relief to find you in good health."

"I'm just fine, thank you, Jim." Millicent settled in her chair of dark leather and nodded to a half-dozen acquaintances in the room. The hotel had resumed its prewar position as the gathering place at tea time for Baltimore's elite.

They ordered tea and, in memory of their childhood, their favorite confection—chocolate cream. Then they discussed Jim's recent activities, a delicate subject in view of his enforced retirement from the army. Nevertheless, he launched enthusiastically into a description of a four-day hunting and fishing trip he had taken in the area of Chesapeake Bay, and it was apparent that in spite of his handicap, he had no intention of changing his way of life.

Not until they had finished their tea and chocolate cream did Millicent bring up the subject that had caused her to ask for this meeting. "By any chance," she asked, her voice a shade too casual, "have you had a letter from Isham since he was sent West by the army?"

Jim shook his head. "Isham Jentry would have no

particular reason to write to me," he said. "Sure, he and I were roommates at the military academy, and we've been close friends ever since, but you're the one who's engaged to marry him, not I." He stared at her. "Do I glean that he hasn't written to you?"

"If he's written," Millicent said, "his letters have gone astray."

"He hasn't been gone all that long, my dear," Jim replied.

She looked at him, her expression mildly accusing. "He left Washington City for Fort Vancouver three months ago!" she told him. "I should have had my first letter from him at least a month ago. But there's been nary a word. By this time, Isham is off with his two civilian partners somewhere in the wilds of the Montana Territory."

"To be honest with you, Milly," he replied, "I see no cause for undue concern. Isham was given a major task to perform by the War Department, and I'm sure he's been concentrating his full attention on it. You'll get a letter from him sooner or later."

She shook her head as she deftly refilled their tea cups. "I'm ashamed of you, Captain Jim Randall," she said. "You're talking utter gibberish, and you know it. You not only introduced Isham to me before the war broke out, but you'd been close friends for years, and I refuse to believe that you can sit there and honestly feel that Isham Jentry would neglect to send a whole stream of letters to the woman he intends to marry."

Jim stirred a half-teaspoon of sugar into his tea. "I must admit that you have a valid point there," he said. "I not only know Isham well, but having served with him all through the war, I also know how much he suffered because of his self-imposed refusal to marry you until peace came and he was sure that he wouldn't leave you stranded as a widow. Yes, Milly, you're right. The more I think of it, the more I'm forced to agree. It's not at all in keeping with Isham's character not to have sent you a letter during these past few months."

"That's all I wanted to hear," she replied. "I believe I'll visit Washington City and see General Grant in order to find out what's become of Isham."

Jim Randall couldn't control the laugh that welled up within him. "I strongly advise against it, my dear," he said. "In the first place, General Grant has other things to do than to keep track of his subordinates for the sake of their wives and fiancées. He's a very busy man, to say the least. Furthermore, he wouldn't think it in the least odd that you've heard nothing when he's sent Isham out on an extremely important mission as recently as three months ago."

"Very well," she replied. "Then I shall not bother to see General Grant. It's not that I'm afraid of making a fool of myself, mind you, but I see nothing to be gained by wasting time on a fruitless mission." Suddenly her voice took on a new, granitelike quality that was at odds with her refined and genteel appearance. "I'm depending on you to tell me how to proceed in this matter, Jim. After all, you spent four years at West Point and also served in the Civil War. So you'd know what the layman wouldn't. Tell me how I can satisfy myself that Isham is well."

"I suspect you're maneuvering me," he said with good humor, "which is something you've been doing all your life."

She contrived to look innocent and wide eyed.

"Knowing you, I'm sure you won't be satisfied until you've seen with your own eyes that Isham is in one piece and is thriving. So that leaves you no alternative. You will have to travel out to the Montana Territory and see him for yourself."

A smile spread slowly across her face, and those who regarded her as plain would have been surprised by how attractive she appeared. "Will you escort me to Montana, Jim?" she asked.

He grinned and shook his head. "You minx! This is what you've been leading me to from the very start of this conversation."

She laughed but made no reply.

"Well, I can't let you go traipsing off to the wilds of Montana alone, can I? I do owe it to Isham, since he carried me unconscious from the battlefield when I lost my eye after the artillery shell exploded, and I am responsible, in a sense, for your betrothal to him. So I will go with you."

She was not the type to squeal with joy and relief and clap her hands together, so she merely continued to smile and sit demurely. "How will we make the journey, Jim?" she asked quietly.

"Offhand," he replied, "I'd say we go by train as far as Independence, Missouri, and there we take a paddle-wheel steamer that will carry us right into Montana by way of the Missouri River."

She nodded, her excitement mounting.

"We'll go as far as the ship will carry us, which is to a place called Fort Benton. It's a trading post, actually, where supplies and mail are sent on their way to Fort Shaw, about fifty miles away. I'm sure we'll be able to get a military escort to take us from Fort Benton to Fort Shaw, which is a relief. I'd hesitate to try crossing the wilderness with a lady unless we had troops to protect us against attacks by savages."

"And we'll find Isham at Fort Shaw?" Millicent asked.

Jim nodded slowly. "We should be able to," he said. "Fort Shaw is the regimental headquarters of Colonel Andy Brentwood, the military commander of Montana. Isham and his civilian companions will be functioning under Colonel Brentwood's nominal supervision, so he's certain to know their whereabouts. If he can't tell us where we can locate Isham, I'm sure he'll be able to get word to Isham that we've arrived at Fort Shaw and are waiting for him there."

His reply satisfied her, and she sighed deeply. "Thank you, Jim," she said, "for indulging my whims."

Her cousin looked at her, a sardonic expression on his face, and shook his head. "I have enough money to do what I please, fortunately," he said, "and heaven knows I have all the time in the world since the army retired me from active duty. I certainly don't mind the prospect of being occupied and going on what promises to be an interesting journey, and I'm glad to oblige you. I might add that, if I didn't, you'd give me no rest, so in a manner of speaking, I'm going to act as your escort in order to get a little peace."

The towering, snow-capped peaks of the mighty Bitterroot Mountains, which ran from the northwest to the southeast, formed a seemingly impenetrable barrier between the Washington and Montana territories. The precise borders were indistinct, with the Idaho Territory claiming a thin strip between them, and no one knew for certain where one territory ended and another began. The region was simply too inaccessible for accurate mapmaking.

But the trio of trailblazers, surveying for the route

of the railroad that would bring civilization to this remote sector of the United States, were undaunted.
Certainly Toby Holt, who led the party after they separated from Andy Brentwood's regiment, seemed completely self-confident as he urged his horse over
exceptionally rocky, rough terrain, finding trails where
none had existed, somehow managing to guide his horse
across land that, at first glance, defied men to occupy it.

Mr. Blake trotted happily beside Toby's mount, accepting the hardships of the trail with cheerful canine
equanimity. As a further testament to Toby's excellent
training, the dog obeyed his master and accepted the
presence of Yale Myers.

Rob Martin's great faith in his partner remained un-
diminished, and he was content to follow wherever Toby
led. Once or twice each hour he called a halt, dismounted, produced his surveying equipment, and took accurate sightings, making a series of marks on the map that
he carried. Occasionally, he and Toby conversed at
length when, from the heights, they saw relatively level
stretches of ground below them. In one way or another,
they would find the best of all possible lines for the laying of the steel tracks that would end the isolation of the
West.

The only member of the party who seemed ill at
ease and uncomfortable was Major Jentry. Exhausted by
the pace that the hard-driving Toby set, and terrified by
the seemingly great risks that the party took, the criminal, Yale Myers, had virtually abandoned his pose as an
expert on the establishment of railroads. He volunteered
no information on the possible location of the railroad
line, and even when asked direct, specific questions on
the subject by his companions, he replied in such vague
terms that they found his so-called advice totally useless.

Toby and Rob did not discuss the failure of Major
Jentry to make a significant contribution to the effort in
which they were involved. They exchanged an occa-
sional glance, and that was sufficient to indicate their
deep disappointment in their colleague. They had no
idea how Major Jentry had won the confidence and support of General Grant and, ultimately, of President
Johnson, but for all practical purposes, he was useless
and was more of a hindrance than a help.

But an all-important job had to be done, and even
though Toby and Rob would have appreciated any help
they had been given, they shrugged off the failure of
Major Jentry to contribute anything of substance to the
effort they were making.

Although Rob Martin was long accustomed to his
partner's knowledge of the mountains, Toby's expertise
continued to be little short of astonishing. Even Yale
Myers had to concede to himself grudgingly that the
leader and guide of the expedition was endowed with a
sixth sense for survival in the rugged mountain wilderness.

Myers had been surprised, when the party had set
out from Fort Vancouver, to discover that each man carried only a small quantity of jerked venison and of
parched corn. He estimated that the food was sufficient to
last approximately three days. It soon became evident
that his companions intended to live off the land, and he
was convinced, as they moved on to higher and higher
ground, that they would undoubtedly fail and that their
entire group would starve to death.

But he soon began to realize that Toby Holt, like
his distinguished father before him, was no ordinary
hunter.

One afternoon they found the trail so steep that the

men were forced to dismount and lead their horses
across the rough, broken ground. They struggled upward, climbing steadily, and suddenly Toby halted and
signaled to his companions to do the same, also indicating that they were to remain silent.

Mr. Blake tensed, and his ears pointed upward as
his whole body became rigid. All at once Toby raised
his rifle to his shoulder and fired a single shot. There
was no need for him to give any commands to the dog.
Mr. Blake sprang forward and soon disappeared behind
some high boulders. Quickly tethering his horse, Toby
scrambled forward on foot.

His companions followed, and they found Toby
standing above the carcass of a large, plump, bighorn
sheep that he had shot.

"I reckon we'll be feasting on mutton for the next
couple of days," Toby said. "If I estimate correctly, we'll
be moving into territory, day after tomorrow, where elk
are plentiful. I guess we're not going to go hungry for
quite a spell."

His estimate proved accurate, and the men enjoyed
hearty meals, as did Mr. Blake. The horses were not
neglected, either, for Toby displayed a rare ability for
finding grassy patches and tiny valleys where the mounts
could graze.

He proved equal to any emergency that arose. Late
one morning, while riding across a high ridge between
two peaks, he glanced up at the sky, which had been
clear and blue but which suddenly had darkened.
"We're in for a spell of bad weather," he announced, and
immediately began to search for shelter.

A short distance below timberline, he found an area
that seemed to satisfy him. Several large boulders were
located in a hollow, forming a natural cavelike effect.

Here Toby dismounted and requested his companions do the same. "We have an hour or two, at the most," he said, "so I suggest we use the time to collect as much firewood as we can carry back here." Offering no further explanation, he began to gather dry brush.

Rob Martin quickly followed his partner's example. Yale Myers hesitated, then did the same.

Toby found a pair of fallen evergreen trees with trunks about six to eight inches in diameter. He hurried back to his bedroll, which he had left in his saddle, and removing his ax, he swiftly cut the dead trees into firewood.

All three men carried the wood back to the crude shelter of boulders. There Toby lighted a fire, and the pines snapped, sent sparks shooting through the air, and crackled as they burned.

Myers could see no reason why it had been necessary to build the fire, but he had to admit that the heat it engendered was welcome. A strong wind had blown up out of nowhere and was cold and penetrating.

All at once the air was filled with snow. The flakes, driven with considerable force by the wind, stung the faces and hands of the men, who hunched closer to the fire.

Toby appeared totally unsurprised by the unexpected snowfall.

"You knew this was going to happen?" Myers asked him, a note of wonder in his voice.

Toby nodded and did not reply until he had spread a blanket over the back of his horse. "I smelled the storm coming," he said.

Myers gaped at him but said nothing.

"My pa," Toby said, grinning, "always claimed that

he could feel the approach of a snowstorm in his bones. Me, I depend on my nose."

Myers was fascinated, in spite of himself. "You actually can smell snow in the air?" he demanded.

Toby shrugged. "I know it sounds foolish," he said, "but I can only tell you that my system does work. I knew this storm was on its way." He waved toward the snow, which was blowing horizontally and was already beginning to pile up on the rocks beyond range of the campfire.

"How long do you suppose this blizzard will last?" Myers made no attempt to hide his apprehension.

Toby squinted as he looked out at the leaden, snow-filled sky. "There's no way of predicting the duration or intensity of a snowstorm in these mountains, especially at this time of year," he said. "But I'd say it's a pretty safe guess that this won't let up until nightfall, at the very least."

Myers's alarm was reflected in his face.

Toby grinned reassuringly at him. "We have plenty of venison left from the deer I shot yesterday," he said. "Our supplies of firewood will last until morning, and we can melt a heap more snow than we can ever use as water. So we'll just sit tight and let this storm do its damndest."

Yale Myers became thoughtful. He had made up his mind that this was not an appropriate time to carry out his original plan. Toby Holt's days on earth were numbered, to be sure, but Myers had the good sense to realize that his own safety depended on the guide's survival. Later, when they had passed through the high mountains of the Continental Divide, he would carry out his original scheme and would dispose of young Holt. Until then, however, the man's presence was essential. If Myers exercised patience, as well as cunning, the time would come soon enough, and then he would be on easy street for the rest of his days.

Andy Brentwood's scouts followed the route that Toby Holt had laid out for them, and the regiment arrived without incident at Fort Shaw, located in the hill country east of the Rocky Mountains of Montana. The fort was situated in the vast and fertile, pie-shaped territory between the Missouri and Yellowstone rivers. On its arrival, the regiment was greeted by the single company of infantrymen, who had been on housekeeping duties there through the long winter months. These men had tended the livestock that would provide milk and other dairy products, and they had planted the large garden that would supply the troops with vegetables for the coming year.

Thanks to the meticulous advance planning of Colonel Brentwood and his regimental adjutant, the troops moved into the barracks that awaited them, the unmarried officers took up residence in the bachelor officers' quarters, and those whose wives and families were following by wagon train moved into the spacious clapboard houses on the post.

The banner of the Eleventh Cavalry was raised, and it floated below the Stars and Stripes on the flagpole located at one end of the large parade ground. Sentry outposts were stationed, and details were assigned to hunt for the meat that would augment the supplies the regiment had carried with it. Men were dispatched into the surrounding hills to search for deer, elk, and moose, and since the colonel had been informed that herds of buffalo sometimes ventured into the vicinity of the fort, he admonished the hunters to keep watch for the all-important animal. If none were found within a reasonable period of time, he intended to send parties considerably farther afield in search of them. Buffalo meat for eating, fat for candles, and hides for clothing and blankets were essential to the welfare of the regiment.

The infantrymen, who were the old-timers at Fort Shaw, had chopped down trees and bushes and then cut the grass short within one hundred yards of the palisades of the fort in all directions. This was done to keep any approaching enemy in the open. As far as the officers and men of the Eleventh Cavalry knew, no one but the soldiers of the infantry company were aware of their arrival. But the newcomers were mistaken.

Thunder Cloud and several of the subchiefs of the Sioux sat motionless on their horses and watched the arrival of the regiment from the heights that lay to the southeast of Fort Shaw. Their faces looking as though they had been carved out of granite, the Indian leaders were expressionless, keeping their thoughts to themselves.

At last Thunder Cloud broke the silence. "Soldiers who wear the uniform of the white man's government are coming to Montana," he said, and his voice was bitter.

"There are many soldiers," one of the subchiefs declared. "I have counted them with care as they passed through the gates, and they number more than six times one hundred warriors."

One of his colleagues spoke contemptuously. "The braves who wear the war paint of the Sioux," he said, sneering, "are far more numerous than are these soldiers.

There are at least three, and perhaps as many as four, braves for each soldier the enemy has."

Thunder Cloud shook his head and spoke vigorously. "Let us not make the grave mistake," he said, "of thinking that we can defeat these troops in battle because our forces are more numerous. Look you well at their horses, which are heavier, stand taller, and are much stronger than ours. Study the firesticks of the troops, and you will find they are marvelous weapons of destruction. For many years, the guns of the white settlers frightened even the most courageous warriors simply because of the loud noise they made when they were discharged. But those days have ended. In the recent great war, when the whites fought their own brothers, the men who make their firesticks perfected these weapons, and the new rifles they carry are far more powerful than are their older guns. A soldier no longer needs to be a great marksman in order to fire his rifle accurately. With only a little practice, any man can use these remarkable weapons. So the fact that the soldiers are badly outnumbered by the braves of the Sioux is of no importance. One man armed with the new rifle of the soldiers is the equal of five of the most courageous of our braves."

His colleagues took his words to heart, and one of them replied softly, "Thunder Cloud speaks words of truth. We must tread with care if we are to overcome the might of these soldiers."

"Let every brave who wears the war paint of the Sioux be warned," Thunder Cloud said. "He who kills and scalps a settler will be followed to the ends of the earth by soldiers who will demand full vengeance."

One of his subordinates frowned. "The chief of

chiefs is not planning to give up his campaign against the white man?"

Thunder Cloud shook his head, and the faint smile that appeared at the corners of his mouth was lacking in humor. "I have taken a sacred vow in the presence of all the warriors of the Sioux," the chief of chiefs said, "and I keep my word. I shall not rest until every settler is driven from this land, and the territory, once again, becomes the exclusive hunting ground of the Sioux! We will try to avoid a war with these soldiers, but if there must be war, we will fight to the death!"

The Indians were not alone in observing the arrival of the regiment. On the heights, hidden from the Indians and much closer to Fort Shaw, Ma Hastings and the members of her band also took in the scene, carefully screening themselves and their horses behind the trees that studded the heights.

"I guess," Slim Davis said harshly, "we'll have to hie us to Utah or Dakota now. The pickins ain't so good in them territories, but we won't have the U.S. Cavalry breathin' down our necks, neither."

Clifford Hastings laughed harshly. "Where's your sportin' blood, Slim?" he demanded. "You don't think that we aim to let the U.S. Army spoil our fun, do ya?"

Ma Hastings chewed on the wad of tobacco that was lodged in one cheek, then spat accurately at a tree stump. "Let me tell ya somethin', Slim," she said, "and this goes for all the rest o' ya, as well. A regiment o' cavalry has just arrived in Montana, and some o' you boys is feelin' a mite edgy. Well, we been cleanin' up good, makin' ourselves some real nice profits, and I don't aim to be lettin' the army interfere in any way with what we're doin'. There's plenty o' ranches still to be visited, and there's a heap more booty to be collected. We ain't changin' our tactics, and we ain't slowin' down none. We'll be careful, o' course, more careful than we ever been, and we'll take pains to make sure that every raid we make looks like it was done by Indians. But the army ain't drivin' Ma Hastings out o' Montana, not for a minute, and don't any o' you forget it!"

A scant two weeks after the cavalry reached Fort Shaw, the wagon train of dependents appeared on the heights to the west. Andy Brentwood immediately relieved husbands and fathers of other duties, then mounted his own gelding and led the welcoming party in person.

Soon he was reunited with Susanna, and they embraced and kissed, as did the other soldiers and their wives. Leaving his gelding in the care of one of his men, Andy climbed up beside his wife on the seat of her wagon to join her for the last stage of her long journey.

"How did you make out?" he demanded anxiously. "The motion of the wagon didn't make you sick and hurt you or the baby?"

His wife shook her head, pleased by his concern. "I've never in all my born days felt better," she told him. "I recommend wagon train travel for all mothers-in-waiting." She laughed happily.

Andy, however, was not reassured, for his wife could have her baby at any time. "As soon as we reach the post," he said, "I'll ask the doctor to examine you."

Such an examination was unnecessary, she knew, but she made no objection. Her husband would feel easier in his own mind when he learned from the regimental surgeon that she had suffered no ill effects on the wagon train journey.

"Did you have any problems on the trail?" he asked. "Any troubles with the weather?"

"We ran into a surprise snowstorm on the heights about ten days ago," Susanna said. "I realized belatedly that the advanced season is no guarantee against such storms, but we made camp and hunkered down for an extra twenty-four hours. There was no harm done to anyone, nor to the animals."

"Good." Andy hesitated for a moment and then asked, "Any fireworks between Beth and Clarissa? I have been imagining all kinds of troubles."

Susanna shook her head, and her auburn curls danced up and down. "Clarissa Holt is not only a wonderful traveling companion," Susanna told him, "but she's one of the most eminently sensible women I have ever known. You can be sure that she saw to it that she and Beth got along well." She thought for a moment, then added, "I've got to say, in all justice to Beth, that she seemed to be conscious of the fact that she is a general's daughter, and she acted accordingly. We've seen her indulging in irrational behavior of late, but there was no sign of it at all on the trail. She behaved admirably."

"Well," her husband replied, "I can only hope that she and Clarissa continue to get along well. We have a tremendous task ahead of us pacifying the Montana Territory, and I'd hate to have anyone in the garrison distracted by a feud between Beth and Clarissa."

"I think you will find that the relations between them are amiable enough, as long as they are separated from their husbands," Susanna said. "The time to watch out for trouble is when Toby and Rob come to the fort."

Her husband looked at her curiously. "What makes you say that?" he demanded.

"I don't know, really," she replied. "It's just a hunch." Susanna dismissed the subject with a shrug.

When the wagon train finally reached Fort Shaw, the proud husbands and fathers conducted their families to their new homes and showed them through the houses, then began the task of unpacking the dishes, linens, and other household goods that had been carried in the wagons.

Since Clarissa Holt and Beth Martin had no husbands on hand, Andy thoughtfully provided them with the services of two privates, who helped them move their belongings from their wagon to their new dwelling. Andy also signed a note allowing the women to acquire supplies to get them started, and while Beth began to put the house in order, Clarissa hastened to the Fort Shaw commissary to obtain foodstuffs. After she returned to the house, she prepared a quick meal on the wood stove in the new kitchen, then she and Beth sat down at the kitchen table for their first meal in their new Montana home.

Clarissa looked out at dusk falling on the snow-dusted peaks that lay to the west. "I think I'm going to like it here," she said as she cut her meat. "What about you?"

"I've lived on so many army posts all my life that I find one exactly like another," Beth replied indifferently.

Clarissa could understand how she felt, and nodded.

"It's people who make the difference at any post," Beth said. "Fort Shaw won't come to life until our husbands arrive here. Don't you miss Toby terribly?" she asked, and her eyes gleamed.

Clarissa had to admit she did miss her husband, but she couldn't help thinking that Beth appeared to come to life when she mentioned Toby's name. Clarissa felt a stab of premonition, a warning that serious, complicating dangers lay ahead.

The arrival of the Eleventh Cavalry electrified the citizens of the sparsely settled Montana Territory. Settlers, most of them from the plains of the eastern portion, began to arrive at the fort, some of them accompanied by their wives or sons, others traveling with neighbors. Few made the journey from their homes alone because conditions in Montana were too unsettled to allow such freedom of travel. All of the visitors insisted on seeing Colonel Brentwood, and they inundated him with complaints.

Andy had known that conditions were chaotic, but the situation was even worse than he had believed possible. He did what he could, assigning individual troops to specific areas for regular patrol duty. On the surface, at least, Montana soon became quieter.

But raids by the Sioux continued, as did the vicious robberies committed by such gangs as Ma Hastings and her followers, who continued to scalp their victims in the hope that the Indians would be blamed for the outrages they committed.

Those citizens who had expected a rapid change in the fundamental situation in the territory following the arrival of the cavalry were bitterly disappointed. But Colonel Brentwood maintained his objectivity.

"Montana has been in an uproar for a long time now," he said, "and we can't change it overnight. What we need is patience, and a lot of it."

Cavalry patrols spread out through the territory, but the raids did not stop. Andy, however, refused to become discouraged.

"It stands to reason," he said to Susanna at supper one night, "that we're spreading ourselves very thin. We have a total of only seven hundred men on the regimental roster, and when you look at a map of Montana and realize the size of the territory, seven hundred men are spread out very thinly. But eventually we will pull this land into shape."

His wife did not seem to be listening to him, and he looked at her more closely. Color had drained from her face, and she appeared to be in distress.

"I—I don't want to alarm or upset you," she said faintly, "but I think my time has come, Andrew. You're about to become a father."

Andy Brentwood had acquired his reputation as a soldier, at least in part, because of his ability to handle an emergency. Now, however, he completely lost his head and stared at his wife in helpless fascination.

Susanna was equal to the emergency. "Send your aide to summon the doctor," she said, "and ask your orderly to fetch Clarissa and Beth."

He dashed out of the room to comply with her requests. When he returned, her labor was even more advanced, and she was gasping. "You might tell the cook," she said slowly, "to put a large kettle filled with water on the fire. We're going to need it."

Again, Andy left the room hurriedly, and his relief was infinite when the regimental surgeon, whose house was only a few doors from that of the commandant, appeared and took charge of the situation. Then Clarissa arrived, followed by Beth, and Andy found himself banished to his small library, which as yet contained only a handful of books. There, too nervous to sit, he restlessly paced the floor, hour after hour. He lit a cigar, but he almost choked on it and hastily stubbed it out. He took a copy of Thackeray's *Vanity Fair* from the shelf and tried to read, but he was unable to concentrate on the words. He decided he needed a drink of whiskey but changed his mind and went to the kitchen for coffee instead. Every few minutes he pulled his watch out of his waistcoat pocket, but time seemed to be almost standing still, and he repeatedly held the watch up to his ear to make certain it was still functioning.

Andy's frayed nerves threatened to snap. But near dawn, when he decided he could tolerate no more, the door opened, and Clarissa Holt stood in the frame smiling at him, her sleeves rolled above the elbows.

Andy gave her no chance to speak. "How is she?" he demanded. "How is Sue?"

"She's fine," Clarissa told him quietly. "In fact, they're both doing quite well. Come along and meet the new Brentwood."

Not until they were approaching Susanna's bedroom, where Andy caught a glimpse of the physician inside the chamber, did it occur to him to wonder whether he had sired a boy or a girl.

Susanna lay in bed propped on pillows and smiling broadly. In one arm she held a tiny human being. "Colonel," she said softly, "come in and meet your son. Master Samuel Brentwood, say hello to your father."

She had named the baby after Andy's father, and he was overwhelmed. He looked down at his wife, then at his child, his eyes suspiciously moist, and then he bent down and kissed Susanna gently on the lips. This was a day he would remember as long as he lived.

The morning after the snowstorm ended, the sun appeared in a cloudless blue sky, and the members of the surveying team resumed their journey. They traveled far more slowly and carefully than usual because a blanket of six to twelve inches of snow covered the ground, and in spite of the sunshine, it was slow to melt.

Toby, who was in the lead as usual, progressed cautiously, letting his horse pick his own way on the precarious trail. Mr. Blake encountered troubles from time to time, too, and sometimes the dog virtually disappeared in the heavier snowdrifts, with only his tail showing.

Suddenly, shortly before noon, Mr. Blake bounded ahead, ignoring the depth of the snow, and barked furiously as he charged toward a boulder. He halted beside it, his legs spread, his ears erect, and his tail extended out behind him.

Clearly something unusual was taking place, and Toby quickly grabbed his rifle, dismounted, and went forward on foot. When he drew closer to the place where the dog was raising a commotion, he saw what appeared to be a bundle of clothing lying on the ground. Suddenly he realized that he was looking at a human body.

"Easy there, Mr. Blake. Easy, boy," Toby said, patting the dog in order to quiet him. Then dropping to one knee, he looked hard at the still figure on the ground. Stretched out in the snow, an old rifle clutched in one hand, was an elderly man with white hair and a week's stubble on his face. His shirt and pants were of good quality, as were his stout leather boots, and his heavy buckskin jacket appeared to be fairly new. It was plain that he was no derelict. His eyes were closed, but his chest rose and fell evenly, indicating that he was breathing, and Toby grasped him gently by the shoulder.

"You ain't the angel Gabriel, that's for sure," the man said, "so I must still be alive." His voice was deep, but he spoke feebly.

Toby smiled and gently pulled the man to a sitting position as he introduced himself.

"MacGregor is the name," the old man said. "I reckon I drifted off to sleep during the snowstorm. I just couldn't go on another foot."

Toby nodded, recognizing the phenomenon, which was common in the high mountains. When a man began to fail, due to a variety of causes, he usually felt an overpowering urge to go to sleep.

"Some hot food will fix you up just fine, Mr. MacGregor," Toby told him, and called to his companions.

Rob Martin immediately handed him a blanket and a small flask of brandy that they had for medicinal purposes. Then Rob went back to kindle a fire and put some snow in a pot to melt. He got out the remains of the previous night's venison and some cornmeal, then began looking for wild onions for the primitive soup that he was preparing.

Toby wrapped the old man in the blanket and gave him a sip of brandy. MacGregor was moved to protest. "You ain't got no call to fuss over me, lads," he said. "Go on about your business, because I ain't gonna live that long."

"Let us be the judge of that," Toby told him, then turned to Yale Myers, who was standing behind him, gaping at the fallen figure. "Major," he said, "we'll be grateful if you'll make yourself useful and gather some more firewood. This man is chilled and needs to have his blood warmed."

Major Jentry galvanized himself into action and made his way across the uneven, snow-littered ground, searching for chunks of wood that could be used in a fire.

MacGregor grinned weakly at Toby. "You'd have done yourself a real favor, boy," he said, "if you'd left me where you found me and just let me die a natural death."

Toby shook his head. "Stop talking that way, Mr. MacGregor," he said. "You're going to be just fine."

The old man peered at him, and his watery eyes looked enormous. "From the looks of you," he said, "you know the wilderness."

Toby nodded.

"In the animal world," MacGregor declared, "when a critter is ailing, he goes off by himself to die. That's true of every beast there is. From a mountain cat to a buffalo, to a moose that's as big as a house."

"That's true," Toby agreed, not yet aware of what the man was trying to tell him.

MacGregor waggled a feeble forefinger under Toby's nose. "You look smart, young fellow," he said, "but you act awful stupid. I woke up yesterday morning knowing I was breathing my last. MacGregor, I told myself, your time has come, and you gotta pack it in. So I left my cabin down yonder, and I headed up here to the high ground, because this is the land I've always loved. I fell asleep during the snowstorm, which is exactly the way I wanted it to happen to me. And then," he said accusingly, "you had to come along and wake me up and spoil everything."

Toby didn't know quite what to reply.

Rob Martin, aided by an inept Yale Myers, built a

roaring fire, and while he continued to prepare the soup, Toby carried the protesting old man closer to the flames.

In spite of his indignation, MacGregor was amused. "You don't persuade easy, boy," he said. "What's the matter with you? Don't you believe me when I tell you I'm on my last legs?" His bony fingers reached out and clutched Toby's arm. "Look at me!" he commanded. "No, look me straight in the eyes! That's it! Keep looking!"

Toby did as he was told and at last recognized the point the old man was trying to make. There was no doubt of it; impending death was in his eyes.

MacGregor's laugh sounded like a cackle. "There, now!" he said. "You know I'm telling you the truth!"

Toby nodded slowly. His own experience, both in the wilderness and in the Civil War, had made it possible for him to recognize death when it was near. Rather than admit that the old man's hold on life was at best tenuous, however, he removed the soup from the fire and produced a tin spoon from his pocket. "Here," he said. "Eat this while it's still warm."

The old man cackled again and then began to eat. He was silent for a time, clearly enjoying the soup, and then he examined Toby carefully, then transferred his attention to Rob, whom he also scrutinized.

"Tell me something that will fulfill my last wish," he said. "Why are you boys bothering and fussing with an old codger like me?"

Toby was surprised by the question. "Hellfire, Mr. MacGregor," he said. "We found you sleeping on the trail. You sure didn't expect us to go on about our business and just ignore you, did you?"

"Most men hereabouts would have done just that,"

the old man told him. "Maybe they'd have stopped long enough to see if I was carrying a wallet, and they'd have relieved me of it if they could. Otherwise, they wouldn't have cared if I was alive or dead."

"My partner and I aren't built that way," Toby responded, and Rob nodded vigorously.

Again the watery eyes were fixed, first on one, then on the other. Yale Myers, who was bored by the conversation, wandered some distance from the fire.

The old man continued to eat his soup, but the effort proved too great for him, and dropping the spoon, he slowly fell back onto the ground in exhaustion. His lips moved, but neither Toby nor Rob could hear him, and they leaned closer.

"I ain't going to be with you very much longer," MacGregor muttered. "I'll have to say this fast. Reach inside my coat and take the oilskin packet that you'll find in my inside pocket."

Toby hesitated, then obeyed the old man's order.

A smile appeared on MacGregor's wrinkled face. "You've been good to me," he said, "so the least I can do is to return the favor."

The statement captured Yale Myers's interest, and he inched closer. The others paid virtually no attention to him.

"That there map," MacGregor whispered, "is worth a heap of money to you. I spent more years than I can count searching for precious metals, and that's a map of a gold mine that will make you rich. . . ." Suddenly he stopped speaking. His features relaxed, and then he died.

"The poor old fellow," Rob said. "His breathing has stopped."

Toby leaned closer to the old man, nodded, and then reaching out gently, closed his eyes. "There's no way we can dig a grave for him in ground this hard," he said. "I suggest we pile rocks over his body to keep wolves and vultures away."

Rob nodded in agreement.

Toby looked down at the document he held in one hand and stared at it blankly.

"That's the map of the gold mine he mentioned, I reckon," Rob told him.

Toby nodded and, mildly interested, unrolled the map and examined it for a few moments. "It looks authentic," he said. "You want to see it?"

Rob shook his head. "Eventually," he replied. "Not now."

Toby absently rolled the map in its oilskin covering and shoved it into his own pocket. He felt exactly as his partner did. If it was indeed authentic, he wouldn't mind acquiring an interest in a gold cache, but there were far more important matters on his mind. First MacGregor's body had to be protected, and then their journey had to be resumed. The building of a railroad across the face of America could not be delayed.

Yale Myers watched in undisguised astonishment as his companions gathered rocks and placed them on the body of the old man who had just died. What left him almost breathless with wonder was their cavalier attitude toward the map of the gold mine that MacGregor had given them. Never had he encountered such an indifferent approach to riches.

Now, more than ever, it had become necessary for him to dispose of Toby Holt. Regardless of the risks involved, he had to gain possession of the map. Had Toby shown a keen, genuine interest in the map and offered

Major Jentry a fair share, he would have felt far different, Myers told himself. Under the circumstances, however, he felt he had no choice. For the sake of his own future, Toby Holt had to die.

VI

For almost three decades, Independence, Missouri, had been the gateway to the West, and it continued to serve the people of the United States in that capacity. Beyond the thriving, bustling city that had become such a vital communications and supply center lay the Great Plains, the Rocky Mountains, the Coast Ranges, and the promised land that bordered the Pacific Ocean.

Here immigrants by the thousands and tens of thousands had gathered to buy supplies, form wagon trains, and make their way westward, following either the northern route that led to Oregon or the southern path that took them to California. Now, in more recent years, with much of the Great Plains tamed and settled by hard-working farmers who had formed territories and then states of their own, a new form of transportation had augmented the wagon train. Now paddle-wheel steamers that carried both freight and passengers navigated the winding Missouri River as far as Fort Benton in Montana.

For years these rugged little ships had brought beaver and fox furs—the great treasures of the Rockies—to civilization. The fur trade had dwindled and become insignificant, but the importance of the Missouri River to the West had kept the river steamers in business. Now they were used to carry vitally needed supplies to the chain of forts maintained by the United States Army in the Dakota and Montana territories, and on their return to Independence they brought the grains and beef that were the produce of the hardy immigrants who were settling in the West.

Millicent and Jim Randall disembarked from the sleeping car of the train that had carried them from Baltimore to Independence, and after engaging a porter to carry their luggage to the river steamer that would carry them on the next stage of their journey, they had time to stretch their legs and wander through the town. Not until that moment had Millicent realized the importance of the assignment that had been given by the army to her betrothed, Major Isham Jentry. The railroad, when it was extended westward from Independence, would speed the civilizing and settlement of the West as no other form of transportation had ever done.

Until that time came, however, the outfitting of wagon trains and the river trade remained the major Independence industries. Holding tightly to her cousin's arm, Millicent was fascinated by what she saw.

There were endless stables where horses, mules, and oxen could be purchased and even rented to haul the wagons to California, Oregon, or the Washington Territory. Looming over these buildings were vast warehouses, where spare axles and wheels were stored, as were such foodstuffs as sides of bacon and sacks of flour and coffee, as well as bolts of cloth for clothing and blankets, kitchen utensils, oil lamps, and the dozens of other products that made life possible on the long trek across the face of the continent. Then there were the wagon shops themselves, large, barnlike buildings, where wagons and carts and carriages were made and repaired.

The customers who poured in and out of these various establishments were as numerous and as varied as the products that were offered for sale. There were artisans from the cities of the East and the Middle West, carpenters and plumbers, masons and bricklayers, tailors and makers of cloth, all of them seeking a new start in life in the vast acreage that was theirs for the taking in return for a token payment to the government, which encouraged such sales by keeping prices of precious land absurdly low.

There were veterans of the Union and Confederate armies seeking to forget the horrors of war and sinking roots for themselves and their families in the West. There were adventure-seekers from all parts of America, brought this far and determined to go farther because of the lure of silver and gold in the mountains. There were immigrants from Europe, too, the oppressed from the slums of the cities of the Old World, who were attracted by the lure of land and the promise of living in freedom and personal dignity in the New World. There were the English, who had been forced to endure wretched working conditions as they had labored for sixteen hours a day in factories; there were the impoverished from Ireland, who had been unable to wrest a living from the soil of their native land; there were Swedes and Germans, Italians and people from the Low Countries and Latin basin of the Mediterranean; and there were the beginnings of the new tidal wave of migrants from Russia and the other lands of eastern Europe, who were seeking to escape tyranny and poverty.

All funneled through Independence and spread out in the West, where the frontier worked its own brand of magic and transformed all of them into Americans

Independence reflected the years of prosperity it had been enjoying, and it in no way resembled a fron tier town. The main street of the community was cobbled, as befitted a thoroughfare that would have done credit to New York or Boston Wooden sidewalks graced both sides of the roads, and the private houses that lined these thoroughfares were substantial struc tures of brick and wood, each of them with white picket fences and well-tended yards.

As Millicent and Jim Randall made their way to their waiting paddle-wheel steamer, the young woman could not help noticing that many of the buildings, in cluding the livery stables, the numerous warehouses, and the wagon manufacturing plants, bore the same legend. All of them said: *Sam'l Brentwood and Associates.*

"This company," she said, "seems to own half the town."

Jim nodded and laughed. "I'm sure they do," he replied. "Mr. Brentwood is the first citizen of Independence. It so happens that he's the father of Colonel Brentwood, the man whose help we'll be seeking in Montana."

"Really," Millicent said.

"Ordinarily," he continued, "we might want to stop in to pay our respects to him and to his wife, but Mrs. Brentwood is the sister of the late Cathy Blake—General Blake's wife—who was killed with Whip Holt in that tragic rock slide in Washington last year."

Millicent nodded somberly "The newspapers were

filled with stories about the tragedy," she said, "and I think you're quite right not to disturb Mrs. Brentwood's privacy. She obviously needs time to regain her equilibrium after her sister's unexpected passing."

As the cousins drew nearer to the waterfront district facing the great Missouri River, the neighborhood gradually changed. Private homes disappeared, and the district was made up almost entirely of huge warehouses, at least half of them belonging to Sam Brentwood. Numerous taverns were located on small side streets, and the presence of painted, sleazily dressed young women loitering in doorways indicated the presence of a number of brothels as well.

The neighborhood had a distinct flavor of the West. Tanned, bearded men, most of them unkempt and wearing buckskins, and all of them carrying either rifles or pistols, seemed to be everywhere. Like all Westerners, these buckskin-clad men were, without exception, scrupulously polite, and when they looked at Millicent, their glances were covert and swift.

This was more than could be said for the dockhands, cargo loaders, and other men who frequented the neighborhood. Dressed in wool shirts and work pants, they filled the taverns, and the few well-dressed citizens who were making their way through the area gave them a wide berth. Occasionally, too, there were Osage Indians, who wore either their native garb or the attire of the dockhands. They were the first Indians Millicent had ever seen, but she was careful not to stare at them.

Millicent instinctively drew closer to Jim, and her grip on his arm tightened.

Suddenly two men loomed directly in front of the couple, blocking their path. Both wore the rough attire of dockhands, and it was obvious from the stench of liquor on their breaths that they had been drinking heavily. Each of them held an iron crowbar in one hand.

"Well, now!" one of them said and smirked. "Look who's here!"

"You're goin' slummin', huh?" his companion demanded. "You're out to see how the common folks live."

"We want no trouble," Jim Randall told them quietly. "Let us pass, please."

"Let us pass, please." One of the pair mimicked him and then laughed raucously. "You ain't goin' no place, mister, until you empty your purse for us."

Jim's right hand dipped into the pocket of his coat, emerging instantly, gripping a nickel-plated six-shooter, the smallest of the modern weapons manufactured by Colt. The click of the hammer sounded emphatically as he cocked the gun. "I assure you," he said quietly, "that I have no hesitation in doing away with scum. So be good enough to drop your iron bars to the ground and then step aside and allow us to pass in peace."

The pair stared hard at him, and one of them, at least, saw from the expression on Jim's face that they had miscalculated. This man was capable of making good his threat, and the dockhand reacted accordingly. Dropping his crowbar to the ground, he instinctively took two steps backward.

His companion, however, either was too obtuse or too drunk to react with such sensitivity. Gripping the iron bar so hard that his knuckles whitened, he faced Jim defiantly.

Knowing her cousin meant every word, Millicent intervened swiftly before Jim could pull the trigger. She raised one small foot, then stamped the heel of her shoe hard onto the instep of the dock worker.

"I suggest," she said gently, "that you do as the gentleman has directed."

The pain was excruciating, and the man howled in agony, his crowbar thudding on the ground as he released his grip on it.

Smiling sweetly, Millicent again took her cousin's arm. To make certain that the risks were kept to a minimum, Jim continued to grip his pistol firmly as he and Millicent resumed their walk.

Both were sufficiently acute judges of human nature that they felt no need to look back over their shoulders to make sure that they were not in further danger. They knew the dockhands had been cowed and rendered harmless, and they were satisfied to let the matter drop.

Their ship, the *Star of Montana*, awaited them at the dock. Built exclusively for river traffic, it was a vessel with a shallow draft, and the cargo of salted meats, grains, and other supplies for the army forts of Dakota and Montana were neatly piled on the port and starboard decks. At the aft end of the ship was the single steam-powered paddle wheel. A large quantity of coal to provide the fuel could be seen just forward of the paddle wheel.

"I hope," Millicent murmured, "that we won't be obliged to sit on sacks of wheat or corn anytime we want to be outdoors."

Jim laughed. "I think not," he said, and pointed to an upper deck. "I'll be very much surprised if there aren't chairs placed in the open for our convenience on the upper level."

A laconic crew member welcomed them on board and went off for the captain, who proved to be equally uncommunicative. He showed them to their cabins, which, as Jim had suspected, were located on the upper deck. These were tiny cubicles, each of them furnished with a surprisingly comfortable bunk, a chair for reading, and a chest of drawers to hold clothing and other personal belongings. They were the only passengers and would eat their meals in the saloon, located amidships, with the vessel's company.

The captain tendered one bit of unsolicited advice. "I hope, ma'am," he said to Millicent, "that you brung a bathin' costume like you was asked to do."

She nodded but seemed mystified. "I didn't understand the instructions," she said, "and still don't."

The leather-faced ship's officer grinned at her. "Travelin' by riverboat," he said, "is a mite more primitive than sailin' on a clipper ship or a trans-Atlantic steamer. When you want a bath, one o' the crew hauls water out o' the river in a bucket and pours it over you. Generally speakin', you'll need one bucket to get yourself soaped, and at least two buckets worth o' river water to get rinsed off."

Millicent looked at him in wonder. "Isn't the water rather chilly?"

The captain indicated surprise. It was apparent that the possibility that the water might be chilly for bathing had not occurred to him. "It never bothered me none, ma'am," he replied politely.

Less than a half hour later a high-pitched whistle sounded, and the ship was ready to begin her voyage. Two members of the crew cast off the lines that held her to her place at the dock, and the paddle wheel began to churn majestically. The captain, steering the vessel himself, headed for the middle of the swiftly moving, brown-green waters of the mighty Missouri River.

Standing with her cousin on the forward deck, Millicent peered out at the flatlands that stretched as far as she could see toward the horizon. She was leaving civilization behind and was entering the untamed wilderness of the West. But she didn't mind because she was confident she would soon be reunited with her beloved Isham Jentry.

There was a flurry of excitement when Troop D of the Eleventh Cavalry, engaging in a routine patrol in the foothills of the Mountains of the Plains, suddenly encountered a stranger who seemed totally out of place. Rounding a sharp bend on the trail, the three advance scouts came upon a young boy, whose horse was tethered nearby. The lad was seated on the ground behind a boulder, his rifle cradled in his arms, and he appeared to be waiting in ambush for someone, although he had fallen fast asleep.

Awakened and startled by the totally unexpected appearance of the horsemen, he raised his rifle to his shoulder, and then becoming aware of the blue uniforms that the men wore, he hesitated. The veteran scouts immediately pounced on him and disarmed him of his knife and guns.

"Here now, sonny," the corporal in charge of the small unit said good-naturedly. "What are you doing up here all alone?"

Hank Purcell set his jaw stubbornly and made no reply. For weeks he had been riding through the territory, making new camps, looking for Ma Hastings and her gang, and now he was embarrassed at having fallen asleep, then being caught by the troops. He certainly had no intention, however, of revealing his plans to the soldiers. They represented authority, and he was afraid they might distract him from his all-important mission.

Obtaining no satisfaction from the youth, the corporal made the boy his prisoner and turned him over to the troop commander.

Annoyed by the intrusion of the army into what he regarded as private business, Hank refused to explain his presence in the hill country and would answer no questions. The captain was mildly intrigued and insisted that Hank accompany him back to Fort Shaw. There, he went without delay to headquarters.

"Colonel," the captain said, "the boy was sleeping on a small hill when we found him. He had a number of weapons in his possession, and he looked as if he was lying in wait for someone. Whatever it was he was doing, I can't get a word of explanation out of him, so I thought I'd haul him and his horse back here and let you try your luck with him."

"I'll talk to him right now and see if I can't persuade him to speak freely," Andy Brentwood replied.

Seeking a less formal atmosphere than his new office in which to conduct his interrogation, Andy deliberately conducted the sullen boy to the officer's mess, a short distance down the main corridor of the headquarters building from his own office. There, an orderly brought him a cup of strong coffee, and he waved Hank to a chair, then said pleasantly, "Make yourself at home, lad. You look a touch peaked to me, so I'll make a deal with you. Tell me plainly and honestly what you were doing out there in the wilderness by yourself, and I'll see that you're fed a good meal. We had some mighty good baked ham for dinner this noon, and my nose tells me the chef's apple pies are about ready to come out of the oven. So, if you're at all hungry—and from the looks of you, you wouldn't mind a good, home-cooked meal—all you've got to do is speak up and then eat your fill."

Hank's mouth watered, but his resolution remained firm. "Colonel," he said, "I ain't talkin', and that's final!"

"Why in the world not?" Andy didn't know whether to be amused or angry. Certainly he had rarely encountered anyone as intransigent as this boy.

"I was mindin' my own business, I didn't break no law, and I don't see why I have to tell some snoopin' soldiers what I'm about!" Hank looked up and was startled to see an exceptionally tall, handsome young woman with red hair standing in the doorway, staring at him with undisguised interest.

Andy Brentwood looked up toward the door and immediately rose to his feet.

"I'm sorry to trouble you when you're busy, Andy," Clarissa said. "Your aide told me where to find you, and he said it would be all right to interrupt. Beth and I wanted to stock up on some things from the commissary—flour, sugar, and bacon principally—and the supply sergeant in charge insists he must have another note from you before he sells any quantities of food to us."

"I'll issue a blanket order," Andy told her, smiling, "authorizing you and Beth to buy as much as you want and need from the commissary at any time."

She thanked him with a smile, and a dimple appeared in one cheek.

Andy, a shrewd judge of human nature, noted that the boy was staring at Clarissa in awe and wonder, as though he had never seen anyone quite like her.

"I'll be on my way then, and thanks very much." She continued to linger, however, and glanced curiously at the stubborn-faced boy.

Andy acted on a hunch, reflecting that it was just possible that this attractive young lady could persuade the silent youth to speak freely. Certainly there was nothing to lose by making the experiment.

Thus he hastily explained how one of his patrols had encountered the boy, seemingly setting an ambush in the higher foothills. But, he admitted, as yet he had been unable to persuade the lad to explain what he had been doing there.

Clarissa's eyes widened. "Surely you don't mean that he's under arrest!"

Andy shrugged. "There are several bands of thieves that are proving a severe nuisance to the settlers of Montana," he said, "and I don't care to take any risks."

Clarissa studied the boy more intently, and as she became indignant, a spot of color burned in each of her cheeks. "He doesn't look even remotely like a criminal to me!" she exclaimed.

Hank's admiration for his unexpected champion grew.

This was beginning to work out even better than Andy Brentwood had hoped. "May I ask what he does resemble, in your opinion, Mrs. Holt?" he asked politely.

"He looks to me like a lonely, frightened child, who is probably half-starved and is dying for a good meal to fill his belly!"

By now she had won Hank completely, although she didn't yet realize it.

"Since the United States Army doesn't make war on adolescents," Andy said solemnly, "and since I have some rather urgent matters that require my attention, I'll be glad to release this mysterious young man into your custody, if you wish, Clarissa."

"I'll be delighted!" she replied.

"I'm releasing you on parole to Mrs. Holt," Andy

said to the boy, and then demanded sternly, "Do you know what that means?"

"Yes, sir."

Not satisfied with the reply, the officer decided to spell out his position. "Your horse will remain in our custody, and we're not releasing your firearms to you until we have a satisfactory explanation of your conduct. What I am doing is to turn you over to Mrs. Holt to deal with as she sees fit. You're on your honor, which means that if you try to escape or violate your parole in any way, you'll be subjected to severe punishment."

Clarissa took a step closer to Hank and put an arm around his slender shoulders. "I wish you'd stop intimidating him, Andy," she said. "He's still a child!"

Delighted by the way his little scheme was working out, Andy excused himself and returned to his own office.

"You would like a good meal, no doubt," Clarissa said.

"Yes, ma'am." Hank moistened his dry lips.

"Then come along, and we'll see what I have in the larder. My commissary order can wait." She started to walk briskly down the corridor.

Her steps were so long that Hank had to hurry to keep pace with her. Dazed by the unexpected stroke of good fortune, Hank knew only that, for the first time in his life, someone other than his late father had come to his defense. This lovely lady who, in ways that he didn't quite understand, reminded him of his mother, or at least what he liked to think of as his mother, had actually stood up to a full colonel of the United States Cavalry on his behalf. Nothing so wonderful had ever happened to him before.

"Did—did I hear the colonel call you Mrs. Holt?" he asked.

They left the building, and Clarissa nodded as they cut across a corner of the parade ground on the way to the house that she and Beth occupied.

"That's a famous name hereabouts," the boy observed.

She smiled at him. "Whip Holt," she said, "was my husband's father."

No remark she could have made would have had the impact of that simple statement. The boy's eyes widened, his mouth opened and shut, and then he whistled without making a sound.

Clarissa took advantage of his astonishment. "Who are you?"

"I am Henry Purcell, ma'am. My pa always called me Hank."

"Called?" she asked, stressing the past tense. "Doesn't he call you that anymore?"

"My pa is dead, ma'am. He was gunned down by robbers two months ago." The bitterness and hatred in his voice were overwhelming.

Certain now that she would learn his whole story without too much difficulty, Clarissa ushered him into the house. Beth had gone out to exercise her horse, so they were alone in the place. Conducting the boy to the kitchen, Clarissa immediately put him to work peeling a large potato and an oversized onion, both of which she sliced and dropped into a frying pan. Occasionally stirring the mixture, she took a large, juicy beefsteak from the larder and dropped it into another pan, where it was soon sizzling.

Standing by the stove, Hank watched her every move.

While the meat and potatoes cooked, Clarissa quickly prepared a salad of lettuce, watercress, and cucumbers, which had come from the fort's garden. "Here," she said, "You can start on this."

To her astonishment, sudden tears appeared in the boy's eyes. She wondered what she had done to hurt his feelings.

Hank, however, explained to her that his father had always made an issue out of the consumption of salad greens.

Even before Clarissa served his meal, the boy began to pour out his whole story, telling her how his mother had died in childbirth and how he had been raised by his father. His voice became ragged when he related the tragedy that had occurred two months earlier and that had resulted in the death of Pete Purcell.

"If it's the last thing I ever do in this world," Hank swore, "I'm goin' to drill a hole in the forehead of that there Slim Davis. I swore on my pa's dead body that I was goin' to avenge his killin', and that's what I aim to do, come hell or high water!"

Clarissa was appalled that someone of his tender years should have such a grim goal in life. Keeping her thoughts to herself, she removed his meal from the fire and put it on a plate for him.

Hank fell silent as he devoured the enormous meal that she had prepared. Then, thawed, replete, and relaxed, he revealed his purpose in concealing himself in the hills where the cavalry patrol had found him.

Clarissa listened but made no comment, preferring not to interrupt until he was finished speaking.

All at once Hank broke off in his recital. "How come you're bein' so nice to me?" he demanded.

Clarissa's smile faded, but her voice remained

gentle. "If a hungry, friendly puppy followed you home," she replied, "would you feed it?"

Taken aback by her candor, he nodded.

"As a matter of fact," Clarissa said thoughtfully, "I believe we can work out an arrangement that will be good for me, as well as for you. I'll have to check it out with the other lady who occupies this house with me, but I'm sure she'll be delighted, too. We have more than enough room here to give you quarters of your own, and we'll be pleased to provide you with your board, as well as with your quarters. In return, there are so many things that you can do for us. We have weeds that need pulling, grass that needs to be cut, and a thousand chores that require doing around the house."

Hank was startled and didn't quite know what to reply.

Clarissa quietly clinched the deal. "This is an army post, you see," she said. "So life here isn't too easy for two women whose husbands are absent most of the time. We have a great and persistent need for a man around the house."

Watching Hank swell with self-importance, she knew he would accept. She realized, too, that she would have to know him better before she could try to dissuade him from his self-appointed mission of lying in wait for Slim Davis and avenging the murder of his father. She intended to repeat the boy's story to Colonel Brentwood—in confidence, of course—and she knew that she could persuade Andy to leave the resolution of the matter to her.

Her maternal instincts were aroused, and Clarissa knew it was wrong for a child of Hank's age to wander, alone and homeless, through the vast Montana Territory, looking for trouble that was certain to be serious. Not only did she intend to provide the boy with a home, a project she felt certain Beth Martin would second, but in time she hoped she could persuade the child to abandon his dangerous scheme.

The hollow, located in a thickly wooded copse a short distance below timberline, was typical of the bivouac areas that Toby Holt almost miraculously found night after night. Ample supplies of cold, clear water, for both men and animals, were available from the mountain stream that ran through one side of the area, and the horses were turned loose to forage in the tall, sweet grass. Spreading evergreens hid the hollow from view, concealing it from the heights above, and it was as snug and secure as any spot in the wilderness could be.

At the end of the day's surveying, Toby and Rob Martin had enjoyed exceptionally good fortune fishing and had hauled in several mountain trout from the stream, which they had fried for their supper. To complete their meal, they had found a number of potatolike roots in the forest, and they had baked quantities of them in the coals of their supper fire.

Now, tired after their long day's work, and comfortably full after their meal, they rolled in their blankets and were sound asleep. The third member of the party, however, was wide awake.

Yale Myers stared unblinkingly at the stars that filled the blue-black sky. He had been patient, but that patience was exhausted, and the time to act had come. Somewhere in these Rocky Mountains, a fortune in gold awaited him if he was bold and acted decisively. His entire future was hanging in the balance, and he realized he could hesitate no longer.

It was obvious to him that Toby Holt and Rob Martin had only a slight, passing interest, at best, in the gold mine that the old man had left to them. It was his private opinion that they were mad, preferring their endless task of surveying for a railroad line to finding the rich metal that would make them wealthy for the rest of their days. Well, if they didn't want to enjoy the benefits of the gold mine, he did!

That meant he had to acquire possession of the old miner's map, which, wrapped in oilskin, rested in young Holt's inner pocket. The map was the first and most important step, and Myers knew he had to take any risk in order to gain possession of it.

After weighing his options carefully, he had decided that he would prefer to avoid violence for the present, if at all possible. He had no idea where the mine was located, and common sense told him to let Holt guide him much closer to it before he acted.

But his greed gnawed at him and gave him no rest. He'd find the mine by himself if he had to. Unlike his foolishly shortsighted companions, he eagerly looked forward to being inundated with great wealth, living a life of ease and indolence. Dreams of that existence tortured him and forced him to take action.

His plan was both basic and simple. Holt and Martin were sound asleep, both of them breathing deeply. So was the shepherd dog, who was lying some distance away from the men. Myers had a natural advantage. He would reach into Holt's pocket and steal the precious map. If the man awakened and tried to struggle, Myers would dispatch him swiftly with his thick, double-edged hunting knife.

He thought it best if he could avoid committing such a murder for the present, however, because he might awaken Rob Martin, and certainly it was possible that Martin could draw his pistol before Myers could neutralize him as well. That, however, was a risk that had to be taken. Myers knew that his sanity depended on his ability to get his hands on the map that very night.

He rose to his feet, stretched sinuously like a cat, and then stood very still to make sure that his movements had not awakened his companions. They continued to breathe deeply and evenly, and reassured, he drew his knife, gripping the hilt in his left hand as he advanced slowly, step by step, over the mossy carpet beneath his feet. He could not have selected a better place to commit his theft, he decided. His feet made no sound on the ground, and in spite of the star-filled sky above, there was no moon to reveal his movements.

All at once a low, menacing sound seemed to reverberate through the night. Mr. Blake had sensed that Myers was up and about and was making known his objection to the man's approach.

Yale Myers cursed the dog. The animal had been a nemesis to him from the time of their first encounter, and he was sick of the beast. Certainly he had no intention of allowing his scheme to be spoiled by the damned dog!

Mr. Blake scrambled quickly to his feet, his ears pointed, his whole body tensed. His low growl challenged the man who was approaching his master.

Myers hastily revised his plan. First, before he did anything else, he would have to dispose of the animal. He took a firmer grip of his knife and crept forward, intending to plunge it into the dog's chest.

The growls of the aroused Mr. Blake had awakened Toby Holt. One moment he was sound asleep; the next he was completely alert, and somehow his pistol was gripped in his right hand, cocked, and ready for action. Myers instantly sheathed his knife and hastily backed away.

Toby sat up, his pistol ready for instant use. "What's wrong, Major Jentry?" he called.

Myers contrived to sound a trifle sheepish. "I couldn't sleep," he said, "so I got up, intending to relieve myself, and I guess this dog of yours didn't care for the idea. He's never liked me, you know."

Toby smiled and reached out with his free hand to pat the dog. "Take it easy, Mr. Blake," he said. "Everything is all right." The dog stopped growling but remained alert as Myers walked past him into the woods.

Toby stretched out on the ground again and settled himself, preparatory to returning to sleep. Mr. Blake moved in a circle and then took his place at his master's feet.

From the vantage point of the woods, Myers could see that Toby continued to grasp his pistol, even though he was lying down and prepared to sleep again. The man cursed under his breath.

It would be very difficult—virtually impossible, in fact—to take the map of the gold mine from a man like Toby Holt. Myers realized he would have to abandon his plan to gain possession of the map that night.

Now he would be forced to resort to a far more complex scheme. The first step, obviously, would be to get rid of the dog. How to dispose of a viciously unfriendly, seventy-five-pound beast was a problem that would require considerable thought.

But one thing was certain: The shepherd dog, like his master, would have to die. They stood in the way of Myers's acquisition of a fortune, and having waited all his life for just such an opportunity, he intended to let nothing spoil it. No matter how much blood he had to shed.

Just as Clarissa Holt had hoped, Beth Martin reacted strongly and positively to young Hank Purcell. Like Clarissa, she was stunned by the realization that the boy had been on his own for two months, wandering aimlessly around the vast Montana Territory in search of his father's murderers.

"He needs so much," Beth told Clarissa at breakfast. "A settled environment, a real home, and adult supervision."

"Not to mention an education," Clarissa added. "I found out indirectly from him when I fed him supper yesterday that he can read and write, but that's hardly enough these days. He needs schooling, as well. And," she added sternly, "he needs to be disabused of the idea that he's directly responsible for avenging his father's murder. I can see him getting into terrible difficulties that way."

"Not only difficulties, but needlessly risking his life," Beth said, shaking her head.

They broke off the conversation abruptly when Hank appeared in the kitchen entrance.

"We were just talking about you," Beth told him.

"Indeed we were," Clarissa added smoothly. "We were wondering whether you prefer ham and eggs or flapjacks for breakfast."

The boy stared at the young women, his expression incredulous. "You mean I have a choice?" he asked.

"Yes, but the easiest solution to the problem is to give you both." Clarissa was on her feet and went to the stove.

"You can start your meal with this." Beth pointed to a bowl with a hot baked apple, covered with cream.

Hank shook his head. "I thank you kindly, ma'am," he said, "but I don't much like baked apple."

"It's good for you, so you'll eat it," Beth informed him.

"Yes, ma'am," he said meekly, and sitting down at the table, he began to eat the baked apple without further ado.

Clarissa busied herself at the stove, preparing his meal.

"It ain't right for you to be cookin' and waitin' on me, ma'am," Hank protested.

Clarissa shook her head firmly. "We settled all that last night," she said. "Beth and I will do the women's work around here, and you'll do the man's work. That's the way it's going to be done."

The boy opened his mouth to protest but thought better of it.

"It so happens," Clarissa said, "that I taught school back in Philadelphia before I came West. So after you've had your breakfast, we're going to give you a little test, and if you're remiss in your reading, writing, and arithmetic—as I suspect you are—we're going to make up for lost time with some daily classes."

Hank was alarmed. "You're aimin' to teach me book learnin'?"

Beth had to curb a strong desire to laugh. "That's about the size of it, Hank," she said. "We are intending to have a talk about you with Colonel Brentwood, and you might say for all practical purposes we're adopting you. Whether you like it or not, you're going to have a home with routines, and schooling to fit."

He tried to object, but Clarissa gave him no opportunity to express himself. "Either you'll agree to our terms," she said, "or we'll have to turn you over to Colonel Brentwood."

"I guess you haven't seen the prisoners' stockade on the post grounds," Beth told him sweetly. "But you will have to take my word for it that you wouldn't like it there."

Hank knew that these lovely ladies had trapped him, that in spite of himself, he was going to be subjected to the influences of civilization. "I'm much obliged to you for botherin' with me," he said. "I ain't one to holler about gettin' three square meals a day and sleepin' in a real bed. I promise you I'll work hard for my keep, and I won't make you sorry you've took me in."

Clarissa was relieved by his acceptance of the situation.

"There's just one thing I want to make awful clear," he went on. "Not for all the good food and soft beds on earth am I givin' up my quest. I swore on my pa's dead body that I'd kill the devil who gunned him down, and I aim to keep my pledge! I'll stay here at the fort with you because the soldiers should be gettin' reports on where the robber bands are operatin', and I tell you flat out and plain that whenever I find out where to find a critter who calls himself Slim Davis, I'm goin' gunnin' for him!"

Clarissa and Beth exchanged a long look. They were in rare agreement that Hank Purcell needed to be protected, but the boy seemed determined to create a serious problem for himself. Perhaps they were more generous than wise in taking him under their collective wing.

* * *

A scant three days after Yale Myers's aborted attempt to obtain the map of the gold mine, the surveyors paused in their work at noon to rest and water their horses in a mountain stream and to eat some cold, smoked venison. Toby and Rob appeared to enjoy the flavor of the meat, but Myers had to choke it down bite by bite. The day would soon come, he hoped, when he would be eating nothing but the finest beefsteak.

When Toby finished his meat, he wiped the grease from his fingers onto his buckskin trousers and then reached into his inner pocket for the oilskin-wrapped map. Unrolling it, he studied it at length.

Watching him, Myers could scarcely breathe.

"You know," Toby said casually, "if this map of old man MacGregor's is at all accurate, we're right in the heart of the region where his supposed gold mine is located. Just for curiosity's sake, do you fellows have any objection if we make a slight detour and see for ourselves whether he was daydreaming or whether there really is a gold mine?"

Rob chuckled. "I don't think we'll delay the building of the railway overly long," he said, "if we do a little private snooping of our own for an hour or two."

Myers sucked in his breath and could only nod. At last the secret of the mine was about to be revealed!

They mounted their horses again, and Toby assumed the lead, with Mr. Blake at his stallion's heels. Following the directions in the map, he climbed to higher and still higher ground, coming at last to a narrow ledge, with a drop of several thousand feet beyond its lip. "Careful of your footing here," he called. "A slip would be disastrous!"

Myers, bringing up the rear, well knew that in rugged terrain such as this, accidents could occur. With a few well-placed shots, he could be rid of Holt and Martin and the dog, killing them and then dropping their bodies off the ledge, never to be found in the rocky chasm below. Each second brought him closer to the wealth about which he had dreamed for so long.

Toby halted, looking alternately at the side of the cliff and at the map. He was frowning, but eventually his expression cleared, and he folded the map, carefully putting it back into his pocket. "Now I have my bearings," he said, leading the way to still higher ground. Then he halted and pointed. Directly ahead, partly hidden behind a jumble of fallen boulders, was a dark opening.

"There," Toby said pointing, "is the entrance to a cave. According to MacGregor's map, this is it. This is the gold mine." He took a large, fat candle from his saddlebag and, shielding the wick, lighted it with a sulfur match. Then he dismounted and, looping his reins over his horse's head, left the animal at the cave entrance.

Mr. Blake followed, close at his heels, as he disappeared from sight. Rob Martin grinned, and then he, too, vanished.

Yale Myers swiftly examined his rifle and pistol to make sure that both were loaded, and then, his mouth set in grim lines, he followed.

Inside the entrance was a large cavernlike chamber, about forty feet long, and perhaps as wide. Its floor, which sloped gently inward from the entrance, was of solid stone, as was the high ceiling. The interior was littered with fallen boulders.

Evading the nearest of these obstructions as he continued to shield the candle whose flame burned brightly in the cave, Toby went to the nearest wall and examined it. "I'll be damned," he said, and pointed. There, about shoulder height, was a gleaming vein of gold approximately two to two and a half inches high. It ran like a glittering ribbon around the circumference of the cavern. There was no way to determine at a glance how deep the vein ran.

In an increasingly tense silence, Toby followed the thick vein of gold as it ran all around the cavern. At the far end it disappeared on the right-hand side into some further semi-impenetrable part of the cave and then reappeared on the left-hand side. Whether the vein continued indefinitely or whether it grew thicker were matters that could only be imagined.

Even Toby, who shared his late father's lack of concern for material belongings, couldn't help feeling excitement over the discovery. MacGregor, whom he and Rob had befriended, had rewarded them handsomely for their kindness.

Toby was incapable of putting a value on the discovery, but he knew that the gold in the cave represented a fortune of considerable magnitude. Clarissa, he thought, would be highly pleased, and for her sake, he, too, was pleased. He would buy her a fancy wardrobe and some jewelry that would set off her beauty.

Rob Martin shared his partner's sense of deep satisfaction. More realistic and practical than Toby, he was quick to recognize the fact that they were suddenly transformed into men of great substance. There was nothing that Rob particularly wanted for himself, it was true, but he imagined that Beth would have many uses for their new wealth. She would probably want a large and imposing home, and he had no doubt that one of her first expenditures would be on a stable of her own riding horses.

Yale Myers was giddy, but his excitement soon evaporated, and he became coldly calculating. His dreams had materialized at last! The vein of gold that was visible would enable him to live in luxury for the rest of his days. The portion that was hidden beyond the end of the chamber might easily double or even triple the worth of the find.

But he had to make certain that the proceeds of the mine became his alone. Some men might be satisfied with one-third ownership of the property, but Myers's greed was so great that he rejected the thought that he might have to share with any partners. He knew now where to find the mine; he had learned that it truly contained the gold that he had sought so avidly; and he was fairly certain he would now also be able to find his way out of the Rockies without a guide.

Very well, then. The moment had arrived to dispose of the two young men who had led him to this place.

Toby and Rob were absorbed by the sight of the thick vein of gold, so they paid no heed to their companion. Recognizing Toby Holt as the more dangerous of the pair, Myers decided to eliminate him first. He drew his pistol, squinted down the length of the barrel in the uncertain flickering light of the single candle, and squeezed the trigger.

The explosion was an ear-shattering roar that echoed and reechoed in the cavern. The shot missed Toby's head by inches, and the bullet ricocheted crazily, striking one wall and then another.

Toby was startled, but thanks to his lifelong train-

ing, he reacted coolly in the emergency, proving once
again that he was truly Whip Holt's son. Reacting instinctively, he instantly blew out the candle.

"Take cover, Rob," he called softly. "I'll handle
this." It might be castastrophic if both he and Rob Martin tried to go after their attacker in the dark; they well
might injure or destroy each other.

Rob understood at once. "I'll keep you covered as
best I'm able, Toby," he replied.

Toby flattened himself against the wall and took his
bearings. His opponent was Major Jentry, and he supposed he should be surprised by the unexpected development. But the truth of the matter was that he
readily accepted the fact that the sullen, ill-informed Major Jentry was a man sufficiently greedy to commit murder for the sake of acquiring a fortune.

Something wet and cool touched Toby's hand, and
he knew he was being nuzzled by Mr. Blake. He
reached out and patted the dog in silence. The shepherd, reassured by Toby's touch, wagged his tail. But he,
too, seemed to sense that they were in danger, and he
remained very silent.

Toby strained for the slightest sound that would indicate that Major Jentry was on the move. This was a
situation in which one either killed or suffered death
oneself. With his and Rob's life hanging in the balance,
there was no question in Toby's mind as to what he had
to do.

Slinging his rifle over his shoulder by its strap, Toby
drew his pistol and, with his free hand, reached down
and grasped Mr. Blake's collar. Then, choosing his direction at random, he began to inch to his left, lifting one
foot at a time and placing it with infinite care on the

floor of the cavern again. Thanks to the great caution
that he observed, he made virtually no sound.

The silence in the dark cave was menacing, its intensity magnified by the deep blackness of the gloom.
There was no light of any kind that filtered into the
chamber, and it was impossible for Toby to see anything
in front of his face.

All at once, Mr. Blake gave a low, faint growl. This
was the signal that Toby had been awaiting. His dog
was growling because they were approaching Major Jentry. Toby wished that he had heeded at the start the
dog's obvious dislike of the man.

Patting the animal in order to silence him, Toby
took stock of the situation. Major Jentry could be no
more than a few feet from him, though there was no
way of determining the man's precise location. The
slightest error would prove fatal.

Wondering how his father would have handled a
similar situation, Toby ultimately found a solution. Finding at least temporary safety behind a large boulder,
Toby tapped his dog once on the back. Mr. Blake was
aware of what he had to do and, obeying his master instantly, sat behind the boulder.

Toby dropped to his hands and knees and began to
search the floor of the cavern. Finally he found what he
was seeking, a rock about the size of his fist. He picked
it up, and then, replacing his pistol in his belt, he un-
slung his rifle and silently slid a bullet home. What he
was intending was a sensitive, delicate maneuver; he
would have only one chance to succeed or fail.

The shepherd dog's growl had indicated that Major
Jentry was somewhere to his right. So Toby dropped to
one knee, swung his rifle to his shoulder, and after again
taking the precaution of patting the dog in order to keep

him quiet, he threw the rock gently into the air and off to his right.

It struck the far wall of the cavern, then dropped to the floor with a clatter and rolled several feet. The ruse proved as successful as Toby hoped it would. Yale Myers, jittery in the silent gloom, heard the sound of the rock and fired his pistol.

Toby had been waiting for precisely this development. His rifle was already raised to his shoulder, and his finger was on the trigger. When he saw the flash from Myers's pistol, he quickly took aim, knowing that his life and Rob's depended on his accuracy. Then he squeezed the trigger.

The roar of the rifle in the pitch-black cave was not loud enough to drown the sound as Myers screamed, Toby's bullet having hit him in the shoulder. But Myers was still very much alive, and he immediately fired his gun in the direction Toby's shot had come from. The bullet hit the side of the boulder, and fragments of stone flew out and hit Toby in the face, causing him to mutter a curse and take a backward step.

For Mr. Blake, this was enough. His master had commanded him to stay put, but that was before Toby had been nearly shot down and hurt by the stone fragments. The love the shepherd dog bore his master was too great and overcame any command. Mr. Blake launched himself in the direction of the hated enemy, and his jaws closed on the murderer's neck. One mighty wrench of the animal's jaw, and the threat to his master was no more. Yale Myers screamed, then fell to the floor of the cave, the shepherd dog still gripping his throat.

At first the silence that followed was deafening. Then the dog gave a sharp bark.

"Are you all right, Toby?" Rob's question sounded somewhere off to the left.

"I'm fine," Toby replied, rubbing a small gash near his eye. "I think Mr. Blake took care of the situation."

Toby called to his dog, and once again Mr. Blake barked. Toby now took the risk of relighting his candle.

In the dim light he and Rob saw the dead, blood-smeared body of Yale Myers crumpled on the floor of the cave. Above him stood the alert shepherd dog, guarding his quarry.

Toby reached down and, patting his dog vigorously, said, "Thanks, friend."

Toby and Rob wanted to put the gloom of the cave behind them, and without any words, they dragged the dead man's body into the open. There, with Mr. Blake standing between them, they stared at the corpse.

"He would have killed us," Rob said hoarsely, "in order to gain possession of the gold mine for himself. It's hard to believe that such a man could have held a special commission from President Johnson and General Grant."

Toby did not reply. Reaching into the pocket of the dead man, he removed a packet of documents and other papers and handed them to Rob. This, in its way, was the most distasteful phase of the whole tragic incident.

Rob began to examine the papers, one by one, placing them on the ground beneath his pistol as he finished perusing them.

The first three or four papers identified the man as Major Jentry, and Rob was aware of nothing wrong. Then, however, he was startled and confused to discover identification under a second name. "Look at these, Toby," he said, and passed the documents to his companion.

While Toby examined them, frowning, Rob continued to go through the pile. "This is odd," he said at last. "Here's a third set of identification papers." After Rob found a fourth set, Toby said, "I think I've got the answer. This man, whoever he really was, was a criminal who either killed people for their identifications or simply stole their documents, which I consider less likely."

"Of course." Rob shook his head slowly. "That explains a great deal. He was no help to us because he knew nothing about railroads. He wasn't Major Jentry."

"I suggest," Toby said, "that we hang on to these papers and turn them over to Andy Brentwood when we go to Fort Shaw. He'll want to notify the authorities that Major Jentry's murderer has been found."

Rob nodded and pocketed the papers. Then they stood and looked down at the still body of the criminal who had succeeded in fooling them and who had come so close to killing them.

The ground underfoot was too rocky and hard for them to dig a grave for him, and they looked at each other, communicating without words. Then Rob nodded solemnly.

Toby displayed no sentiment as he nudged the body with his foot, and it slid off the precipice, hurtling down several thousand feet to a chasm below. There, they knew, wolves and vultures would do the rest and would pick the bones clean.

The incident and all that it had implied left them unsettled. They walked slowly to their mounts, and Rob picked up the reins of the dead man's horse, which he intended to lead. "For whatever it's worth," he said, "the discovery of this mine is going to make us wealthy, Toby."

"I reckon it is," Toby replied, "and we really owe our good fortune to Mr. Blake." Patting the shepherd dog, he then mounted his stallion. "But no matter how much money we're worth, we still have a duty to complete for the government. The building of a railroad is waiting on the information that we're going to supply."

Far to the east, unaware of the tragic events that were ultimately destined to touch their lives, the Randall cousins continued on their journey, eager to reach their destination. Day after day the riverboat sailed up the broad waters of the Missouri River, anchoring at nightfall and resuming the journey at daybreak the following morning.

Millicent had brought several books on music and musicians with her, intending to spend her days reading. But she quickly discovered that the scenery so enchanted her that her books remained untouched.

The West, she realized, was not one land, but many. The Missouri River delineated the border that separated Iowa and Nebraska, rich farmland, settled within the past quarter of a century and just beginning to come into its own as an area producing a major share of crops for the rapidly increasing population of the United States.

Cutting abruptly toward the northwest, the mighty stream passed through the huge, undeveloped realm of the Dakota Territory, a land so vast that it equaled the square mileage of a large number of Eastern Seaboard states. Certainly Maryland would have been completely lost within its borders. Here the Great Plains still seemed endless, and the soil that someday would yield corn and wheat in great abundance now boasted only grass as an agricultural product. The sea of grass, knee-high in most places, extended all the way to the horizon in every direction, and not a tree was to be seen anywhere.

In Dakota the ship's captain adopted new tactics: Two crew members were assigned to sentry duty, fore and aft, during every halt, and were relieved at regular intervals until daylight came again. This was necessary, he explained, because Dakota was truly a wilderness, a land where the Sioux roamed in large numbers and where the Cheyenne had moved eastward from their own home in the Wyoming Territory in their search for the abundant game that the Dakota wilderness provided.

Making an abrupt forty-five-degree cut to the west, the Missouri River entered Montana. Here, although the ground gradually rose higher, the terrain seemed to be a continuation of the Great Plains, and most of the settlers whose homes could be seen from the riverboat were farmers. Gradually, however, Millicent and Jim became aware of a change in the occupation of the pioneers.

As the ship carried them northward to the border of Canada and westward toward the towering Rocky Mountains, they found the farms giving way to ranches where the raising of cattle was proving to be more prosperous than the growing of crops.

On the final leg of the voyage, Millicent was perplexed one day when she heard a sound like that of thunder but, looking up, saw that the sky was a cloudless blue.

The sound became louder still, and when she saw her cousin hurrying onto the deck to join her, she looked at him questioningly.

Jim grinned at her. "The captain told me we're in for a rare treat," he said. "Watch!"

The young woman's sense of mystification grew when she saw the captain and two members of his crew emerge from the pilothouse on the forward portion of the deck. All three were armed with rifles, and she could only think that an Indian attack was impending. But that could not account for the strange noise that continued to swell and made conversation almost impossible.

Jim shouted something unintelligible as he again pointed upstream. A cloud of thick dust was rising from the far bank of the Missouri River, and as Millicent tried to understand the peculiar phenomenon, she saw clods of earth thrown skyward, too. She peered more closely at the approaching dust cloud, then gasped as the mystery explained itself.

She was witnessing an event about which she had read in numerous newspaper and magazine articles over the years. She was actually seeing a buffalo stampede!

Leading the wild, headlong charge eastward along the far bank of the Missouri were perhaps twenty young bulls, each of them mature and fully developed, yet sufficiently young to be able to sustain great speed for long periods. Directly behind them were a number of mature cows, great creatures, each of which weighed at least nine hundred pounds. They appeared to be directing the mass movement.

The charge was so savage, so primitive, that Millicent could not help feeling uneasy, even though she realized that she was safe on board the riverboat and that the broad expanse of water separated her from the herd of buffalo.

Behind the vanguard of young bulls and cows came

the main body of the buffalo, the massive, mature bulls, with their large, glistening horns, each of the shaggy creatures weighing at least two thousand pounds. There were huge cows, too, with their calves at their heels, as well as countless adolescents of both sexes doing their best to maintain the pace set by their elders.

A number of agile, young bulls patrolled the outer fringe of the thundering mass movement, and whenever a calf strayed or a cow began to veer out of line, a nudge from the horns of one of the young bulls forced the animal back into line again. Millicent could see in the distance that this same principle of utilizing sentries was observed at the rear end of the column, where a line of young bulls forced stragglers to exert themselves and not lag behind their fellows.

The young woman found it literally impossible to count the number of beasts in the herd. All she knew was that there were many hundreds of buffalo, all of them in motion simultaneously. Here, she thought, was the West incarnate, the raw power, the surging tide of brute strength, the mystical quality that no author had yet been able to capture on paper.

Eventually Millicent realized that Jim, like the captain and the members of his crew, was armed with a rifle. As she watched, he raised the weapon to his shoulder, and so loud was the thunder of the buffalo hoofs on the prairie that she could scarcely hear the sound of the rifle shot. She saw a bull stumble and drop out of the line; Jim had found his target. He reloaded with great but deliberate haste, and she watched him as he again raised the rifle to his shoulder.

His second shot brought down the bull, which slid partway down the embankment toward the river and lay still, beyond the path of the hoofs of the other members of the herd, which would have crushed and mangled the dead beast beyond recognition.

Again Jim reloaded, and this time he required only a single shot to bring down a young calf. Its mother, Millicent could not help noticing, did not falter or slacken her speed as she continued her headlong plunge forward.

All at once the tail end of the column passed the riverboat, and the thundering sound began to recede. Soon, all that remained of the terrifying incident was the sight of the churned ground, the grass trampled into the earth, and on the slope that led to the river, the unmoving carcasses of the two buffalo Jim had shot.

The captain directed the riverboat engines to be cut and prepared to send some of his crew ashore in three small boats to tend to the felled buffalo. As he came down the deck, he called to Jim in admiration, "You be right handy with a rifle, Mr. Randall. You looked like a Westerner the way you was shootin'." He could have offered no higher praise.

A grinning Jim made no reply but was privately relieved that having only one good eye had not hurt his aim. "You and the crew may keep the bull and do with it what you please, Captain," he said, "providing you'll butcher the carcass of the calf for me. I'm sure the soldiers at Fort Shaw will be grateful for the meat and as a result won't mind so much escorting a couple of civilians to the post."

The captain's nod indicated that Jim Randall thoroughly undestood the ways of the West.

Feeling ill, Millicent retired to her cabin so she would not have to watch the butchering of the dead animals. She had seen enough violence, enough brutality, for one day. The West, she concluded, was incompara-

bly beautiful, with breathtaking scenery. But life was
lived here on a primitive level, and the forces of nature
were close to the surface, no matter how civilized its
people might seem.

VII

The education of Hank Purcell was a project that was pursued vigorously. Clarissa Holt, who was more or less in charge, taught him writing and arithmetic. Beth Martin accepted the responsibility for instructing him in geography and history, and Susanna Brentwood, who had been a highly successful newspaper writer and editor before her marriage, became the boy's teacher in the study of the English language. The chore was complicated for Susanna because of her baby, but she solved the problem by teaching Hank during the time the infant was napping.

Hank graciously accepted the earnest endeavors of his teachers. Realizing their only goal was his improvement, he plunged into the work with an energy and a fervor that surprised them. He did homework without a murmur of protest, and his speech improved noticeably. He made himself useful around the house, too, accepting every chore that he was assigned, and volunteering for many others.

The young women engaged in a continuing subtle campaign to dissuade the youth from his aim of seeking revenge for the murder of his father, and they lost no opportunity to try to persuade him to act sensibly. Hank listened to all that they said, never raised his voice in argument, and on the surface, at least, appeared to agree with them. But his mind was made up, and nothing would change it. He regarded the vow he had taken to avenge his father's death as sacred and was determined that nothing would dissuade him from finding and killing Slim Davis.

He was lucky, he knew, and he appreciated his good fortune. He had a comfortable bed in a substantial dwelling, and he ate three very large meals each day. His duties were light, and he was undoubtedly improving his mind, preparing for a future vocation in the years that stretched out ahead. But what made him particularly fortunate, he felt, was the convenience of Fort Shaw for his own private purposes.

He soon learned that individual troop assignments were posted on a bulletin board at regimental headquarters, and he made it his business to go each day to the building and look at the latest orders. Eventually he hoped the Hastings gang would be located and a troop would be assigned to run down the band and render it harmless. When that time came, he intended to disappear for as many days as would be necessary to accomplish his mission.

He appreciated all that his mentors were doing for him. He particularly looked up to Clarissa, whom he regarded with a mixture of love and awe, having substituted her for his mother in his imagination. But even she failed to sway him or dampen his resolve to even the score with the man who had shot his father in cold blood.

Sensitive to the boy's moods, Clarissa was aware of his silent resistance whenever she brought up the topic of abandoning his goal. Realizing that her words were falling on deaf ears, she deliberately dropped the subject and tried taking a different approach.

One morning after Hank had spent over an hour struggling with some problems in long division, Clarissa sat back in her kitchen chair and pushed a thick strand of red hair back from her forehead. "I'm inclined to doubt that you'll ever be a professor of mathematics, Hank, or for that matter, that you'll ever become a surveyor like Rob Martin. Mathematics doesn't seem to be your natural activity."

"To be honest with you, ma'am," he replied, giving her a painful smile, "I'd rather dig post holes for a new fence than do problems in division."

"No matter what you'll become in life, you'll need familiarity with arithmetic," she told him. "Otherwise, you could be badly cheated by everyone who does business with you."

"Yes, ma'am," he said without conviction.

"Just what do you want to do when you grow up, Hank?" she asked, hoping to inspire and stir him.

Hank ran a brown, sinewy hand through his sandy hair. "Blamed if I know," he confessed.

"You've seen quite a bit of military life here at Fort Shaw," she said. "How does an army career strike you?"

The boy shrugged. "It wouldn't be so bad if I could be an officer," he said, "but I don't have the book learning for that. To tell you the truth, ma'am, I never thought of being anything except a rancher, like my pa.

But now I'm not so sure. There's a heap of other things in the world that could be a lot more exciting."

"What do you have in mind?" Clarissa demanded.

Hank's grin was shy. "You said you were related to Whip Holt," he replied. "I'd rather be like him than anybody! He was an explorer and a hunter and a trapper and a guide, and he knew the wilderness like it was the palm of his hand."

"That's true," she said, "and Toby—my husband—is like his father in many ways. But as he'll be the first to tell you when he comes to visit us here at the fort, the day of the mountain man is ending. Civilization is making major inroads in the wilderness, and the frontier that we've known for so long will soon be a thing of the past. Why, the coming of the railroad virtually guarantees it, and that's what Toby and his partner are doing now, laying out the route for a line that will join the Pacific Northwest with the rest of the United States. So I'm afraid you're a bit late if you want to emulate Whip Holt."

"Then I don't rightly know what I want, ma'am," he said flatly.

"Why don't you wait until Toby comes here and talk it over with him?" Clarissa suggested, at a loss as to how to proceed. "I'm sure he'll be able to steer you in the right direction."

Having worked steadily for weeks without taking as much as a single day's respite, Toby Holt finally proposed to his partner that they take a break. "We are within easy enough range of Fort Shaw now," he said, "and we can give ourselves a holiday of a few days. Besides, I don't want to delay in registering our claim to the gold mine."

Rob was quick to agree. Although it was unlikely that anyone else would stumble across the mine and learn of the riches it contained, there was so much money at stake that it was wise to take no unnecessary risks.

Neither Rob nor Toby broached the subject, but both were anxious to be reunited with their wives, even if only for a few days. Although they were as close as two young men could be, they avoided the subject that was foremost in their minds. To Toby and Rob, raised to accept hardship and adversity, it wasn't seemly to talk about such things as missing one's wife or being homesick.

They descended rapidly from the high mountains, arriving without incident in the rolling hill country of the central portion of Montana. Knowing they would reach the army post in another twenty-four hours, they unconsciously spurred their mounts to a faster gait.

Directly ahead of them stood a corral, and beyond it was a farmhouse made of unpainted clapboard, with several outbuildings, including a barn and a separate kitchen. A single glance told the two riders that something was very much amiss. The corral was empty, and the gate was open, creaking as it swung to and fro in the breeze that blew down from the heights. The barn door was open as well, and when they drew nearer, they saw that the entrance to the kitchen was also ajar.

There was no need for words. Exchanging a quick glance, Toby and Rob instinctively slid bullets into the chambers of their rifles.

Mr. Blake growled and advanced slowly, cautiously, his hair ruffled. He stayed close to his master, and his step was wary, as though he did not quite know what to expect next.

The men stopped at the entrance and pounded on

the open door, then shouted to determine if anyone was at home. There was no reply. Gripping their rifles, they went in. The first room that they entered was the parlor, and they saw at a glance that the place had been ransacked. Furniture was knocked over, the contents of a table were scattered on the floor, and it appeared that bric-a-brac was missing from the mantlepiece above the hearth.

Toby and Rob went into the dining room, where similar chaos met their gaze, and then hurried upstairs. There were three bedrooms, all of them empty, and all of them ransacked. Closets and wardrobes had been opened, and their contents were spewed everywhere.

"I don't like the looks of this," Toby said.

"I'm uneasy," Rob agreed, and led the way downstairs again.

The pair went to the barn, and there, just inside the entrance, the body of a man in his early thirties was sprawled on the ground. He had been scalped, and Toby estimated the man had been dead for a day or two.

The barn was empty. Whatever animals had been there had been taken by the intruders.

"Come on," Rob said urgently, leading the way into the kitchen outbuilding. There he stopped short. Huddled on the floor in front of him were the bodies of a woman and of two small children, a boy and a girl, whom she obviously had been trying to protect, but in vain. They, too, had been scalped.

"My God," Rob muttered. "The Sioux have been here. They're responsible for this."

Toby made no reply. Instead, he stared down at the bodies for some time, then knelt beside them and examined them more closely. Standing again, he spoke quietly.

"I'm not so sure this was the work of Indians," he said, "though it was meant to look that way. I think we were meant to believe that the Sioux were responsible for this outrage."

Rob looked at him blankly. "What do you mean?"

Toby dropped to one knee again and pointed. "You'll note that this poor lady was shot behind one ear," he said. "The same thing happened to her youngsters. And it appears to me that the shots were fired from a modern-day firearm, probably a Colt. You'll note that all three wounds look virtually identical."

Rob nodded.

"The Sioux," Toby said, his voice harsh and grating, "aren't equipped with modern-day firearms. Repeating Colt pistols were issued to army officers in the last two years of the Civil War, and they're still mighty difficult for civilians to get. They're also damned expensive. Too expensive certainly for the Sioux."

Rob nodded; his friend was making sense.

"Now look at the heads of the victims," Toby commanded. "Their scalps were almost literally torn off their heads, as you can tell by the ragged condition of what's left."

Rob forced himself to examine the head wounds of the woman and the two children, and he saw that Toby was right.

"If you've ever seen the body of a person who is scalped by an Indian—and I've seen plenty of them in my day—they don't look like this."

"What do you mean?" Rob asked.

"The Indians of just about every tribe on the continent," Toby told him, "and that includes the Sioux, naturally, scalp their enemies. An experienced warrior," Toby went on, "does a clean, slick job when he removes a scalp. This, unfortunately, looks like it was done by a boy in his early teens who couldn't even qualify as a junior brave."

"I'm beginning to see the picture," Rob said.

"Wait," Toby said. "Let's be good and sure before we make any definite conclusions." He led the way back to the barn, and there he examined the corpse of the dead man.

"Same thing here," he said. "He was shot behind the ear, and my guess is that the wound was also made by a Colt repeater. His scalp was cut away and removed by someone just as amateurish as the fiends who scalped that poor lady and her young ones."

Conquering his distaste, Rob bent low and examined the body of the man. Then, rising to his feet again, he nodded slowly. "It seems to me," he said, "that this property was attacked and robbed by men who then killed all of the inhabitants—using modern firearms. They then went to extreme lengths in an attempt to make it appear that the murders had been committed by Indians."

"Exactly my thinking," Toby told him.

"Who—"

"It's useless for us to speculate," Toby said, interrupting his friend. "But it wouldn't surprise me any if Andy Brentwood has a pretty good sneaking hunch, and I think we ought to collect every scrap of information that we can give him."

Rob agreed, and for the next hour they traced and retraced their steps, going over the house and outbuildings thoroughly and making copious notes on everything that they saw. When they finished the task, Toby hesitated.

"I'd like to show my respect for the poor devil and

his unfortunate family," he said. "I think we ought to bury them."

Rob shook his head. "We'd be doing them no favor, I fear. Andy Brentwood has the unsavory and unenviable job of rounding up the thieves who were responsible for this outrage, so I don't believe we should touch anything. We can report our findings to him, but he'll want to send a troop of his own here and get a report from them."

Toby knew he was right, so they returned in silence to their waiting mounts. They rode on, and not until they were some miles from the scene of the tragedy did they speak.

"Folks who claim that the West has been civilized don't know what they're talking about," Toby said.

Rob nodded somberly. "This part of the country," he said, "has a long way to go before it will be tamed."

Clarissa Holt descended the stairs from her second floor bedchamber, a lighted oil lamp in one hand. She was on her way to the kitchen to prepare supper for herself, Beth, and young Hank Purcell.

Suddenly a man stepped out of the shadows at the foot of the stairs and addressed her.

"If you please, Mrs. Holt," Toby said, "I'll relieve you of that lamp. You might drop it while you're getting yourself kissed."

Clarissa stared at him in momentary astonishment, and then her joyous laugh seemed to fill the whole house. "I believe you'll be too busy holding your wife to be encumbered with a lamp, Mr. Holt," she replied demurely, carefully placing the oil lamp on the newel post.

Toby embraced and kissed her, and she melted into his arms.

The reunion of Rob and Beth Martin was less joyous, less dramatic. Rob learned the location of his wife's bedchamber from Hank, who was stoking wood in the kitchen range, and he hurried up the stairs.

Reaching the second floor, he made his first mistake, an error of consequence: Instead of bursting unannounced into the bedroom, he hesitated outside it and then tapped on the door.

Beth requested him to enter and then stared at him, the element of surprise having been blunted.

"Well!" she said, and then added a trifle foolishly, "If I'd known you were coming, I could have worn something more festive."

Rob chuckled as he kissed her. "I regret to inform you, my dear," he said, "there's no mail service as yet in that portion of the mountains that I've been frequenting."

Beth joined in his laugh, relieved that humor was lightening the load of intimacy. Certainly she did not intend to reveal to him what she had been thinking during the weeks of their separation. The marriage of her father to Eulalia Holt had changed everything for her, and she had discovered, as well, that once she had snagged Rob for her own, she had lost interest in him. He was an unexceptional, unexciting lover, and it was far more interesting to speculate on what life would have been like had she married Toby Holt instead. Even though Toby had a wife of his own now, and Beth had gained a certain measure of respect for Clarissa, she felt confident that Toby would still come to her if she wished him to do so.

At the moment Toby was fully occupied. Accompanying his wife to the kitchen, he listened to her recital of the latest news, the most important items being the birth of Susanna and Andy's son, and her own "adoption" of

Hank Purcell, whose background she hastily sketched for him.

Gleaning that Toby was extremely anxious to speak with Andy Brentwood, Clarissa immediately proposed that she invite Andy and Susanna to join them for supper.

Toby approved of the idea, and she sent Hank to the Brentwood house with a brief note that she scribbled.

"The boy's useful," Toby said. "It appears you've made an arrangement that suits everyone."

"Indeed it does," she replied. "But I must warn you. He worships your father's memory, and the mere fact that you're Whip Holt's son is sure to bring on a severe case of hero worship."

Toby laughed as, one arm around her shoulders, he stood with her beside the kitchen table. "Seeing as you are going to have company for supper," he said, "I'll help you in the kitchen."

"There's no need for that," she protested, "especially on your first night here. Beth should be downstairs any minute."

"I want to help," Toby told her. "Besides, it won't be long before you have a maid to fix meals for you." He proceeded to tell her about the kindness that he and Rob had shown the old miner, MacGregor, and how they had been rewarded beyond their wildest expectations. "Of course," he said, finishing his recital, "it will be some time yet before the money we make from the mine begins to show. I've got to finish my present assignment from the government, which is going to take a number of months, and then—presumably after this coming winter—Rob and I will be free to work the mine ourselves. So I'd guess it'll be some time next year before we realize any hard cash from it."

"It will be nice to have a cushion for emergencies," Clarissa said. "But we're certainly in no rush for it. We have everything we could possibly need and want."

Smiling at her, Toby realized that he was fortunate to have Clarissa for a wife. She was the least mercenary woman, other than his mother, whom he had ever known.

Certainly Clarissa's attitude contrasted strongly with that of Beth Martin, who, seated at her dressing table as she applied makeup, listened avidly to the recital of her husband, who perched on the foot of her bed as he told her about their acquisition of the mine.

Beth was thrilled. One thought filled her mind and seemed to encompass her entire being. The acquisition of wealth meant that she would be able to escape from the life she had been leading. She could be independent, free of any association with her father and his new wife. Moreover, the money would help her overcome her dissatisfactions with Rob by allowing her to live grandly, to travel, to go wherever she wanted.

Clutching her rouge pot in one hand, Beth twisted on her dressing stool until she faced her husband, and she regarded him with shining eyes. "Do you mean we're truly going to be rich?" she demanded.

"Very rich," he told her.

"How wonderful! Then we can move East. I've always wanted to own a home of my own somewhere near New York or Boston."

Rob was startled. He had been born in Oregon, and he had grown up in the territory, now a state. Not only were his roots firmly implanted in the West, but the thought of settling permanently in another part of the country had never occurred to him.

"We don't have to make any final decision now," he said. "I suggest we wait until the time comes and then make up our minds where we want to live."

Beth was insistent. "My mind is already made up," she told him firmly. "I want to go East."

Taken aback by her vehemence, Rob could only blink at her. He knew better, however, than to become embroiled in a senseless argument with her so soon after being reunited with her. Rather than allow an issue to be created where none existed, he would bide his time, and if Beth continued to insist on moving to the alien Eastern Seaboard, he would deal with the problem then.

Thinking she had won her point, Beth's mood improved, and she slipped her arm through his as they started down the stairs.

The Holts awaited them in the kitchen, and Rob exchanged a pleasant, warm greeting with Clarissa; they embraced lightly and kissed each other on the cheek.

Beth, however, was prompted by an inner devil who saw to it that her greeting to Toby was one that he would long remember. Curling both arms around his neck, she pressed her body against his, and with one hand held securely at the back of his head, she parted her lips for his welcoming kiss, her tongue darting in and out.

Toby was dazed and certainly was made uncomfortable by her inappropriate greeting, though the unsuspecting Rob was aware of nothing wrong in his wife's behavior. Clarissa, however, was conscious of the deliberate eroticism that Beth had displayed, but she contained her anger. Virtually certain that Beth was not even remotely in love with Toby, she knew that the woman was trying to stir up excitement for herself out of a basic sense of dissatisfaction with her own existence.

Nevertheless, as she had already determined, Beth Martin would bear close watching. Clarissa had established a solid rapport with her husband, loving him and feeling certain that he loved her in return, and she intended to allow nothing and no one to come between them.

The tension soon eased. When Beth learned that the Brentwoods had been invited to supper, she pitched in with her customary vigor, and soon she and Clarissa were busily engaged in preparing the evening meal. Their husbands lingered in the kitchen with them, helping where they could, and Beth led the conversation, chatting excitedly about the gold mine that Rob and Toby had acquired.

Accompanied by Hank, Andy and Susanna finally arrived, bringing their sleeping baby along in his bassinet. The entire party adjourned to the parlor while the meal continued to cook. There, the men drank small tumblers of whiskey, the ladies contented themselves with glasses of sack, and Hank consumed a special concoction of apple and berry juice. Mr. Blake, meanwhile, lay on the floor and gnawed contentedly on a bone Toby had given him as a special reward.

"Mr. Blake here is quite a hero," Toby began, and then he and Rob told the grim story of their experience with the impostor who had taken the place of Major Jentry. They had no idea of the criminal's identity, but they gave Andy the entire packet of identification papers that Yale Myers had used at one time or another.

Clarissa put her hand to her mouth, alarm registering on her face. "I should have spoken up," she said, her voice pained. "I distrusted that man from the start."

"Don't put any blame on yourself, honey," Toby said gently, taking his wife's hand. "None of us liked the man. But we had no idea of his treachery until he acted up in the mine. Anyway, it's all taken care of now."

Andy promised to wire the War Department at once and said he would also send personal communications to General Grant and to the President, as well as to territorial and state authorities. Eventually the identity of the impostor would be revealed.

"We have some more official business to pass on to you, Andy," Toby said, then turned apologetically to the ladies. "You'll have to forgive the grisly details that I'm forced to relate, but there is no other way that I can repeat what Colonel Brentwood has to be told."

Mincing no words, he and Rob told about what they had found at the ranch house they had visited on their journey to Fort Shaw. Alert and interested in every detail, Andy questioned them at length.

They were so intent on relating what they had discovered that they did not realize, for a time, that Hank Purcell was fascinated by what he heard. His eyes shining, Hank moistened his dry lips with the tip of his tongue. "Are you sure, Mr. Holt, that the thieves used a Colt repeater?" he asked.

Toby was surprised by the question but tried to reply honestly. "I wouldn't swear to it," he said. "The only way to be certain of the make and caliber of weapon would be to remove the bullets from the bodies of the victims."

Hank looked at the colonel, then at Toby and Rob, and it was plain that he was finding it difficult to control his emotions. "I spent a lot of weeks in the saddle," he said, "after my pa was killed, and I reckon I rode just about everyplace there is in Montana Territory where people live. I kept my ears open, and I learned a few things. First off, I learned that Slim Davis, the no-good crook who killed my pa, is a member of the Ma Hastings gang, if that means anything to you."

"Indeed," Andy Brentwood said. "I've had complaints from a half-dozen settlers about the Hastings gang. Apparently there are no thieves operating in the entire territory who are more vicious or greedy. Or more elusive. Our patrols have yet to come upon their trail."

The boy nodded, his eyes smoldering. "Maybe you didn't know, then, Colonel," he said, "that it's a favorite trick of the gang to pretend that Indians are responsible for their raids. That's why it's so hard to track 'em down. What Mr. Holt was just saying about the poor folks at the ranch house being shot and then scalped so's it would look like Indians did it—well, the whole time I've been listening, I've been thinking that it had to be the Hastings gang that did it."

"It's quite possible that you're right," Andy told him, "which explains why only a few of the supposed Indian attacks involve scalping and murder. In any event, I'll send a troop to that ranch tomorrow and have them make a thorough search of the entire property. It's always possible they'll find some clues that will lead us to the guilty parties."

Hank sucked in his breath and held it for a moment. "Can I ride with the troop, if you please, Colonel?"

Clarissa was openly shocked by the request, and Susanna was deeply perturbed, too. "You have your studies to attend to, Hank," the former said instantly.

The boy shook his head. "There're things in this world more important than book learning," he said, "and getting a line on the whereabouts of the scum that killed my pa comes ahead of everything else!"

"I appreciate the way you feel, Hank," Andy Brentwood said gently, "and I certainly sympathize with your attitude. I'm sure all of us do. But I wish you'd keep in mind that the Hastings gang, or whoever it was that killed the poor rancher and his family and ransacked their property, are tough desperadoes. They are mean, they are ruthless, and they have the morality of voracious mountain lions. Frankly, I'm afraid they are too much for you to try tackling."

Hank's eyes were hard, and he shook his head vigorously. "I'm willing to take any risk that's needful," he said. "Anyway, I don't have much choice."

Toby, who had been unfamiliar with the boy's background and attitude, was impressed by his courage. But his common sense left something to be desired. "Lad," he said, "let me remind you of something that my pa taught me long ago. You don't argue with a bullet that comes out of the business end of a gun. It's impersonal, and it's lethal."

"I know, Mr. Holt," Hank replied firmly, "and it's something I intend to teach the feller who goes by the name of Slim Davis."

Aware of Clarissa's deep concern, Toby continued to intervene for her sake. "You might be smart," he said, "if you let Colonel Brentwood's regiment handle this problem for you. They're professional marksmen, and they can meet any gang on equal terms."

The boy was adamant. "I don't take second place to anybody with either a rifle or a pistol," he said flatly.

Toby flicked a glance at Rob, indicating that he saw a way out of the dilemma. "That's interesting, Hank," he said calmly. "Maybe we could do a mite of target shooting together tomorrow morning." He could reason with the boy, perhaps, after showing him up as an inferior marksman.

Hank nodded calmly. "Glad to oblige you, Mr. Holt."

The building of the railroad line came in for its share of discussion after the party moved to the dinner table. Talk was animated, and the prospect of the railroad coming to the territory was exciting.

"Once the trains start rolling through Montana," Rob said, "you're going to see such changes in the territory that you won't recognize it anymore. Just think, cattle cars will transfer beef on the hoof to stockyards. The mines of the territory will open up, and the Lord, in His wisdom alone, knows what minerals will be found and will make the citizens of the territory richer. There will be towns where none exist now—the whole region will be tamed."

"In a way," Toby said plaintively, "I'll be sorry to see the passing of the frontier. I spent so much of my boyhood with my pa in one wilderness or another that I feel at home here, and it makes me kind of sad to think that once civilization comes to the area, the wilderness will disappear for good."

"That's the story of the development of America," Susanna Brentwood said. "I've seen it happen twice in my lifetime, and I still think of myself as being a young woman. I saw civilization come to California and then to Colorado. And they're both better for it."

"I'll welcome the day when civilization comes to Montana," Clarissa said. "Then ranchers, like the poor people whose tragedy Toby and Rob discovered on their way here, will be safe from the thieves and robbers and marauders—all the desperate people who seem to thrive in the wilderness."

Andy grimaced. "I'm here," he said, "to establish law and order in the territory, even before it becomes civilized. And believe me, I have my hands full!"

Later that evening, after the dinner party came to an end, Toby and Rob reveled in their unaccustomed domesticity by helping clean up the dining room and washing and drying the dishes. The two couples parted for the night, and when Toby and Clarissa were alone in the privacy of their bedchamber, he looked at her in the soft light cast by a flickering candle. Because this was a special occasion, she had lighted a smokeless French taper, which she regarded as an extravagance.

They continued to look at each other in the soft light and lost consciousness of everything but their need for each other. With one unspoken accord, they embraced and kissed, then parted breathlessly. Somehow they disrobed and found themselves stretched out on the bed, feverishly making up for weeks of loneliness as they made love, kissing, caressing, and exploring, leading each other to new heights of passion.

Clarissa realized only that Toby was her man, that she yearned for him with all her being. He was aware of her desire, which rekindled and sparked his own, and he wanted her more than he had ever wanted anything on earth.

When he took her, a deep sigh rose up within her and escaped her lips. Then as they moved in unison toward the climax that both sought so avidly, Clarissa screamed, and her fingernails raked Toby's back. His response was a groan that indicated much more than pleasure. It was a sign that his satiation, like hers, was complete.

At last they parted, then kissed again, and Clarissa was at peace within herself. Let Beth tease and flirt and make advances to Toby all she wants, she thought. He's mine!

After they had rested for a short time, they started to make love again, hungrily, greedily, each of them filled with a yearning to possess, even devour, the other.

Again they achieved a simultaneous climax, and this time they so exhausted themselves that they fell asleep in each other's arms. They awakened some hours later—neither was sure of the time, and they knew only that dawn had not yet broken—and once again they made love.

Toby's deep chuckle sounded in the dark.

"What's so funny?" Clarissa demanded.

"We seem to be making up for lost time," he told her, "and we appear to have made up our minds to do it all in one night."

She, too, began to laugh, and soon both were roaring. Afraid they would awaken others in the house, they buried their faces in the pillows as they clung to each other, but merely feeling each other shaking sent them into new paroxysms of laughter.

It occurred to Toby that he had been far lonelier than he had known. He had never taken his wife for granted, but he also had never realized just how much he needed her. She was an extraordinary woman, more precious to him than he had known or recognized.

At last morning came, but not until they had bathed and dressed, then gone down to the kitchen, did they engage in a sensible conversation.

For a time Toby watched Clarissa expertly frying a thick slice of ham and several eggs in a sizzling pan. Then he said, "Today I'm going over to headquarters and register our claim to the gold mine. Andy Brentwood tells me that he'll have his warrant officer make a copy of it, and that's all we'll need to tie down the claim. That way you will be protected if anything happens to me."

"Nothing is going to happen to you, sir," she replied, "and I forbid you to talk that way."

He smiled and shook his head. "I appreciate your feelings, but there's too much involved here to take risks. We're going to be rich. In fact, we're going to have more money than just about anybody we know."

"As long as you're safe and well," Clarissa said, "that means far more to me than wealth."

They were interrupted by the arrival of Beth and Rob Martin in the kitchen, and Clarissa promptly added more ham and eggs to the food that was frying in the pan. The new arrivals were hollow-eyed and gaunt, and Toby grinned, thinking they, too, had been kept awake by ardent lovemaking. He soon discovered he was wrong, however. The atmosphere was strained, Beth was coldly furious, and Rob seemed to be having a hard time controlling his own anger.

Neither Beth nor Rob mentioned the subject that had caused their estrangement, and in the days ahead, both took great pains to avoid any mention of the topic. The facts were plain: They had argued again about the wealth they would accumulate from the gold mine. Beth had insisted that she wanted to move to the Eastern Seaboard and establish permanent residence there. Rob, disliking the idea intensely, had made the grievous error of telling her that she was simply trying to escape from her father and his new wife. She had reacted explosively to this airing of the truth, and both had lost their tempers, saying harsh things and making accusations for which they were subsequently sorry.

For the present, however, the damage was done, and the atmosphere was strained. Toby was relieved when they were joined by Hank Purcell, and the boy's enthusiasm glossed over the hard feelings between Rob and Beth.

"I hope you ain't forgettin'—I mean, I hope you *aren't* forgetting—we have a shooting contest this morning, Mr. Holt," Hank said.

"I'm looking forward to it," Toby replied, relieved by the respite. "Rob, what do you say if we pick up some targets over at regimental headquarters this morning when we go to register the mine?"

"Good idea," Rob replied, glad of an opportunity to put some distance between his wife and himself for a time.

The registration proved to be a simple matter. They filled out a brief but comprehensive form, submitted a map showing the exact location of the mine, and then took an oath in which they swore that the property was theirs alone. The formalities completed, they went to the office of the regimental operations officer, and from his sergeant obtained a half-dozen paper targets. Some were in the form of concentric circles, and others showed the outlines of human figures.

Hank was waiting for them behind the house when they returned, and his face lighted when he saw the targets. Toby was privately amused by the boy's eagerness, though he also realized how much was at stake. Young Hank needed to be taught that he could not act with impunity when it came to using a gun, that there was always someone who was a better shot.

Hank produced the pistol that had belonged to his

father. "If it's all the same to you, I'll use this gun," he said. "But if you have any objection, I'll be glad to borrow any weapons you want."

"That's quite all right," Toby told him, admiring the boy's sense of fair play. "Use what you will."

Hank pinned an outline of a human figure to one tree and a series of concentric circles to another. "Any special distance that you want?" he inquired.

Toby shook his head. "Suit yourself," he said. "Whatever you like will be fine with me."

Hank carefully counted off one hundred paces from the targets, which were within a few feet of each other. "Anything less than this distance wouldn't be a fair judge of shooting," he said.

Surprised by the boy's knowledge, Toby nodded. "Fair enough," he said.

Rob went into the house, returning with a gun for Toby.

Hank was surprised. "Aren't you going to join in this here contest with us, Mr. Martin?" he demanded.

"I'm not in my partner's class," Rob replied, "so he'll represent both of us."

The boy nodded, then turned to Toby, who said, "You shoot first, Hank. And to make this a little bit better than the usual contest, suppose we shoot first at one target, then fire again as fast as we can and try our luck with the second target? How does that strike you?"

Hank remained very much in command of himself. "Sure," he said. Moving forward to the line he had chosen, Hank raised his gun and squinted at the target of concentric circles. He squeezed the trigger and, not pausing to examine the accuracy of his initial shot, fired again, this time at the silhouette of the human figure.

Toby and Rob accompanied him as he moved

toward the targets in order to examine them. Hank's first shot had pierced the target no more than an inch from its center, and the second shot had struck the human figure in the forehead, just above the left eye.

"That's fine shooting," Rob said. "If the second target had been a man, he'd be a goner."

Hank grinned, satisfied with his shots. "Your turn, Mr. Holt," he said deferentially.

Toby's mind was working rapidly. He was in a peculiar spot, and he well knew it. He had agreed to this contest for the simple purpose of teaching Hank Purcell a lesson. But the marksmanship that would be required to beat the boy's remarkable performance would have to be nothing short of extraordinary.

Although confident of himself, Toby wasn't certain he could outshoot the boy. He had to calm himself, and the best way he knew was to remember advice his father had given him. "Remember," Whip Holt often had said, "a weapon—be it a rifle or a pistol—is an extension of your hand and your arm. Treat it as such, and don't regard it as something alien. As long as it is part of you, it will respond to your mind and your will."

Toby nodded, and his tension vanished. He squeezed the trigger, shooting first at one target, then at the other, and he was scarcely conscious of firing at all.

Hank walked with him to the targets and stared at them in astonishment. Toby's first shot had scored a perfect bull's-eye. His second was equally accurate; he had placed his shot in the heart of the human silhouette.

"Nice shooting!" Hank said, and his voice was filled with awe. "I've always thought of myself as a sharpshooter, but next to you I'm a greenhorn."

Toby kept his thoughts to himself and looked the boy in the eyes. "Just remember this, Hank, and you'll do fine: No matter how good you are, there's always somebody out yonder who can outshoot you. That's the way you stay alive, and that's why it's not a good idea to spend your life as a gunslinger."

Hank nodded, and from the look in his eyes, it was clear he felt nothing but admiration and respect for Toby. But the hard, set expression on his mouth indicated that he had not given up his vow to even the score with his father's killer.

Toby believed he had made his point with the boy, and what Hank did now was up to him. "What do you say we go back to the house?" Toby said, smiling. "I wouldn't be surprised if Clarissa's baked a special treat for us."

Concealing herself behind the curtains in the kitchen windows, Clarissa watched the trio approaching. All three were laughing and chatting, and somewhat to her surprise, she sensed an unusual degree of camaraderie among them.

When they came into the kitchen, she drew a pan of hot, freshly baked cookies from the oven, which attracted Hank's full attention. Both he and Rob paused to eat some cookies, and Clarissa was able to draw Toby into the adjoining pantry.

"Well?" she demanded in an urgent whisper. "Did your scheme work? Were you able to persuade him to abandon his suicidal plan?"

Toby grinned at her and shook his head. "That youngster," he said, "is one of the best gunslingers I've ever encountered. He's as good a shot as my father, as good as Sam Brentwood, and it took all I had to outshoot him. No, I don't think he's changed his mind, Clarissa. And after seeing his shooting, all I can say is, when

he goes gunning for Slim Davis, may the Lord have
mercy on Davis's soul!"

"There are more than thirty-eight million people in
the United States now," Toby Holt said, "and blame
near all of them are clamoring for the establishment of
railroad lines that are going to stretch from the Atlantic
to the Pacific. We've had three days and nights of holi-
day-making, but we can't keep thirty-eight million
people waiting any longer!"

Rob Martin was quick to agree with him—a trifle
too quick, Clarissa observed—and the partners decided
to leave Fort Shaw early the following morning to
resume their surveying duties.

"When are you coming back?" Clarissa asked her
husband when they were alone that night. "When will I
see you again?"

Toby held her in his arms. "I'll be here the first
chance I get," he told her, "but I can't set a date. The
weather has been favorable, and as we're no longer
struggling through the highest passes of the mountains,
we can make really good time now. We have President
Johnson and General Grant riding on our backs, prod-
ding us, you know, and there's no time like the present
to finish our work."

She looked at him with respect, tinged with a sense
of wonder. The acquisition of the Montana gold mine
made Toby independently wealthy, and he no longer
had to rely on the percentage he earned from the lum-
bering operation in Washington or on wages he earned
from the U.S. government for his surveying mission. But
even the ownership of the gold mine did not deter him
from finishing the important task he had accepted.

She knew now what it meant to be a Holt: His duty

came first, regardless of his own preferences or his family's situation. He thought only in terms of doing what had to be done.

"I'll try not to be too impatient," she said.

"Good girl," he replied. "We won't be working all that far from the fort, so one way or another we ought to be able to grab a day here and a day there. I doubt if we'll be able to take as long again as we took this time, but I don't think I'm going to be separated from you for so long again, either."

"That's good to know," Clarissa replied, and clung to him.

The atmosphere at the other end of the house was far different. The rift that had separated Beth and Rob Martin had deepened into a chasm, and the air was chilly.

Had their relationship been more physical, their misunderstandings might have been overcome. But they were not inclined toward the physical. They tried to make love only one night, but the hurts that had driven them apart rose up and came between them again, and the failure of their effort made it virtually impossible for people of their temperament to try again.

Now, with only a few hours remaining before Rob departed at dawn, he and Beth made a final effort to tear down the obstacles that they themselves had created.

"I was goaded beyond endurance the other night," Rob said slowly, "and I went too far when I called you money-mad. I'd never known you to be so interested in material things, and your insistence that we move to the Eastern Seaboard unsettled me."

"I'm glad," Beth replied carefully, "that you don't

really think I'm a money grubber. That's a relief to hear."

He looked at her in silence, trying to understand her.

Beth wanted to make certain that she did not lose whatever advantage she had gained so painfully. "Before we're separated again," she said carefully, "let me make my position very clear to you. I'm delighted that you are half-owner of a lucrative gold mine that's going to earn us a great deal of money. The money itself doesn't mean a thing to me. I have no craving for expensive clothes or fabulous jewels. I don't crave a carriage and a team of horses of my own."

He nodded, wondering if he had done her an injustice.

"I'm very pleased, however, because the money we will get from the mine gives us a degree of financial independence that we otherwise wouldn't have known. I am eager to resettle on the Eastern Seaboard as soon as you are done with your present surveying assignment. My reasons are very simple. I lived in Washington City with my parents when my father was stationed at the War Department, and I traveled with my mother to New York, Philadelphia, and Baltimore many times. I feel far more at home in those places than I do in any other part of the country."

"Your desire to resettle in the East," Rob said slowly, "is a certain cause of conflict with us. I was born in the Northwest, I grew up there, I went to school there, and the only time I've been elsewhere in the country was during the Civil War. And frankly, the East didn't appeal to me, although I saw it under battlefield conditions, which weren't exactly conducive to making that part of the country very appealing. I wish I could take you at your word that you want to go East because you like that part of the country so much better than you like Oregon or Washington or even Montana. I've known you for a long time, and I never heard you express such a preference—never."

"I daresay the subject never came up," she interjected lightly.

He ignored the interruption. "As I mentioned before," he said, "it seems to me that your real aim is to put as much distance as you can between you and your father, not to mention his new wife."

"I already told you," Beth said, controlling her temper, "that that is irrelevant to my motives."

"Is it?" he demanded, raising an eyebrow. "I wonder."

"You're in no position to judge me," she said, now becoming annoyed. "Both of your parents are still alive, still together."

"I know," Rob replied soberly. "I've tried to put myself into your situation. My mother and father are devoted to each other, and I'm sure if one of them died, the survivor would be devastated. All the same, I'd be elated if he or she found a new mate who could create a sense of contentment and give my parent a happy marriage for as many years as he or she had left on this earth."

"That's very noble of you, I'm sure," Beth said bitterly, "but perhaps I lack your nobility. My mother and father had a perfect marriage. Perfect! I don't really blame him for what's happened. He was devastated, completely broken up by the tragedy that took my mother's life. I blame that woman for taking advantage of his condition and stealing his affections when he was confused and hurt and lonely. I'll never forgive her for conniving so cold-bloodedly—never!"

Every word she said added to his conviction that she had become pathological on the whole subject of her father's remarriage. What he was not aware of, however, was that her dissatisfaction with her own marriage was compounding the problem, causing her to become nearly hysterical.

Beth was indeed working herself into a frenzy. "I hate the woman!" she cried. "I hate her! As for my father, the great General Blake, the strong hero of the war with Mexico and the Civil War—his heroism and strength are nothing but big jokes. He's a milksop, a weakling who lets a greedy woman haul him around by the nose. He's forgotten all those wonderful years of his marriage to my mother!"

As her fury grew, she launched a new tirade that—experience had taught Rob—would last for hours until she became so worked up and so exhausted that she would cry herself hysterically to sleep. He had no one but himself to blame for initiating the discussion, but he knew full well that it would be impossible to achieve a meeting of the minds now. In his wife's present condition, she would not listen to reason and would spew out her hatred for Eulalia and her contempt for General Blake until she virtually lost her voice.

Any hope of achieving a true rapport, of drawing closer to her, would have to await his next visit to Fort Shaw, whenever that might be.

On the final day of the voyage, with the riverboat about to arrive at Fort Benton, Millicent was enthralled when the early mists cleared away and she saw, rising at a distance, the majestic, snow-capped peaks of the Rockies. The grandeur of the mountains was indescribable, and the young woman was stirred as she had seldom been in all of her life. She felt an urge to take her flute from its case and to improvise a tune that could best express the wild sense of exhilarated freedom that suffused her.

Suddenly the steamboat whistle blew, announcing they had reached Fort Benton, the small trading post that stood at the head of the navigable waters of the Missouri River. Within moments, the boat was docked, and Millicent was ashore, dressed in her city best. Her flute case tucked under one arm, she was wearing a dark straw hat with a veil, a short cape, and white gloves. She remained unaware of the startled glances directed toward her by the few workmen at the trading post, who had never seen a lady from the East in the rugged Montana Territory.

A detachment of cavalry appeared to take charge of the supplies destined for Fort Shaw, and Jim Randall immediately introduced himself to the commander of the unit, Lieutenant Elkins, to whom he explained the nature of the mission that had brought him and his cousin so far from home.

"I know better than to offer a bribe to an officer of the U.S. Cavalry," Jim said lightly, "but we encountered a stampeding herd of buffalo last week, and I brought down a calf. We butchered and salted the meat, and there's more than enough available to the men of your unit for their supper tonight if Millicent and I are allowed to tag along with you."

The lieutenant nodded his head. "You'd be welcome to join us under any circumstances, Mr. Randall," the young officer replied, grinning broadly, "and you're also welcome to use a couple of our horses. As for the meat—well, sir, I've got to admit I'm partial to buffalo steak, and I hope you'll join me in eating it!"

So the cousins had an escort that would assure their safe arrival at Fort Shaw. Jim was given a spirited mare for Millicent and a gelding for himself, and they set out with the cavalry unit, their luggage piled into one of the carts in which the military supplies were packed.

The troopers who had thought their return to the fort would be delayed by the presence of a woman were surprised to discover that she was completely at home in the saddle and handled her mare with consummate ease. A further surprise was in store when Millicent insisted on taking charge of the supper preparations, scrubbing potatoes and roasting them in the coals of the fire, and cooking the buffalo steak with the expertise of a professional chef.

After the meal was done, Millicent picked up her flute case and drifted off a short ways by herself, and Jim, long accustomed to her moods, made no attempt to follow her. He watched her as she climbed to the crest of a small hill and stared off at the distant peaks, their snow-capped surfaces gleaming blue-white in the soft moonlight.

This was the country that had always come to her mind when she had thought of the West. The air was crisp but not cold, heavy with the sweet smell of pines and the more pungent scent of wood smoke. The harsh outlines of the mountains looked softer by moonlight, and the intervening hills, dark and brooding, seemed gentle and in no way menacing.

At last Millicent opened her case, removed her flute, and began to play a flute sonata by Scarlatti.

The troopers, still gathered around the campfire, where they were sipping coffee from tin mugs and smoking, broke off their conversations abruptly and listened as the sweet sounds of the flute drifted into the air.

The music of Scarlatti had never been played in a stranger atmosphere. Yet Millicent's interpretations were so sensitive, her techniques so brilliant, that the soldiers who had never before heard a flute played—and certainly had never heard the name of Scarlatti—felt that the scene for the impromptu concert was natural and right.

Millicent herself knew that music, as it always did, gave her a sense of serenity, of being at peace within herself. She was lonely and had traveled far from her Baltimore home to learn the whereabouts of the army officer to whom she was betrothed. She had no idea if he was all right, and she wondered if and when she would see him again. But her questions, although unanswered, for some reason no longer gnawed at her. She felt rested, confident of herself and of the future.

VIII

The day began early at Fort Shaw. Susanna Brentwood fed her baby, while her husband sat in the dining room, eating his breakfast, reading the night report written by the duty officer. The situation in Montana was becoming increasingly grim. The regiment had failed to track down the elusive Ma Hastings and her gang, even after a visit to the ravaged ranch house that Toby and Rob had discovered. What was more, the Sioux attacks were continuing unchecked, for the regimental patrols simply were unable to cover such a vast territory. It appeared more and more that Andy Brentwood was going to have to send his regiments into the field to launch a major assault against the Sioux.

Susanna joined her husband for breakfast, which was prepared by Mrs. Ford, the wife of a sergeant. Anxious to earn some extra money, she eagerly performed such duties.

Susanna helped herself to a slice of toast but ate very little of it, and when her eggs were served, she scarcely touched them. Andy looked up from the report he was reading and raised an eyebrow. "No appetite today?" he asked.

Susanna shook her head.

"You're feeling okay, though?" he persisted.

She nodded, then took a deep breath. "Yes and no," she confessed. "I'm getting restless, Andy."

Her husband was anything but surprised. Susanna had been a newspaper editor and writer for years before their marriage and had acquired a large and enthusiastic following. He knew it had been difficult for her to acclimate to the life she led as the wife of an army officer, and he realized that her existence had become even narrower since the birth of their son. Putting his report aside, he looked across the table at her. "I reckon we've got to do something about you," he said. "The big question is what?"

Relief showed in Susanna's violet eyes. "You don't know how good you make me feel, Andy," she said. "I didn't know how you were going to react."

He grinned at her. "I know you fairly well," he said, "so I can imagine what you've been feeling, and as I'm aware of your needs, the question now is how to fulfill them."

She sipped her coffee as her husband slowly filled his pipe with tobacco. "I'm a fortunate woman, and I'm the first to realize and admit it," she said. "I have a wonderful, successful marriage, and I have a marvelous baby who helps to fulfill me as a woman. But I was spoiled, I suppose, because I started to work at such an early age. I can't be really happy unless my mind is occupied, too, and when it isn't, I grow restless. I'm restless every day now."

The colonel attempted a touch of levity. "I'm

afraid," he said, "there aren't enough people as yet in Montana to sustain a newspaper. So I'd advise against starting one."

Susanna laughed. "That's the farthest thought from my mind. But I've been thinking a great deal about the problem, and I believe I know what needs to be done."

Andy busied himself lighting his pipe.

"The newspapers of the United States," she said, "are always printing articles about Montana, and there are a surprising number of pieces that appear in the national magazines, too. People all over the country are interested in life here, and the frontier atmosphere fascinates them."

"Of course," Andy said, nodding in agreement. "Folks in Montana are leading a real wilderness existence."

"Exactly," she said eagerly.

"I hadn't thought about it before," her husband said, "but you're absolutely right. The frontier existence of people in Montana is a mirror of life everywhere in the yesterdays of history."

"The more the realization dawned on me," Susanna told him, "the more convinced I became that there would be a large and responsive market for a book on the subject."

"That's a first-rate idea!" Andy observed.

She smiled. "That's what I thought, but I had to be sure of my ground. So—without mentioning the subject to you or to anyone else—I sent off letters to several publishers in New York and Boston. The results are overwhelming. Without exception, they want me to write a book for them on life in the territory, and, in fact, two of them have even gone so far as to offer me contracts."

"That's wonderful," her husband said.

Susanna's smile faded slowly. "If I'm going to sign a contract," she said, "I've got to make certain that the book I write is worth what I'm being paid. That means I've got to get out into the countryside and interview ranchers and other settlers."

"I see," he said.

"Obviously," she went on, "it wouldn't be practical for me to try to cover the entire territory or to wander too far from Fort Shaw. I couldn't do that and fulfill my obligations to you and the baby. The way I have worked it out in my own head, I can devote approximately two days a week to traveling and interviewing, leaving little Sam during the day with Mrs. Ford. Since her own little one is nearly weaned, she has been able to take over the nursing of Sam more and more. So I can go out, interview a settler and his family, and get back here in time to put the baby to bed and to prepare dinner for you. It isn't easy to have one's cake and eat it as well," Susanna concluded, giving Andy a quick smile, "but this is as close as I know how to come to managing the feat."

Andy puffed on his pipe and then spoke slowly. "You'll have to pick your locations with care," he said. "You'll be taking too much of a risk if you try to wander aimlessly and freely throughout Montana. Just keep in mind that there are still gangs of robbers and even murderers we haven't captured or subdued as yet, and, in addition, Thunder Cloud and his Sioux are creating more and more trouble."

"There's the problem in a nutshell," she said. "I am neither foolish nor naive, and I realize that the wife of the commanding officer of the Eleventh Cavalry will make a prime target for bands of criminals and for the Sioux, as well. They'd like nothing better than to take me prisoner and force you to negotiate with them."

Andy nodded thoughtfully. "Unfortunately, that's the situation," he said. "I'd gladly assign you a cavalry escort if I could. But, I'm sorry to say, I can't spare the personnel at the moment. Under our present scheme of operations, we're establishing a far-flung dragnet, and every trooper is needed for the purpose. And as you can see readily enough yourself, I can't allow my wife to roam through the wilderness of Montana without appropriate guides."

"Do I assume correctly," Susanna wanted to know, "that you'd agree to my going out if I stayed close to the fort and if I had an escort?"

"I suppose I would," he said. "I think that, by and large, the area within a day's riding of the fort is safe—if you were escorted."

"In that case," she said, "I may have found a solution. What would you say to the idea of Hank Purcell acting as my guide?"

Andy was taken aback. "The boy?"

Susanna nodded. "He may be very young, but he does know Montana as few people, other than Toby Holt, know it. Remember that after Hank's father was killed, he spent weeks roaming from one end of the territory to the other. What is more, he's an excellent shot—just in case there's trouble."

Andy nodded but was reluctant to commit himself.

"I'm also sensible enough to realize," she continued, "that there's safety in numbers. And I think I have a solution for that, too. I asked Beth and Clarissa if they'd like to come with me. Beth jumped at the chance, as you can imagine. The truth of the matter is that day-to-day life here at the fort bores her, and I can't say that I blame her, what with her husband off in the mountains

all the time. She jumped at the chance to spend a couple
of days a week on outings."

"I'm not sure that Beth's company is any recommen-
dation," Andy said. "She's quite capable of getting herself into trouble, not to mention involving you with her.
Is Clarissa willing to go with you?"

Susanna chuckled. "You know Clarissa," she said.
"Always cautious. She asked me to make my definite
plans first, and she said she'd think about the idea in the
meantime. I don't believe she's any too anxious to make
a series of one-day jaunts, but she's so nice and accom-
modating that I believe she'll do it as a favor to me."

"Good," Andy replied. "I'll be far easier in my own
mind if I know Clarissa is with you."

"You approve of my making these trips, then?" she
asked.

He sighed, then smiled in spite of himself. "I know
you, Sue; you're a former newspaperwoman. One way
or another, you'd find a way to get your story, with or
without my approval. So I guess I should content myself
with the fact that you've agreed to stay close to the fort
and that you've got others to go with you. It's a far from
perfect system, but I guess it will have to do."

The ranch was located in the Montana foothills of
the Rockies, the main house and barns nestling in a hollow protected on all sides but the south by rugged hills.
The place was unpretentious but solid, the settler and
his sons having cut and finished the wood that they had
used in construction. Made of unpainted clapboard that
had turned gray as it weathered, the one-story ranch
house was snug, a home that stayed warm in winter,
thanks to the enormous fireplace that ran almost the en-

tire width of the kitchen, and yet was cool when the windows were opened in summer.

The settler, his wife, and two grown sons went out of their way to treat Susanna Brentwood hospitably. After showing her and her companions around the extensive property, they returned to the house with Susanna and patiently answered her many questions.

"Our cattle, hogs, and chickens provide us with all the meat we want and can eat, and also give us milk, butter, and eggs. Most of our vegetables come from my wife's kitchen garden, and now that we have a system of snares that keeps the rabbit population down, we grow just about everything we need. You might say we're pretty much self-sufficient."

As always when conducting an interview, Susanna took voluminous notes, having discovered years earlier that even the most unlikely details occasionally improved a story immeasurably. "Your nearest neighbors live miles away. What do you do for recreation?"

The rancher and the younger men looked at each other and laughed. Then the elder son said, "We start our day around five in the morning before sunup, ma'am, and most days we ain't finished until at least seven at night. By the time we've eaten our supper, we're ready for bed."

"Once every month or two, when Ma insists," the younger son said, "me and my brother, we ride to the town of Helena together and stay there for a day or two."

"How far is Helena?" Susanna asked.

He shrugged. "About seventy miles I reckon." Noting that she was impressed, he added hastily, "But we don't travel none to speak of. We got friends who go twice as far in order to get to town."

"What do you do there?"

"Mainly," the elder son said, "we make deals to sell our cattle that's come of age. We buy nails and other hardware that we need, and we meet our friends down to one of the saloons for a sociable gabfest." He was too polite to mention the visits to a local bordello that almost every male visitor to the town made.

Susanna was gaining an accurate picture of the way the family lived but was still curious about some aspects of their existence. "It strikes me," she said, "that you're terribly isolated here."

The settler's wife shrugged. "A couple of times a year, maybe," she said, "we get company for a day or two. Folks that happen to be passin' this way."

"Your security problems must cause you a great deal of concern," Susanna persisted.

The settler laughed aloud. "Not so's you could notice," he said. "We got four expert shots here, including my wife, who's as good as any man. Let a band of thieves come nosing around the place or let some of them no-good Sioux braves show up, and they'll get a volley of lead that'll make them wish they'd kept their distance."

His wife smiled calmly. "I don't rightly know how it happened," she said, "but word gets around as quick on the frontier as it does in a big city. It seems like the Indians hereabouts all know we're good rifle shots on this ranch and that we don't stand for no messin' around. The criminals seem to have heard of us, too. Leastwise, they keep their distance, and that's all that we ask."

"It's been four years, maybe five," the elder son said, "since we last had to get tough and teach the Indians a lesson. We ain't been bothered none from that day to this."

Deeply impressed by the family's courage and stamina, Susanna realized that the most remarkable facet of their existence was their refusal to regard themselves as heroic. They did simply what they considered necessary for survival.

Members of the family tried to persuade Susanna and her companions to stay for supper and accept overnight quarters. But they understood completely when she told them that it was necessary for them to return to Fort Shaw by sundown.

"My husband has his doubts about these jaunts into the wilderness that we're making," Susanna explained, "and if we're not on time, I'm afraid he'll send the whole regiment searching for us."

The members of the family joined in the laugh, then graciously consented to the departure of their guests.

"When you leave my property," the settler said, "turn sharp left after you close my gate behind you, and when you come to the ridge, follow it due west. That'll provide you with a handy shortcut, and it'll take you to Twin Hills on the road to Fort Shaw in about half the time that you'd need otherwise."

When the party finally left the ranch house and began their homeward journey, Susanna Brentwood had good cause to feel satisfied with her day's activity. She had gathered considerable information about the way that a ranch family lived in the wilderness, and equally important, she had gleaned for her readers their casual attitude toward the dangers that they faced.

Her companions had enjoyed themselves, too. Hank Purcell was proud of the adult role he was playing in guiding the women through the territory. Beth was pleased by the outing, which she found a welcome respite from the routines of daily existence at Fort Shaw, and her boredom was very much relieved. Only the ever-practical Clarissa found any fault with the situation, for she would have preferred staying at home, either educating young Hank or doing necessary household chores. But she kept her views to herself, for she knew she was being helpful to Susanna.

After closing the rancher's gate behind them, they headed left, as they had been instructed, and climbed toward higher ground as they made their way up to the ridge that they would follow for the better part of their more than three hour ride back to Fort Shaw. But as they rode, it became increasingly clear that they were going the wrong way. Rather than heading west, toward the fort, the trail veered eastward, and by the time the sun was about to set, they were still going in the wrong direction.

"Darn it all," Hank exclaimed as they pulled their horses to a halt. "We made a wrong turn somewhere."

"We should never have tried to take a shortcut," Beth said anxiously. "We're lost, and it's getting dark!"

"Don't you worry," Hank broke in, acting more confident and adult than he felt. "I'll get us out of here. But we'll have to wait till morning. We can't go looking for the right trail in the dark."

They all agreed to bed down for the night and resume their journey as soon as it was light. What Colonel Brentwood would say or do when they didn't show up that evening was only a matter for speculation, and they all hoped—Susanna in particular—that they'd find their way back to the fort early the next day.

At first light, the quartet was awake, though in truth, no one had gotten much sleep, having had to lie on rocky ground with no blankets to keep away the chill. They mounted their horses and headed back the way they had come, and Hank, thinking he recognized a little-used trail heading off to the right, led them onward.

The trail grew narrower as they made their way upward, with the walls of a canyon pressing in on them from both sides. Hank, who was in the lead, rode warily, his rifle resting across the pommel of his saddle. Suddenly he heard approaching hoofbeats, listened intently, and realized that there were more horses in the approaching party than he could readily distinguish. Not knowing whether the unseen newcomers were friendly, he knew it was best to take no chances and, raising a hand, silently waved his companions off the trail.

They obediently followed him and, still mounted, moved behind some high boulders, making themselves more or less invisible to those on the road.

There were nearly a dozen riders in the party, and the concealed group, peering out from behind boulders, could see that all were heavily armed, with braces of pistols in their belts, as well as the rifles that they carried. Leading the group was a gray-haired woman in man's attire, who seemed very much at home in the saddle.

The thought occurred to Hank that perhaps he was looking at Ma Hastings, and his pulse began to race. It was almost too much to hope that in the next few moments he might see the man who had murdered his father.

Curbing the wild excitement that surged within him, Hank forced himself to remain calm. In one corner of his mind he realized that even if the man he knew as Slim Davis should suddenly materialize in front of him, he would be wise to forget the killer's proximity and to wait for a more propitious moment to gain his revenge.

By no stretch of the imagination were the three young ladies he was escorting the equal in strength of Ma Hastings's notorious band. And if the gang knew that Colonel Brentwood's wife was a member of the party, they wouldn't hesitate to seize and hold her for a ransom, so he would be best advised to keep silent and allow the gang to move on unmolested.

Suddenly in the narrow, slitlike open space between two boulders, Slim Davis appeared on horseback. There was no mistaking the man's swarthy lean face. It was a face that had haunted Hank in his dreams for months.

Here, within reach at last, after an eternity of waiting, was the villain who had shot down his father in cold blood.

Common sense was forgotten. It no longer mattered to the boy that he was responsible for the safety of three young ladies, that wisdom demanded that he and they remain silent and invisible. His soul cried aloud for vengeance.

Scarcely realizing, and no longer caring what the consequences of his rash act might be, Hank raised his rifle to his shoulder and squinted down the barrel. His sense of excitement was gone now, and in its place was a cold-blooded determination to keep the promise he had made to his father. He felt no elation, no sense of satisfaction, and even though he knew that Slim Davis would pass from sight within a moment, he felt no need to rush. He was being presented with a heaven-sent opportunity to even the score, and he intended to avail himself to the utmost of the advantage that had come his way.

Slim Davis's face was partly turned toward him, giving Hank a nearly full-faced view. It was impossible for a marksman to miss his target at such a range, and

Hank was an expert who had been taught the use of firearms by Pete Purcell, whose memory he was about to purge.

The blood that flowed in Hank's veins seemed transformed into a fluid as icy as the mountain streams that cascaded down the slopes of the Rockies from the snow-laden heights. "This is for you, Pa," he whispered. "I've kept my word to you." He squeezed the trigger.

The shot echoed and reechoed up and down the narrow canyon, and Slim Davis slumped in his saddle, the avenger's bullet neatly placed between his eyes.

Hank felt no joy, no sense of triumph, no feeling of accomplishment. At most, he was relieved that he had kept his word to his father.

The totally unexpected rifle shot jarred Hank's three companions and simultaneously startled Ma Hastings and the members of her band. The gang, long accustomed to crises, reacted quickly. Ma Hastings wheeled in the saddle and bawled an order. Clifford, her elder son, immediately raised his own rifle to his shoulder.

Several members of the band had moved on to lower ground down the trail and, wheeling their mounts around, saw the three women and the boy hiding behind the high boulders. Now Clifford Hastings shouted a command.

The young women were stunned by Hank's totally unexpected violent act. None of them cared that he had kept his vow to his father and had killed Slim Davis. All they cared about at the moment was that they were themselves being menaced by a hard-faced band.

One of the robbers shouted an obscenity and raised his own rifle to his shoulder. Clarissa Holt reacted instantly, and raising her own rifle, she quickly took aim and fired.

By no stretch of the imagination was she an accomplished markswoman. But on this occasion, at least, she enjoyed great good fortune, and her bullet caught the bandit in the shoulder, forcing him to drop his weapon.

Hank, in the meantime, had come to life with a vengeance. Automatically the boy reloaded his own rifle, and when he saw the bandit aiming at the women, he, too, fired, his shot following Clarissa's by a second or two.

The boy's aim, as always, was superb. The robber barely had an opportunity to realize that he had been wounded in the shoulder when Hank's shot lodged in his brain.

Clifford Hastings was outraged. Two members of the band had been killed, and one of them was the best marksman in the gang, Slim Davis. Half-standing in his saddle, he called, "Shoot them down, boys! Now! Before they do more damage!"

Ma Hastings had other ideas, however, and her deep, husky voice rose high in the air, drowning the orders her son was giving. "No!" she shouted. "No! Don't shoot 'em down! I want 'em taken alive. All of 'em!"

Hank mechanically reloaded his rifle again. But Beth was too shocked to react, and Susanna was stunned, too. Only Clarissa retained her wits, and she quickly realized that she and her companions were hopelessly outnumbered. She herself had been fortunate beyond belief and knew that her luck could not hold. There was virtually no chance that her next shot would be accurate. Beth, she knew, was a fair markswoman, but Clarissa knew nothing about Susanna's ability to handle firearms. That left Hank Purcell to protect the entire group, and in spite of his expertise, she realized the boy was incapable of performing miracles, particularly when the odds against him were so great. He was greatly out-numbered, and they would all be killed if they insisted on putting up a fight.

Clarissa vastly preferred to take her chances after she found out what the bull-voiced woman commanding the band had in mind. "Don't resist!" Clarissa called. "The odds against us are overwhelming!"

Susanna recovered sufficiently to evaluate the situation for herself and agreed with Clarissa. "We'll have to surrender," she said, speaking loudly and succinctly. "Put down your rifle, Hank. I'm afraid that you've already done enough damage for one day."

The sound of Susanna's voice brought Hank to his senses. He suddenly realized that he had brought the wrath of the Hastings gang on his own head and on the unprotected heads of the ladies he was supposed to guard. It was too late now for recriminations, however, and he slowly lowered his rifle.

"Collect their firearms!" Ma Hastings ordered.

Three members of the gang rode forward slowly, cautiously, and relieved the ladies and the boy of their weapons.

Clifford Hastings rode to his mother's side, ignoring his younger brother, Ralph, who was taking advantage of the preoccupation of the others by surreptitiously drinking a colorless liquid from a small bottle that he produced from a pocket.

"Ma," Clifford said urgently, "they deserved to be killed in cold blood. Do you realize they shot down Slim Davis and Augie Hinds?"

Ma Hastings nodded and smiled grimly. Then she called out, "Guard 'em close, boys, and don't let 'em pull no shenanigans, but I don't want any o' 'em hurt. They're our prisoners, and if anythin' happens to any

one o' 'em, the one who's responsible will answer to me
for it." Still smiling, she turned back to her son. "Ya better take the lead, Cliff, and we'll go on to the campsite
ya had in mind for the night. The sooner we get to it,
the better."

"What about buryin' Slim and Augie?" he demanded.

She shrugged indifferently. "We'll take their horses,
and the boys can cast lots for their firearms and other
property, the way we usually do when we lose somebody. There's enough vultures in the mountains hereabouts, and plenty o' coyote, so I don't think we'll need to
waste any time buryin' 'em."

Clifford was still not satisfied. "I can't believe you're
lettin' that boy and those three women live," he said.
"Not after two faithful members o' the gang were killed
before our very eyes."

"You ought to know that I never do anythin' without reason," Ma replied, chiding him. "Just do as you're
told and make camp, and we'll talk later."

Disarmed and surrounded, the four prisoners were
forced to ride in the center of the line. They were silent
as they took in their surroundings and observed the hard
faces of the members of the gang. When they came to
the bivouac area that Clifford had chosen for the night,
the captives were made to dismount, and two members
of the band stood guard over them.

The quartet huddled together beside a fallen log
and looked at each other bleakly.

Hank Purcell broke the silence. "It's all my fault,"
he said. "I saw Slim Davis, the fella who killed my pa,
and I couldn't think of anything except the solemn vow
that I made when my father died. Well, I rid the world
of Davis all right, but we've been taken by the Ma

Hastings gang, and there's no worse, more heartless crooks in the whole of the Montana Territory. For all the good it does, I'm sorry."

"Don't apologize, Hank," Susanna said softly. "What's done is done, and I can't say as I really blame you for acting the way you did. You waited a long time to avenge your father's death, and when the opportunity presented itself, you took it."

The boy swallowed hard and appeared to be on the verge of tears. Clarissa impulsively put an arm around his shoulders and hugged him.

Hank straightened, swallowed again, and shook his head. He could not afford the luxury of weeping like a child now. The ladies were depending on him, and he had to act like a man.

Beth Martin was seething. "I don't know who these people think they are," she said, "but they can't treat us like cattle!"

Clarissa and Susanna tried in vain to quiet her as a guard approached them and silently handed them plates of cold roasted meat and mashed, cold peas.

"I—I'd like to throw this food in their faces!" Beth exclaimed.

"I wouldn't advise it," Clarissa said quietly. "We're fortunate that we're being given anything to eat, and there's no way of telling when more food will be available. I suggest that we conquer our pride and eat what we're given."

"Amen to that," Susanna said.

Beth did as she had been told and managed to cram down some of the food, but it was obvious that her bad temper was getting the better of her. One of her feet tapped furiously, incessantly, and she glowered at her captors, making no secret of her contempt for them.

All at once, her temper boiled over, and she turned to an unshaven, shaggy-haired member of the band who sat on the ground, a rifle held carelessly in his lap as he guarded the prisoners. "Tell your captain, or whoever is in charge, that I demand to see him instantly!" Beth said.

Ordinarily the man would have ignored such a request, but the authority in Beth's voice was unmistakable, and before the bandit quite realized what he was doing, he rose to his feet and went in search of Ma Hastings.

Her thumbs hooked into her broad belt, the older woman approached at a casual saunter, an amused half-smile on her face. "What's on your mind?" she demanded gruffly.

"I don't know what you think you're doing," Beth said haughtily, "but you're making a mistake, a very large and expensive mistake, by taking us as your captives. We're honorable, law-abiding people, and you have no call to treat us in this manner!"

The smile faded slowly from Ma Hastings's face. Thrusting her chin forward, she said, "Suppose I admit every word ya say is true? What of it? What are ya gonna do about it?"

Beth did not retreat. "It's obvious," she said coldly, "that, inasmuch as we're your prisoners and have been disarmed, there isn't much that we can do to look after ourselves or protect our rights. But we're far from helpless."

Ma Hastings deliberately spat on the ground, inches from the woman's feet.

Beth remained unflinching. "It so happens that I'm the daughter of General Leland Blake, the commander of the Army of the West," she declared, then gestured toward Susanna. "And this is the wife of the colonel who commands the Eleventh Cavalry at Fort Shaw. It's safe to predict that the military will go to any length to win our release, and I can assure you they won't be gentle with our abductors."

Ma looked at her through narrowed, glittering eyes, but her face remained expressionless.

Clarissa could not help wondering whether Beth had made a major error when she had identified Susanna and herself. She had probably saved the party from being casually murdered or maimed, but, on the other hand, by revealing that they were persons of consequence, she had possibly made them much more valuable to their kidnappers.

"So I demand that you release us instantly!" Beth demanded. "Now! Without delay!"

Ma Hastings continued to regard her with eyes that reflected hatred for all that the young woman represented. "Lady," she said harshly, "ya ain't in no position to be callin' tunes. If ya know what's good for ya, you'll shut up and do what you're told." She spat again, narrowly missing Beth's foot, then turned abruptly and sauntered off.

Her followers, uncertain of her mood, gave her a wide berth. Long experience had taught them to avoid her when she became aroused.

Ralph sighed and stared at her dully, then sneaked a swallow from his ever-present bottle. He shrank from confrontation, as well as conflict, and was taking refuge in the only way he knew.

Only Clifford had the courage to face his mother openly and challenge her. He followed her to a knot of birch trees out of the hearing of the other members of the gang and well beyond a point where they could be overheard by the captives.

"I think," he said, "we bit off a bigger hunk o' buffalo steak than we can digest. The daughter o' General Blake and the wife o' Colonel Brentwood are too rich for our blood. The army will have every cavalryman at Fort Shaw lookin' and gunnin' for us, and they won't be satisfied until they nail us."

Ma shook her head in mock exasperation. "To think that one o' these days you're gonna be the leader o' the Hastings gang," she said. "I feel right sorry for the fellers who are gonna cast their lot with ya."

Color rose to Clifford's face. Unable to tolerate ridicule, he became annoyed. "I don't rightly like havin' my hide nailed to a wall, Ma," he said. "And I want no part o' the holdin' o' these women and that boy. The boy is a deadly shot anyways, and I say good riddance to him!"

Ma Hastings was disgusted. "If you wasn't my own kid," she said, "I'd swear you was the son of a natural jackass. You got no more brains in your head than the gunslingers who work for us!"

No man could insult Clifford Hastings, but he meekly tolerated the abuse heaped on him by his outraged mother.

"Use your head," she said. "Instead o' thinkin' o' ways to protect your skin, think o' ways to line your purse with more gold. We're in this business for only one reason—to make money! And don't ya forget it!"

He did his best to avoid backing down. "Honest, Ma," he said earnestly. "If we try holdin' these women for ransom, there's gonna be hell to pay. This here Colonel Brentwood has a reputation for bein' tough and mean and ornery, and if we hurt one hair on his wife's head, he'll come after us, hammer and tongs!"

She nodded calmly. "I already know every word you're sayin'," she told him, "and I've taken it into account. But it's like I've tried to teach ya for so long. There's more than one way o' holdin' up a stagecoach, and there's more than one way o' robbin' a bank!"

Clifford's hostility dissipated, and he told himself that he should have known his mother would have a sound, well-laid scheme in mind that would be safe, yet eminently practical.

"Just about everybody who lives in the Montana Territory," Ma Hastings said flatly, "knew that the comin' o' the cavalry regiment was goin' to mean trouble for the Sioux nation. Sooner or later they're goin' to go to war against the Sioux, when it appears that's the only way to stop 'em. And I know Thunder Cloud don't want to tangle with the U.S. Cavalry, and I can't say as I blame him. They're tough, they shoot straight, and when they come after ya, they keep a'comin'."

Clifford nodded.

"It'll be worth plenty to Thunder Cloud to keep the troopers from startin' a full-scale war." Ma chuckled aloud. "I'm sure he's willin' to pay through the nose to avoid that, and I aim to oblige him."

The man looked at his mother in awed respect. "Ya mean," he said softly, "you're gonna sell these people we captured today to Thunder Cloud so's he can use 'em as hostages to force the regiment to leave him and his warriors alone?"

"Exactly," his mother replied proudly. "That's why I plan to send Sonny off to arrange a private meetin' with Thunder Cloud for the first thing tomorrow mornin'."

Clifford's admiration for his mother grew rapidly. She was succeeding once again in turning wrath away

from herself and the members of her band, while leaving
them with a handsome profit.

"I don't know what it's goin' to be worth to Thunder
Cloud to take possession o' these prisoners," she said
comfortably, "but I promise ya, before I'm through with
him, he's goin' to pay through the nose."

IX

Wary in all of his dealings with whites, Thunder Cloud
did not believe in taking needless risks. To be sure, he
knew of the notorious white female bandit, Ma Hastings,
and was dismayed about her gang's brutal raids, though
it was true that in their own way, they caused no little
trouble for the Montana settlers. But although his curiosity led him to accept the invitation of Ma Hastings to a
private meeting with her, he was accompanied to the site
by a strong escort of fifty young warriors, all of them
mounted on swift, small horses, all of them armed with
bows and arrows and the deadly lances that they used
with such skill.

The braves arrived early at the appointed rendezvous high in the Mountains of the Plains, and needing
no instructions, scoured the countryside looking for hidden armed gang members. Finding none, they conceded
that Ma Hastings truly wanted a meeting with the principal sachem of the Sioux, and they relaxed their vigil
somewhat.

Indian scouts hidden on the heights followed Ma Hastings's progress for miles as she rode toward the rendezvous, and they dutifully reported to Thunder Cloud that, precisely as she had promised, she was traveling alone.

The leader of the Sioux nation hated all whites and felt the traditional contempt of the warrior for members of the opposite sex. But he was forced, much against his will, to feel a reluctant and grudging respect for Ma Hastings. She was a coyote who survived by preying on her own kind. But she nevertheless had courage, and equally important, she was always scrupulous in keeping her word, at least in her dealings with the Sioux.

Continuing to take no chances, Thunder Cloud remained concealed in a thick grove of evergreens a short distance below timberline, and there he waited until Ma Hastings arrived on the small plateau where they had arranged to meet. Then he nodded to his escorts, who immediately took up positions near the fringe of the wooded area, deliberately covering Ma from every possible angle.

Well aware of the activity of the braves in the forest, Ma nevertheless remained imperturbable. The Indians were reacting precisely as she had anticipated. As a matter of fact, the strength of her position, as usual, depended on her almost uncanny ability to predict precisely how others would react in any given situation.

Thunder Cloud rode slowly into the open. Under one arm he carried an ornamental lance decorated with dyed eagle feathers that matched those in his war bonnet. As he approached the tough old woman, he felt a sudden surge of revulsion, but his face remained placid, revealing none of his feelings. He raised the palm of his left hand upward in the universal Indian gesture of a friendly greeting.

Ma Hastings hastened to reply in the language of the Sioux. One of her many accomplishments was her ability to speak the tongue fluently, although few of her associates were aware of her talent. "Hail to the mighty Thunder Cloud, leader of the Sioux nation," she called.

The principal sachem of the largest and most powerful Indian nation west of the Mississippi River did not deign to reply in words. A friendly gesture was required, however, and he had no intention of being remiss in his duty. So he inclined his head, then folded his arms across his chest. This gesture was significant because it indicated he had no intention of using his weapons.

Ma promptly replied in kind. She was wearing a large bandanna handkerchief, loosely knotted around her neck. She immediately removed it and, placing it on the muzzle of her rifle, extended the weapon, offering the bandanna to the Indian chieftain as a gift.

In spite of Thunder Cloud's aversion to whites, he had no objection to accepting gifts of property from them. He had no use, however, for a bandanna, which was far too small to be utilized as a shirt. Thus he rejected it with a haughty shake of his head and a wave of his hand.

Ma Hastings reacted instantly to the rebuff, dealing with the matter with the indifference of an Indian. Her face wooden, she took the bandanna away and stuffed it into her hip pocket, where it remained out of sight. She knew Thunder Cloud had taken pains to emphasize that this was no meeting between old friends. Ma Hastings had suggested that the sachem meet her on a matter of business that would prove profitable to him and his people, and his mere presence at the rendezvous showed his willingness to hear whatever she had to say. That did not mean, however, that he regarded her as a colleague or a friend.

Judging her adversary shrewdly, Ma lost no time in getting down to business. "It so happens," she said, speaking succinctly and clearly for the benefit of his subordinates, who she knew were crowded into the wooded area behind him, "that four white persons came into the custody of me and my followers yesterday. Three of them are young females. One is the daughter of General Blake, the chief of the American Army of the West. A second is the wife of Colonel Brentwood, who leads the troops at Fort Shaw. The identity of the third I have not yet learned, but I have reason to believe that she, too, is important. The fourth member of the party is a mere boy, who acted as the guide for the ladies. But I can tell you plainly that he is a gunslinger of great promise and would serve the Sioux well if he could be persuaded to shift his loyalty to them."

The quick-witted Thunder Cloud grasped the situation instantly and nodded. He deliberately elected to reply in English. "Do I understand that you offer me the custody of these persons?"

Ma Hastings, having initiated her speech in the language of the Sioux, refused to switch to her own tongue. "That is so," she conceded.

"You wish to be rid of them," Thunder Cloud observed complacently, "because it would be very difficult for your small band to hold them hostage for any length of time."

She knew better than to lie or strike a bold pose with a man of his intelligence. "It is true, the members of my band are few in number," she said. "We can't go about our business with four prisoners in tow."

He inclined his head, indicating that he accepted the point she was making.

"The Sioux," she continued, "have many homes, many towns and villages, even in the wilderness of Montana. When they are pursued by troopers, they can retire to their secret dwellings in the mountains and the hidden valleys, and there they can take refuge from their foes. But my band and I lack such protection. When we are pursued, we must run and run until exhaustion forces us to halt. We could not possibly escape from our enemies who wear the uniform of the army if we were saddled down with the four whites."

The point she was making was both simple and legitimate. It was not possible for her to retain possession of the captives, not only because they would hinder the gang's movements but also because the gang was certain to be pursued and caught by the authorities. But the prisoners could be easily sheltered and guarded by the Sioux, who could keep them safely, no matter how hard the regiment of cavalry tried to get them back.

But the more important issue, as Thunder Cloud and Ma Hastings well knew, was that Thunder Cloud could use the hostages to strike a bargain with Colonel Brentwood and prevent the regiment from taking punitive action against the Indian nation. This was obvious to the Indian chief, who weighed the question seriously. He knew it was only a matter of time until his worst fears came to pass: Army troops, unsuccessful up to now in putting an end to Sioux attacks in Montana, would strike out against the Indians in force. There would be a full-scale war, which the Sioux could not hope to win.

There was no doubt in Thunder Cloud's mind that the possession of the captives would be effective in calling a halt to the regiment's activity against him and his people. What remained to be decided now was the price that Ma Hastings demanded for transferring the captives into the custody of the Sioux.

"My nation does not know wealth as white men count wealth," Thunder Cloud declared. "We have discovered no rivers of gold and no mounds of silver. We have none of the precious metals that white men cherish. We have few pelts of the beaver, the fox, and the lynx. We can acquire the hides of large numbers of buffalo, but those with skin of your color place small value on them. So I do not know what the Sioux, who are poor in worldly goods, can offer to you for the persons of these captives."

He was shrewd, to be sure, but Ma Hastings was equally clever. "You forgot to mention firearms," she said. "But no matter. We have all the rifles and pistols we need."

"Then what can we offer to you in order to strike a bargain?"

This was the moment that Ma had been awaiting, and although she spoke lightly, the greed in her voice was thick. "I have long admired the ability of the Sioux to ride with the speed and ease of the wind," she said. "I have long coveted your fine horses."

He was relieved that they had already found a basis for bargaining, but he indicated no relief, no pleasure. "How many horses do you want in return for these captives?" he demanded.

She preferred that the offer originate with the Sioux. "How many would you give me?" she countered.

Thunder Cloud replied rapidly, almost too easily. "I propose to give you twenty swift horses, each of them no more than two years of age. Therefore, you will receive five horses in return for each captive."

Ma hid her elation. That many horses, sold on the black market to some unscrupulous horse dealer, would earn the gang a tidy sum. The negotiations were progressing far more smoothly than she had anticipated, but still the bandit leader attempted to strike an even better deal. "Human beings, if they have any worth, are worth more than mere animals," she said. "A fair bargain would be an exchange of ten horses for each prisoner."

His expression unchanging, Thunder Cloud shook his head vehemently.

"We will accept thirty horses for all the captives. No more and no less," Ma Hastings said.

His nod was almost indifferent. "It is agreed," he declared. The bargain, he thought, was sound. The offspring of wild horses that the Sioux had captured had cost the warriors nothing. But in return, they would gain possession of hostages who would prevent the U.S. Army regiment at Fort Shaw from engaging in all-out war. The bargain was all that the principal sachem of the Sioux could have hoped it would be.

Ma Hastings was equally delighted, and they agreed that the exchange would take place early the following morning—the earlier the better, Ma felt, and that the transaction would take place at the present meeting site. They parted casually, with Ma Hastings riding off alone, while the Indians waited until she disappeared from the sight of their lookouts before they abandoned their position on the heights and moved on to the bivouac area they had established near timberline.

Both parties had reason to feel thoroughly satisfied with the bargain they had struck.

Still guarded by two rifle-carrying members of the Hastings gang, Clarissa Holt spent a sleepless, restless night at the gang's bivouac. Beth Martin obtained little rest, and Susanna Brentwood was too overwrought to sleep, too. Only Hank Purcell dozed off and soon was sleeping soundly. It was ironic, Clarissa thought, that Hank, who was responsible for the group's predicament, was the only one who was able to rid himself of fears, at least for the night. She supposed she had every right to be furious with Hank, but in her heart she could not blame the boy for behaving as he had. The avenging of his father's murder had become an obsession with him, and he had been unable to resist the opportunity that had presented itself to him so suddenly and dramatically.

Although it was useless to speculate on the fate that awaited them, Clarissa was positive of certain things. Chief among them was that Toby would swing into action like a whirlwind when he learned his wife's fate. He was a Holt, and she could not forget a statement that Whip had made only a few short days before his untimely death. "There's a time to sit back in the weeds, twiddle your thumbs, and wait for events to catch up to you," he had said. "Then there're other times when you've got to act fast and hard and sure, knowing what you're doing and not giving a damn about the consequences."

This, she knew, was just such a situation.

She suspected, too, that Andy Brentwood would waste no time in seeking his wife and securing her safety. She didn't know Rob Martin all that well, but she recognized him as being direct and forthright, and she had an idea that he, too, would leave no stone unturned in his attempts to rescue Beth.

The future, then, was far from hopeless. Clarissa realized that she and her companions had to stay together and stand together, doing nothing to antagonize their captors into killing or injuring them. That was easier said than done. Not only was Hank impetuous, but Beth, who had blurted out Susanna's identity and her own, had proved that she, too, was capable of impulsive action. Clarissa realized that somehow she and Susanna would have their hands full in the days to come, whatever their fate might be.

The guard was changed every few hours, which allowed those who had been standing sentinel duty to sleep. The members of the band took their responsibilities seriously and kept sharp watch on the prisoners.

Observing them through half-closed eyes, Clarissa realized that the chances of escaping from the Hastings gang were remote. It was possible, she reflected, that by devising a bold and clever plan of action, one or two of the captives might manage to get away. But it was too much to hope that all four would be able to make good their escape, and the risks, particularly when dealing with a gang of unscrupulous criminals, were too great. She finally decided it would be the better part of wisdom to await developments and not to plan too far ahead.

To the astonishment of Clarissa and her cohorts, the entire camp was stirring long before daybreak. The captives were given a breakfast of sizzling bacon, hot biscuits, and strong black coffee. Discovering she was ravenously hungry, Clarissa was forced to concede privately that the food was delicious.

The meal heartened her and had the same effect on her companions. It was apparent to them that if they were being fed so generously, Ma Hastings had no intention of killing them.

At least an hour before dawn, Clifford Hastings appeared on the scene and quickly ordered the captives to mount their horses.

They complied because they had no choice, but Beth's curiosity got the better of her, and she asked boldly, "Where are you taking us?"

"You ask too many questions. Just do what you're told," he replied curtly. In secret, however, he admired the young woman's spunk. She might be the daughter of a general in the U.S. Army, but it was plain that she had a mind and a will of her own. Clifford found himself staring at her speculatively.

Beth became aware of his interest, and her instinct prompted her to smile at him. Any advantage that she could gain was worthy of exploration. But Clifford suddenly became all business again, and putting the young woman out of his mind, he rode to the front of the gang.

Before the captives quite realized what was happening, they were on the march, surrounded by the gang, who rode with their rifles laid in front of them across their saddles. The band was taking no needless risks.

"Where do you suppose they're taking us?" Susanna muttered.

Clarissa shrugged. "All I know is that we're moving higher into the mountains. I don't think I like this." She glanced at Hank Purcell and saw the stubborn set of his jaw, the expression of hostility and resentment that blazed in his eyes. An inner voice warned Clarissa to keep an eye on him. His masculine pride had been wounded, and she knew he was determined to find some way to wipe the slate clean. She tried to warn him with a glance not to attempt any foolish heroics. But the boy did not understand her meaning and stared beyond her at the snow-covered peaks that were beginning to glisten in the light of the first break of day.

At last they came to a wooded area, and Clarissa felt rather than saw many eyes peering at her through the screen of evergreens.

At an order from Ma Hastings, the members of her band dropped their rifles into the slings attached to their saddles for the purpose, and Clarissa regarded the gesture as strange, not understanding why the gang would go to such pains to appear unarmed.

Suddenly an imposing figure, mounted bareback on a horse, emerged through the trees. Broad shouldered and tall, his face and torso streaked with war paint, an intricate feathered bonnet settled firmly on his head, he approached the party. His skin was walnut colored, and in the early morning light, he looked middle-aged. What impressed Clarissa about him was the aura of power that he exuded. Her late father-in-law had been that type, and so was General Blake. Obviously this was no ordinary Indian; he was accustomed not only to giving orders but also to being obeyed promptly.

A half-dozen other braves, all of them a generation younger than their leader, all of them armed with bows and arrows, as well as with light lances, came into the open.

Hank Purcell lost his composure. "These here are Sioux!" he shouted in alarm and disgust. "They're the dirtiest, most treacherous savages on earth. They're nothing but scum!" Even though he was unarmed, he spurred his mount in the direction of the Indian leader.

Thunder Cloud appeared to be anything but upset. In fact, a gleam of humor appeared in his eyes.

His subordinates, who were sworn to protect the principal sachem of their nation, did not share his sense of humor. One of them drew a length of rope from his belt and twirled it in the air expertly above his head.

Before anyone could intervene, the line had dropped down over Hank's head and shoulders, pinning his arms to his side. The noose tightened, and the warrior jerked on the loose end. The boy was helpless and tumbled to the ground. One of the braves laughed and, moving forward, prodded Hank with the sharp point of his lance.

All at once four or five warriors were engaging in the sport, forcing the helpless boy to scramble madly, twisting and turning and running before being jerked from his feet again, in a futile attempt to evade the cruel spears of his tormentors.

Thunder Cloud made no attempt to halt his braves. The young white boy deserved to be punished and was being taught a lesson he would not forget.

Clarissa watched in horror, sickened by the spectacle. Suddenly she could tolerate no more. Scarcely aware of what she was doing, she jumped to the ground, ran to the boy, and threw her arms around him. "Stop, you contemptible savages!" she shouted angrily. "How dare you molest a child like this!"

The Indians were stunned by her intervention, as were the members of the Hastings gang, and everyone stared at her as she stood defiantly, breathing hard as she cradled Hank in her arms.

Thunder Cloud was the first to recover, and he addressed her in English. "Who are you, woman, that you dare to interfere with Sioux justice?" he demanded.

Her eyes blazing, she looked at him contemptuously. "You call this justice?" she asked scornfully. "Do you call yourselves men? My father-in-law would have spat upon you, and if he were here, so would my husband!"

"Ah, you are the wife of the American colonel," Thunder Cloud said.

Still clutching and shielding Hank, Clarissa drew herself up proudly. "I am Mrs. Toby Holt," she declared.

The principal sachem of the Sioux stared at her intently. "Holt?"

"My father-in-law," she said, "was Whip Holt."

The revelation struck its listeners with the impact of a bombshell. The warriors, who knew little or no English, nevertheless were quick to recognize the name of the renowned mountain man, and they stared uneasily at the flushed, angry young woman. The members of the Hastings gang were even more impressed and, stirring in their saddles, exchanged surreptitious glances.

Thunder Cloud turned accusingly to Ma Hastings. "You did not tell me that the daughter of the old eagle was among your captives," he said.

Ma Hastings's composure was badly jarred. "I—I didn't know it until just now," she muttered.

Thunder Cloud spoke coldly and decisively. "It has been related," he said, "that the wings of the young eagle are as powerful as those of the old eagle. That his vision is as keen and his claws as sharp. I did not want the old eagle to become the enemy of my people, and I do not now want the young eagle to become their foe." He paused, then seemed to make up his mind. "I will take the other captives from you, as we have agreed, and I will still pay you the price of thirty Sioux horses for them. But the squaw of the young eagle I will not take."

Ma Hastings was aware of the consternation, bordering on panic, of the members of her band. One of her strengths long had been her ability to read the minds and the tempers of her followers, and she knew they would either rebel or desert her if she agreed to retain custody of Toby Holt's wife. "I can't keep her, either," she said flatly. "I've got to hold you to your original bargain. And you can't simply turn her loose, because she'll go straight to Fort Shaw and tell the army everything she's learned about all of us—which is far too much."

Thunder Cloud faced a dilemma and seemed to be trapped. If he refused to accept custody of the young Holt woman, he would be breaking his sacred word to Ma Hastings, and his reputation would be ruined. An Indian chieftain was no better and no worse than the promises he kept or broke. If he made the young woman his prisoner, however, he was virtually guaranteeing that her husband would join in the search for her, and he emphatically did not look forward to a confrontation with the son of the redoubtable Whip Holt.

Still, he would never allow himself to appear as if he were afraid of a Holt or of anyone else. As principal chief of a nation of fighting men, he supposedly had the heart of a lion, the stamina of an elk, the tenacity of a moose. He would lose standing with his own warriors if they detected a cowardly streak in him, and that would mark the beginning of the end of his reign. Therefore, he had no choice.

At the same time, however, he knew he could not treat this young woman as he would an ordinary captive.

"I have given my word," he said, "and Thunder Cloud of the Sioux always keeps his pledges. Therefore, I will accept custody of this woman, as well as of the other captives."

Ma Hastings hid her relief, but her son forgot himself and sighed aloud.

Thunder Cloud turned to Clarissa, whose anger was cooling sufficiently for her to realize that she had inadvertently created a new, and perhaps favorable, situation for herself and her companions.

"The Sioux," he said, "are struggling to regain land that was taken from them by force and by cheating. Therefore, all that we do to regain it is fair. I regret that you must become the guest of my people for a time. But rest assured that the daughter of the old eagle and squaw of the young eagle will not suffer. You will have a tent of your own made of skins, and you will be given all you wish to eat. Your hands and feet will not be bound. You will not be beaten, nor will you be led with a noose around your neck. You will be treated with full honor at all times."

Clarissa quietly marveled at the power that the Holt name exerted on the frontier. But Whip himself would have been proud had he seen her reaction: She accepted Thunder Cloud's statement as though it was her due and pressed her advantage calmly and quickly. "My companions also must be treated with dignity," she said, "and this boy must not be abused again."

Anxious to bring the entire incident to a conclusion, Thunder Cloud readily agreed.

As the captives were surrounded by warriors mounted on their horses, Susanna was privately amused by the influence that the Holt name had exerted. Beth was also impressed and regarded her housemate in a new light. But Hank Purcell was the most deeply affected. As Clarissa removed the lasso from his shoulders, setting him free to return to his own horse, he whispered fiercely, "You saved me when I didn't deserve it, and I won't forget it. One of these here days I'm gonna have the chance to return the favor, and no matter what happens, you can depend on me!"

Colonel Andy Brentwood was deeply concerned by his wife's disappearance and sent a full troop of his cavalry out to search for her. The captain in command of the unit traced Susanna to the remote ranch house of the settler whom she had visited and interviewed, but following the shortcut the rancher had recommended to his visitors, the captain lost their trail in the rugged terrain.

There was nothing more that Andy could do for the present, and he hoped that his wife and her companions, being resourceful, would be able to extricate themselves from whatever difficulties they were encountering. Until he learned more about them, however, his hands were tied. At least there was the sergeant's wife, Mrs. Ford, to look after little Sam, and this was some consolation.

In the meantime, Andy was totally occupied with preparations for a full-scale campaign that he intended to launch against the Sioux. The Indians' widespread destruction of property was causing havoc throughout Montana, and they had to be stopped once and for all.

Despite Andy's preoccupation with the absence of the women and the upcoming campaign against the Sioux, the colonel nevertheless turned his attention to the arrival of two newcomers to the fort. Lieutenant Elkins had told Andy the story of the two cousins, whom his men had escorted from Fort Benton, and the colonel received Jim and Millicent Randall cordially, according the former the hospitality due a retired brother officer in the regular army. He made a small apartment on the post at Fort Shaw available to them, and realizing that he alone was responsible for notifying them of the death of Major Isham Jentry, he invited them to dine with him.

On a number of occasions during the war, Andy had been compelled to inform the parents or wives of various subordinates that their loved ones had been killed in action, and he supposed he should be accustomed to the difficult task by this time. All the same, he shrank from it and somehow managed to keep up a patter of small talk throughout the interminable meal.

When they moved to the living room for coffee after dinner, Andy knew, however, that he could procrastinate no longer. So he took a deep breath and began to talk about Toby Holt and Rob Martin.

"I know their names," Millicent said brightly. "Isham was assigned to work with them."

Andy drew a deep breath. "They were associated for a period of many weeks with a man who presented himself to them as Isham Jentry, and they assumed that was his identity. Not until his greed got the better of him did they realize that he was actually a criminal—a murderer—whom they killed in self-defense. I telegraphed the essentials to the War Department sometime ago, and received word back that the murderer's name was Yale Myers. As I find this very painful—and I'm sure it isn't easy for you either—I think you may find it simpler if I give you to read a copy of the report I wrote up after all the information came in."

"By all means, Colonel, and thank you," Millicent said, reaching out to accept the sheaf of papers from him. Her cousin moved to a place behind her so he could read over her shoulder.

Millicent read steadily, pausing only once, briefly, to shield her eyes with a hand. Then, managing through supreme willpower to remain calm and collected, she picked up the document again and finished it.

"I'm terribly sorry, Miss Randall," Andy said simply.

"Thank you, Colonel," she replied, and she seemed to be staring at a single spot on the carpet near her chair.

Jim Randall put a consoling hand on her shoulder. "Would you like a brandy, Milly?" he asked softly.

She shook her head. "No, thank you, but I would appreciate a cup of tea, I think."

Andy, relieved because he had something to keep him occupied for a moment, went to the kitchen himself and fetched her the tea.

"You say, Colonel," Jim declared quietly, "that you were informed by the Army of the West that Major Jentry's body was located in a small town in eastern Oregon. That the sheriff there had sent out telegrams to post offices and army posts and that the murder victim was finally identified as Major Isham Jentry."

Andy nodded and reached into his pocket, producing a long telegram. He handed it to Millicent, and as she perused it, her cousin looked at it over her shoulder.

"It's almost needless for me to tell you this," Andy said, "but you may rest assured, Miss Randall, that Major Jentry will be given full military honors."

Millicent bowed her head to indicate her assent.

"I'm sorry," he said, "that you've had to travel such a very long way from home to be given such crushing news, and it's a small consolation to assure you that the War Department will send his remains wherever you may direct for burial."

Millicent nodded. "I'll need a little time to digest all this and to reach a decision, if you don't mind, Colonel."

"Of course," Andy said. "Let me know at your convenience, and please don't feel under any pressure."

There was an awkward pause. Then Jim said, "If it's all the same to you, Colonel, I think I could tolerate a drop or two of that brandy just about now."

"I'll join you, Captain Randall," Andy said, and poured brandy into two bell glasses.

Jim took a large swallow of the liquor. "Do you happen to know any details of Isham's death?" he asked.

"I'm afraid headquarters sent me only a summary of the autopsy report, indicating that he died very quickly after receiving a lethal knife wound. If you wish, I'll obtain a full report for you."

"I'll appreciate that," Millicent said. Her voice was still steady, and she remained dry eyed.

Andy Brentwood privately admired her. She demonstrated the steel in her backbone that the wife of a regular army officer required, and he thought it was a great shame that Major Jentry was lost to her.

"In no sense will this compensate you for your loss, Miss Randall," Andy said, "but at least you can have the satisfaction of knowing that your fiancé's murderer has paid the supreme penalty for his crime. Toby Holt and his dog disposed of him under conditions that I can best describe as brutal."

"I'm very much obliged to Mr. Holt," she replied.

"If these were ordinary times," Andy said, "I'd offer you an escort immediately to Fort Benton and enable you to return East on the same riverboat that brought you to Montana. But I'm afraid the times are far from ordinary. We're about to engage in a full-scale campaign with the Sioux, and in addition, I have patrols out searching for a party that includes my own wife. They've been missing from the fort for a few days now."

"Oh, dear," Millicent said. "Under those conditions, I couldn't accept an escort. Please, I urge you, forget about my problems for the present."

"You won't mind staying on at Fort Shaw, then, until I can spare the troops to take you as far as the riverboat?" Andy asked.

Millicent shook her head. "Not at all," she said. "As a matter of fact, I rather welcome a period of respite. It will give me the opportunity to get a better grip on my emotions."

Still standing behind her, Jim Randall nodded to corroborate her words. He knew her sufficiently well to realize she was being completely truthful and that she would indeed welcome a period of time that would enable her to regain her equilibrium.

"As for me, Colonel Brentwood," he said, "if you have any need in your coming command for a one-eyed veteran from the Corps of Engineers, I'll gladly volunteer my services."

"Thank you, Captain Randall," Andy replied warmly. "If you were either a scout or a cavalryman, I'd take you up on your offer without delay. Under the circumstances, however, it's the terrain that will dictate the nature of our campaign, so I think you'll be better off if you stay at Fort Shaw and look after Miss Randall."

Like his cousin, Jim was expert at concealing his feelings. If he was hurt by the rejection of his offer, nothing in his manner showed it.

Andy Brentwood felt boundless admiration for both of the Randalls and wished he had the time to devote to their future welfare. It was not enough, he thought, merely to wish them well. But his hands were tied. Not only was his own wife in danger, but the campaign against the Sioux that had brought him to the Montana Territory was about to erupt into full-scale battle.

What was more, there was little doubt in Andy's mind, or in the minds of his staff members, that the gangs of thieves and robbers, who were roaming at will through the territory, were also creating a great menace, inasmuch as they were murdering with abandon. However, the staff fully supported Colonel Brentwood in his decision to subdue the Sioux before turning the regiment's attention to the gangs.

The day after the arrival of Jim and Millicent Randall, Andy held a meeting of the heads of staff to consider the problem. "The way I see it, gentlemen," Andy said to his subordinates, "the Indians constitute by far the greater danger because there are so many of them. According to the estimates of our own scouts and reconnaissance patrols, there are approximately two thousand or more Sioux warriors at large in the territory under our jurisdiction. They're playing a very careful, cagey game at present, destroying homes, livestock, and property, but taking no lives. That policy is typical of the cunning of Thunder Cloud, who seems to feel that we'll let him do as he pleases, provided he doesn't resort to killing and scalping."

"On the other hand," his operations officer said, speaking to the group, "we estimate that there are no more than six gangs of outlaws who are traveling throughout the territory, killing and plundering. We've weighed the matter at length, and the section has recommended to Colonel Brentwood that we first pacify and control the Indians. Once their menace is removed, it should be a relatively simple matter to get rid of the criminal gangs."

"As a matter of fact," Andy said, "the citizens of Montana may well take care of at least a portion of that problem for us. Any place that two or more ranchers gather, they invariably talk about establishing vigilante justice, and I can't say that I blame them. I think you'll find that the question of how to rid Montana of the bandits will be eased considerably after the good people of the territory hang some of the scoundrels."

The heads of all staff sections expressed themselves as being emphatically in favor of first conquering or otherwise pacifying the Sioux.

The commanders of battalions and troops were then called into a separate meeting of their own, and the choice was explained to them. They agreed that the nuisance of the criminal gangs had to be eliminated, but recognizing the need for concerted action against a potentially far greater foe, they, too, cast unanimous votes in favor of a campaign against the Sioux.

So, trying to hide his worry in work, Andy prepared for a major thrust against the Indians. The Eleventh Cavalry would bear the brunt of the attack and would be aided wherever possible by the sparse militia units that the settlers were able to muster. "One thing is clear," Andy said repeatedly. "Montana has got to be made safe, not only for the folks who have been moving here, but also for the railroad that's going to transform this wilderness into a civilized land!"

Haggard from loss of sleep and inability to eat, Andy drove himself unmercifully. His concern for his wife was ever present in his mind, but he took care not to mention her to his subordinates, feeling it was unfair to burden them unnecessarily with what he regarded as his own problem.

One morning an aide came into Andy's office in an

obviously excited state. Saluting, he said, "Sir, there is an envoy from the Sioux, who insists on seeing you in order to deliver a personal message."

Andy raised an eyebrow. "What does that mean?"

"Damned if I know, Colonel, but I'll tell you this much. The brave is one of the most persistent devils I've ever seen. He has made it very clear to everybody who's seen him that he's prepared to stay here indefinitely until you agree to receive him."

"Under the circumstances," Andy replied, sighing, "we might as well see what's on the rascal's mind."

A few moments later a warrior in his early thirties, his scalp lock decorated with five crow feathers that denoted his high rank, was led into Colonel Brentwood's office.

The aide, taking no chances, stayed in the office and took up a position near the windows, where he could keep watch on the warrior. The young officer kept one hand on the butt of his pistol, ready to draw it and fire instantly if the Sioux resorted to trickery.

The warrior raised his left hand in an open-palm greeting. Andy returned the gesture by nodding and waving the visitor to a chair.

The Sioux had never before used the furniture of the whites, but he did not let that faze him as he lowered himself into the chair, gripping the arms awkwardly. Then he reached into a large rawhide pouch he carried in his belt and handed a folded document across the desk.

Andy glanced at it and then grew pale. "By God!" he muttered. "That's my wife's handwriting!"

The communication itself was brief and to the point:

Dearest Andy,

This will introduce an emissary from Thunder Cloud, leader of the Sioux, who will deliver his message in his own way.

I am well, as are Beth, Clarissa, and Hank. Thanks to Clarissa's stature as a Holt, we are being treated as honored guests, so we have no complaints.

I miss you and our dear little one and pray we will soon be reunited.

Your devoted wife,
Susanna

Andy scanned the letter quickly, then reread it with great care, devouring every word. He was relieved beyond measure that his wife was alive and in good health, but the knowledge that she and her companions had fallen into the hands of the Sioux infuriated him. He knew better than to demonstrate his feelings to Thunder Cloud's emissary, however, so he deliberately adopted a cool, remote stance. "You have come to me from your principal chieftain," he said. "What is the message he sends to me?"

"Thunder Cloud knows," the warrior declared, "that the soldiers are filling their firesticks with lead and that they plan to empty them, making the braves of the Sioux their targets."

"That is so," Andy conceded, "because the Sioux are raiding the ranches and farms of the settlers. They are burning down homes, destroying property, and slaughtering cattle and livestock."

The emissary looked at him indignantly. "White men build their homes on the hunting grounds that the tribes of this area have used for many years. The grandfathers of today's warriors, and their grandfathers before them, hunted for deer and antelope and mountain sheep on the very land that the white men have stolen. Let them return to their cities and towns in other parts of America, and the Sioux will raid their homes no more."

Andy had to admit to himself that there was a strong measure of justice in the demands of the Indians. At the same time, however, he knew they were seeking retribution in the wrong way. "The day will come," he said, "when the representatives of the people of the United States and the representatives of the Sioux nation will sit down together and talk. They will reach a compromise that is fair to all men, and when they sign a treaty, there will be peace for all time between your people and my people. I urge Thunder Cloud to agree to such talks now, before many of his young men and our young men are killed needlessly in battle."

The emissary had to admit, privately, that the war chief of the whites made sense. What the colonel failed to take into account, however, was the spirit that motivated the Sioux. Their pride had been severely injured, and until it was restored, no self-respecting brave could hold his head high again.

"Let the soldiers withdraw," the brave said, "and let them be followed by those who have settled in our hunting grounds. Then there will be peace."

"Let my squaw and the squaws of my friends be released at once as a sign of the good faith of Thunder Cloud and the Sioux nation," Andy said firmly.

The emissary shook his head, his eyes hardening. "If the war chief of the whites gives his solemn word, which he will put on paper and will sign, that the soldiers will not make war against the Sioux, those who are held captive by my nation will be released. If there is no such

pledge given, they will be held as captives until the war
ends in victory for the Sioux."

Andy had felt virtually certain that Thunder Cloud
would try to use the hostages to force the army to abandon its campaign, and the brave's flat statement con-
firmed his worst fears. Not for a moment did he consider
giving in to the demands of the Sioux, however. He
could not equate the safety of his wife with the duty
that he was required to perform on behalf of his country. The one had no connection with the other, in spite
of Thunder Cloud's attempt to use blackmail as a
weapon.

The aide, standing across the office from Colonel
Brentwood, felt sorry for his superior, knowing that he
faced the most difficult choice that a man could be
called upon to make. But his pity gave way to open admiration because the colonel made up his mind instantly, as soon as he heard the terms proposed by the
Sioux. His eyes gleamed, and he struck the desk smartly
with his fist.

"Take my words to Thunder Cloud and to all the
warriors of the Sioux," Andy declared in a ringing voice.
"Repeat them loudly and often until all who wear the
war paint of the Sioux know and understand what I
have said. I hold Thunder Cloud personally responsible
for the welfare and safety of the three women and the
boy, whom he holds as captives. I also hold every warrior of your nation personally responsible. If any harm
should befall these captives, I will make unremitting war
on the Sioux! I will not stop until your warriors have
been slain, your women and children have been driven
from their homes, and your towns have been reduced to
ashes. Let Thunder Cloud and every brave of the Sioux
heed my warnings!"

It was apparent to the emissary that the colonel meant every word. The plan of Thunder Cloud to have the army call off its campaign had ended in obvious failure. The emissary wanted to counter the words of the white war chief with a warning of his own. But he thought better of it. The man's wrath would become all the greater if the safety of his wife and the other captives should be threatened.

Toby Holt and Rob Martin found it far easier to conduct their survey for a railroad route in the flat, plains country of eastern Montana than it had been in the heights of the Rocky Mountains. The worst of their chore was behind them now. They could make far better time in this region, with less personal risk, and by looking out across the plains for miles ahead, they could choose their route visually and then map it accordingly.

They continued to encounter many difficulties, to be sure, not the least of which was the risk of running into bands of roaming Sioux warriors hunting for game. The pair realized all too well that they were considered fair prey by the Indians and that they would more than meet their match if they encountered a group of twenty or more heavily armed braves.

They appeared to lead a charmed existence, however, thanks to Toby's uncanny ability to spot the presence of parties of Sioux hunters. Again and again he called his companion's attention to the nearby presence of a band of braves, and then it was a simple matter to avoid them. To be sure, Mr. Blake also played a large part in alerting the pair to an Indian trail or an extinguished camp, but by and large it was Toby who sensed the presence of Indians, even when there were apparently no signs to be seen.

One evening, as they sat at their campfire sipping coffee after consuming a meal of venison steak and baked beans, Rob became curious. "How do you do it, Toby?" he asked. "How do you always know when there are parties of Indians within a radius of ten or fifteen miles of us? All you've ever told me is that you've inherited your father's ability to sniff them out. But there must be more to the story than that."

Toby was amused, and he chuckled. He patted Mr. Blake's head and fed him a chunk of roasted meat, then said, "What I told you was right, Rob—as far as I went. I do owe my ability to ferret out the presence of warriors to my father, who taught me some very simple tricks. For one thing, I keep watch on the land that we ride through for signs that others have been in the vicinity, and twenty or thirty Indian horses usually leave a heavy trail of trampled grass behind them."

Sipping his coffee, Rob nodded thoughtfully.

"Whenever we stop to decide where we're going next," Toby said, "you concentrate on the best route to lay railroad tracks. Maybe you haven't noticed it, but I use my glass to scan the horizon in all directions. There are all kinds of telltale signs that show up. Such as the smoke from cooking fires. Indians have a reputation for making themselves invisible when they're in the open countryside, but that's a myth. They reveal their presence, just as white men do." Toby reached for the coffee pot, which rested near the coals of the fire, taking care to wrap his hand in a protective bandanna before grasping the handle and refilling his tin cup. "Let's just say that we have been fortunate and not go patting ourselves on the back," he said. "Judging from the messes we've run into at ranches that the Indians have overrun and destroyed, I'd guess they are in a pretty foul mood, and it's just as well that you and I avoid them."

"I've got to admit," Rob said, "that when I see the damage they wreak, I get terribly angry."

"So do I," Toby said, "but there isn't much that the two of us can do against a whole nation. I reckon we'll be wise to leave the job of teaching them a lesson in good manners to Andy Brentwood and his boys."

He broke off suddenly, listened intently, and reaching for the rifle that rested on the ground within easy reach, he slid a bullet into the chamber. Mr. Blake also heard something and, standing rigidly, stared in the direction of the sound. Rob had heard nothing, but he immediately followed his friend's example and readied his rifle.

Toby continued to listen intently. "Party of three riders heading this way," he muttered, and suddenly Rob saw in the distance the approaching figures.

Rising to one knee, Toby aimed his rifle as the three men on horseback neared the camp. "Halt and identify yourselves!" he shouted.

A deep baritone sounded in the dark night. "Sergeant Harry Allen and two troopers of his patrol, Eleventh Cavalry," was the reply.

Toby did not relax his vigil. "Advance and be recognized," he called.

The three uniformed men rode up to them, and not until their blue uniforms could be seen in the light of the campfire did Toby and Rob lower their weapons.

"We had sort of a rough idea where to find you," the sergeant said, "and we've been looking for your campfire. When we saw the smoke in the distance, we played on our hunch that it was you."

Sergeant Allen dismounted, ordered his troopers to do the same, then hesitated before he seated himself on the ground. "I'm under orders from Colonel Brentwood to find you gentlemen and to deliver messages to both of you." He hitched up his pistol belt, reached into an inner pocket, and removed two envelopes addressed in Andy Brentwood's handwriting to Toby and to Rob, respectively.

"Help yourselves to coffee," Toby said as he accepted his communication and opened the envelope.

The sergeant, familiar with the contents of the communications, felt sorry for the recipients. Toby grew pale beneath his heavy tan, while Rob clenched and unclenched his fists in impotent rage.

"When were these letters written?" the former demanded hoarsely.

"Day before yesterday, sir," Sergeant Allen replied. "An emissary from the Sioux showed up at the fort, and the colonel sent us out to search for you as soon as the Indian left."

Toby and Rob exchanged an intense, quick glance that immediately told both of them they were of one mind. The crisis that had erupted so suddenly necessarily took precedence over the survey for a railroad route. The safety of their wives was paramount, and as men who had now spent a considerable period of time in the mountains and foothills of Montana, they were in the best position to locate the Sioux, who had made captives of Clarissa and Beth, Susanna and young Hank.

"Sergeant," Toby asked, "are you and your horses too tired to get a start tonight?"

Allen, who was not surprised by his reaction, gulped his scalding coffee. "No, sir," he said. "We'll hit the trail with you and keep up with you for as long as you want to ride."

Toby and Rob were already busy packing their belongings, saddling their grazing horses, and otherwise preparing for an immediate departure.

Gray Wolf often was mentioned as a potential successor to Thunder Cloud. The younger man had accumulated a record as a warrior of note, as a diplomat in dealings with the Cherokee, the Arapaho, and the Ute, and as a man who was highly educated.

Schooled by missionaries, Gray Wolf could not only read, write, and speak passable English, but he had also become thoroughly familiar with Americans and American ways, which made him that much more valuable to the Sioux nation.

Gray Wolf was the natural choice, then, of the Sioux council of state to take charge of the four prisoners, who, it was hoped, could still be used as pawns in order to avoid an outbreak of actual hostilities with the U.S. Army. Even though Colonel Brentwood had refused to call off the attack in exchange for the release of the hostages, there were other ways he might be persuaded. It was true that Thunder Cloud had promised to treat the hostages with dignity, but he had said nothing about keeping them alive. Perhaps if one of the hostages were killed, the colonel might begin to see reason and call off his troops.

Gray Wolf was in charge of twelve warriors who guarded the captives night and day, and he devoted his own time exclusively to the task of keeping the prisoners safe, while, at the same time, preventing their escape.

The captives slept in two tents of animal skins, a very large one, used by the three women, and a small, cramped one, in which Hank Purcell slept.

The tents were located in a semipermanent camp that the Sioux had established in a narrow valley. The

Yellowstone River cut through the floor of the valley, providing the Indians with ample water supplies. and the forest not only afforded firewood but also shielded the Indians from the sight of any whites who might wander into the area.

High, rocky ledges loomed on both sides of the valley, protecting those who took shelter there from unexpected attack, and the head of the valley opened onto an even larger forest area where game was plentiful. A minimum of fifteen hundred Sioux made their headquarters in the concealed valley, and here the prisoners were held in loose confinement. It would be difficult, at best, for them to escape, and even if they managed to slip away, it would be a simple matter to follow and recapture them.

Gray Wolf was rightly proud of his assignment when he first received it, feeling correctly that his appointment indicated the faith of his colleagues in his abilities. His euphoria was short-lived, however, and he soon began to wonder if Thunder Cloud was deliberately testing his patience and his mettle.

The tall, red-haired woman called Clarissa, who towered at least half a head above Gray Wolf, was a very difficult woman with whom to contend. Following the firm directive he had received from Thunder Cloud, Gray Wolf served the captives the best meals that were available. When trout were caught in the Yellowstone River or some of its tributaries, he acquired them for the prisoners' meals. Similarly, he badgered the returning hunting parties for the choicest cuts of venison and antelope, elk and moose, and when they returned to the bivouac area with wild geese and ducks, he always obtained a fair share.

The redhead, however, soon indicated her extreme dissatisfaction with the arrangement.

One evening, shortly after the captives had been served their meat in the open near their tents, Clarissa had jumped to her feet and approached Gray Wolf, brandishing the large wooden spoon she had been supplied as a utensil. "This is ridiculous, absurd, and unnecessary!" she exclaimed, waving the spoon beneath the young war chief's nose.

Gray Wolf reacted wearily. "You do not like your venison steak?" he asked. "You may accept my word that not even Thunder Cloud has been given a better cut of meat for his own supper."

"I'm in no position to tell you whether I do or don't like the meat," she replied angrily. "I haven't tasted it, and I have no intention of being reduced to the level of an animal in my eating habits."

He had no idea to what she was referring, and although he remained alert, he looked at her blankly. "What is it you want?" he asked.

Clarissa made no attempt to hide her utter exasperation. "A knife, naturally! You certainly can't expect any of us to hold the meat in our bare hands and tear it apart with our teeth like dogs."

At last her predicament dawned on him. "It is the direct order of Thunder Cloud," he said, "that no captive be given any weapon that can be used to harm the guards. A knife is a sharp, dangerous instrument, and it could do much damage to a warrior if it were plunged into his back."

Clarissa brandished the wooden spoon wildly. "You call yourselves warriors?" she demanded scornfully. "You who are so afraid of three women and a young boy that you will not give us knives to cut our meat?" She laughed loudly and shrilly.

The contempt that Gray Wolf heard in her laugh made him cringe.

Hurling the spoon to the ground, Clarissa stood with her arms akimbo. "While you are trying to decide whether we can be trusted enough to use knives when we eat, our supper is getting cold, and I know of nothing less appetizing than cold venison steak. Be good enough to inform Thunder Cloud immediately that we demand someone in charge here who has greater courage than a mouse."

Gray Wolf could tolerate no more. Apprehensive about what might grow out of the experiment, he nevertheless ordered knives brought to the captives, and then assigned several warriors to stand close watch over them, instructing the braves that they were to snatch the instruments out of the hands of the prisoners at the first sign that they were going to be used for anything other than cutting and eating meat.

His fears proved ill grounded, however. The behavior of the captives was exemplary. They used their knives to cut off small pieces of meat, which they then speared and ate. At the end of the meal, Clarissa collected the knives, and with two braves following close behind her, she took them to Gray Wolf and presented them to him. "This," she said, "is with our deep thanks for enabling us to eat a meal in a civilized manner." She handed him the knives, then totally disconcerted him by curtsying deeply.

Feeling himself incapable of dealing with ridicule, Gray Wolf thereafter avoided the young red-haired woman whenever possible. Obviously it did not pay to tangle with her.

It soon became apparent to him that the daughter of the American general was equally dangerous in her own way. One morning after he had consumed a hearty breakfast of fish and cornmeal cakes, Beth approached him as he sat in the sunlight, his back to one wall of their tent, smoking his pipe. At the sight of her, his feeling of contentment vanished, and although he maintained an imperturbable façade, his nerves became jangled.

"I'm learning to have far greater respect for the Sioux than I've ever had," she remarked conversationally. Then, without waiting for an invitation, she lowered herself to a sitting position on the ground beside him.

Gray Wolf looked at her, waiting for a fuller explanation.

"This summer weather is lovely," she said, "and I really can't imagine finding any nicer climate anywhere. But at night it's dreadfully chilly!"

He had to admit the nights were cool but saw nothing out of the ordinary in that fact.

"My friends and I feel half-frozen," she said, still smiling amiably. "In fact, we get so chilly, we can't sleep." Seemingly unaware of their proximity, she leaned closer to him so that her shoulder touched his. "I know you've told us that there are no blankets in the entire bivouac area that are available to us," she said. "But surely, with all the hundreds of Sioux who are gathered here, it must be possible to find four simple blankets that will make the nights more bearable for us."

Gray Wolf stirred uncomfortably, disturbed by the nearness of the young woman. He knew she was married because she wore a gold ring on the fourth finger of her left hand, as was the custom with white women, and he had no idea whether she took her marriage vows seri-

ously. She didn't appear to be a flirt, much less a totally
wanton woman, however, and he had to assume that the
aura of intimacy that she created was inadvertent.

Beth looked up at him, her eyes limpid. "I'm sure
that you could arrange—somehow—to find blankets for
us. You're so clever that you've been made a war chief
years before it's customary for such a promotion. So I
have faith in your ability to do it." Still seemingly unaware of what she was doing, she put a hand on his bare
arm.

Knowing that the braves assigned to guard duty undoubtedly were watching them, Gray Wolf flinched. He
would be disgraced and would face certain demotion if
Thunder Cloud was led to believe that he had taken advantage of the position he held to become intimate with
one of the female captives. He rose to his feet effort-
lessly, if a trifle too rapidly, his face masklike. "I will see
what can be done," he said without emotion.

Later that same day, Beth's efforts were rewarded
when Gray Wolf appeared at the tents, followed by a
brave who carried four folded blankets, all of them new
and unused.

"I've known Indians everywhere we've been stationed," Beth confided gleefully to her companions later
that same day, in private. "It all boils down to knowing
how they'll react to the way a thought is presented to
them. I told you I'd get us these blankets!"

It was Susanna Brentwood, however, who caused
Gray Wolf the greatest grief. She came to him early one
morning and expressed her mind bluntly. "I want to see
Thunder Cloud as soon as an appointment can be arranged with him," she said.

"I am in charge of the captives," he replied. "If you
have complaints, you will make them to me."

She shook her head. "I have no complaint other than the basic unfairness of our captivity, which you already know, and Thunder Cloud is also aware of our feelings in this matter. That isn't why I want to speak to him, however."

"What is your reason?" he demanded.

Susanna smiled sweetly, but her voice was very firm. "That," she said, "is a matter between Thunder Cloud and me. If he wishes you—or anyone else—to know it, it is his privilege to tell you in due time. Will you notify him, please, that I am eager to speak with him? If you refuse, I shall have to find some other way of getting in touch with him."

Gray Wolf cursed silently, wishing he had never been given charge of the captives. "All right," he said wearily, "I will give your message to the principal chieftain."

That evening, when Thunder Cloud returned to the bivouac, Gray Wolf repeated the conversation word for word. The leader of the Sioux was intrigued. He was spending his days inspecting the patrols and sentry outposts of the Sioux in anticipation of the combat with the Eleventh Cavalry that seemed unavoidable, but he agreed to receive Susanna that same evening.

Gray Wolf escorted her to the principal chieftain's tent a short time later, and when he would have stayed nearby intending to hear what she had in mind, she had the audacity to wave him away. "I wish to speak to Thunder Cloud in private," she said.

Impressed by the squaw's courage, Thunder Cloud waved the young war chief away, and even though the sentries on duty at the entrance to his tent spoke no English, he ordered them to leave the premises, too.

"I have gathered," Susanna said to him, "that the reason your braves have been attacking the homes of settlers and causing so much damage in Montana is because you believe that the Americans who are moving into the territory are usurping hunting grounds that rightfully belong to your nation and to other tribes that have held those privileges here for many generations."

He nodded, surprised by her grasp of the situation.

"You may be right and justified in your claim," Susanna told him. "I honestly don't know enough about the subject to speak authoritatively on it. But it strikes me that it's imperative that you present your case to as large an audience as you can muster."

"White men," he said, "will not listen to painful truths about their brothers."

"That's where you're wrong—very wrong," Susanna told him forcibly. "Americans have their faults, just as Indians have theirs. But I must say in defense of my people that they're always willing to listen to another side of a story and to be fair in their judgments."

Thunder Cloud was puzzled. "Why do you say these things to me?" he wanted to know.

"Before I was married," she explained, "I wrote for newspapers, and I am a writer still. I am currently preparing a book on the Montana Territory that I have good reason to believe will be read by many Americans who are interested in the West and in the frontier. If you will tell me your story—the story of the Sioux claim to Montana and your reasons for it—I will present that story in your own words in my book."

The principal chieftain of the Sioux was stunned. "You joke," he said.

"I speak the absolute truth," Susanna told him with a depth of sincerity that was difficult for him to deny.

"Tell me your side of the case. Explain why the Sioux feel as they do, and I promise you that every word you speak will appear in my book in the spirit in which you told it to me."

Had anyone told Thunder Cloud that a white person would make such a fair and generous offer, he wouldn't have believed it possible. That the suggestion had come from the wife of his principal opponent, the commander of the army troops whom he was obliged to fight, made the miracle all the more remarkable. "You are sure there is no trick in this?" he asked.

Susanna shook her head. "I carry writing materials in my saddlebag," she said. "If you'll permit me to go to where my horse is being kept, I'll get them. Then I'll not only put your words on paper, but I'll read to you what I've written, and you may make whatever changes or corrections you wish."

Overwhelmed, he nodded slowly. "I accept," he said, and he could not help wishing that this open-minded woman were in charge of the United States forces in place of her husband. Perhaps, if she were, an accommodation could be reached, and lives could be spared.

To the astonishment of Gray Wolf, Susanna went off to where the hostages' horses were being kept and then returned to the tent of the principal chieftain of the Sioux.

Thereafter, she spent at least an hour each morning with Thunder Cloud and another hour in the early evening.

His subordinates soon learned that the young woman was acquiring data for a book she was writing, and most of the Sioux were not impressed. They agreed with Gray Wolf, who said that this woman, like her colleagues and compatriots, was clever beyond compare, and that it had been an unfortunate day for the Indians when their party had been taken prisoner. Their presence in the Sioux camp would not avert bloodshed, and they were causing innumerable and needless complications.

Haggard and tired, with their skin and clothes covered with dust after the long hours they had spent on the trail, Toby and Rob, accompanied by the three troopers, finally arrived at Fort Shaw three days later, in mid-evening. The headquarters was closed down for the night, with no one on duty but the officer of the day and his assistant, so the two civilians immediately went to the house of Colonel Andy Brentwood.

A grim-faced Andy offered them a drink, which they refused, and instead they went to the kitchen with him while he put a pot of coffee on the stove to heat.

"Have you found any leads since you wrote to us?" Toby asked tersely.

Andy shrugged. "Yes and no," he said. "We're pretty certain that the main bivouac of the Sioux is located high in the mountains of central Montana. But exactly where in the mountains is anybody's guess. As to the women and Hank, we have no idea where they are. They've simply disappeared from the face of the earth."

"Have you thought of taking a couple of Sioux as captives and squeezing the truth out of them?" Rob asked.

"I've weighed that precise question very carefully," Andy replied, "and although I've been strongly tempted, I'm afraid that such an act would do more harm than good."

Toby nodded slowly in agreement. "I reckon you're

right, Andy," he said. "No Sioux could be persuaded to give us any information voluntarily. That would be too much to hope or expect. You'd have to resort to torture—which I disapprove of wholeheartedly on principle—and even then, I think you'd find that any warrior worthy of the name would die before he'd break faith with his own people."

Andy rubbed his chin. "I wouldn't consider resorting to torture," he said. "That would be reducing ourselves to the level of the savages we're trying to beat. No, we can't break our own rules, no matter how difficult the task that awaits us."

"What are your plans?" Rob asked.

"The entire regiment, plus the small units of Montana militia that have been mustered, will be ready to move by the day after tomorrow," Andy said.

"Move where?" Toby demanded.

Andy smiled sourly. "That's the big question," he said. "Into the Mountains of the Plains, of course, but after that, I'm at a loss as to how to proceed."

"It strikes me," Toby said thoughtfully, "that your biggest need right now is an accurate scouting report."

Andy Brentwood laughed unhappily and ran a hand through his hair. "How right you are!" he said. "Unfortunately, we don't have any scouts in the regiment who are sufficiently accomplished to glean the data that we so badly need."

"You have them now," Toby told him quietly. "When I was retired from the army, I kept my commission, and the orders from the War Department state specifically that I am liable to recall to active duty in the event of an emergency. I consider the abduction of my wife and the wives of my good friends as a sufficient emergency. I volunteer to return to duty immediately and to assume command of your scout unit."

Colonel Brentwood's spirits rose. "That's generous of you, Toby," he said. "I appreciate it."

"Nonsense," Toby replied. "The lives of our wives are at stake in all this. Rob, do I assume correctly that you're willing to serve with me?"

"You bet!" Rob replied promptly.

"How much of a free hand will you give me, Colonel?" Toby asked formally.

"You tell me what you want, and it's yours, Lieutenant Holt," Andy replied.

"Very well, sir." Toby thought and spoke quickly. "There are four or five veterans of my old platoon on whom I know I can depend, and I'll want them detached immediately from their present units for service with the scouts. I'll go through the present roster of scouts, and I'll keep only those men who I think will be useful. The others can be reassigned to regular troop duty."

Andy took the pot from the stove and poured steaming coffee into three cups. "You have a blanket approval," he said. "How soon do you want to get going?"

Toby looked at him in surprise. "Right now, tonight!" he said. "There's no time to be lost. By dawn tomorrow morning, I intend to be well on the move with my scouts."

Andy wanted to protest, to insist that Toby get a long night's rest before undertaking such strenuous new duty. He knew, however, from Toby's military record, that he would be wasting his breath. Like his father before him, Toby Holt ignored his own feelings, his own welfare, when more important factors weighted the scales.

The house quickly became a beehive of activity. Five of Toby's wartime subordinates were summoned, and all were delighted at the opportunity to serve again under his command. The roster of the scouts, thirty strong, was called, and for his present purposes, Toby chose fifteen of the men. A cook was awakened and was ordered to prepare a huge breakfast for the members of the departing unit. Similarly, a quartermaster was aroused and procured uniforms and fresh mounts for Toby and Rob, as well as supplies that the men of the unit could carry with them in their saddle rolls.

Before Toby and Rob went to their own house to change into their uniforms, Andy told them briefly about the arrival of Millicent and Jim Randall and what had brought them to Fort Shaw. Toby listened, somber-faced. Though harried and distracted, he felt it his duty to go see the cousins and explain to them how Yale Myers had masqueraded as Isham Jentry and had fooled them.

He and Rob hastened to the house where Millicent and Jim were occupying a small apartment. Though it was late, the cousins were still awake, finding sleep difficult in light of all the unsettling news of recent days. Jim answered the knock at the door, and after Toby and Rob introduced themselves, he led them to the living room, where Millicent was sitting, wearing a plain house-dress. She looked somewhat tired, though her expression remained resolute and strong.

The cousins listened to Toby and Rob's account, especially that portion of the story that had to do with Myers's grisly death. "Perhaps it's wrong," Millicent said, "but I'm glad Myers died the way he did. A man like that deserves nothing but contempt and loathing."

The others nodded in agreement. Toby and Rob

expressed their sympathy to the cousins, then excused themselves in order to carry out the final preparations for their upcoming mission. They all shook hands, and as the two men left, Millicent called after them, "Thank you for coming to talk to us. I know you have a great deal on your minds right now, and maybe someday I'll be able to do something for you to return your kindness."

Toby and Rob went immediately to the dwelling that their wives had occupied. There, they changed into their uniforms. Tugging at his broad-brimmed hat and adjusting the ammunition belt from which a brace of pistols dangled, Toby put the cousins out of his mind as he readied himself for action. He felt completely at home; it was almost as though he had never retired from the army and had continued to serve as a first lieutenant.

Rob was similarly at ease as a second lieutenant. "What are your specific plans now, Toby?" he asked.

"We're going to head for the Mountains of the Plains as fast as we can," Toby replied emphatically. "Then we're going to spread out and find—once and for all—where the Sioux are camped. Once we find them, we'll familiarize ourselves with every approach to their hideout, and we'll report back to Colonel Brentwood, who will then go on the march himself with the whole regiment."

Toby became thin-lipped, and his eyes narrowed. "Next," he said, "we'll lead the regiment to the enemy, and then all hell will break loose. If our wives are still alive, we'll find some way to rescue them, and if they've been killed, may the Lord have mercy on the souls of every Sioux who I sight down the barrel of my gun!"

X

Arranging for a rendezvous on a plateau in the mountains, Toby dispersed his scouts over a wide area, sending them out in pairs to specifically designated zones. He chose one of the most inaccessible areas for himself and Rob, and accompanied by Mr. Blake, they set out at once for the location.

They had not slept all night, but they felt no need for rest. The knowledge that the rescue of Clarissa and Beth depended strictly on their efforts aroused them, and they were alert and filled with energy.

Mr. Blake sometimes ranged as far as fifty to one hundred yards ahead of the two men as they rode through the mountains, but when they neared the region that Toby intended to explore in detail, he called the dog to heel, and the shepherd obediently trotted beside his master's mount.

"I'm betting on this site," Toby said. "I remember it so well from our explorations for the railroad line."

Rob nodded thoughtfully. "I know what you mean,"

289

he said. "If I were a leader of the Sioux and wanted to hide a very large war party, I think I'd head right for this same valley. It seems a natural for the purpose."

"We can't afford to take even the slightest risk," Toby said. "The lives of the women will be in double danger if the Sioux know that we've located their hiding place, so I think we've got to assume that we've found their hideaway and act accordingly."

Rob seemed puzzled for a moment, but then his face cleared. "Ah! I see what you mean," he said. "You mean we dismount, proceed on foot, and keep our eyes and ears open for any sentries the warriors might have posted."

"Exactly," Toby said grimly. "We may be wasting our time, but better we lose an hour than lose precious lives."

As they drew nearer to the entrance to the valley, they dismounted and tied their reins to trees. Then Toby turned to the shepherd dog.

"Mr. Blake," he said, "whether you go with us for the rest of the way depends strictly on you. If you think you can be quiet and behave yourself no matter what may happen, you may come with us. If you're going to get excited, however, and bark or otherwise create any distraction, you'll have to wait here with the horses."

The dog looked up at him, ears flattened against his head, his tail slowly wagging.

"From the way that dog acts," Rob said, shaking his head, "I swear that he understands every word you say to him."

"I reckon he does," Toby replied, patting the dog. "He knows there are times to raise a commotion and times to be as quiet as if he were stalking a rabbit. Come along, Mr. Blake, and mind your manners, sir."

Sliding bullets into the chambers of their rifles, the two men moved about ten or fifteen feet apart and made their way swiftly through the forest, making no sound as they advanced. The shepherd dog ranged back and forth between them, veering first toward Toby, then toward Rob. He, too, was quiet, his instinct telling him that his master was playing no game.

All at once Toby halted and raised a cautionary hand. Rob could see nothing and hear nothing. He could not help noting, however, that Mr. Blake was aware of an alien presence, too. The dog had become taut, his ears pointing sharply upward and his tail extended.

Rob had the uncomfortable sensation that someone was watching him, and his blood froze. He broke into a cold sweat when he realized that that was precisely what was happening. Through the dense foliage of ever-green boughs and bushes, a pair of dark, glittering eyes was inspecting him carefully. A Sioux sentinel had seen him and was taking in every aspect of his appearance.

Rob quietly snapped the fingers of his left hand, and when he had alerted Toby's attention, he inclined his head a slight fraction of an inch in the sentry's direction.

The dog became aware of the Indian's proximity and, facing him, began to quiver. But he obeyed the strict orders he had received and was silent.

Realizing that Toby's hunch had been correct and that they had stumbled onto a Sioux hideaway of some sort, Rob knew that he could make no overt move to protect himself. He could raise his rifle to his shoulder and put a bullet between those gleaming eyes, but the sound would alert the Sioux to the fact that their hiding place had been discovered.

So Rob, feeling he had no real choice, stood quietly,

his rifle gripped in his right hand. He had the virtually impossible task of pretending to be unaware of the presence of the brave and somehow managing to look through the man without revealing any of the alarm that he felt.

It was Toby's place to eliminate the danger. The warrior, still concentrating on Rob, was unaware of his companion's presence, and that was all to the good.

Knowing that the use of firearms would create more problems than would be solved, Toby gripped the handle of one of a pair of throwing knives in his belt, and balancing it in the palm of his hand, he slowly raised his arm. He had never acquired his father's uncanny ability to wield a whip, but he had been taught the art of knife throwing from the time that he had been a very small boy and had achieved a remarkably high degree of accuracy. His problem was that he had not thrown a knife, even in practice, for some time. But that could not be helped; the situation called for the use of a knife. He measured the distance to his target carefully, then let fly, and the blade flashed through the air.

Rob breathed an inaudible sigh of relief when the face of the brave suddenly vanished.

"Mr. Blake," Toby said, "if anybody shows up, you raise a rumpus. Stay near that Indian's body and don't move." He started forward through the underbrush, and Rob followed close behind him. The dog obeyed instructions and continued to stand with his front paws on the dead sentinel's chest.

Toby advanced swiftly for about fifty yards and then halted. From here, the whole of the long, narrow valley stretched out ahead of them, and it was as good a vantage point as he could find to study the terrain. Rob came up beside him, and they peered through the trees together.

At first glance the area appeared totally uninhabited. Then Toby noted thin, gray plumes of smoke rising from six or eight separate locations in the forest ahead. It was obvious to him that a number of campfires were burning. That was all he needed to know. Signaling silently to his companion, he withdrew, and Rob followed.

They faced a dilemma when they reached the body of the Sioux sentinel whom Toby had killed. If they left his body lying on the ground, it was sure to be discovered by his fellow sentries, and an alarm undoubtedly would be given. Toby looked down at the body that the shepherd dog was continuing to guard, then glanced at Rob and shrugged. They bent down and picked up the brave, with Toby hoisting the body over his shoulder, then made their way slowly back to their horses.

Placing the dead Indian in Toby's saddle, they started back in the direction from which they had come. After they had gone no more than a mile or two, however, Toby pointed ahead, and Rob nodded. They understood one another perfectly.

Looming ahead was a cliff with a drop of at least one thousand feet beyond its edge. The spot was perfect for their purposes, and without further ado they approached the edge, then carried the body to the cliff and threw it as far as they could into the void. Neither looked down, but Toby smiled grimly when he heard a distant thudding crash that indicated the body had landed below.

It would be difficult, at best, for the Indians to retrieve the body of their fallen comrade from the base of the cliff, and even if they succeeded in such an effort, it was unlikely they would discover that he had been killed with a knife. His body would be badly battered from the fall, and they would think that he had misjudged his distances in some way and had stepped into thin air and then fallen to his doom.

Their unsavory task accomplished, Toby and Rob mounted their horses, and with Mr. Blake now frolicking more freely, they descended from the highlands into the lower, rolling hill country. They arrived at the plateau just in time to meet the other scouts at the rendezvous, and then the reunited troop set out with all possible speed for Fort Shaw.

It was late the next night when they finally reached the fort and promptly adjourned with Colonel Andy Brentwood to the officers' mess, where hot meals awaited them. While they ate, they described what they had seen in the hidden valley, and Andy leaned forward anxiously.

"You think, then, that you've discovered the principal bivouac area of the Sioux," Andy said.

Toby and Rob exchanged a glance, and the former shrugged. "I have no way of knowing whether it's their main camp or not. All I can tell you for sure is that there were at least half a dozen campfires burning in those woods, and that means that one whale of a lot of warriors are hiding out there."

Andy drew in a deep breath. "Obviously, if you had seen any sign of our wives, you'd have mentioned it right off," he said in a heavy voice.

"Obviously," Rob replied curtly.

"We have no idea where they're being held, and we have no way of even guessing," Toby said. "It stands to reason that they'd be wherever the main body of Sioux warriors are bivouacked, but in a situation like this, logic doesn't necessarily apply."

"All we can do," Rob added, "is to hope they're there and try to rescue them when the time comes."

"The time is coming in a mighty hurry now," Andy said, and while his companions devoured their steaks served with potatoes, bread and butter, and salad greens, he unrolled a map. "Can you show me the precise location of this valley on the map?"

"You bet," Toby replied, touching the appropriate spot with the sharp tip of his knife.

Andy pulled an oil lamp closer and carefully scrutinized the map. "If this representation is accurate," he said, "the terrain is far too hilly to send cavalry into the valley."

"There's no doubt of that," Toby told him. "Attackers would have hell's own time getting in there, and even the defenders would have a rough time, including those who are mounted on the small Indian horses."

"What do you suggest, then?" Andy asked.

"We'll have to go in on foot," Rob said flatly. "It's the only way."

"I'm afraid that's about the size of it, Colonel," Toby said. "This is one time that horses won't do us too much good."

Andy frowned as he continued to scrutinize the map. "Am I right in assuming that the valley is roughly shaped like a long bowl?"

"Yes, sir," Toby replied. "That's a pretty accurate description."

"Suppose, then," Andy said, "that I send about one-third of our troops into the valley on foot, and that along with the regulars, I include every Montana militiaman who has volunteered for service. That'll give me about four hundred men in all.

"This makeshift infantry will penetrate into the mouth of the valley as far as they can manage; then they'll split into two groups, each unit flanking one or the other side of the bowl. That is, two hundred of them will infiltrate to the left, and the other two hundred will go to the right. The two groups will try to get their formations as close to the opposite end of the valley as possible; then they'll swoop down in a united attack."

"I'm not so sure that four hundred men are enough to do the trick," Toby said. "It depends on whether or not Thunder Cloud has his entire force in the valley."

"Hold on a minute or two," Andy said, "and let me finish. These four hundred foot soldiers will make hell's own noise. They'll fire their rifles until they run out of ammunition. Their object is to flush out the Indians."

"That's sound thinking," Toby said approvingly. "My pa always said that Indians are a good deal like a herd of buffalo. Once you fill them full of a sense of panic, they'll stampede."

"Exactly the tactics that I have in mind," Andy said. "The two units will exert as much pressure on the flanks as they possibly can. I hope the Sioux will explode in the center, so to speak. They'll want to get away from those pressures, and they'll try to leave the valley—preferably on their horses. They'll stream out of the opening at the head of the valley, and beyond that, if this map is accurate, there's a large plateau."

Toby nodded, and Rob chortled. "I think you've hit on it, Colonel," he said.

"There are a great many boulders and smaller rocks scattered on the plateau," Toby said, "but all the same, it's an area where cavalry can operate."

Andy smiled faintly. "I'll have the bulk of the cavalry waiting as a reception committee there for the Indians, after they've been driven out of the valley by the foot soldiers. What do you think?"

"I can see some possible flaws," Toby said thoughtfully, "but none of them are necessarily serious. Everything considered, I think it's a sound plan."

"Very well, gentlemen," the colonel said crisply, "that's our plan, and I'll pass the word along to battalion and troop commanders. We'll leave at daybreak tomorrow, so I urge you to get some sleep. You'll be badly needed for purposes that I'll outline to you tomorrow. But you won't be worth a lead nickel to me if you don't get some rest first."

The small troop of scouts was in the lead, following a simple directive. "We'll advance into the valley ahead of the infantry," Toby told his men, "and we'll follow the principle of trying to maintain secrecy as long as possible. The farther we can creep into the valley along the flanks of the Indians, the better we'll be in a position to drive them out. So kill the sentries silently, but don't use firearms. This is a situation that calls for knives and axes and strips of rawhide that you can use as garrotes. Just remember that a single shot is all that is needed to spoil the element of surprise."

Andy Brentwood had suggested it might be wise to leave the dog behind, but Toby had protested. "I'm sorry, sir," he said, "but Mr. Blake is a full-fledged scout, and he goes where we go."

Andy did not press his point.

Prior to the action, Toby and Rob made a careful analysis of the enemy dispositions and decided that the sentinels posted by the Sioux undoubtedly would be

clustered in the forest at the entrance to the valley. It
would avail the Indians nothing to station their sentries
farther to the rear. Consequently, Toby and Rob determined that their best tactic would be to deploy all of
their scouts simultaneously, with the men ordered to dis-
able or kill all sentries they encountered.

This was done, and for the second time Toby and
Rob, along with the scouts, crept forward through the
underbrush searching for hidden foes.

Following the example set by their commander, the
veterans of the scout troop were as efficient as they were
ruthless. Three times Toby encountered a Sioux sentinel
and struck swiftly and surely. His throwing knives found
their targets, and the enemy sentinels were eliminated
before they could give an alarm. Now there was no
question of disposing of the bodies. Before they were
discovered, the attack would have begun.

Noting the technique used by their leaders,
whereby Rob acted as a decoy while Toby threw his
knives at the distracted target, the men of the scouting
unit followed their example, and the results they
achieved were equally effective. Had they chosen to uti-
lize such methods regularly, the Indians would have certainly caught on to the system and reacted accordingly.
But as a one-time system, the technique was beyond
reproach.

The secret of the operation, Toby knew, was to
keep moving, no matter what might happen. Thus, he
set a rapid pace, and his scouts spread out along the
breadth of the valley's entrance. They used their knives
to good advantage whenever they encountered a Sioux
sentry, but under no circumstances did they pause or
hesitate.

As Toby well knew, luck was playing a major role

in the enterprise. There were scores of ways in which a
sentry stationed by the Indians in the forest could have
become aware of the approach of a large body of attackers and could have given the alarm. But with his own
ability to detect the whereabouts of sentries, and with
Mr. Blake also alerting him to the presence of Indians,
Toby and his subordinates managed to get through un-
detected.

He would have been happy had they penetrated no
farther than one hundred yards into the valley before
their presence was discovered. As it happened, however,
they were able to travel almost three times that distance
before a sentinel, whom no scout saw in time, raised his
voice in a loud, prolonged war whoop that alerted his
colleagues to the extreme danger they faced.

The infantry was massed directly behind the lead
unit, following close on the heels of the scouts, and
when the Sioux sentinel raised his voice, the need for
silence vanished.

Then, in accordance with the prearranged plan, the
scouts split into two units, half of the men swinging to
the left flank behind Toby and Rob, while the remainder
followed their first sergeant, Dan McDevitt.

The infantry also broke into two augmented companies, each of them under the command of a major. Their
rifles ready for instant discharge, the dismounted troopers maintained loose formations as they ran on either
flank toward the rear of the valley.

The whine of arrows, sounding like a swarm of angry bees, told Toby that the Sioux were rallying to their
own defense and were initiating a move to repel the invaders. "Spread out and take cover!" he called, and following his own advice, he dropped to the ground and

tried to locate the most persistent of the enemy marksmen.

The infantry moved up to bolster the scouts and eventually to replace them. The task of Toby's men was now accomplished, and for all practical purposes, they would be absorbed henceforth into the infantry companies.

Toby had good reason to be satisfied with the performance of his scouts. They had achieved what had been required of them and had fulfilled their mission brilliantly. They had led the foot soldiers into the valley without being detected and had moved into a position so the infantry could conduct a major thrust. They had, in brief, done everything that Colonel Brentwood had asked of them.

But Toby felt no sense of accomplishment. He still had no idea whether his wife and the others who had been made prisoner were being held somewhere in the valley or were being incarcerated elsewhere, and, at least for the moment, he had no way of learning anything more about their situation.

He and Rob had a far more difficult and complex assignment now: They were relieved of all other responsibilities in order to locate the captives and, if possible, set them free. For the moment, however, the pair could do nothing to further that goal. Mr. Blake, too, could not be sent out to find his mistress and her companions. They were tied down, forced to remain where they were in the forest by a large and determined force of braves, who were doing their utmost to repel the invaders who had sneaked into their sanctuary.

The air overhead was filled with arrows, and the intermittent sounds of rifle fire to the left, to the right, and behind Toby and Rob indicated that the infantrymen were responding vigorously.

It would not only accomplish nothing to push ahead into the enemy lines now, but it was also too dangerous to do so. If Toby and Rob tried to advance farther without the enemy being weakened first, they could be killed or severely wounded by the arrows or even the thrown lances or tomahawks of the warriors.

Raising his rifle to his shoulder, his elbows resting on the ground, Toby looked down the length of the barrel and waited patiently. He was rewarded when he saw a movement in the underbrush about thirty yards ahead, and he knew he was right when an arrow emerged, as if from nowhere, out of a clump of bushes. He took careful aim and squeezed the trigger.

Even above the increasing din of the battle, he heard the scream of the mortally wounded warrior. That was one less brave who stood between him and Clarissa!

Gray Wolf cursed his fate as he stood guard duty in the early morning sun. Other war chiefs roamed through the mountains and the hill country of Montana searching for game. At the very least, they directed the activities of fishing parties that provided the army of braves with food. Some were in charge of the horses that the Sioux rode, and still others directed the war games that the army utilized in order to keep ready for the coming emergency. But Gray Wolf's present lot in life was guarding a group of whites who acted more like captors than captives.

There was no doubt in the minds of Thunder Cloud and his war chiefs that the time for decisive action was fast approaching. Thunder Cloud had delivered his ultimatum, and the leader of the white soldiers had de-

livered his. Now they were about to engage in a fight to
the death.

Let the soldiers come, Gray Wolf thought; we will
take care of them when the time comes. In the meantime, however, he regretted his own inactivity, his inability to participate in full measure in the war
preparations of the Sioux. It was as though he were
hobbled, as though his hands and ankles were tied with
stout thongs.

The accursed captives were responsible. How he
hated them! He despised the three young women, none
of whom behaved in a manner that the Sioux regarded
as seemly, and he felt nothing but contempt for the
young boy who was their companion, even though he
had been told that the youth was a remarkable rifle shot.

Gray Wolf heartily agreed with those of his comrades who said that the captives were a burden on the
Sioux and should be killed. Those who argued in the
councils of war that no good was being accomplished by
preserving the lives of the prisoners were right. The
chief of the army at Fort Shaw had been notified that
his wife and the other two women were prisoners and
would suffer accordingly if full-scale war broke out.
Well, perhaps there wouldn't be any war at all—perhaps
the army troops would call off their campaign completely—when they received first one, then another of
the bodies of the hostages. And when the time came for
the killing, it would be Gray Wolf who would be per-
mitted to sink his knife into the hearts of the captives,
one by one. Soon thereafter he would add four scalps to
those already dangling from his belt. The prospect was
pleasing.

Glancing idly at the captives, Gray Wolf saw they
were standing on the bank of the stream, busily washing

up. He resented them, he guessed, because they paid no attention to the three braves who stood guard over them with ancient muskets. In fact, they acted as though their guards didn't exist; they were chatting gaily and laughing, and even the young boy giggled and nodded at their humor.

Suddenly the ominous crackle of rifle fire interrupted the war chief's reverie, and Gray Wolf was instantly alert. To his astonishment, the fire sounded to the left and to the right, too.

The three young women paused in their ablutions and stared at each other, equally stunned. Only young Hank Purcell was grinning broadly.

Gray Wolf needed no one to tell him the meaning of that gunfire. The inevitable had happened; the army troops from Fort Shaw had successfully invaded the hidden valley, somehow passing the outposts of sentries who had been selected for their duty because they were so alert.

There was no time to lose. Gray Wolf was quietly grateful for the foresight of Thunder Cloud, who had prepared a contingency plan to be followed in the event that a surprise attack should take place.

An angry shout from Gray Wolf aroused the three guards, who stood listening in open-mouthed wonder to the barrage of rifle fire. Giving the captives no time to protest the treatment they were being accorded, Gray Wolf had the guards surround them and, with himself bringing up the rear, directing operations, started off into the woods with them.

Beth Martin, as always, spoke her mind and accused her captors of barbaric behavior. But Gray Wolf was in no mood for the sound of the young woman's voice, and he gestured sharply, angrily, with his toma-hawk.

Clarissa knew she would have to intervene before her friend went too far. "You'd best be careful, Beth," she murmured. "Our keeper is furious."

"Small wonder," Beth replied. "It appears that the cavalry has found the hiding place of the Sioux."

"Quiet!" Gray Wolf shouted, making himself heard above the thunder of the rifle fire. "You will not talk!"

Susanna sensed that there was a strong hint of des-peration in his mood, and she gestured to her compan-ions to heed his wishes.

Breathless and stumbling, occasionally sent sprawl-ing by a hidden tree root, the three women and the boy were herded unceremoniously through the forest, the sounds of battle plain on both flanks of the Indian posi-tion.

At last they came to the base of a cliff and followed a course parallel to it for a considerable distance. Then the guards stood aside, and Gray Wolf gestured impa-tiently to the captives. "You go inside!" he ordered.

They had no idea what he meant, but Susanna, star-ing hard at the wall of solid granite beside her, suddenly saw an opening in the rocks and understood. "It's a cave," she said. "They want us to go inside."

Gray Wolf herded them into the entrance to the cave. The light in the interior was dim, but the war chief did not waste the time to light a bundle of rushes to use for illumination. Instead, still gesturing men-acingly with his tomahawk, he kept them in motion ahead of him.

The light that seeped in through the entrance was increasingly dim as they penetrated deeper into the in-terior, and Susanna was forced to slow her pace to a crawl. She planted one foot in front of the other on the hard, pebble-covered flooring of the cavern, and only when she was sure of her footing did she advance step by step.

Clarissa suggested they clasp hands, and the idea met with instant approval.

They heard a faint but distinct rustling sound overhead, and Beth, quietly fearing the presence of bats in the interior of the cave, covered her long blond hair with her free hand. To her credit, however, she neither expressed her fears aloud, nor did she give in to a sense of panic. She would not give Gray Wolf the satisfaction of seeing that she was very much afraid.

As they penetrated deeper and deeper into the interior of the cave, Clarissa found herself automatically counting the number of strides that she was taking. She half sensed, half heard Hank, who was gripping her left hand tightly and doing the same thing. At the very worst, they would have some idea of how far they were from the cavern entrance.

The sounds of the battle raging in the forest could be heard only faintly, and Clarissa realized that the Sioux high command was being very shrewd in its treatment of the captives. They were completely concealed from view now, and it seemed unlikely that any of the cavalry troopers could find them, much less rescue them.

To the amazement of Susanna, who was in the lead, the light grew brighter, and she discovered they were in a large cavern with a high ceiling and walls that dripped with moisture. Overhead was an opening, perhaps two or three inches in circumference, in the ceiling of the cave. As nearly as she could gather on this cursory examination, the hole opened aboveground, enabling the

light of day to seep into the cavern below the surface of
the earth. In any event, the opening was convenient because it made the use of candles for illumination unnecessary.

Gray Wolf issued specific orders in a curt, harsh
voice. "You will stay here in the cave," he said, "until I
return for you. Warriors will guard the entrance to the
cave. If you prisoners try to leave, the warriors will
shoot to kill with muskets. It is better if you prisoners
obey and stay here until I come back." Nodding grimly,
he looked at each of the captives in turn, then left, his
moccasins making no sound on the floor of the cave as
he took his departure.

The quartet instinctively huddled close together in
the small, relatively bright pool of light cast by the hole
in the ceiling of the cavern. For what seemed like a long
time, no one spoke.

Then Susanna Brentwood broke the silence. "Our
prayers have been answered," she said. "My husband
has been as busy as I assumed he would be, and his regiment has found the hiding place of the Sioux and is attacking it."

"I've dreamed of this day," Beth said, laughing bitterly. "But I had no idea that when it came I'd be hidden away so that no one in the regiment knows whether
I'm alive or dead."

"And none of us knowing, either, what the Indians
have in store for us," Hank Purcell said morbidly.

"I'll grant you the Indians are clever," Clarissa said,
"but they may be a mite too clever for their own good.
It strikes me they have outsmarted themselves."

"What do you mean?" Susanna demanded.

Hank seemed to grasp Clarissa's meaning at once,
and he came to life again. "That there hole," he said,

pointing to the small opening in the ceiling, "leads to a
place where there isn't a tree around. It's a nice open
area, and to judge from the shape of the roof of this
place, it's kind of flat, too."

Beth immediately challenged him. "How do you
know there are no trees in the vicinity of the hole?" she
demanded.

Clarissa peered thoughtfully at the light that
flooded through the small opening. "I believe I know,"
she said. "If there were trees, they would block the light.
You can tell by the brightness and intensity that it must
be direct sunlight."

"Exactly," Susanna declared.

"Let's assume your supposition is accurate," Beth
said. "What of it? I fail to see anything significant in it."

"We have no idea what may be above us on the
ground," Susanna said. "Inasmuch as the Sioux took
great care to conceal themselves in the forests of the valley, I'd say it's a fairly good bet that they've avoided an
open place, such as the one that's above us now.
Whether there are troops stationed anywhere near the
opening is impossible to judge, and there's no way we
can look out."

Hank looked up at the ceiling and shook his head
regretfully. "Even if you were to stand on Clarissa's
shoulders," he told Susanna, "and somehow I managed
to balance on your shoulders, I still don't think I'd be
able to reach that high."

Beth's shrug and sigh of exasperation expressed her
sentiments far better than she could have done in words.

"Hold on a minute," Clarissa said, and seemed lost
in thought. "If it's true, as I assume it must be, that
there's an open area directly above us, then there's at

least a chance that some members of the regiment will be stationed not far from there. So our job, it seems to me, is to find some way to signal to them that we're being held here."

Hearing the continuing rattle of rifle fire in the distance, Beth said, "Quite plainly, it would do us no good to shout in unison. The gunfire is too loud."

"The simplest and most direct way," Clarissa said thoughtfully, "would be to build a fire in such a way that the fumes go up through the opening."

Beth looked at her scornfully. "How on earth are we ever going to build a fire here?" she demanded.

The freckles that dusted Hank's face seemed to merge when he grinned. "That isn't going to be near as hard as you think it is," he said. "You remember a couple of days ago that no-good Gray Wolf was bragging about all the property he'd grabbed when he last led a patrol against a settler's house?"

The young women nodded silently. Unfortunately they recalled the words of the war chief all too well.

The boy reached into a pocket and produced a handful of sturdy sulphur matches. "See these?" he asked. "I took them off Gray Wolf after he bragged how he swiped them from the settler's kitchen. I had no idea what we could do with them at the time, but I figured maybe they might come in useful, and anyway I didn't want him to have benefits from them."

Clarissa smiled softly. "This is the first time in my life," she said, "that I've ever congratulated anyone for stealing!"

Susanna reached into the apronlike front pocket of her dress in which she carried the precious notebook filled with her observations and her interviews for her coming book. "I'd be inclined to say that I'll be using this paper for a good cause—a better cause than using these notes for my book." She took a match from Hank, struck it on the sole of her shoe, then carefully set fire to the notebook, moving it from one location to another until she was certain that the plume of smoke it sent up rose directly to the opening and disappeared from the sight of those in the cavern.

"That paper won't burn very long," Clarissa said. "We'll need something more."

"There isn't a scrap of wood or anything else flammable in this cave," Beth said in disgust. "You can bet on that!"

Clarissa took a small handkerchief from her sleeve and carefully added it to the flames. "This isn't much," she said, "but it will help."

"So will this," Hank added, and threw a large, crumpled bandanna that he took from his hip pocket, onto the fire.

"We can contribute our petticoats," Susanna said to Clarissa and Beth, and nimbly stepping out of her underskirt, she began to shred it. The other women realized this made good sense and immediately followed suit, adding the strips of their garments to the growing fire. Suddenly Susanna paused in her efforts and pointed toward Beth. "Your stockings! They'll help."

"So they will," Beth said, and bending down, removed them.

A column of black smoke began to rise from the built-up fire. Some of the fumes escaped into the cavern, and the captives began to cough.

"Oh, dear," Susanna murmured. "It didn't occur to me we'd be depriving ourselves of air."

Clarissa had a coughing spasm and then sucked air into her lungs, "I think," she said, "we'd better move toward the entrance to the cave. It's darker there, but at least we'll be able to breathe!"

The others agreed, and leaving the fire burning behind them, they began to move in single file back in the direction from which they had come.

The dismounted troopers and Montana militiamen on the left flank of the Indians' roughly drawn defense perimeter maintained a steady rifle fire, shooting whenever they saw the slightest movement in the forest directly ahead of them. They were following the example of Toby Holt and Rob Martin, whose experience in Indian warfare convinced them that they were doing the right thing.

Ultimately their tactic succeeded, partly because their marksmanship was superior and in part because the Sioux, who were profligate in their use of arrows, began to run out of ammunition.

The first sign that a break was at hand came when a heavy flurry of arrows filled the air. Simultaneously there seemed to be considerable movement within the enemy lines.

"Major!" Toby called to the sector commander. "I think the braves are pulling out and are covering their withdrawal with heavier than usual fire."

The officer commanding the left flank agreed and set his troops in motion. "Advance, boys!" he called. "And pump them so full of lead that they won't try to halt you!"

The rate of rifle fire increased markedly, and the troops moved forward, individuals racing from tree to boulder, and tree to tree, concealing themselves as best they could while nevertheless advancing steadily.

Toby and Rob went forward with the first wave.

With Mr. Blake at their heels, they ran jagged courses, dashing from the shelter of a tree trunk to that of a large bush, then advancing to the near side of a heavy boulder. The whole point of the operation was that they continue to move forward, no matter how heavy the arrow fire of the enemy. If they succeeded in this, they knew, the Sioux line eventually would collapse, and the defenders would retire in panic, thus perhaps setting off a chain reaction that could mean victory for the Eleventh Cavalry.

Toby and Rob were not concerned with the question of victory or defeat, however. They were concentrating their full attention on trying to locate their wives and the other captives, and they appeared to have a hopeless task. Off to their right was a barren, treeless area, the ground covered with moss, and they took care to avoid it because of the absence of cover there to protect them from enemy arrows. A small fire appeared to be burning in the middle of the open field, and Toby, noting it absently, assumed that the Sioux might be using flaming arrows now in an attempt to hold off the advance of the soldiers. It would be wise, he thought, to be prepared for this added danger.

Suddenly Mr. Blake moved forward, out into the open. His ears were pricked up, and he was sniffing the air. Toby, alarmed, began to call out to his dog, but even as he did so, a thick stream of arrows came out of the trees. Before Mr. Blake could run back to safety, he was struck in the side, and to Toby's horror, the dog stumbled, then collapsed on the ground.

"I've got to get Mr. Blake!" he shouted. Rob tried to hold him back, but Toby broke free and ran out into the open, ignoring the danger. Another volley of arrows flew from the trees, but Toby, crouching low, was not hit. In an instant he was by the side of his dog, and lifting him in his arms, he dashed back to the cover of the trees.

Gently Toby put Mr. Blake down and removed the arrow. Rob stood over them, watching the scene, praying silently that the wound was not serious. Though hurt, the shepherd dog was still conscious, and as Toby ripped his bandanna into strips and tied them around the dog's middle, Mr. Blake looked up at his master and feebly wagged his tail.

"Now save your strength, Mr. Blake," Toby said quietly. "You're going to be all right. We'll take you to an army doctor who will look after you."

Toby carefully lifted the dog in his arms, and with Rob in the lead, they made their way back to the rear of the infantry lines. The dog occasionally licked his master's arm, and Toby, worried about the condition of the animal, was too distracted even to wonder why Mr. Blake had gone out into the open in the first place.

So it happened that Toby and Rob had passed within a few feet of the hole that led to the cavern where their wives, Susanna, and Hank were being held hostage. Mr. Blake had detected their presence, but because an arrow had shot him down, the brave dog had been unable to alert his master.

Clasping hands in the dim passageway, the captives groped their way toward the entrance to the cave. Again they heard a muted rustling sound of bats overhead, and the terrified Beth again clasped her hair but refused to cry out or to give an alarm.

Turning a bend in the passageway, the quartet stopped short. The cave entrance was directly ahead of them now, and plainly visible in the daylight were the three familiar Sioux who guarded them. Gray Wolf was not among them.

The warriors had no idea their charges were near at hand. In fact, all three were totally absorbed in watching the progress of the battle on the far side of the clearing. As nearly as they could make out, their brothers were being forced backward, and they longed to take part in the fray themselves, but they knew they would be punished severely by Gray Wolf if they deserted their posts. They had to content themselves with merely watching.

The realization dawned slowly on the prisoners that they remained unobserved, for the three warriors appeared to be completely absorbed in whatever it was they were watching. One of them walked far away into the open, leaving the other two standing just inside the cave entrance.

A glittering prize lay temptingly within reach on the floor of the cavern, and Hank Purcell's heart beat wildly when he saw it. There, lying on the ground, was a musket that belonged to one of the guards.

Granted, the weapon was old-fashioned and rather clumsy. From a distance it looked as though it dated back more than two decades to the Mexican War, and it could hardly equal the infinitely more accurate rifles of Civil War vintage that the Eleventh Cavalry carried. Nevertheless, as Hank knew all too well, it was a weapon that commanded respect, and if he could gain possession of it, he might be able to turn the tide on their captors.

The boy tapped Clarissa on the arm and pointed. She saw the musket and, realizing his intention, caught her breath. Susanna and Beth became aware of the weapon's presence and of the boy's intentions, too, but they could not in good conscience try to halt him, no matter how great the risks involved. If they could give their captors the slip during the heat and confusion of battle, there was always at least a chance that they might make good their escape. But if they remained helplessly in the hands of their captors, their future promised to be bleak. At any moment the Indians could come for the hostages and use them in an eleventh-hour measure to hold off their attackers. That meant death for at least one of them, and perhaps for all. Therefore, Susanna thought, it was best to let Hank do what he could to alter their situation, and she nodded slowly in approval.

The boy moved toward the near wall of the cave and, dropping to his hands and knees, began to crawl toward the musket.

The attention of the women was riveted on the two Sioux guards who stood in the entrance. Their companion, who was out in the open, was much too far removed from the scene to be of any concern.

Hank drew closer, then closer still, to his goal.

All at once one of the guards stirred. Perhaps he caught a glimpse of the boy's careful movement out of the corner of an eye; or possibly the attention of the young women that was riveted on him aroused his consciousness. Whatever the reason, he turned.

The Sioux saw the three young women standing together, which surprised him, but he did not yet notice Hank, who was crawling still closer to the musket and had almost reached it.

Beth Martin knew that something would have to be done to attract and hold the attention of the warrior until Hank had the weapon safely in his grasp. She had to do something!

Her mind seemed paralyzed, incapable of rational thought. So she acted instinctively.

Her inner tension and fright were so great that she was numb, incapable of feeling, as she slowly raised her icy fingers to the top button of her blouse and slowly opened it.

The warrior gaped at her, scarcely able to reconcile what he was seeing with reality. The pale-haired young woman, whom he and his companions secretly admired because she was different from the squaws of the Sioux, was smiling at him seductively, and her hands slid to the second button of her blouse. Inconceivable though it seemed, she appeared to be on the verge of baring her breasts for his benefit. He continued to watch her in dazed wonder.

Hank Purcell lunged forward and had the musket in his grasp. He knew at a glance that it was loaded, and although he had not been reared religiously, he thanked the Almighty as he rose to one knee, took aim at the gaping warrior, and squeezed the trigger.

The shot made an ear-splitting noise as it echoed back through the vaulted cave. Perhaps the musket was old-fashioned, but it was still a deadly weapon when wielded by a gunslinger of Hank's proficiency. The bullet slammed into the left side of the brave's chest, and he clutched his body in sudden agony, then slumped to the floor and died.

As Hank well knew, there was no time to lose. He had no opportunity to get ammunition and gunpowder from the supply that the dead brave carried, so he had to do the next best thing. Grasping the long musket by its hot barrel, he leaped to his feet and, wielding it like a club, swung it in a vicious arc as he raced toward the second of the guards, who had turned in amazement at the sound of the musket shot behind him.

Too late, the warrior recognized his danger. He raised a hand in order to ward off the blow, but he could not stop it, and the heavy oak butt of the musket crashed into his head, felling him instantly and sending him sprawling.

Clarissa Holt knew only that Hank desperately needed help, that it was unreasonable to expect a boy in his mid-teens to face and defeat three adult Sioux warriors unaided. Hardly aware of what she was doing, she picked up her skirt, gathering it around her with one hand, and raced forward. Not until much later did she recall precisely what she had done, and then she was filled with amazement because none of her actions were planned.

Scarcely pausing in her dash, she reached down and plucked a double-edged, bone-handled knife from the belt of the brave whom Hank had shot. Grasping it tightly by the hilt, she moved forward a few paces to the body of the second brave. He was unconscious but was stirring, and it was apparent that within a few moments he would be able to regain his feet.

With no time to lose, Clarissa unhesitatingly plunged the sharp blade into the warrior's heart.

Even when she later recalled the incident in full detail, she had to admit to herself that she felt nothing as she killed him in cold blood. Never before in her life had she attacked, much less murdered, another human being. But in this precarious situation, it was either kill or be killed, and she disposed of the savage without regret and without remorse.

In the meantime, Hank found the ammunition and powder horn of the warrior he had shot, and quickly, with his fingers flying nimbly, he reloaded the weapon. Then he stood, his feet apart, and took aim at the back of the head of the third warrior, who was still quite a distance away, engrossed in the noisy battle being fought before his eyes, unable to hear what was taking place behind him.

The brave never knew what hit him. He died from a bullet that penetrated his brain from the rear.

Hank ran out into the open and retrieved the third brave's musket and knife, as well as the musket of the brave who had been killed by Clarissa. Going back into the cave, he distributed the weapons to the young women, and no one could blame him if there was a boastful note in his voice as he said, "I reckon now we'll be fighting on more even terms."

Directly ahead, beyond the open patch, lay a heavily wooded section, and there a battle was raging fiercely. The young women and the boy could hear the steady roar of rifle fire, and occasionally they caught a glimpse of arrows flashing through the air, but they could see nothing of the combatants.

One unfortunate fact, however, could easily be surmised. The Sioux would be directly ahead, and beyond them would be the U.S. Army troops. In other words, the group nearest to the quartet was comprised of their captors. Consequently, they knew that, as yet, they were far from having achieved even a measure of safety.

They stood indecisively for several moments, and then Beth suddenly called, "Come on!" Picking up her voluminous skirts, she dashed across the open space above the cave where they had been incarcerated.

The others followed her and found her kneeling beside the hole from which smoke was still emerging in a thin, steady stream. The fire they had made below obviously was still burning.

Using a portion of her skirt to control the smoke, Beth held the cloth over the hole in the ground for several seconds, removed it, let the cloud of smoke escape, and then capped it again. She repeated the gesture again and again in no particular order.

"I'm taking the chance," she said, "that someone in the regiment will see this strange pattern of smoke signals and will be curious about their meaning. I do not know that anyone will pay any attention to what's happening, but it's worth the effort to find out."

The others agreed. "We had enough trouble making and building the fire," Susanna said. "We might as well try to use it for our own good now."

The troops engaged in a vicious battle in the forest did not see the irregular pattern of smoke puffs rising in the air. But, as luck would have it, several braves noted the strange phenomenon and were curious about it. Three of them detached themselves from the rear echelon of the Sioux formation in the woods and proceeded toward the open space in order to investigate.

Hank, who was quietly keeping watch, saw them coming and spoke urgently. "Get down, all of you!" he ordered. "Hug the ground! You will make less of a target that way than if you are standing up."

The women obeyed instantly, and Hank dropped to one knee beside them, peering down the barrel of a musket. "Mrs. Holt," he said urgently, "you seem pretty familiar with firearms. Do you reckon you can load a musket in one whale of a hurry?"

"I can certainly try," Clarissa replied, looking up at him.

"Good," the boy replied coolly. "I'll hand you a gun

as soon as I fire it, and you load it for me again. Keep loading them and handing them to me as fast as you can."

He suited action to words and squeezed the trigger. Hank's shot found its mark, and his bullet slammed into the shoulder of one of the warriors, wounding and incapacitating him.

The brave was courageous, however, and in spite of the pain he was suffering, he managed to crawl behind the trunk of an oak tree, which he used for cover, and somehow succeeded in fitting an arrow into his bow and letting fly with it. His companions, too, reacted swiftly. One ducked behind a boulder, and another took refuge behind the trunk of an evergreen. They were far from defeated.

Hank handed the musket he had fired to Clarissa, and she instantly gave him another, then reloaded the first. She was glad she could be of help to this astonishing young boy who somehow was able to maintain his poise, even though the odds against him were so great.

The warriors were cunning, making small, elusive targets of themselves, as they concentrated on the boy who was wielding the firearms and the young woman who was loading and reloading the weapons for him.

Hank managed to keep them at bay, but the effort required all of his skill and concentration. A musket shot chipped away the edge of the boulder behind which one of the warriors had taken refuge and removed a portion of the bark from the evergreen tree behind which another was hiding.

Hank's remarkable, almost uncanny aim kept the braves off balance, but all of them—including the one who had been wounded—sent arrows in the direction of the boy and the young woman who was assisting him.

As every one of the beleaguered quartet knew all too well, time was on the side of the Sioux. Sooner or later other warriors would become aware of what was happening and would join in the combat, and eventually the tiny force would be overwhelmed. As long as they were able to continue to fight, to hold the Indians at bay, a spark of hope remained. So they fought on, doggedly determined not to give in.

Sitting around a campfire on the plains of eastern Montana, Ma Hastings had reason to be well pleased with herself. The fine horses she had acquired from the Sioux had already been sold to a dealer from Virginia City, and the gang had never had more money, had never been in a better position. Best of all was that the Eleventh Cavalry was busily engaged in battle with the Sioux, so there was no one to stop Ma Hastings and her men from continuing to raid and plunder to their hearts' content.

Ma tore apart with her hands a piece of roasted chicken. "We're in the clover now," she said, smacking her lips. Ralph Hastings, who was sitting beside her, waiting for an opportunity to take a swig from his concealed bottle, said nothing in reply.

Suddenly the gang was alerted to the approach of two men on horseback. They all grabbed their guns and stood waiting, but it was soon clear that there was no cause for alarm. It was Clifford Hastings and one of the other gang members, who had been out on patrol, looking for a prosperous ranch house to attack.

"I got us a real plum," Clifford said as he dismounted, a big smile on his face. "Just half a day's ride from here—big house, lots o' good horses, and cattle and sheep, to boot."

Ma chuckled and turned her back to Ralph. "I do declare, Clifford, seein' you ride in just now, you were the spittin' image o' your pa."

Clifford laughed loudly and handed his horse over to one of the other men. "I guess I am at that," he said, and went to the cooking fire to help himself to some food.

Ma beamed as she watched him, and she was so absorbed that she took no notice as Ralph uncorked his bottle and took a long swig of gin. Someday, he silently vowed to himself as the alcohol began to numb his brain, he, too, would show his mother what kind of a man he was.

XI

Toby and Rob had brought the wounded shepherd dog to the army surgeon, working behind the lines. The man was already busily attending to the wounded fighting men, but Mr. Blake was fighting for the army, too, and he equally deserved the doctor's attention.

Luckily, the arrow had not punctured any vital organs, and the army doctor told Toby the dog would recover fully if he lay quietly for a few days. Bandaging Mr. Blake's wound and giving the dog a few sips of brandy to help him sleep, the doctor then handed the animal over to an orderly, who would see to it that Mr. Blake didn't move about, thus aggravating his wound. Toby and Rob felt confident the animal was in good hands, so, after gently patting his head and reassuring him, they returned to the front lines.

Shooting sporadically at the unseen enemy in the forest, Toby and Rob knew that the infantry on the left flank of the army's line had no real need for their assistance. The troops were doing better than holding their

own now, and it appeared likely that soon they would
have the Sioux where they wanted them.

Increasingly restless, Toby withdrew from the line,
aware that he had to take some definitive action soon to
try to discover the whereabouts of his wife and the other
captives. He edged toward the open area beyond the
forest, then paused as he waited for Rob Martin to catch
up with him.

Suddenly Toby cocked his head to one side and listened intently. "Well," he muttered, "did you hear that?"

Rob listened, too, and eventually made out the
sound of ragged rifle fire from somewhere beyond the
forest. There was no pattern to the discharges; a shot or
two sounded and was followed by some moments of
silence.

"That's not rifle fire," Toby said. "Those shots are
coming from a far older weapon than any of the regiment is using."

Rob grinned and shook his head. He wouldn't have
believed it possible that his friend could be endowed
with hearing so acute that he could tell the difference
between the sounds of modern rifle fire and the noise
made by older firearms.

"It's rather odd," Toby said. "I want to see what this
is all about." He made his way to the edge of the woods
and peered out across the open space. Rob came up
beside him and did the same.

They stared in open-mouthed astonishment, reacting
as though they had been struck by bolts of lightning.
There, no more than two hundred and fifty yards from
them across the open plateau, were Clarissa and Beth,
Susanna and young Hank. The boy was on one knee, firing muskets that Clarissa was loading for him, while a
trio of braves was concealed behind trees and a boulder.

The joy that Toby and Rob felt at finding their wives alive and healthy was transformed almost instantly into anxiety and anguish, however. A party of heavily armed braves had taken note of the combat just prior to its discovery by Toby and Rob, and a group of warriors moved into the open area, carefully taking cover behind natural obstacles as they formed a semicircle facing the beleaguered women and their youthful companion.

The Indian reinforcements numbered at least a dozen braves, and the odds against Hank and Clarissa became overwhelming. They had done superbly, managing to hold their own against the three braves whom they had been facing, but now they were hopelessly outnumbered.

Their courage did not desert them, however, and they did not give in to a natural impulse to flee from the scene. Instead, they continued to remain close to the ground, and Hank increased his rate of fire, with Clarissa frantically reloading muskets and handing them to him.

"I reckon our women and the boy could stand some help," Toby said softly as he swung his rifle to his shoulder.

Only those who witnessed Toby in action could truly believe and appreciate what they saw. The events of the next quarter of an hour did much to enlarge and solidify the growing legend of Toby Holt. He was a wild whirlwind, a human tornado that suddenly was unleashed on the Montana plateau.

Throwing himself to the ground, Toby fired three times before rising swiftly to his feet and running forward in a zigzag pattern. He again dropped to the ground and repeated his shots. His marksmanship was little short of uncanny. In fact, he disposed of two of the braves, killing each of them instantly, before the rest of the Sioux party actually realized that another force had entered the battle.

By this time Rob Martin had joined in the fray, too, and moved forward stolidly in a direct line, crouching as he ran, then dropping to one knee and firing his rifle and again advancing.

Susanna Brentwood was the first of the beleaguered quartet to become aware of the unexpected presence of reinforcements, and she grinned broadly as she announced that Toby and Rob had come to their aid.

Beth knew that her prayers had been answered. Not relaxing her own efforts, Clarissa smiled quietly as she again reloaded a musket for Hank. For the first time since the battle had begun, her hope soared. All things were possible to Toby, as she well knew, and with him participating in the fray, it was likely that they would emerge unharmed and victorious.

Hank continued to demonstrate his remarkable composure, and firing at yet another warrior, he brought him down, wounding him severely.

The tactics that Toby adopted were so daring, they were breathtaking. He instinctively headed for the center of the Sioux formation, realizing that if he could make a dent in the middle of the line, the flanks necessarily would buckle.

His height and build were similar to his father's, and he bore a strong resemblance to him, so it was small wonder that one of the mature Sioux warriors, gaping at the dervish who was firing steadily as he advanced toward them, gasped aloud, "The ghost of Whip Holt is upon us!"

Ghosts played a large role in the mythology of the

Sioux, and virtually every member of the nation believed that such creatures truly existed.

No shot had yet been fired at Rob or at Toby,
which accounted in large part for the rapidity of their
advance. But the braves failed to take this fact into consideration. The wild rifleman was firing with such accuracy that even the warriors who had never set eyes on
Whip Holt were ready to believe that his spirit had
materialized from the afterworld and was attacking
them.

But Toby was no ghost. He was very much flesh
and blood, and all the worry and anxiety he had felt for
days was released in the sudden spurt of action in which
he was engaging. As he drew nearer to the foe, he slung
his rifle over his shoulder, drew his revolvers, and fired
them simultaneously, then fired them again in the same
smooth, unending movement.

The petrified Sioux gaped at him, so frightened they
could not move.

This respite was of great help to Rob, and, on the
far side of the field, to young Hank. Both of them found
targets while the attention of the braves continued to be
riveted on Toby.

One of Toby's guns jammed. Rather than take time
to find the fault and correct it, he stuck the weapon into
its holster and drew one of his throwing knives. Taking
swift, careful aim, he threw it at a warrior who was
half-visible, crouching behind a boulder.

The high-pitched scream of pain and terror emitted
by the Sioux as he died echoed across the little plateau.

The unearthly sound of that agonized scream was
the last straw. The shaken Sioux survivors had no wish
to face the fury of Toby Holt further—regardless of
whether he was a flesh-and-blood man or a ghost. They

retreated hastily, disappearing into the forest. Their withdrawal was so abrupt that they failed to take their dead and wounded with them, which was unusual in battle for a nation that boasted of its ability to look after its own.

Toby raced the length of the plateau and, reaching down, pulled Clarissa to her feet, embracing her with his free arm as he kissed her. Then he greeted the others, as well, his eyes searching the edge of the woods for any sign that the Sioux were preparing to renew the battle.

Rob approached, too, and when he kissed Beth, her relief was so great that she responded to him with greater warmth and more emotion than she had displayed in many months.

As Toby well knew, explanations would have to wait. "We've got to get out of here and join forces with the troops before the Sioux come back," he said. "Their honor has suffered a blow, so you can be sure they'll return with enough reinforcements to overwhelm us."

He hastily organized the party, moving Hank to a forward position beside himself, placing the women in the center, and asking Rob to bring up the rear.

"Do exactly what I tell you, when I tell you," he said, "and there's a fair chance we'll get out of this scrape with our skins whole. Stay close behind me now, and if I go too fast for any one of you, don't be bashful. Just let me know, and if I have to, I'll carry you!"

He started off without further ado. Clarissa, managing with difficulty to remain close behind him, looked at him in wonder. It was typical of her husband, she thought, that he should take for granted the extraordinary role he was playing in their rescue. He was not the sort of person to regard himself as a hero. He was unique in all the world, and Clarissa loved him with all her heart.

Glancing at Beth, Clarissa saw that she, too, was gazing at Toby, and the expression in the other woman's eyes disturbed her. Granted that Toby deserved gratitude, but Rob was playing an active part in the rescue, too, although Beth didn't seem to know it. Her expression was almost a sure promise of trouble ahead if they emerged intact from this dangerous experience.

Toby plunged into the forest with Hank close beside him, the others following, and Clarissa had to devote her full attention to his movements in order to ensure that she could keep up with him. She marveled at his ingenuity and at his sixth sense.

More often than not he moved straight ahead, but sometimes he paused, then went either to one side or the other, and sometimes he doubled back on himself. The key to the erratic course he was taking, however, was that he drew ever nearer to the positions occupied by the troops, yet managed to avoid a direct confrontation with the Sioux. The walk seemed interminable, and Clarissa's skirt was torn by thorns, with brambles scratching her legs, but she had no real cause for objection. Not once did they encounter any Indians. Later, when she had more time to think about the whole adventure, this aspect seemed the most marvelous of all the deeds that Toby performed.

Eventually the party reached safety, moving inside the infantry's lines. Toby led his charges to the rear, where they were beyond the reach of the Sioux's lances and arrows. A courier was dispatched to carry the good news to Colonel Brentwood, and the former captives could at last rejoice in the certain knowledge that they had been saved.

They had virtually no opportunity to celebrate their deliverance, however. Almost as soon as they arrived behind the army lines, the infantry on both flanks managed to achieve the breakthrough that Colonel Brentwood had sought from the beginning of the engagement.

The foot soldiers punched gaping holes in the defensive cordon set up by the Indians, and the braves, true to their heritage, proved once again that although they could wage agile warfare on the offensive, they were sadly lacking in defense. They retreated so swiftly that their fall back soon amounted to a rout, and the infantry increased its pace accordingly.

In the confusion that followed, the warriors fled to the temporary corrals they had established deep in the woods, and there they mounted their horses, re-formed their ranks, and made a desperate effort to break out of the valley in which they were trapped.

Toby proved to be something of a magician, acquiring Indian horses for the women and for Hank. Then, surrounded by a platoon of Montana militiamen who were no longer needed in the operation, he and his charges followed the infantry toward the head of the valley.

Colonel Brentwood was relieved beyond measure when the courier brought him word that his wife was safe. But he had to postpone his reunion with her while he maneuvered for the climactic phase of the battle.

The pass that stood at the head of the valley opened onto a vast, rolling field, and there the bulk of the Eleventh Cavalry, mounted, armed, and ready for combat, awaited the fleeing Indians.

But Thunder Cloud was too wise, too experienced, too cunning, to be caught in so obvious a trap. The brilliant maneuvers that he devised were studied by future cavalry leaders at the United States Military Academy for the next generation. The most experienced Indian riders—with Gray Wolf among them—moved forward in unison, forming a phalanxlike wedge, as though they were going to attack the soldiers. Meanwhile, the bulk of the Sioux, including the women and children who had accompanied the warriors to this camp, followed them and dispersed on horseback as soon as they emerged from the pass. Shielded by their veteran comrades, the Indians were able to take advantage of the great speed of their small horses, and they managed to escape the wrath of the Eleventh Cavalry.

The troopers held their lines, waiting for the Indians to attack, but the Sioux veterans had no intention of engaging in battle. Their strategy was just a feint devised by Thunder Cloud, and what appeared to be an attacking Indian wedge turned into a retreat as soon as the leaders knew their people were safe.

The deeply chagrined Colonel Brentwood realized that although his foot soldiers had obtained a substantial lead, his horsemen had not been able to capitalize on it. Due to the generalship of Thunder Cloud and the riding skills of his subordinates, the Sioux had made good their escape. He could pursue them, to be sure, but such a gesture would be wrong, because he would not fire if women and children were among the braves.

Andy had to be content with the knowledge that even though the Sioux force had escaped, he still had won a firm victory by driving them out of their hidden valley. The power of the Indians in the Montana Territory was broken, and never again would the nation's warriors be able to conduct raids, killing and plundering at will from an inaccessible stronghold.

The casualties suffered by the cavalry were very light, approximately one-tenth of the number of dead and wounded that their foes had sustained. Mr. Blake, reunited with Toby and Clarissa, was still very sore, but he wagged his tail and even let out a little bark to let his master and mistress know he was going to be all right.

The troopers were tired after their long day of battle; Andy ordered them into bivouac for an overnight rest prior to their return to Fort Shaw. Only then did the colonel ride to the rear and seek his wife. He saw Susanna from a distance and rode to her, jumping to the ground and helping her to dismount. She melted into his arms, and those who witnessed their reunion smiled and were happy for them.

At last Andy turned to Toby Holt. "Thanks, Toby," he said. "I might have known you'd fulfill your assignment and save the lives of our wives. I just wish there were a half-dozen of you, because if there were, the Sioux would no longer exist as a military force."

The Eleventh Cavalry was on the march all the following day, the wounded, including Mr. Blake, riding in an empty supply wagon. The regiment paused late in the afternoon for a light meal and finally arrived at Fort Shaw soon after sundown. The troops were dismissed and would have a two-week rest before they were sent out once again, this time to put an end once and for all to the roving bandit gangs.

Toby and Clarissa were the first to reach the house that they called home on the fort's grounds. They brought Mr. Blake with them and made him comfortable on a blanket on the kitchen floor. They were delighted to see the dog had an appetite, and Toby fed him pieces of dried meat that Clarissa had taken from the larder and chopped up into small bits.

The hunger they felt for each other was too great to be expressed in words, and realizing that Mr. Blake was well taken care of and that they were truly alone, they retired to their bedchamber. There they exchanged a few words but soon indulged in lovemaking that was simultaneously passionate yet gentle, aggressive but mutually respectful.

Their yearning was at last satiated, and Clarissa, slipping into a robe, went down to the kitchen. The others were not yet at home, having gone to the Brentwood house, and she quickly made coffee, then returned to the bedchamber with a tray. There she and Toby at last were free to talk.

"I have a confession to make to you," he said, "and I hope you won't be offended. I've always had the highest regard for you, but I had to come within an eyelash of losing you before I realized how very much I love you."

"That's good to hear," Clarissa replied, smiling, "because all that's happened has solidified my love for you, too."

"Looking back," he said, "I realize now that something happened to me the very first time I saw you. It became stronger and stronger until it overwhelmed me, and I didn't even have the good sense to realize it."

She tried to interrupt, but he held up a hand to silence her. "Wait," he said, "let me finish. This isn't easy for me. First off," he said, "I was disturbed when Beth announced that she was going to marry Rob. You've got to understand that from the time that Beth and I were born our mothers decided it would be a grand idea if we married each other when we grew up, so we were thrown at each other constantly. But when I knew that she belonged to someone else—to my closest friend at that—I couldn't help wondering whether I'd made a mistake, whether I didn't really want her after all."

He was not telling Clarissa anything she didn't already know, but she wisely listened to him, nodding from time to time.

"Then my mother and General Blake decided they'd be married, and I guess you know how I felt about that. I felt as if I was on a racing horse that I couldn't get off. I didn't know whether I approved or whether I hated them because I thought they were being disloyal to my father. In fact, I'm still not sure of exactly where I stand on the question of their marriage."

Clarissa raised an eyebrow as she sipped her coffee but said nothing.

"Of course," Toby went on hurriedly, "I wish them all the best of everything in the world. I think Beth's refusal to have anything to do with them is forced and unnatural and causes unnecessary hard feelings. I wish my mother all the happiness in the world, and I want the same thing for General Blake. I've been keeping my own uncertainties to myself because what I really think and feel about them is irrelevant. I simply don't want to be the cause of any unhappiness on their part."

"That's wise of you, and thoughtful, too," Clarissa said.

"The important thing to me is you and me," Toby told her earnestly. "I'm aware of that as I've never been aware of a relationship in my life. I don't put my thoughts into words too well—that seems to be a failing of Holt men—but I know deep inside myself that you are responsible for any happiness that I know in this world." He reached for her hand.

Clarissa allowed him to take it. "You have no idea how I've waited to hear you say those words."

"My father once told me," Toby said, "that he almost let my mother slip away from him. I guess that's another failing of Holt men."

She grinned up at him. "No, you've come around quite nicely—and just in time."

He looked at her blankly.

"It's time," she said, "to tell you a secret that only the post doctor and I know. I'm going to have a baby."

He stared at her for a moment, then wrapped his arms around her and gingerly gave her a tentative hug and kiss.

Clarissa exploded in laughter. "I'm not going to break in two, you know," she said.

"You'll have to go back to Oregon right off," he said. "This wilderness is no place for you to have a baby."

"Where will you be?" she demanded.

"I'm not sure," Toby said. "Rob and I are almost finished with our surveying job for the railroad here in Montana. In fact, we've already laid out a preliminary route in the easternmost part of the territory, and all I've got to do is to check it over, which I can do in a trip of a few days' duration. Rob's wanted back in California to lay out the track for the western terminus of the Central Pacific Railroad. But I wouldn't be much use to him there."

"Why not?" she demanded.

He chuckled. "It's no reflection on my ability, so you needn't get huffy," he said. "The route through the California mountains has already been surveyed, so there's no need for a guide. That means maybe I can go back to the ranch in Oregon with you."

"Maybe?" she asked gently.

He drained his coffee cup, then ran a hand through his sandy-colored hair. "Well," he said, "just tonight when we left the Brentwoods off at their house on our way here, Andy said something about having a new assignment for me. He said he'd talk about it as soon as we get squared away on our present business."

"Do you have any idea what he has in mind?" Clarissa asked.

He shrugged and shook his head. "I have no idea, and it's useless to speculate. He'll spell it out for me when the time comes."

"Well," she said, "it's comforting to know that you don't have to accept. After all, you're a civilian again—or are you?"

He grinned at her. "You bet. I reverted to civilian status again the minute the ruckus with the Sioux ended."

"There's one issue we can settle now," Clarissa declared. "When we go back to Oregon, how do you react to the idea of our taking Hank Purcell with us?"

"I think that's just great!" Toby said earnestly. "As a matter of fact, I've been very much concerned about Hank's future."

"So have I," Clarissa replied. "He may be too old for us to adopt formally, but he's far too young to be left to his own devices."

"Particularly when he's as expert a shot as he's proved to be," Toby said soberly. "Montana is still a mighty rough country, and a boy who can shoot as well as Hank shoots could wind up becoming a professional gunslinger in no time at all."

"That's what I'm afraid of," she confessed.

"I think he has a crush on you," Toby said, chuckling. "It shouldn't be too hard to persuade him to come to Oregon with us."

"Well, he's in absolute awe of you," she told him. "In fact, your word is law to him. So we should have no problem in sending him to school, getting him to finish his education, and somehow supervising him sufficiently so he stays out of trouble until he's old enough to make his own way in the world."

Toby spoke soothingly. "Hank will not only come to Oregon with us, but he'll behave himself. I don't want you worrying about him. In fact, from now on I don't want you worrying about anything!"

The Holts were asleep by the time that Beth and Rob Martin, accompanied by young Hank, neared the house. Beth seemed slightly uncomfortable, as though unwilling to be alone with her husband, and she asked Hank if he was hungry, even though they had just dined at the Brentwoods.

The boy shook his head. "I ate double portions at supper tonight, but thanks all the same." He yawned and stretched. "I never thought I'd be looking forward to a night's sleep in a civilized feather bed, but that's what I've been thinking about all the same, and tonight I'm going to do it."

As they approached the house, they heard a man and a woman calling Rob's name from the direction of the parade ground, and Rob turned to see who was hailing him.

"It's the Randalls, the cousins I told you about from Baltimore," he explained to Beth. "Come, let me introduce you to them."

"I'm in no mood to meet strangers now, thanks all the same," Beth said impatiently. "Come along, Hank."

Without further ado she hurried into the house, with young Hank trailing after her.

Rob removed his hat and took the hand that Millicent Randall extended to him. Then he released it and shook Jim Randall's hand.

"We've heard your good news about the recovery of your wife, and we're delighted for you, Mr. Martin," Jim said warmly.

"Thanks very much," Rob replied.

"Be sure and tell Mr. Holt how pleased we are that Mrs. Holt is alive and well, too," Millicent added.

"I certainly will," Rob said.

"We know you have better ways of occupying your time than to stand here chatting with us," Millicent said, "so I'll make this brief. It may interest you and Mr. Holt to know that we've decided to stay in the West for a time."

"That's good!" Rob replied enthusiastically.

"We think so," Millicent said. "Neither of us has any pressing reason to return to Baltimore, at least for the present, and fortunately we have sufficient funds to indulge our whims. So we intend to see San Francisco and Portland and the Washington Territory, and if it isn't too inhospitable, we may even travel down to the southern portion of California, as well."

"What my cousin has failed to mention," Jim said softly, "is that she has written to General Blake, asking him to hold Major Jentry's remains at Fort Vancouver."

"That's right," Millicent said. "He had no family back East, and I've decided that I want him buried at the headquarters post. He was assigned to duty in the West, and I think it's only fitting that he be buried in the West."

Rob nodded, struck by her sensitivity. "When will the burial service be held?" he asked.

"I'm not sure," Millicent replied. "It depends on our schedule, and that's still fairly uncertain at the moment. All we know for sure is that we've accepted Colonel Brentwood's hospitality for far too long. He's sending a small military unit to Fort Vancouver in the next day or two with dispatches relating to your battle against the Sioux, and he's told us we're more than welcome to join the group. So we'll be leaving for the Pacific Coast in the immediate future."

"I hope our paths cross again," Rob said, and meant it. He was mildly astonished to discover that Millicent Randall wasn't as plain in appearance as he had thought when he and Toby had first met her. On the contrary, she not only had an exceptionally attractive figure, but her character was stamped in her face and she had an inner glow, a radiance that most young women lacked.

Rob again shook hands with Jim, then took Millicent's hand and held it longer than custom deemed appropriate. As the cousins turned and walked away across the parade ground, he watched them as they disappeared into the night and felt a strange tug, a sense of loss.

Then he sighed, took a deep breath, and followed Beth into the house. Hank had already gone to bed, and Rob and Beth were alone. "Do you want some coffee?" he asked.

She shook her head. "No," she said, "but I would not mind taking a drink upstairs with me."

Rob was startled; he hadn't realized that she enjoyed an alcoholic beverage at bedtime. But he decided not to mention it. "Brandy, gin, or whiskey?" he asked. "We have all three in the cupboard, I believe."

She considered the question, then settled for whiskey.

"I'll keep you company," Rob said, and poured two drinks to which he added water, then followed her up the stairs to their bedchamber.

Closing the door behind them, he raised his glass to her. "Here's to you and me," he said.

Beth forced a smile, then took a large swallow of her drink.

"I have a number of things to tell you to bring you up to date," Rob said. "First of all, I'm sure you remember Chet Harris. He was a boy on the original wagon train that took our parents out to Oregon. You probably know he became wealthy as a miner in the rushes of California, and again in Colorado."

"I remember him very well," Beth replied demurely.

"Well," Rob said, "when Toby and I came to Fort Shaw after discovering the gold mine, we wrote a letter to Chet in San Francisco, telling him about our find and asking him if he'd take charge of the property for us. After all, he knows mining, and we don't."

"That was smart," Beth murmured, and propping the pillows at the head of the bed, she leaned against them. Anything concerning the gold mine was of primary interest to her.

"There was an answer from Chet waiting for us when we returned here a few days ago," Rob told her. "He's agreed not only to manage the property for us, but he says for old time's sake he won't take a penny of the profits. We'll see about that, of course. It's decent of him to offer it, but we'd rather not be in his debt. Anyway, he's heading out here to inspect the property, and he should arrive anytime now."

"We're really going to be rich, Rob? It's almost too good to be true," Beth said, her eyes shining.

"It's true, all right," he replied, "and we should start receiving substantial sums of money just when we need it most. Just in time to buy us a nice property and house in Oregon."

"Why Oregon?" she asked blankly.

"I haven't even had the opportunity to tell you," Rob said, "that I've just about completed the Montana assignment. While Toby checks out my survey lines for the eastern part of the territory, I'll be getting my affairs in order, and then I'll be heading to California. The government now wants me to oversee construction for the Central Pacific Railroad line that's now being laid through the Sierra Nevadas, and I thought that while I'm on that assignment, you could settle down in Oregon."

She made no attempt to hide her irritation. "I distinctly recall a conversation," she said, "in which I told you flatly and unequivocally that I want to settle on the Eastern Seaboard."

He, too, became annoyed. "I made it clear to you," he replied, "that I have no intention of making my home in New York or Boston or anywhere else back East. The West is home to me!"

They glowered at each other, all of their previous animosities aroused anew.

Rob was the first to buckle. "We don't have to reach any final decision this minute," he said consolingly. "My work in the Sierra Nevadas is going to take at least six months, so we can wait until that's done before we make up our minds definitely where we want to settle for good."

"All I know for certain," Beth said stridently, taking another large swallow of her drink, "is that there's no way on earth that I'm going to make my home in Oregon. I refuse to be within shooting distance of Fort Vancouver!"

Rob knew it was impossible to argue with her, to reason with her, to make her see sense. She was still obsessed, filled with hatred by her father's marriage to Eulalia Holt. The passage of time had not in any way softened her attitude or caused her to change her mind. Under the circumstances he realized he could do nothing other than ignore the subject and hope that some day, in one way or another, she would relent.

Beth looked off into space, glowering, but suddenly she brightened. "If we're really going to have a great deal of money," she said, "then we can afford for me to live in San Francisco while you're in the Sierra Nevadas." Recognizing her need to cajole him, she looked at him flirtatiously and smiled. "That way I'd be relatively nearby, and perhaps you could take time to come to the city and see me occasionally, as you've done here during your present assignment."

"I'd like it very much," Rob admitted, "but what I don't understand is why you'd want to go to San Francisco."

Beth continued to smile engagingly. "If you remember, when I was young, my father was stationed there as commandant of the Presidio. I always liked the town, even in those rowdy days, and I was fascinated by the comings and goings of the wealthy people who had found gold. People like Chet Harris, as a matter of fact. We couldn't afford to eat meals in the fancy new hotels, but I dreamed of the day when I'd live there and I'd be wealthy, too. This would be a dream come true!"

It would be easy enough to restore domestic peace by indulging her fantasy, and Rob nodded. "If it'll make you happy," he said, "we'll find you a place to live in San Francisco, and you can wait for me there."

She replied by moving toward him, curling her arms around his neck, and kissing him emphatically.

Beth had been soothed to the point where she was no longer on the verge of hysteria, and Rob was infinitely relieved. He realized that now was the time to make love to her, that it would bring them closer together. Taking her into his arms, he repeatedly kissed and caressed her, but the subtle ghosts of past failures rose up silently and came between them.

Rob was too gentle, too tentative, and eventually, as she had done so often in the past, she became restless, squirming in his embrace. Finally she quietly pushed him away.

They looked at each other, and in his misery, he saw a look of boredom in her eyes that long had haunted him. Once again, he literally didn't know what to say, what to do. She reached past him to the table, picked up her glass, and drained the last of her drink.

"Do you want more?" he asked politely. "Take some of mine."

She shook her head and yawned. "Not really. I find I'm terribly sleepy."

The air was heavy with thoughts that neither of them expressed.

Ten days after the regiment's return from the campaign against the Sioux, Clarissa and Toby were invited to the Brentwood house for dinner. Millicent and Jim Randall were already on their way to Fort Vancouver, and Clarissa had met them briefly before they set out. She liked the independent, courageous cousins immensely and said she hoped they would all meet again in the future.

When the Holts arrived at the Brentwood house, they found Susanna sitting with her baby cradled in her arms, and she grinned up at them. "I haven't let my son out of my sight since I've been home," she said.

"I don't blame you," Clarissa said.

Susanna laughed. "While we were living through the nightmare," she said, "I literally didn't allow myself to think of him. Every time he came to mind, which happened constantly, I deliberately turned my thoughts elsewhere. I knew I'd really fall apart if I allowed my mind to dwell on him. But now that I'm home, I find I keep him with me constantly. He's going to be badly spoiled, you know."

"I very much doubt it," Toby said.

The women had formed a close bond during the experience they had shared, and they were on easy, intimate terms. They chatted all through dinner, while their husbands sat back and listened. Susanna indeed still intended to write her book on the West, even without her notes, and she hoped that her account would eventually do some good in explaining Indian and white relations, and perhaps even in helping the two races to get along with each other.

After they consumed a chocolate cake that Susanna had baked for the occasion, Clarissa accompanied her hostess while she put the baby to bed. Andy Brentwood and Toby remained at the dining table, each of them with a glass of port in front of him.

"I'm glad we're alone," Andy said. "I have some important matters to discuss with you."

"Fire away," Toby told him.

"First, as you know, my troops will be sent out in a

few days' time to scour the countryside and rout out all the bandit gangs. That and the fact that the settlers themselves are forming vigilante groups should put a stop to the gangs' activities."

Toby nodded thoughtfully.

"Second, and much more serious, is the matter of the Indians," Andy said. "I'm afraid we haven't heard the last of the Sioux, not by a damned sight, and I'm sure I'm going to regret our inability to deliver a final blow to them that would have finished them once and for all."

"Look at the bright side of things," Toby replied. "We dislodged them from a seemingly impregnable mountain stronghold, and I think it's unlikely that they'll do much more damage in Montana."

"I've had them followed by scouts," Andy told him, "and strictly between us, they appear to have vacated the Montana Territory."

"Really?" Toby was highly pleased.

"They crossed the border into the Dakota Territory, to other Sioux villages there, and they didn't stop until they came to the Red River."

Toby was impressed. "That's a long march. They must have been badly shaken after their encounter with us."

"I'd like to think that we jarred and frightened them pretty badly," Andy admitted, smiling ruefully, "but maybe I'd be indulging in wishful thinking. No, I'm afraid that there's something far more serious afoot. I sensed it as soon as I learned that they marched into Dakota."

A puzzled frown appeared on Toby's face. "Now that you mention it, Andy, it is rather odd that they would cross the border. Many of the Sioux subtribes that joined up with Thunder Cloud reside in Montana. Why would they go to Dakota?"

Andy became grim. "My worst fears," he said, "appear to have been realized."

"You mean," Toby said somberly, "that the Sioux are planning a war strategy?"

"It's even worse. The Sioux are entering into a new alliance. From the bits and pieces that my scouts and I have been able to put together, Thunder Cloud of the Sioux has sent messengers to Big Knife and Red Elk, the principal chieftains of the Cheyenne to the south and the Blackfoot to the north."

"Good Lord!" Toby exclaimed, then took a swallow from his glass of port. "Other than the Sioux, the Blackfoot and the Cheyenne are the two most prominent tribes in the entire Great Plains area, and they've been enemies for as far back as anyone can remember."

"Exactly. If they're getting together, it means just one thing," Andy said.

Toby nodded gravely. "They're forgetting their differences, burying their past because they've found a mutual enemy whom they hate far more than they hate each other. The United States of America."

"Exactly," Andy said. "I can't swear that they're forming an alliance, but it sure looks that way."

"A combination of the forces of the Sioux, the Cheyenne, and the Blackfoot," Toby said, shaking his head, "would give the alliance an army of several thousand warriors. I hesitate to think of the number, much less let my mind dwell on the mischief they can create. They not only can turn all of Dakota into a living hell for the settlers there, but they can disrupt communications between the East and the West, and I'm referring to everything from the railroad lines that are going to be built to the telegraph lines that already exist."

"You have a good grasp of the picture, as I knew you would," Andy said. "Let me stress, however, that, for the moment at least, we're dealing with a purely hypothetical situation. We don't know for certain that the Plains tribes are forming an alliance, and if they are, we don't know the nature of the partnership."

"True."

"Almost needless to say," Andy declared, "I've been in constant touch, by telegraph, with the War Department on the situation. It's sufficiently serious that General Grant has taken a strong personal interest in the developments."

"I'm sure he has," Toby replied.

"It's not accidental that I'm revealing all this to you," Andy said. "General Grant has directed that I find out—as expeditiously as possible—the true nature and extent of the alliance that may or may not exist among the Sioux, the Cheyenne, and the Blackfoot. Obviously, this is an assignment that can be performed only by someone who is thoroughly familiar with the Indian tribes and their ways, not to mention equally familiar with the Dakota Territory." Andy paused and took a deep breath. "I am authorized by the chief of staff of the army to inquire whether you will make yourself available for the purpose and accept the assignment. General Grant made it emphatically plain to me that he thinks you're better qualified than anyone else in the country to do this enormously important work for the army and for your country."

Toby flushed beneath his tan. "I'm flattered," he said, "that I have the confidence of General Grant."

"You certainly have that. As the son of Whip Holt,

you've had the best training any man can have. And because of your own inestimable abilities, you should not only be able to learn much about what the Indians are planning, but also you might be able to dissuade them from forming an alliance. I might add that while you're in the Dakota Territory, you'll also have a chance to meet with army surveyors now laying out the route for the railroad lines there."

"I see," Toby said, and grinned. "It appears that General Grant is fairly confident I'll accept the assignment." He paused, then exhaled slowly. "Well, I guess he knows me about as well as I know myself. I can't very well turn down a request like this, knowing that my country has need of my services."

The sound of their wives' voices in an adjoining room awakened Toby to the practical aspect of his future. "I'll have all the money that I'll want or ever need, and Clarissa will want for nothing," he said. "I will send her out to my mother and General Blake in Oregon, and they'll look after her. I'll be ready to leave for Dakota whenever you like."

"Thank you, Toby," Andy said, rising and extending his hand. "The country is in your debt. But you don't have to be in that all-fired a rush. Certainly you have time to complete your present assignment first and check out the railroad lines that have been tentatively mapped out in the eastern portion of the Montana Territory."

"I'll get started on that in the next day or two," Toby replied, "and I believe I'll take young Hank Purcell with me to put him through a series of tests before he acts as an escort for Clarissa."

"That's wise," Andy said.

Toby grinned. "The reason I'm in such a hurry, between you and me, is that Clarissa is going to have a

baby, and the sooner I put her traveling days behind her
and get her settled at home, the more peace of mind I'm
going to have!"

Rob Martin and Toby Holt had laid out a route for
the railroad that followed the course of the Yellowstone
River as it wound its way toward the northeast through
the Montana Territory until it reached its junction with
the still mightier Missouri River at the Dakota border.

The lowlands of Montana marked the beginning of
the Great Plains, and Toby, accompanied by young
Hank, found it a simple matter to ride fifty to sixty miles
each day, rechecking the maps and charts that Rob had
already plotted.

The summer weather was warm, and the ride
through the tall grass was as pleasant as it was easy and
uneventful. Game was plentiful, and Toby deliberately
allowed Hank to act as the hunter for the party. The
boy, still showing uncanny skill with a rifle, brought
down a variety of animals, from a deer to rabbits, to a
buffalo calf that he managed to detach from a large
herd.

In all, Toby was more than satisfied with Hank's
conduct. The boy had been thoroughly drilled by his
father in what Toby called "frontier manners"; he was a
first-rate hunter, he always made camp in a protected
spot near a body of water, and even when relaxing in
the saddle, he kept his eyes open for possible trouble in
the wilderness. Toby was more than satisfied that the
boy would provide Clarissa with a competent escort on
her journey to Oregon.

The last of the charts Rob Martin had drawn covered the area directly west of the Montana border, and
when Toby finished checking out the proposed location

of the railroad line, he sighed in quiet relief. "That's that," he said. "It's a job well done."

"Do you want to stop and make camp, Mr. Holt?" Hank asked. "There's plenty of firewood hereabouts, and I'll fry up those buffalo steaks that we've been saving."

"I'm tempted," Toby replied, "but we have a couple of hours of daylight left, so we can get a good start on our ride back to Fort Shaw. I'd just as soon not lose all that time." Toby was anxious to get back to Fort Shaw as rapidly as possible. He wanted to spend several days with Clarissa prior to her departure for Oregon and his own in the opposite direction to Dakota.

Hank nodded cheerfully. "You bet, sir," he said. "And I suppose you want to follow the trail that goes parallel to the river, that being the easiest and quickest."

"You get the general idea, Hank," Toby said. "I suggest that you take the lead because in that way you can set the pace. I'm afraid I'll be inclined to keep pushing faster and faster if I have my own way."

The boy laughed and maneuvered his horse ahead of Toby's on the trail.

Mr. Blake, fully recovered, trotted beside his master's mount, as always. Toby was going to miss his old friend sorely when he was sent off with Clarissa to Oregon. But the dog would be needed to guard his wife on her journey, and Toby reconciled himself to the separation.

Hank rode easily at a slow, steady canter, and Toby, staying several paces behind him, let his mind wander. Pushing his broad-brimmed hat to the back of his head, he let the sun shine on his face. Its warmth felt good, as did the cool breeze. He had been subjected to strains of one kind or another for a long time now, and it was good to know that he had completed one assignment on time.

It was a relief to realize, too, that he and Clarissa, with parenthood approaching, would have no serious money worries to trouble them. As for his next task for General Grant, he refused to worry about it prematurely. How well he remembered his father's words: "When you have a tough job awaiting you, don't fret yourself and stew about it. Never borrow trouble. You will find that any problems that arise will come your way all by themselves."

"Mr. Holt!" Hank called sharply.

Suddenly alert, Toby heard a quality in the boy's voice that caused him to reach instantly for his rifle.

"Look yonder," Hank said, and pointed.

Toby saw an ordinary ranch house and outbuildings several hundred yards away. Gathered on the near side of it were approximately a dozen mounted men.

Hank's voice seethed with such excitement and hate that he found it difficult to speak. "That there is the Hastings gang!" he said. "The ones who killed my pa and stole our horses! I recognize them!"

Toby stared at the boy, uncertain whether his youthful imagination was playing tricks on him.

The mounted band gathered around a tall, lean, dark man, who gestured as he spoke and seemed to be unaware of the proximity of Hank and Toby.

"I'm not dreaming!" Hank insisted. "I know it's them! You see that big one who's doing all the talking? He's the one who gives all the orders."

As Toby watched, the group split up, with several of the men moving toward the ranch house, while others headed toward the corral and the barn.

"They're going to rob some poor settler and murder him in cold blood, just like they did my father!" Hank said in horror.

Toby noticed that, without exception, those in the group were carrying firearms, which they held ready for instant use. Clearly they were up to no good, and he knew that Hank was right. Having made up his mind, he promptly took action. "I reckon we'll have a little surprise in store for them," he said softly. "Stay close behind me now." He spurred forward and took care to seek cover behind a clump of bushy evergreens that stood between him and the buildings.

When the tall leader directed two of the men, in a swooping gesture, to open the corral door, which would give them access to a dozen or more horses gathered inside, Toby calmly and deliberately raised his rifle to his shoulder, slid a bullet into the chamber, and took a bead on the leader. Then he squeezed the trigger, and the sound of his shot echoed across the vast prairie.

Hank Purcell was not to be denied his own aftertaste of revenge. He raised his rifle, and determined to do as well as his friend and mentor, he aimed at another member of the band and fired.

Clifford Hastings fell sideways and toppled to the ground, felled by Toby's shot. One of the other members of the gang slumped in his saddle, hit by Hank's bullet. Both men died instantly.

Toby quietly slid home another bullet in his rifle, and Hank, reacting to his lifelong training, automatically did the same.

It proved unnecessary for either to fire again, however. The members of the gang, stunned by the accuracy of the sudden, unexpected attack, had no desire to engage in combat with enemies who obviously were crack shots. So they abandoned their plans and galloped off.

Toby tied a white handkerchief to the barrel of his rifle, and waving it back and forth slowly over his head, he began to ride toward the ranch house, where he could see several people standing at the windows, peering out anxiously. "We'll tell the folks who live here what happened," he said, "and we'll make them a present of a couple of horses and saddles."

Following close behind him, Hank grinned. He knew of no more satisfactory ending to his feud with the Hastings gang.

Night had come to the Montana Territory, and the sky was star-filled, with a half-moon casting a bright, silver light on the ground below. The disheveled, dispirited group that sprawled around a small fire in the vast prairie plainly was very tired and in low spirits. They had cooked a meal, but they had no appetite and had left it uneaten. The meat remained on forked sticks over the fire, gradually shriveling and burning to cinders, while fried potatoes congealed in grease after the pan in which they sat had been removed from the flames.

Only the pot of strong, oily coffee proved popular. It had been refilled twice, and every member of the Hastings gang held a mug. Only coffee, it seemed, was capable of clearing their minds and helping them recover from the sense of shock they had suffered.

One member of the band did not touch the coffee in his mug, and a single glance at Ralph Hastings was sufficient to tell the well-informed that he had already consumed more than a fair share of gin.

His mother, Ma Hastings, vowed that Ralph had consumed his last alcoholic drinks. With his brother gone, he was the natural heir to the leadership of the Hastings gang, and henceforth, he would be required to act accordingly.

No member of the band had ever known Ma

Hastings to be in such a deplorable state. Her eyes were badly bloodshot and red rimmed, as though she had been weeping, although no one had actually seen her shed tears. Her face was drawn, making her look older than her years, and she appeared to be tired to the point of utter exhaustion. Her hair was messy and snarled, thanks to the hundreds of times she had run a hand through it in her grief. When she rose to her feet, using her last reserves of strength, she wavered slightly from side to side until she could gain her proper balance.

One of Ma's gang members had looked back as they were riding off and had seen the killer of Clifford Hastings heading toward the ranch house. The bandit was sure he knew who the man was. He had heard too many descriptions of Toby Holt and his shepherd dog, and there was no question who had murdered Ma Hastings's son.

Ma's voice, when she spoke, was harsh and flat, as husky as the voice of a man and totally expressionless because she was drained of emotion. "Well, boys," she said, "we ran out o' luck today, and I'm the first to admit it. We've had success after success. More than any other gang that's ever operated in Montana. I suppose you could say we got too big for our boots and didn't take proper precautions."

Clenching her fists, she looked slowly around the fire. "Nah, that just ain't true. It was sheer luck that put that damn Toby Holt on our trail—may his soul rot forever in hell! He ain't an officer o' the law, and he don't wear no army uniform, either. So he has no call to interfere with what we do or how we live."

Controlling a sob that welled up deep within her, she spoke with increasing bitterness. "He killed my Clifford, and I'll make him pay for it if it's the last thing I ever do. He had no call to shoot Clifford down like a dog in cold blood or no call to murder Sonny, either. If he thinks he can stop Ma Hastings that way, he's wrong. Nothin' on earth can stop Ma Hastings, nobody can stop me! You boys are the nucleus of this band, and I'm gonna make you rich. That's what you get in return for your loyalty to me! But that's just the beginnin'. We're gonna build up the band. We'll get recruits until we're twice the size we are now—three times the size."

The members of the gang were listening carefully. If they had wondered whether Ma intended to disband the group and retire, they had their answer. They should have known that nothing, not even the death of her elder son, could discourage or stop her.

Only Ralph Hastings paid no attention to his mother's words and stared vacantly into the fire, lulled into a false sense of security by the gin he had consumed.

Planting her feet apart, Ma Hastings raised a clenched fist and began to shout defiantly. "Hear what I tell you, boys, and don't ever forget it! I believe in takin' an eye for an eye, a tooth for a tooth! That damn Toby Holt killed my Clifford in the prime o' life, and I won't rest until I take his life in turn! I won't rest until I have Toby Holt's head on a platter and I deliver it to the commander o' Fort Shaw!" Her voice rose to a piercing scream. "Hear me, Toby Holt, and heed what I say— your days are numbered! Ma Hastings swears on the soul of her Clifford to take your life, just as you took his!"

★ WAGONS WEST ★

A series of unforgettable books that trace the lives of a dauntless band of pioneering men, women, and children as they brave the hazards of an untamed land in their trek across America. This legendary caravan of people forge a new link in the wilderness. They are Americans from the North and the South, alongside immigrants, Blacks, and Indians, who wage fierce daily battles for survival on this uncompromising journey—each to their private destinies as they fulfill their greatest dreams.

☐	24408	INDEPENDENCE! #1	$3.95
☐	24651	NEBRASKA! #2	$3.95
☐	24229	WYOMING! #3	$3.95
☐	26072	OREGON! #4	$4.50
☐	26070	TEXAS! #5	$4.50
☐	24655	CALIFORNIA! #6	$3.95
☐	24694	COLORADO! #7	$3.95
☐	26069	NEVADA! #8	$4.50
☐	25010	WASHINGTON! #9	$3.95
☐	26073	MONTANA! #10	$4.50
☐	23572	DAKOTA! #11	$3.95
☐	23921	UTAH! #12	$3.95
☐	26071	IDAHO! #13	$4.50
☐	24584	MISSOURI! #14	$3.95
☐	24976	MISSISSIPPI! #15	$3.95
☐	25247	LOUISIANA! #16	$3.95

Prices and availability subject to change without notice.

Buy them at your local bookstore or use this handy coupon:

Special Offer
Buy a Bantam Book
for only 50¢.

Now you can have an up-to-date listing of Bantam's hundreds of titles plus take advantage of our unique and exciting bonus book offer. A special offer which gives you the opportunity to purchase a Bantam book for only 50¢. Here's how!

By ordering any five books at the regular price per order, you can also choose any other single book listed (up to a $4.95 value) for just 50¢. Some restrictions do apply, but for further details why not send for Bantam's listing of titles today!

Just send us your name and address and we will send you a catalog!